TRACKING THE MASTERMIND

UNOFFICIAL GRAPHIC NOVEL #2
FOR FORTNITERS

NATHAN MEYER
ILLUSTRATED BY ALAN BROWN

Sky Pony Press
New York

This book is not authorized or sponsored by Epic Games, Inc. or any other person or entity owning or controlling rights in the Fortnite name, trademark, or copyrights.

Sky Pony Press books may be purchased in bulk at special discounts for sales promotion, corporate gifts, fund-raising, or educational purposes. Special editions can also be created to specifications. For details, contact the Special Sales Department, Sky Pony Press, 307 West 36th Street, 11th Floor, New York, NY 10018 or info@skyhorsepublishing.com.

Sky Pony® is a registered trademark of Skyhorse Publishing, Inc.®, a Delaware corporation.

Visit our website at www.skyponypress.com.

10 9 8 7 6 5 4 3 2 1

Library of Congress Cataloging-in-Publication Data is available on file.

Cover design by Brian Peterson
Cover illustration by Alan Brown

Paperback ISBN: 978-1-5107-4521-6
E-book ISBN: 978-1-5107-4523-0

Printed in the United States of America

TRACKING THE MASTERMIND

UNOFFICIAL GRAPHIC NOVEL #2
FOR FORTNITERS

CHAPTER 1: CLASS REUNION, PART 1

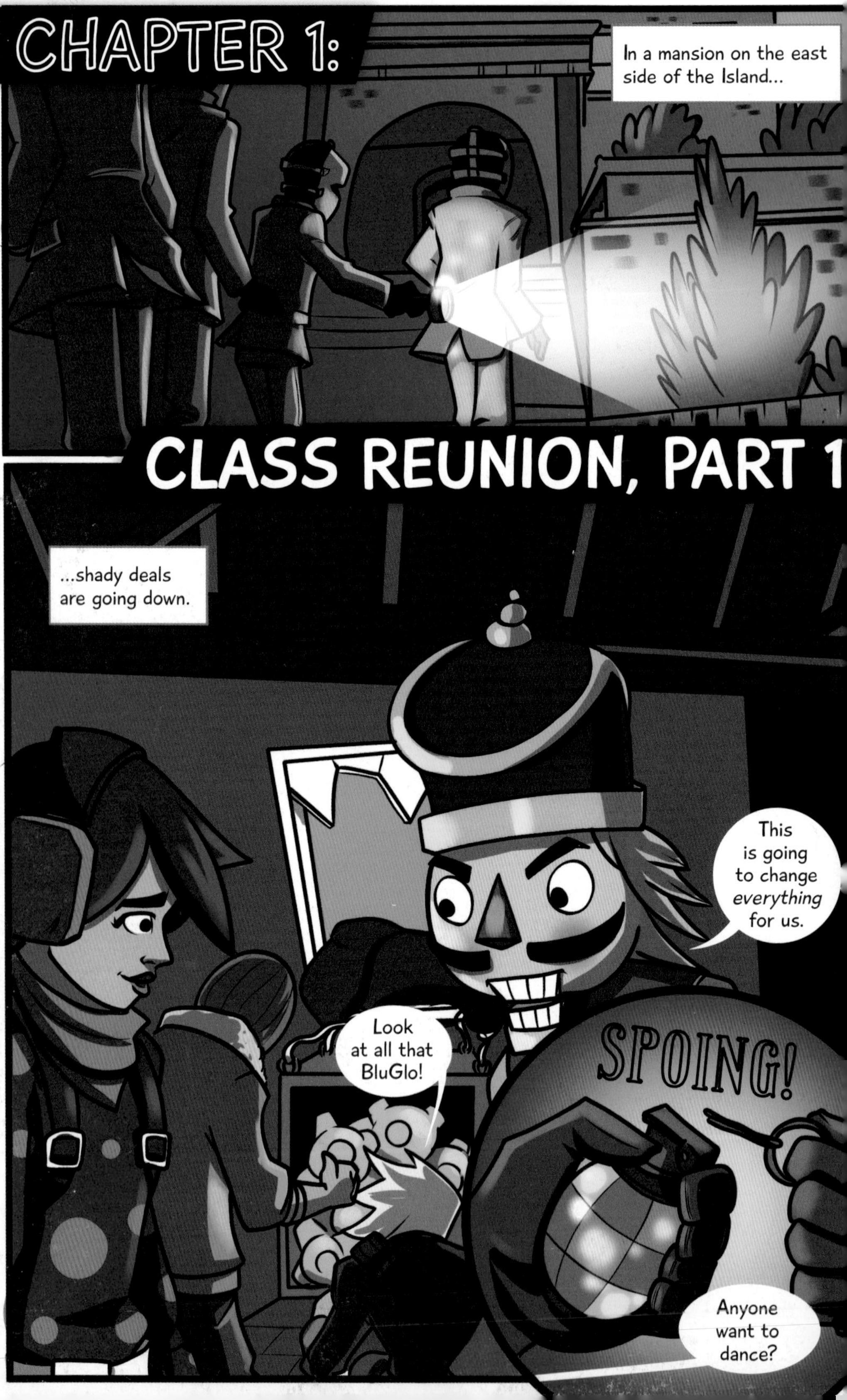
In a mansion on the east side of the Island...
...shady deals are going down.
This is going to change *everything* for us.
Look at all that BluGlo!
SPOING!
Anyone want to dance?

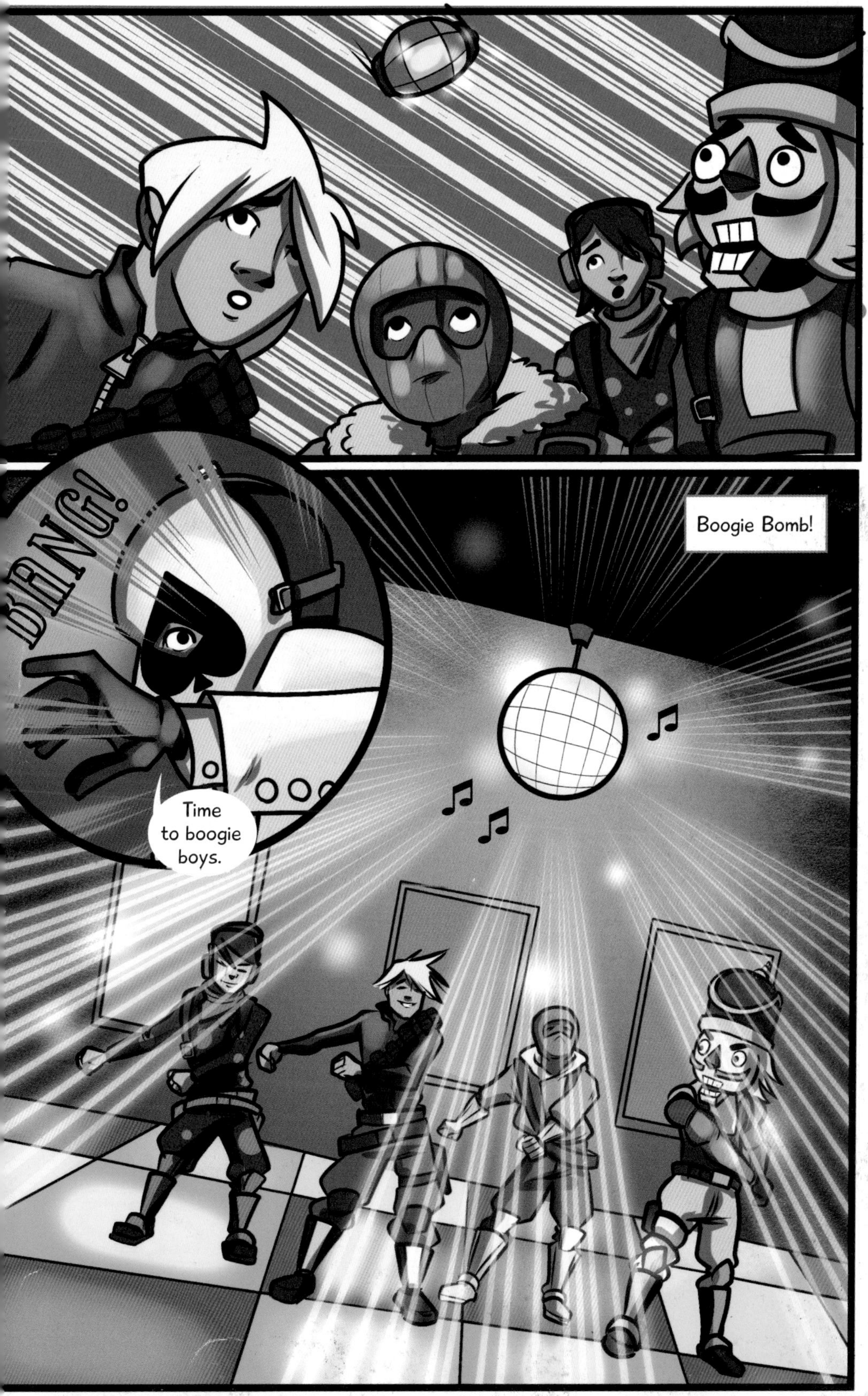
Boogie Bomb!
BANG!
Time to boogie boys.

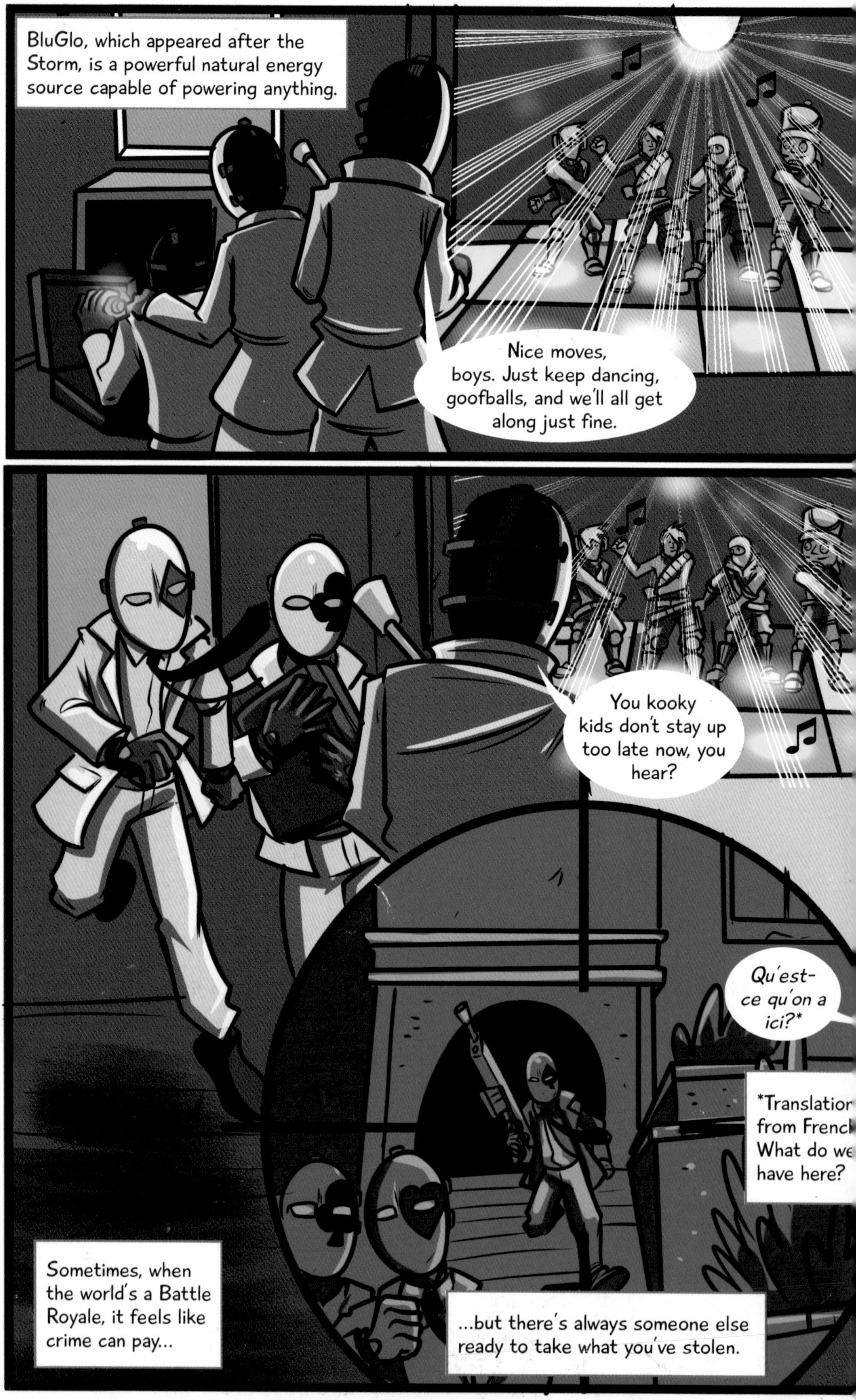
BluGlo, which appeared after the Storm, is a powerful natural energy source capable of powering anything.
Nice moves, boys. Just keep dancing, goofballs, and we'll all get along just fine.
You kooky kids don't stay up too late now, you hear?
Qu'est-ce qu'on a ici?*
*Translatio from Frenc What do we have here?
Sometimes, when the world's a Battle Royale, it feels like crime can pay...
...but there's always someone else ready to take what you've stolen.

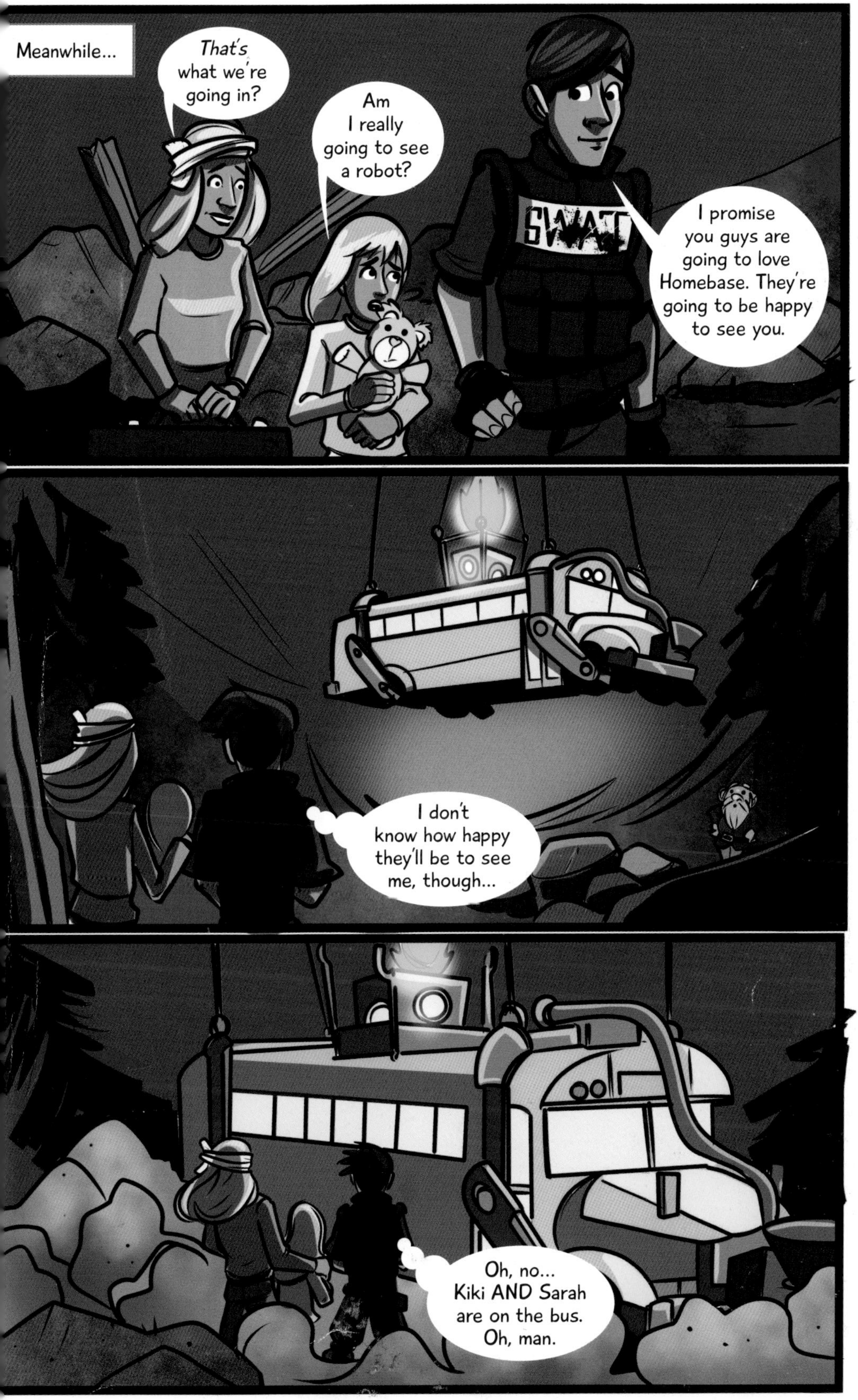
Meanwhile...
That's what we're going in?
Am I really going to see a robot?
I promise you guys are going to love Homebase. They're going to be happy to see you.
I don't know how happy they'll be to see me, though...
Oh, no... Kiki AND Sarah are on the bus. Oh, man.

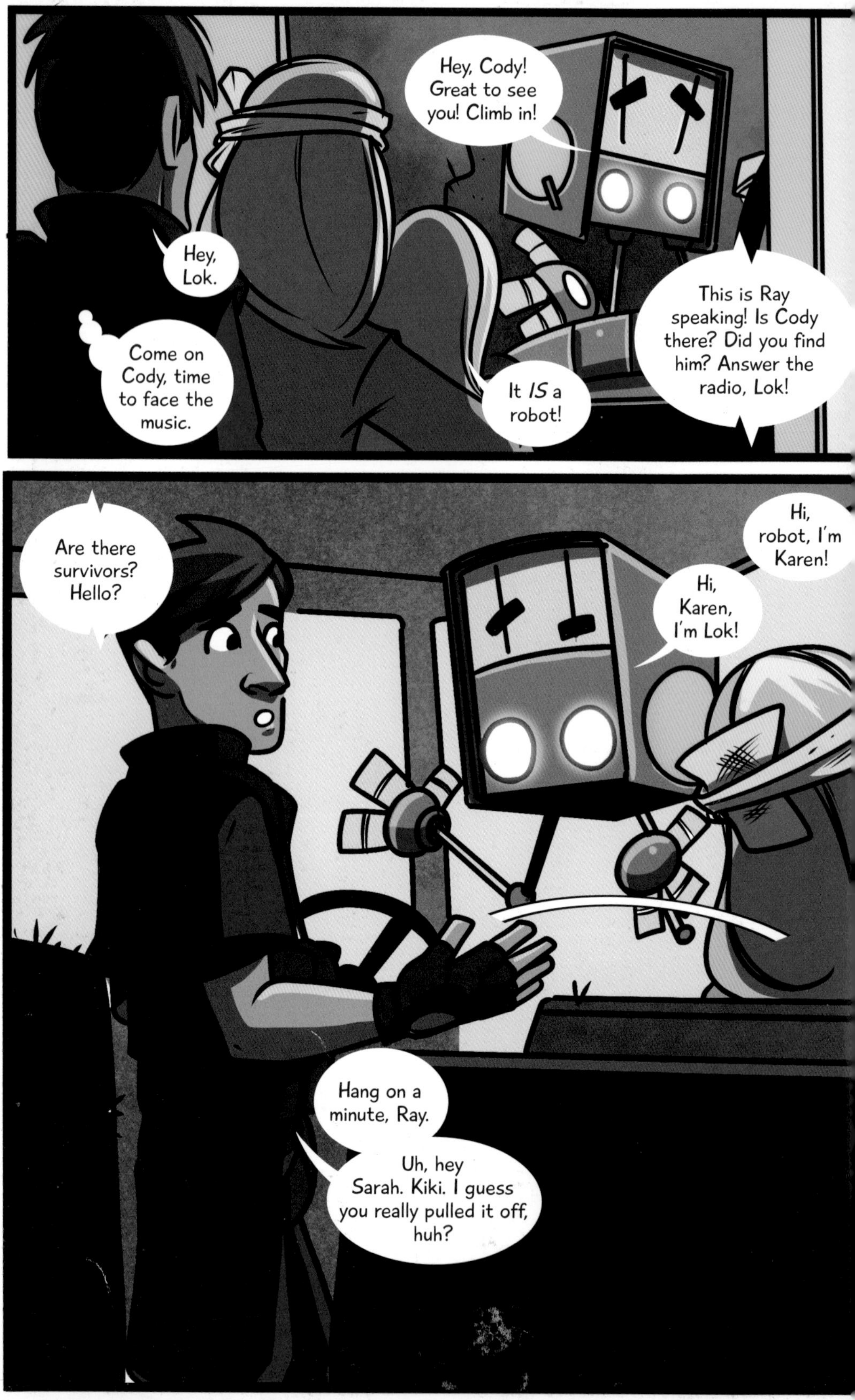

Hey, Cody! Great to see you! Climb in!
Hey, Lok.
Come on Cody, time to face the music.
It *IS* a robot!
This is Ray speaking! Is Cody there? Did you find him? Answer the radio, Lok!
Are there survivors? Hello?
Hi, robot, I'm Karen!
Hi, Karen, I'm Lok!
Hang on a minute, Ray.
Uh, hey Sarah. Kiki. I guess you really pulled it off, huh?

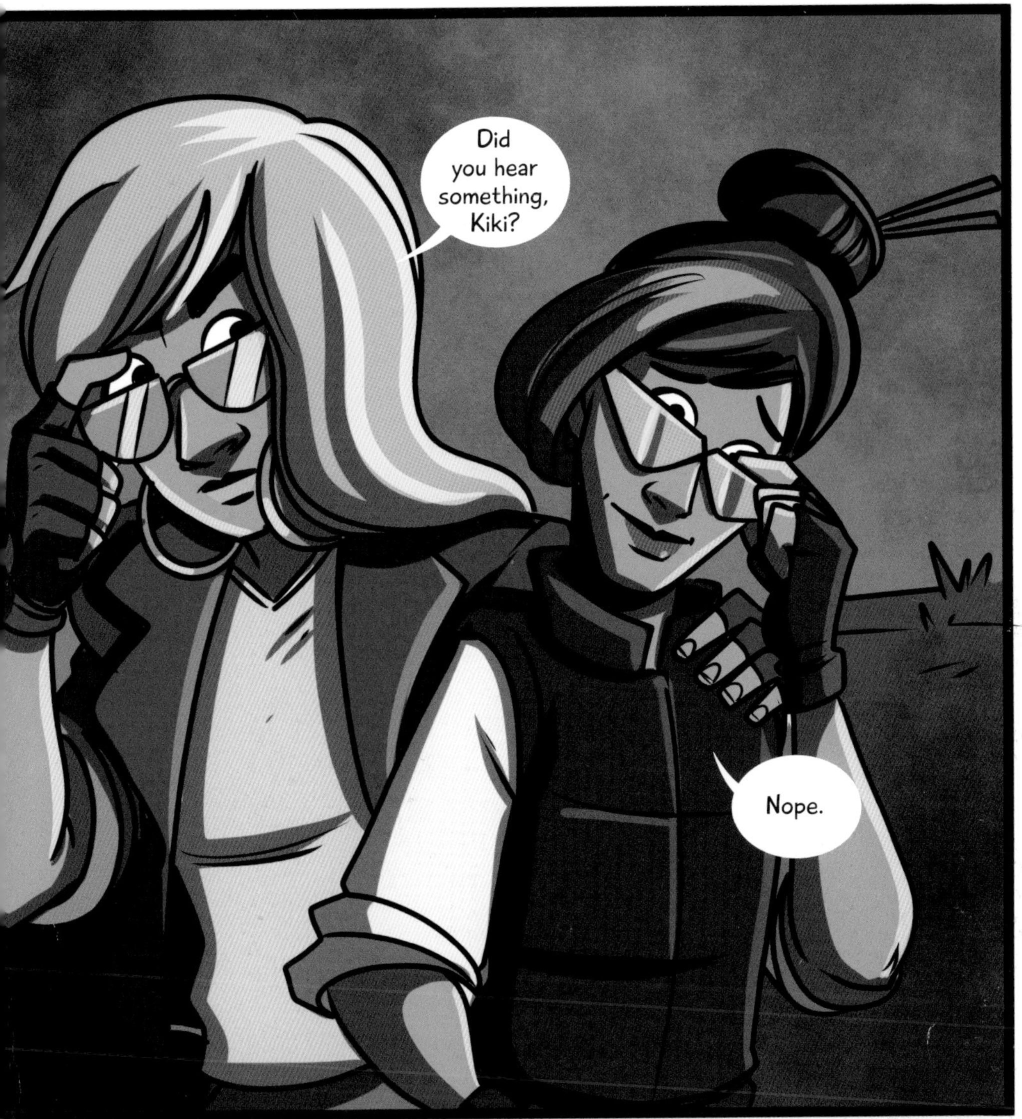
Did you hear something, Kiki?
Nope.
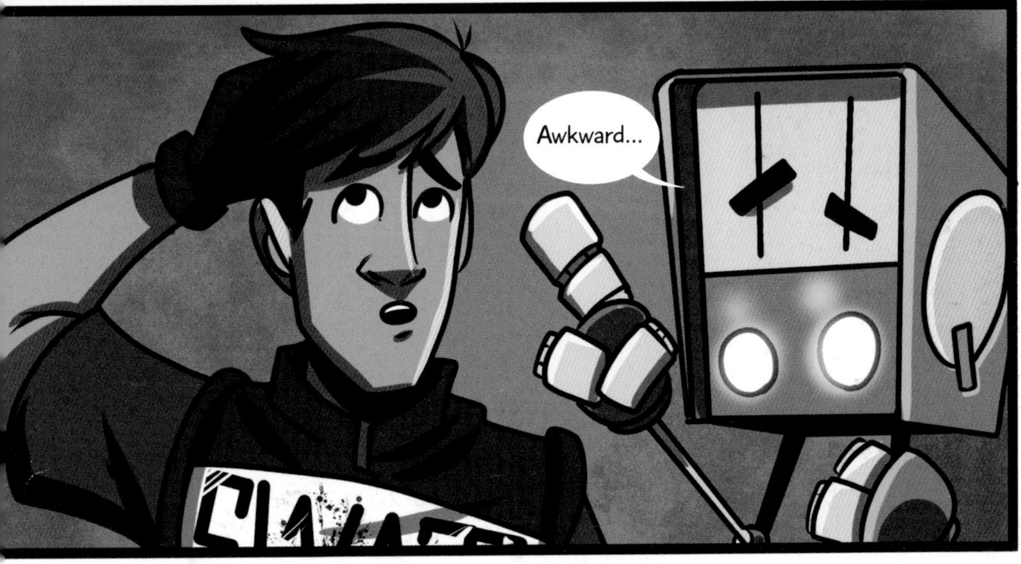
Awkward...

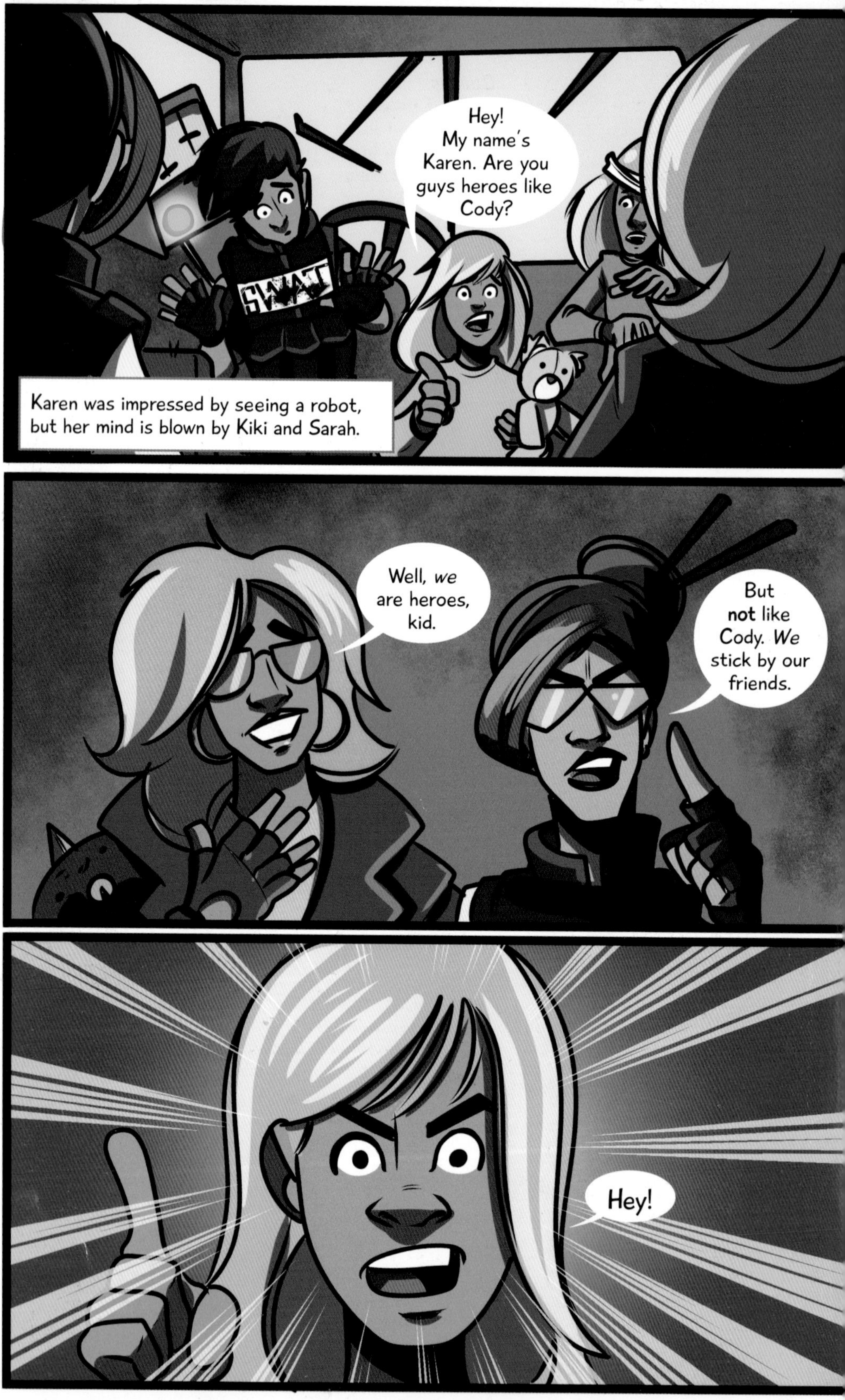

Hey! My name's Karen. Are you guys heroes like Cody?
Karen was impressed by seeing a robot, but her mind is blown by Kiki and Sarah.
Well, *we* are heroes, kid.
But **not** like Cody. *We* stick by our friends.
Hey!

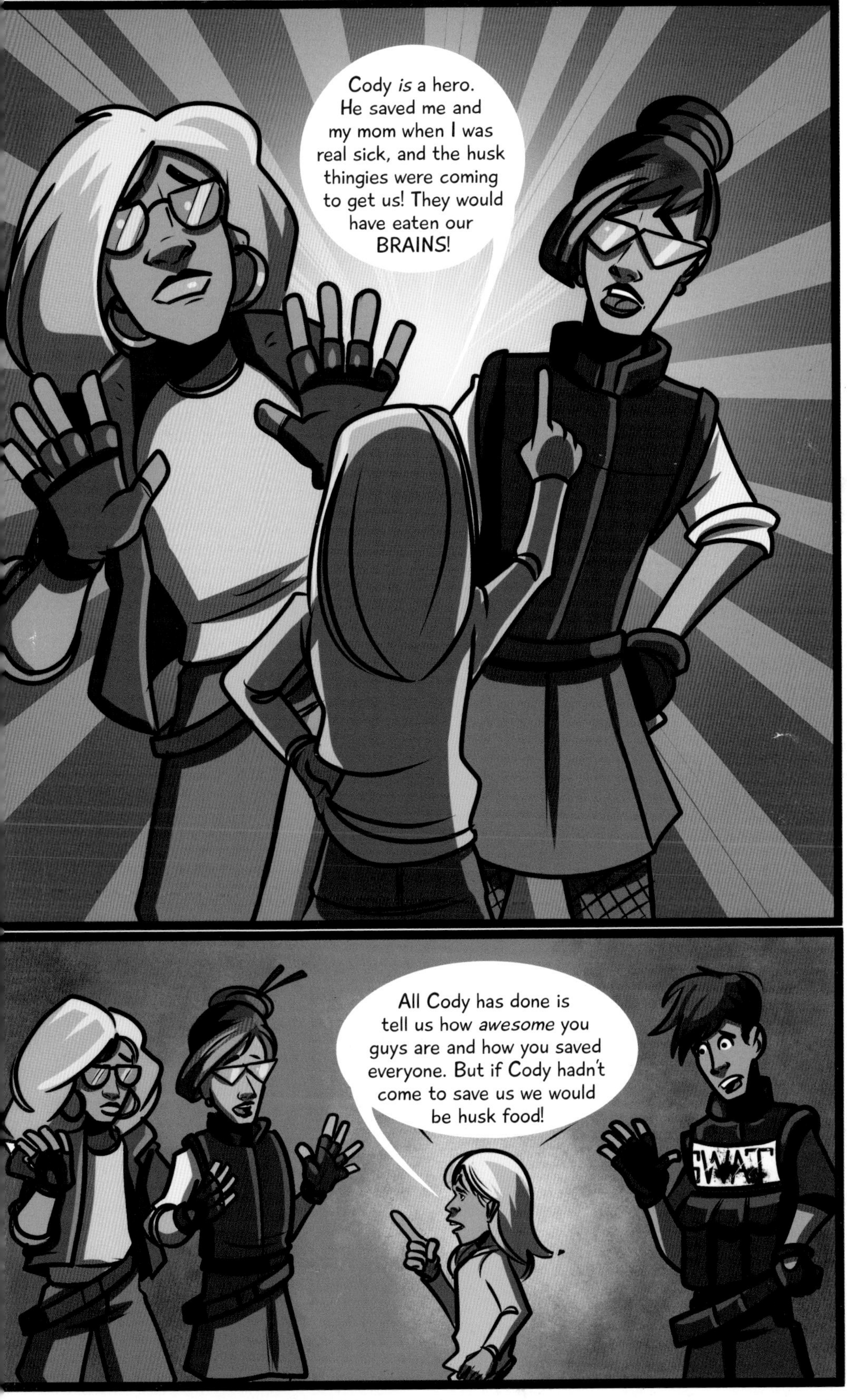
Cody *is* a hero. He saved me and my mom when I was real sick, and the husk thingies were coming to get us! They would have eaten our BRAINS!
All Cody has done is tell us how *awesome* you guys are and how you saved everyone. But if Cody hadn't come to save us we would be husk food!
SWAT

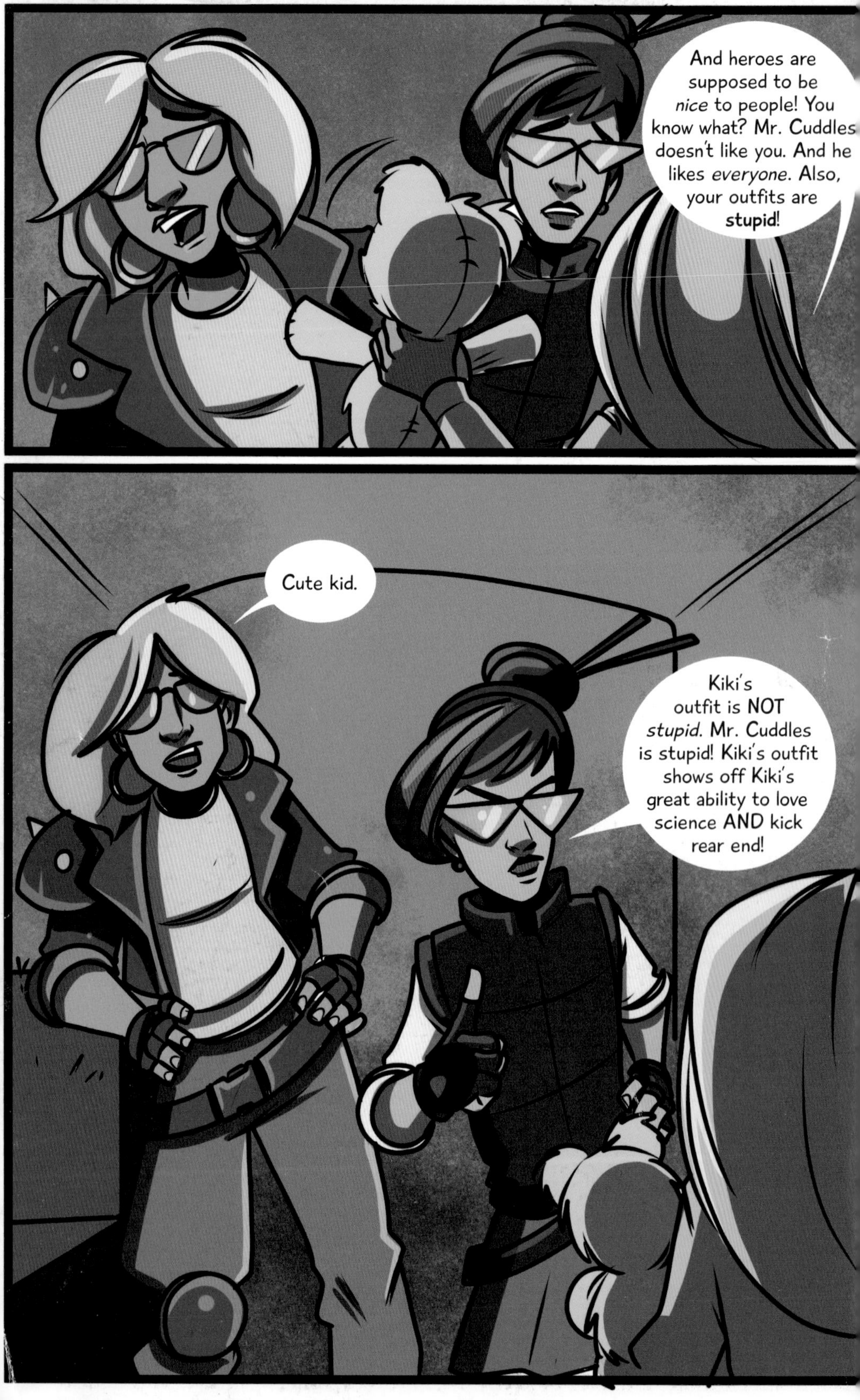
And heroes are supposed to be *nice* to people! You know what? Mr. Cuddles doesn't like you. And he likes *everyone*. Also, your outfits are **stupid**!
Cute kid.
Kiki's outfit is NOT *stupid*. Mr. Cuddles is stupid! Kiki's outfit shows off Kiki's great ability to love science AND kick rear end!

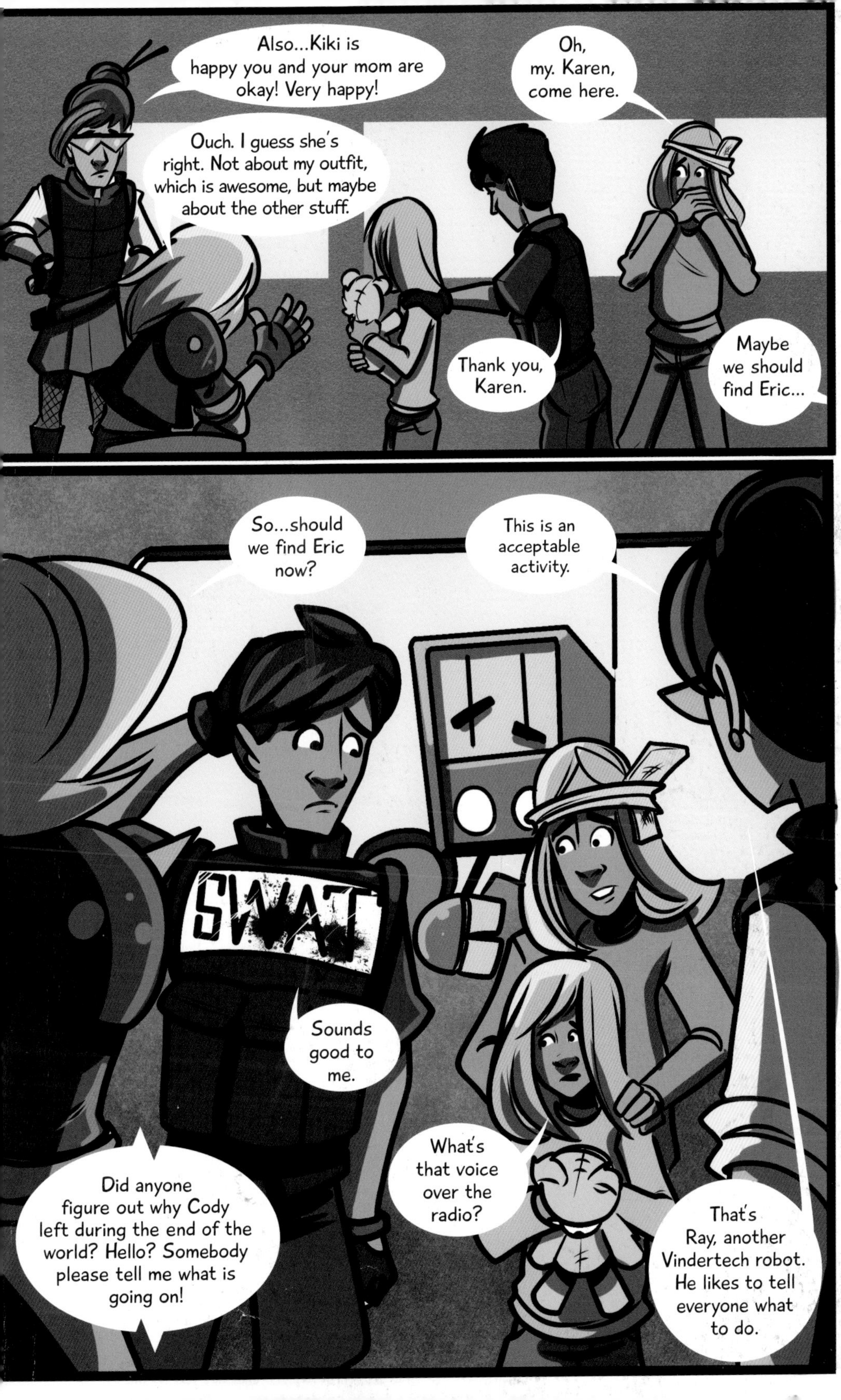

Also...Kiki is happy you and your mom are okay! Very happy!
Ouch. I guess she's right. Not about my outfit, which is awesome, but maybe about the other stuff.
Oh, my. Karen, come here.
Thank you, Karen.
Maybe we should find Eric...
So...should we find Eric now?
This is an acceptable activity.
SWAT
Sounds good to me.
Did anyone figure out why Cody left during the end of the world? Hello? Somebody please tell me what is going on!
What's that voice over the radio?
That's Ray, another Vindertech robot. He likes to tell everyone what to do.

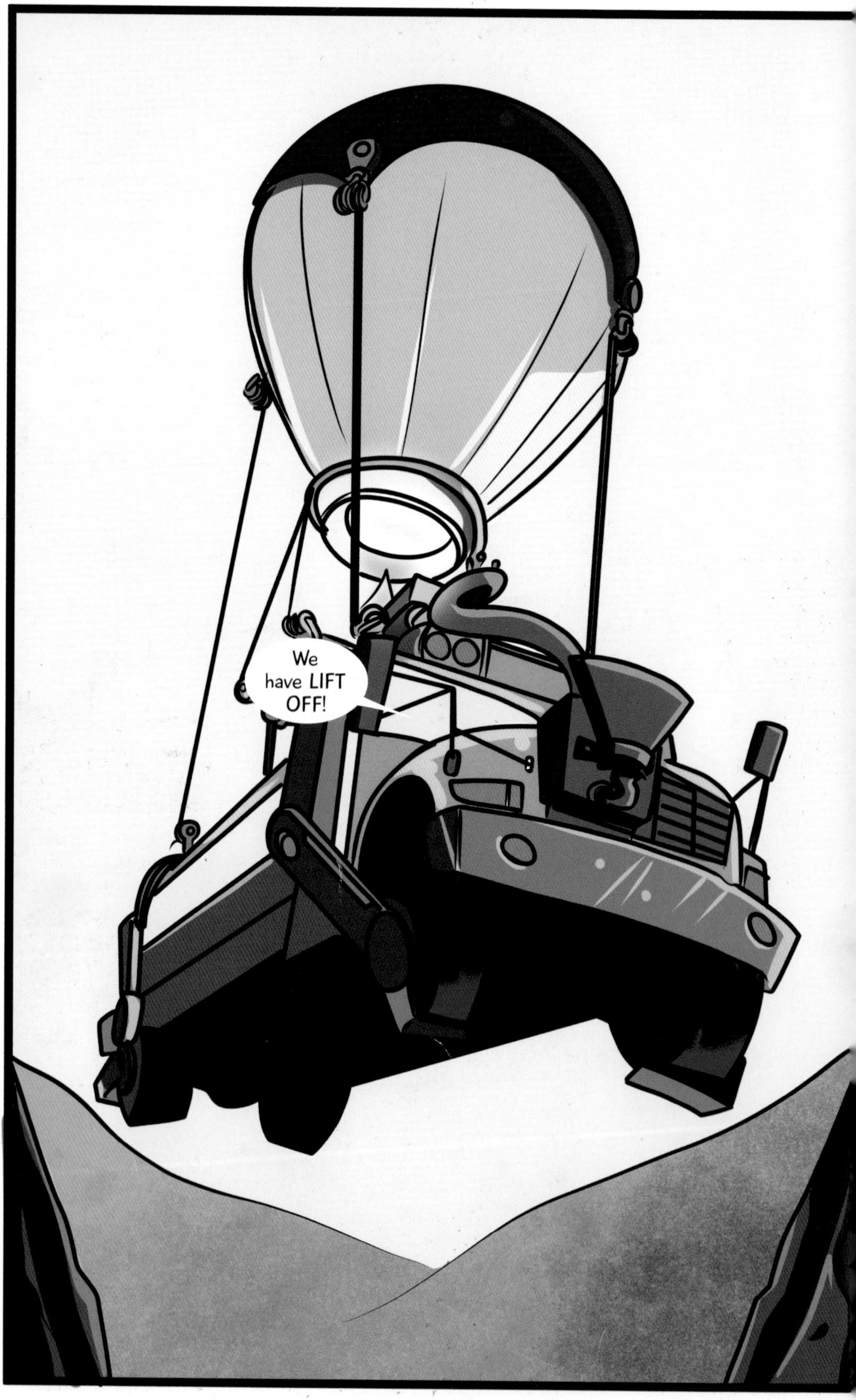
We have LIFT OFF!

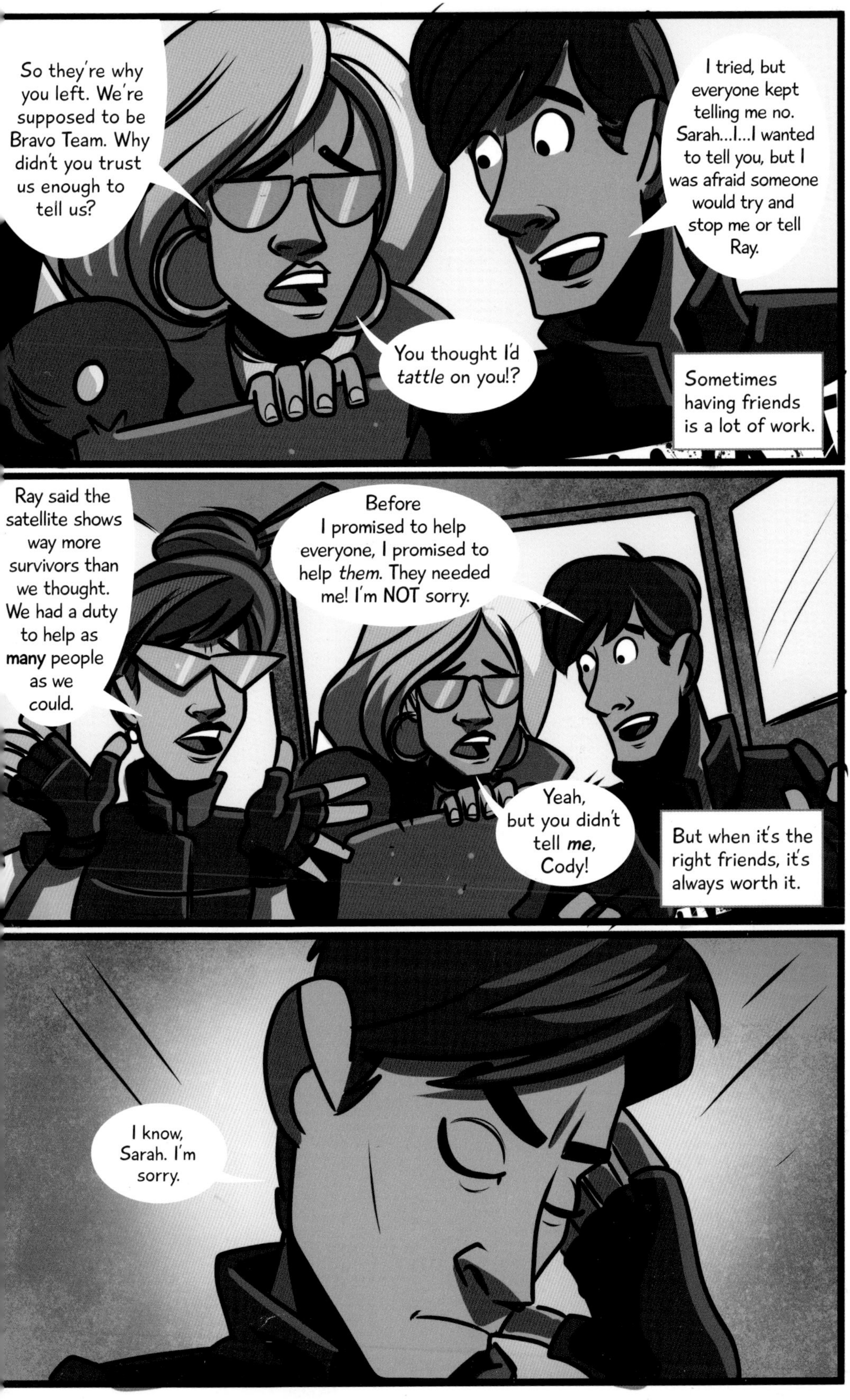
So they're why you left. We're supposed to be Bravo Team. Why didn't you trust us enough to tell us?
I tried, but everyone kept telling me no. Sarah...I...I wanted to tell you, but I was afraid someone would try and stop me or tell Ray.
You thought I'd *tattle* on you!?
Sometimes having friends is a lot of work.
Ray said the satellite shows way more survivors than we thought. We had a duty to help as **many** people as we could.
Before I promised to help everyone, I promised to help *them*. They needed me! I'm **NOT** sorry.
Yeah, but you didn't tell ***me***, Cody!
But when it's the right friends, it's always worth it.
I know, Sarah. I'm sorry.

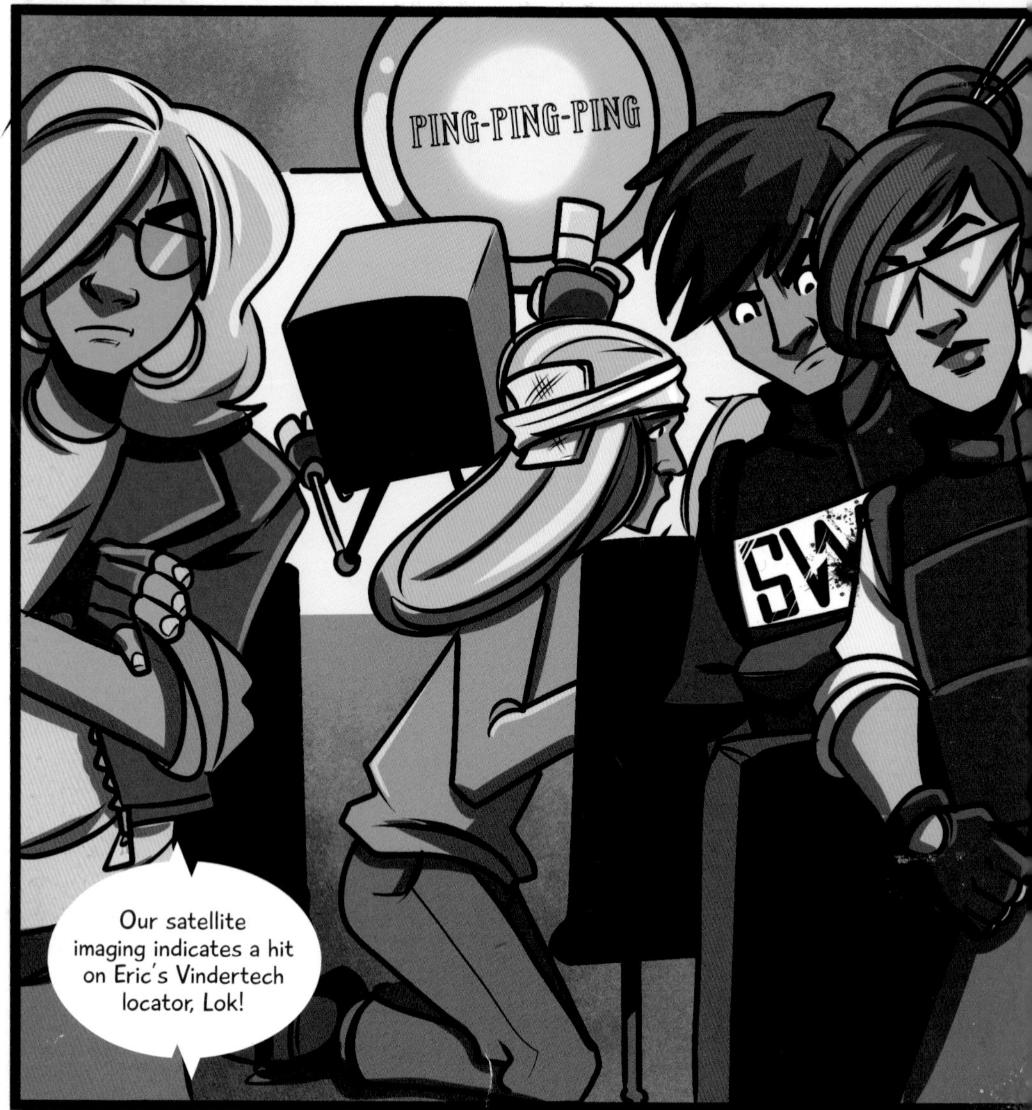
PING-PING-PING
Our satellite imaging indicates a hit on Eric's Vindertech locator, Lok!

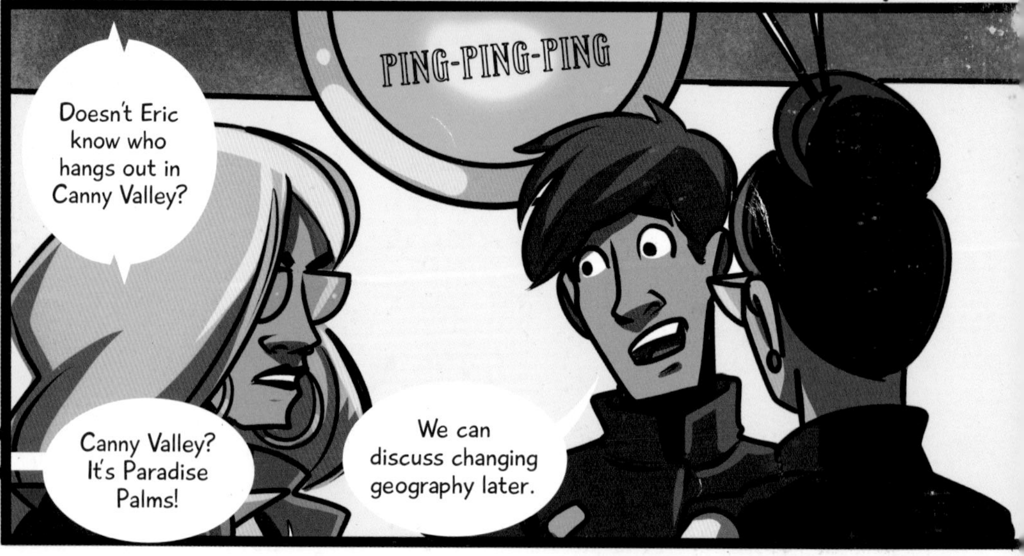
PING-PING-PING
Doesn't Eric know who hangs out in Canny Valley?
Canny Valley? It's Paradise Palms!
We can discuss changing geography later.

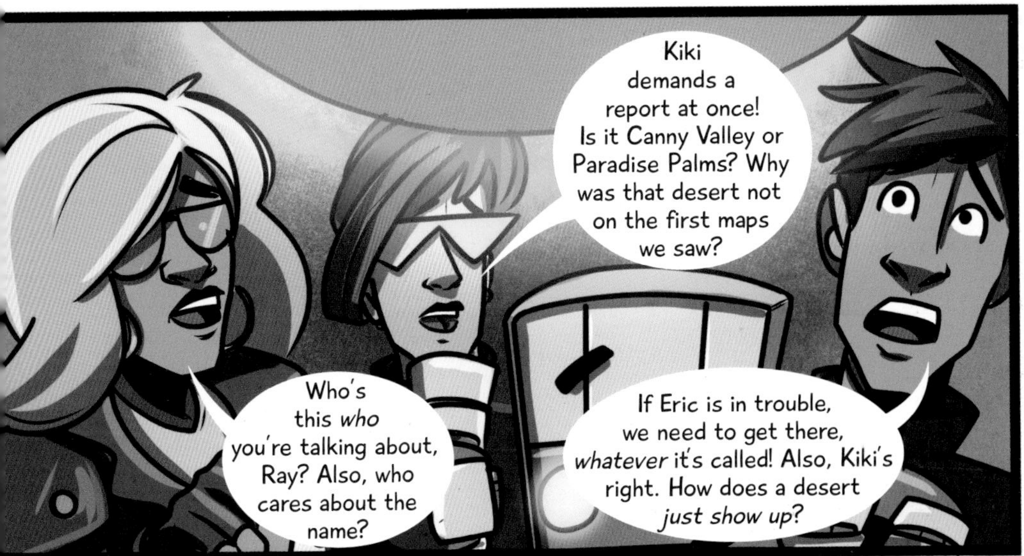
Kiki demands a report at once! Is it Canny Valley or Paradise Palms? Why was that desert not on the first maps we saw?
Who's this *who* you're talking about, Ray? Also, who cares about the name?
If Eric is in trouble, we need to get there, *whatever* it's called! Also, Kiki's right. How does a desert *just show up*?

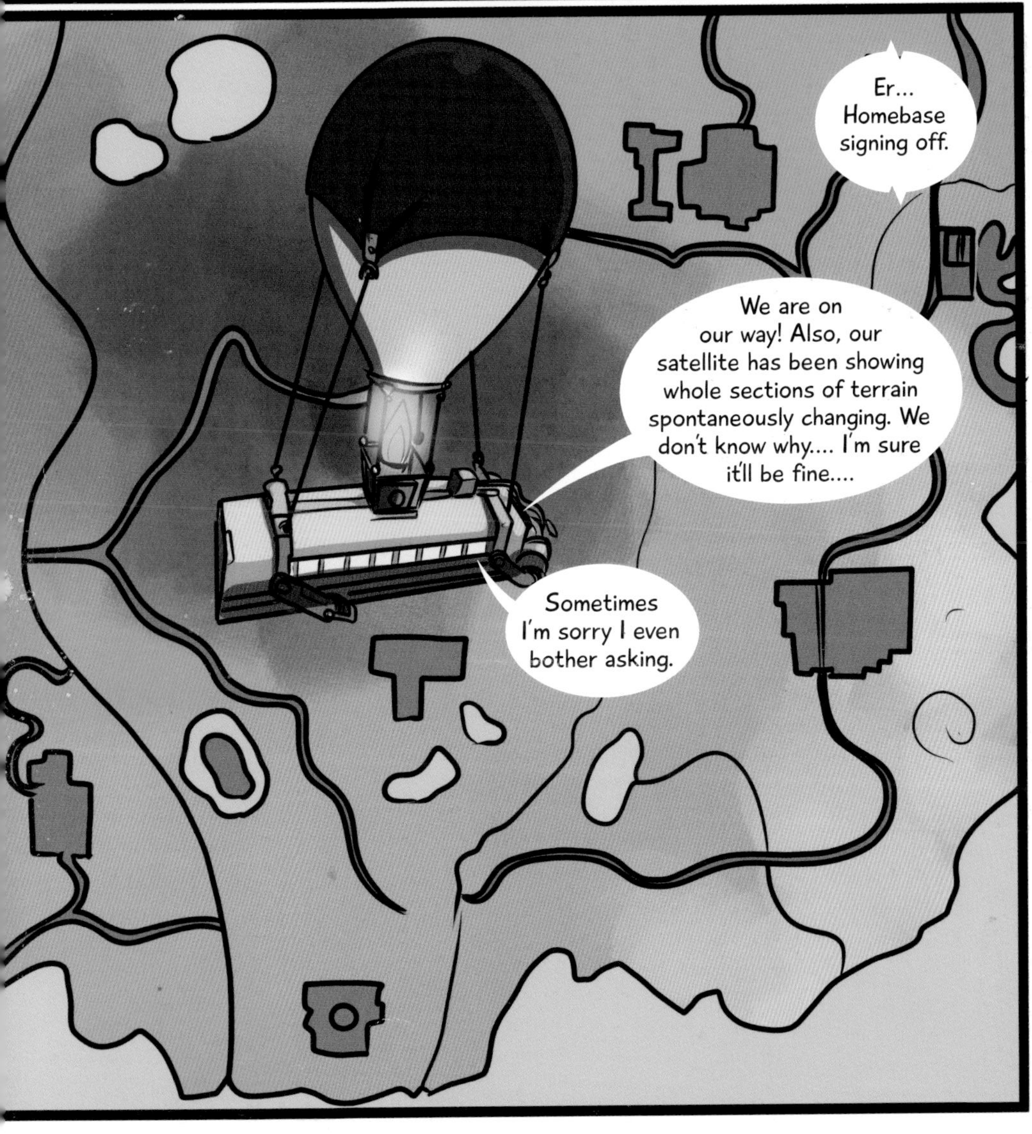
Er... Homebase signing off.
We are on our way! Also, our satellite has been showing whole sections of terrain spontaneously changing. We don't know why.... I'm sure it'll be fine....
Sometimes I'm sorry I even bother asking.

CHAPTER 2: CLASS REUNION, PART 2

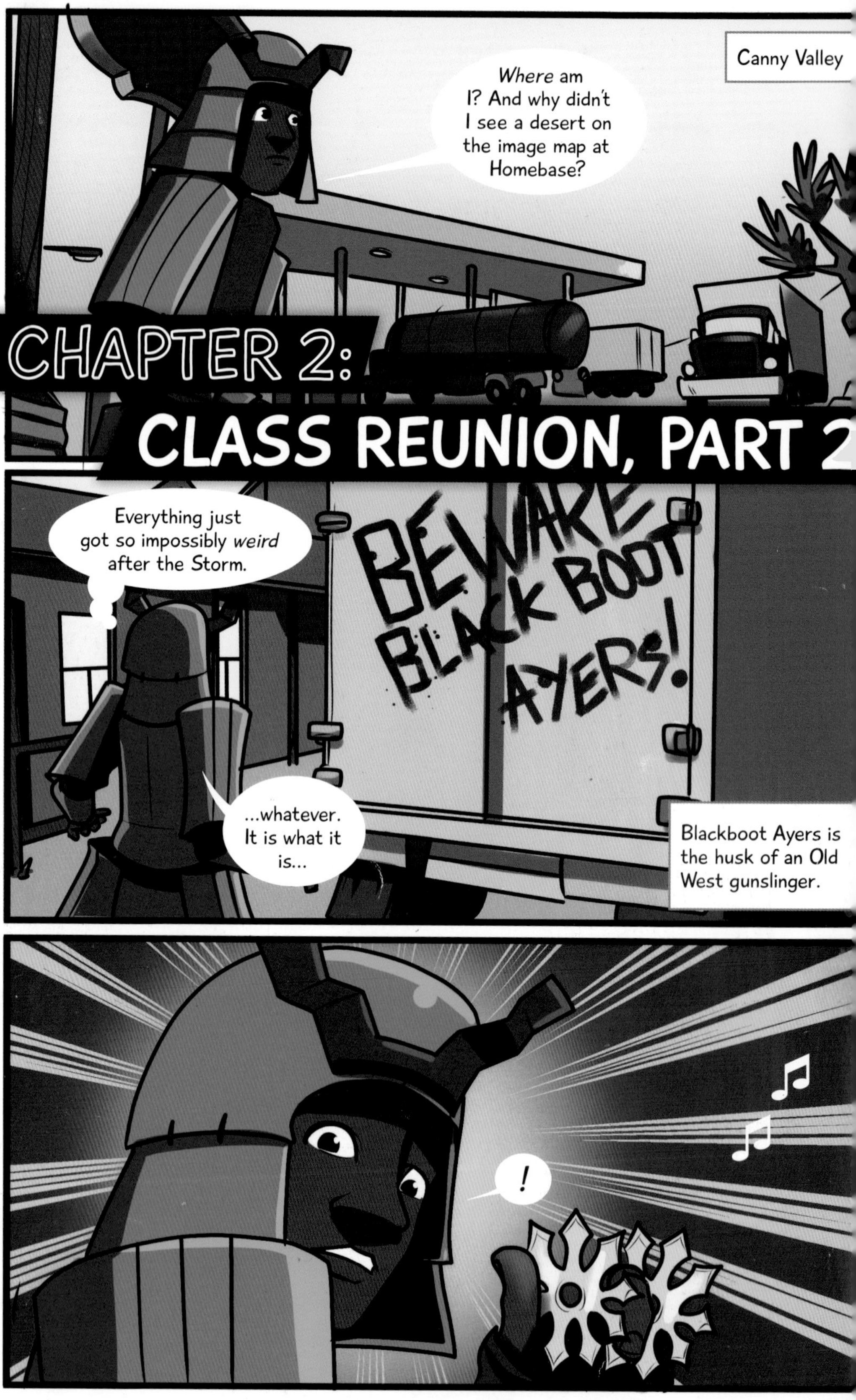

Canny Valley
Where am I? And why didn't I see a desert on the image map at Homebase?
Everything just got so impossibly *weird* after the Storm.
BEWARE BLACK BOOT AYERS!
...whatever. It is what it is...
Blackboot Ayers is the husk of an Old West gunslinger.
!

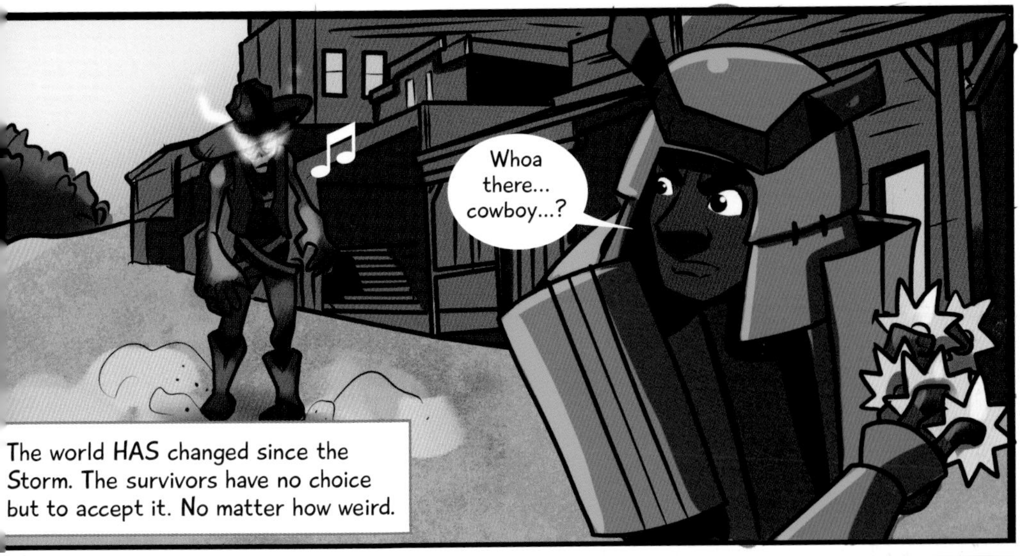
Whoa there... cowboy...?
The world HAS changed since the Storm. The survivors have no choice but to accept it. No matter how weird.

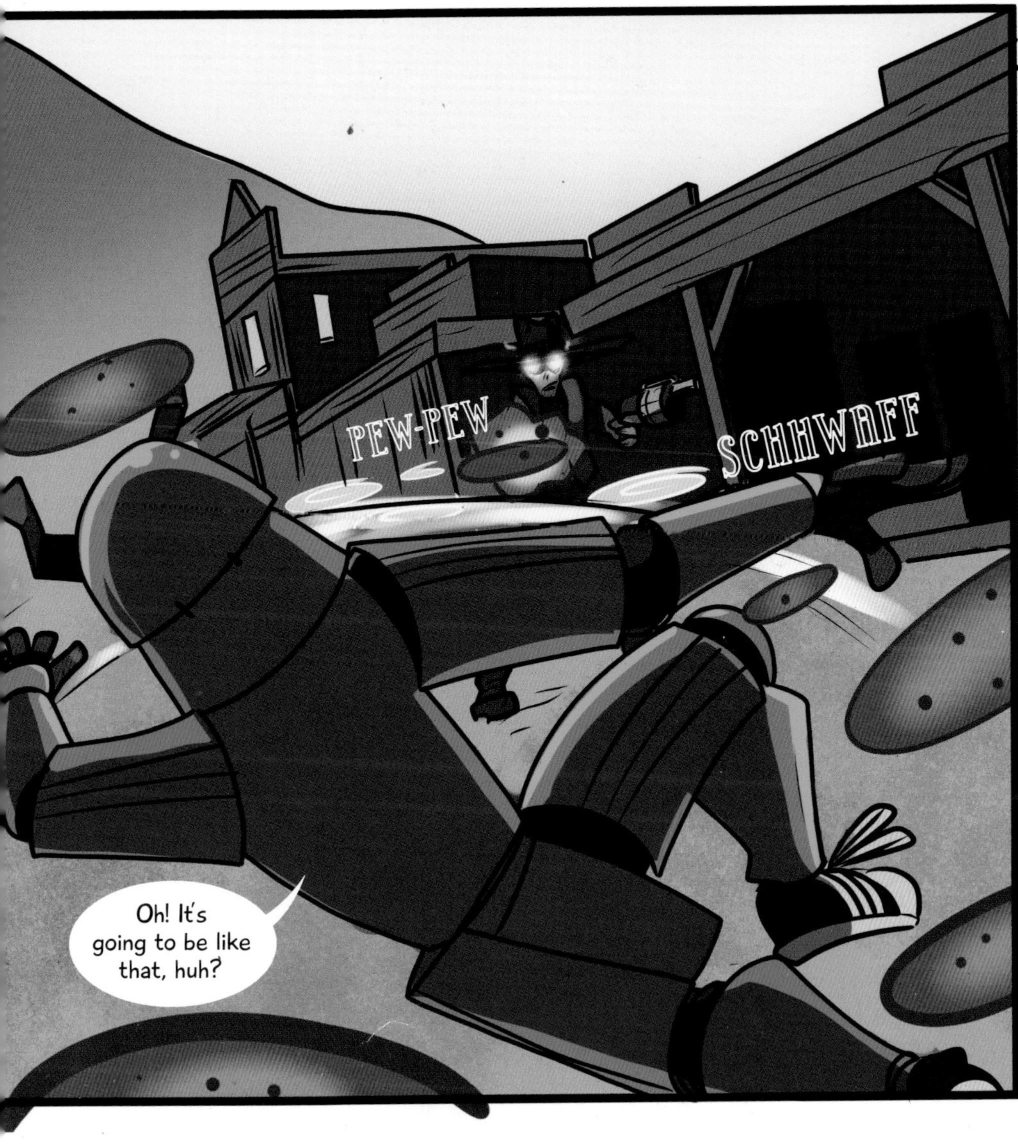
PEW-PEW
SCHHWAFF
Oh! It's going to be like that, huh?

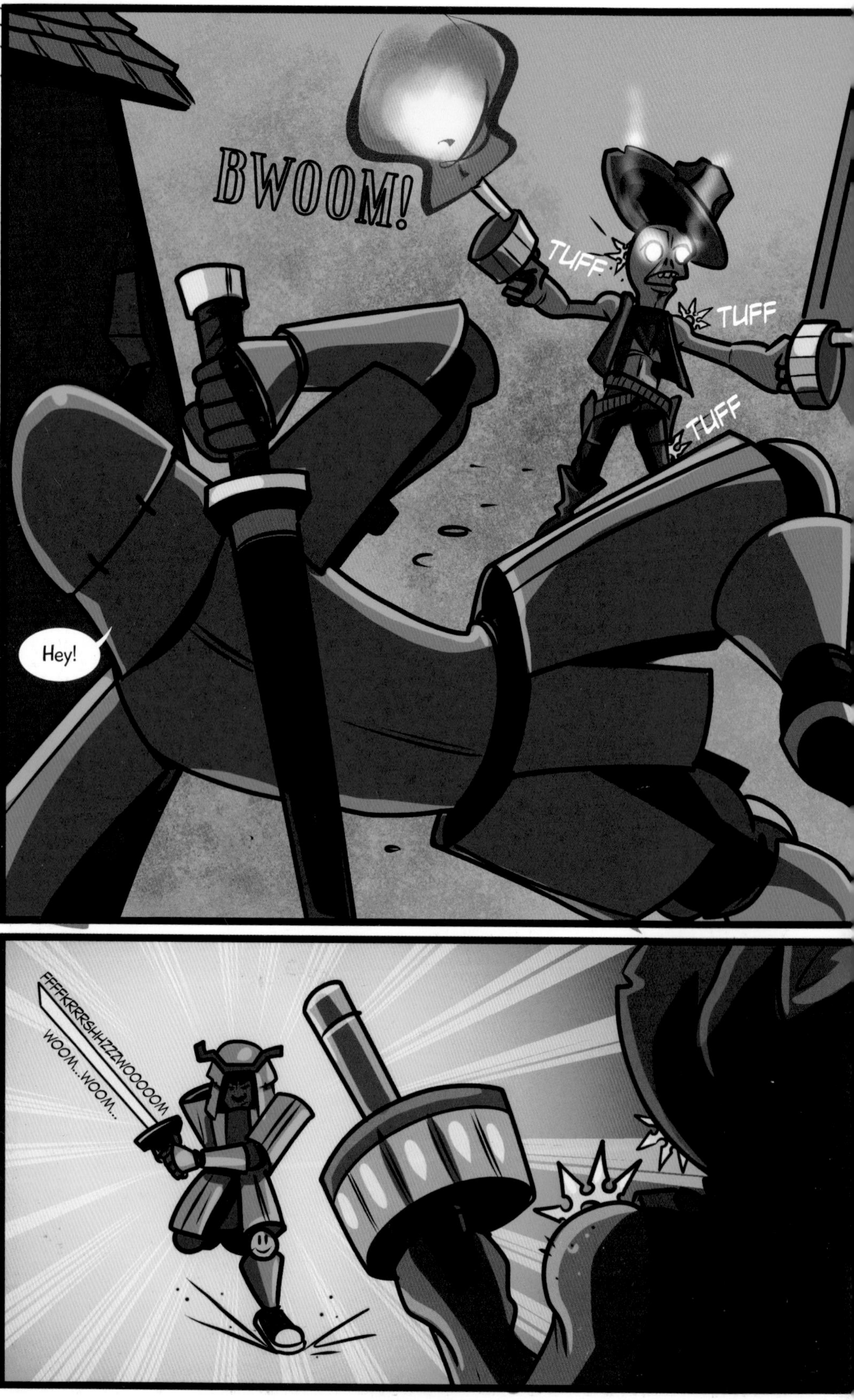
BWOOM!
TUFF
TUFF
TUFF
Hey!
FFFFKRRRSHHZZZWOOOOOOM
WOOM...WOOM...

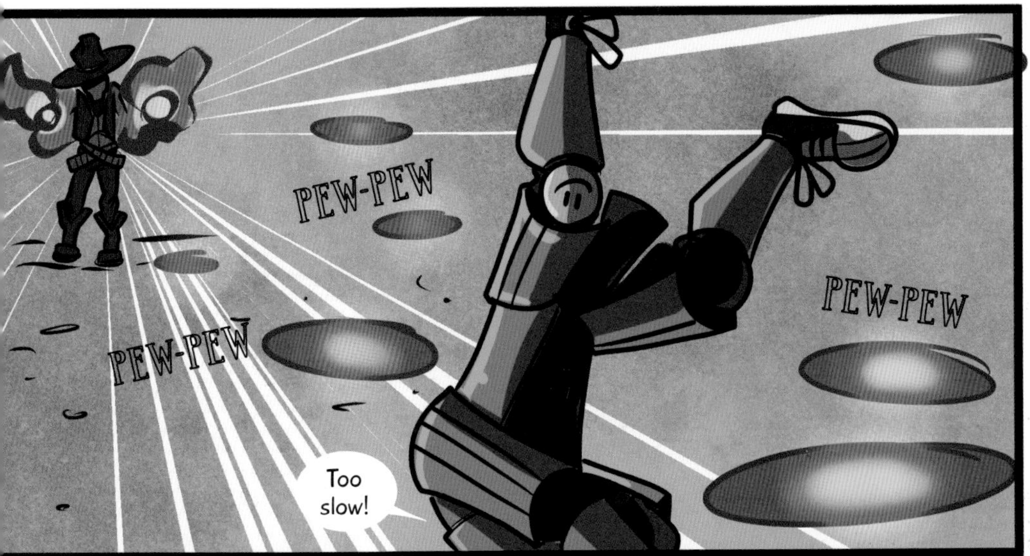
PEW-PEW
PEW-PEW
PEW-PEW
Too slow!

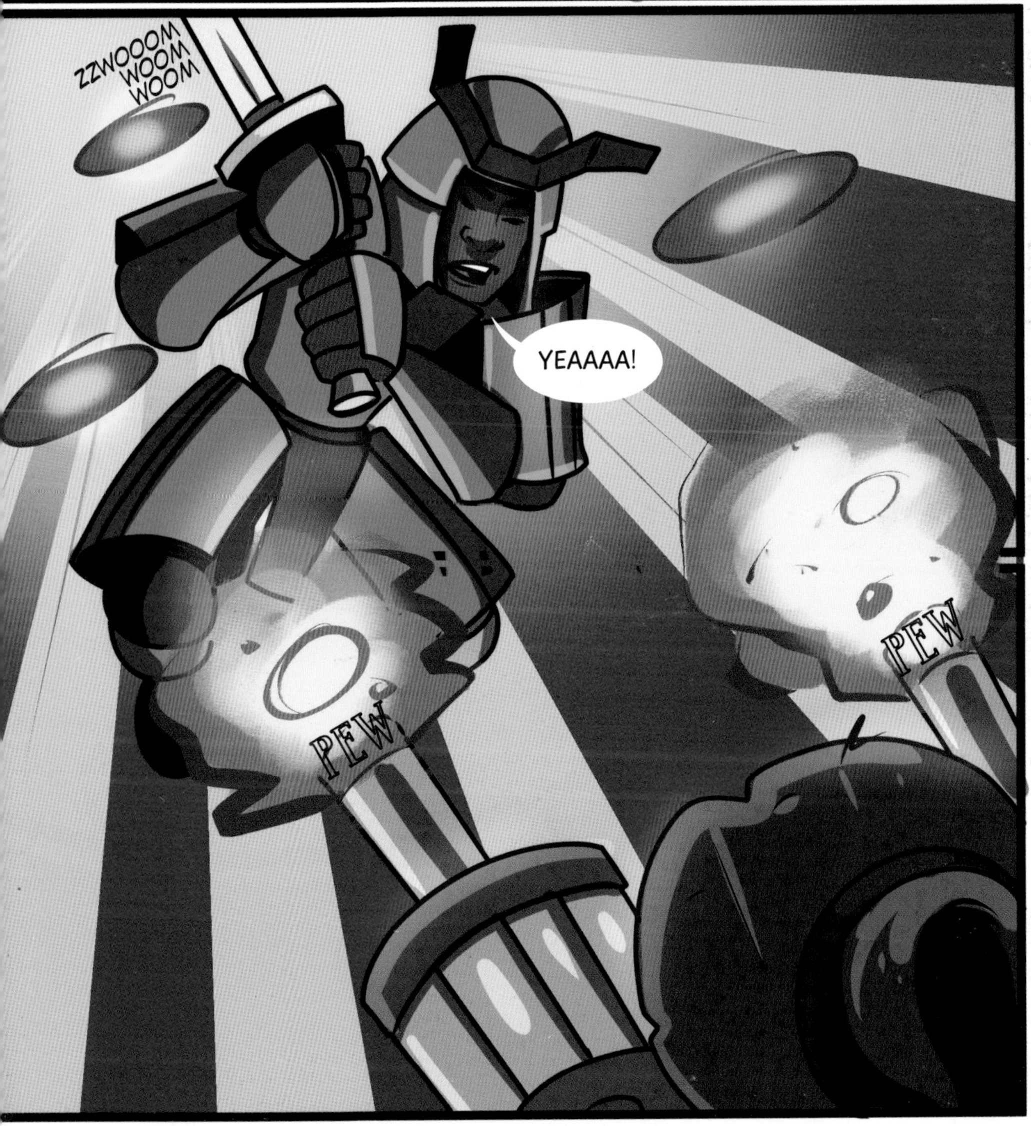
ZZWOOOM WOOM WOOM
YEAAAA!
PEW
PEW

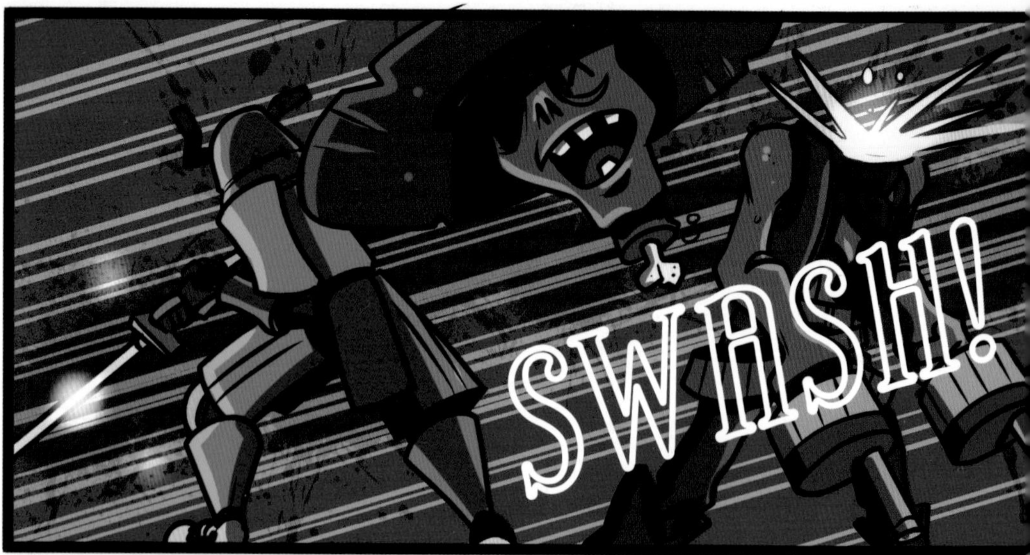
SWASH!

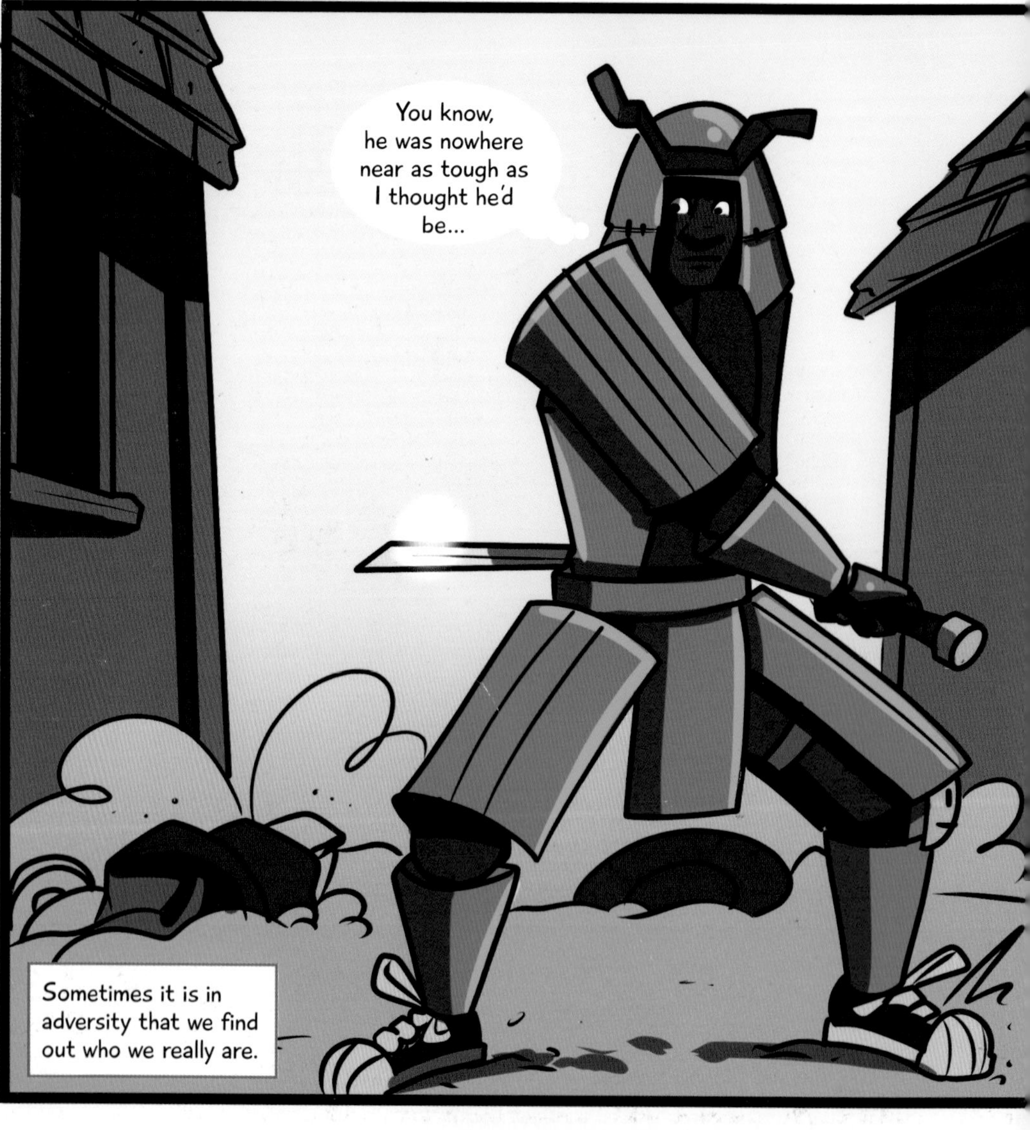
You know, he was nowhere near as tough as I thought he'd be...
Sometimes it is in adversity that we find out who we really are.

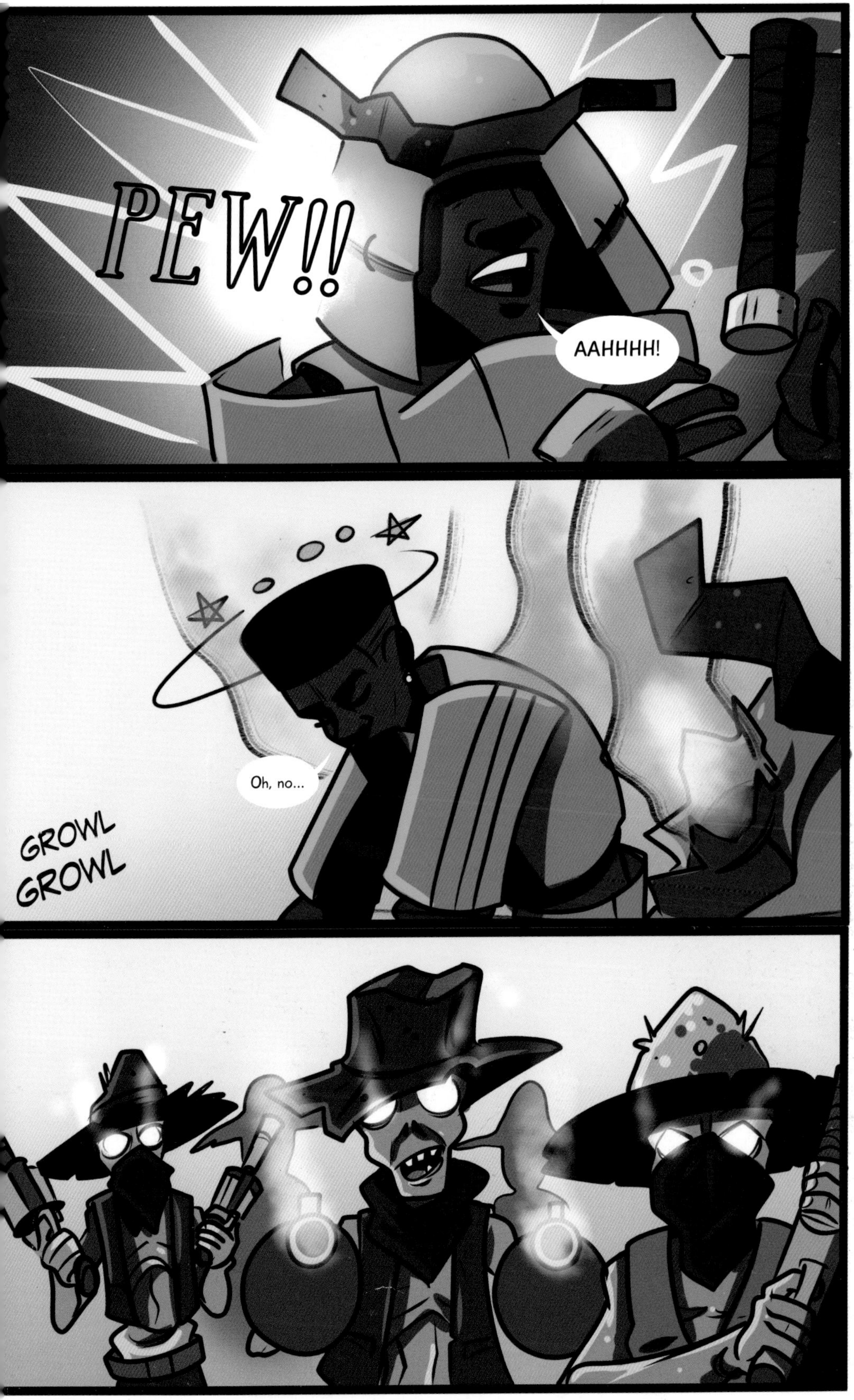
PEW!!
AAHHHH!
Oh, no...
GROWL
GROWL

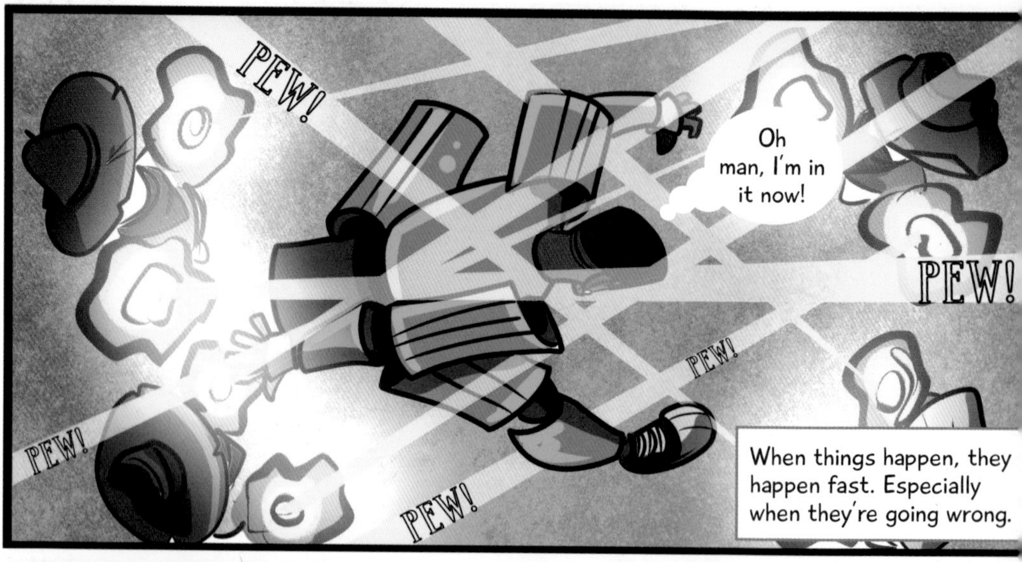
PEW!
Oh man, I'm in it now!
PEW!
PEW!
PEW!
PEW!
When things happen, they happen fast. Especially when they're going wrong.

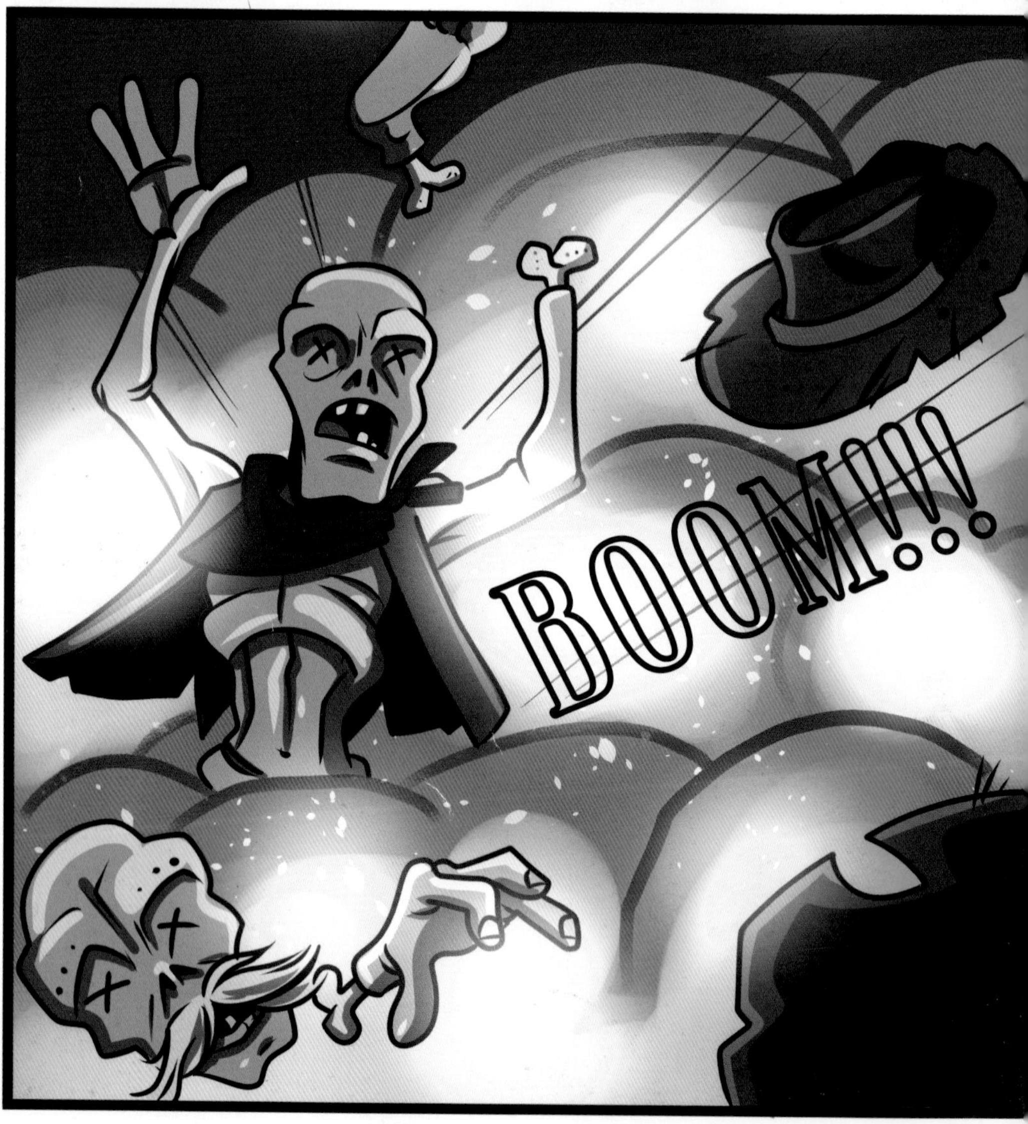
BOOM!!!

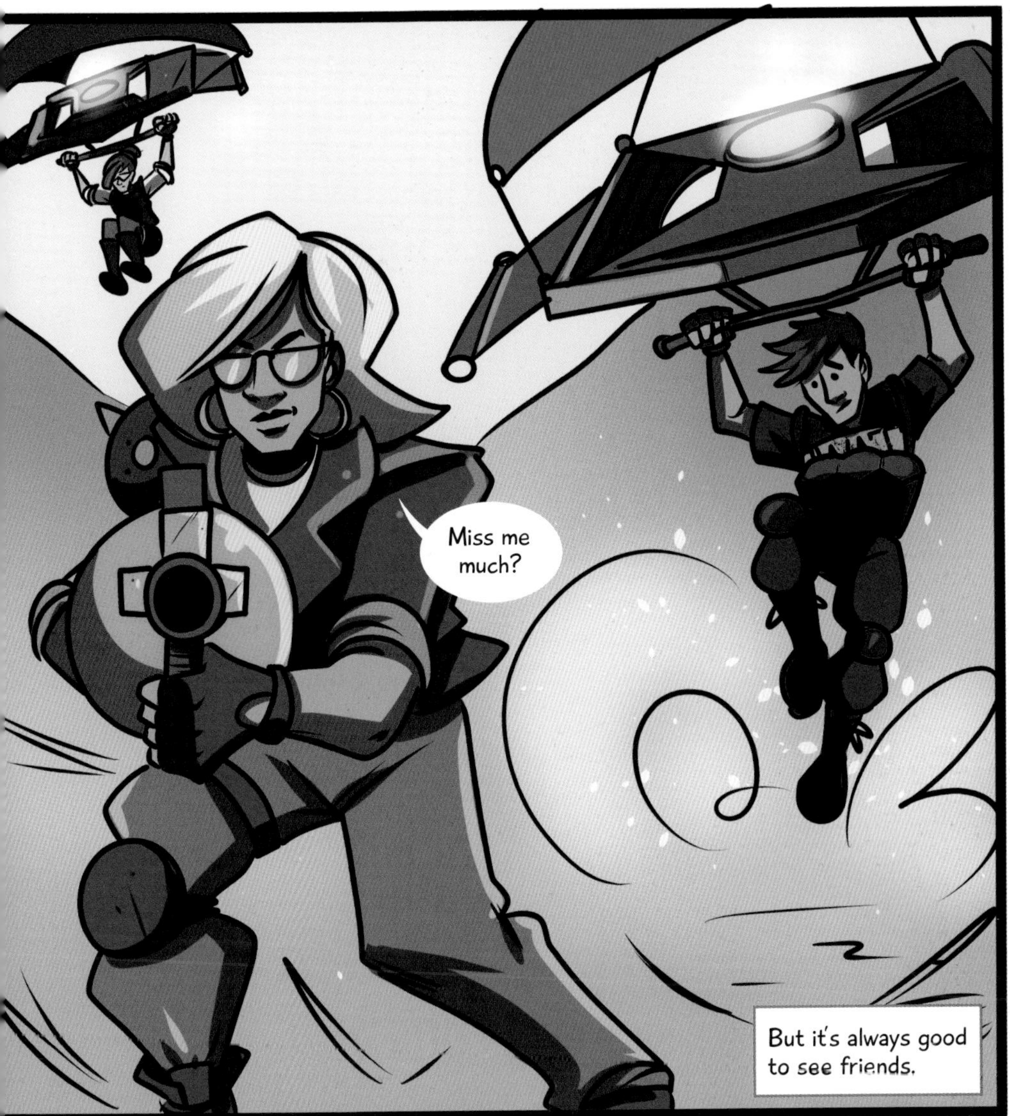
Miss me much?
But it's always good to see friends.

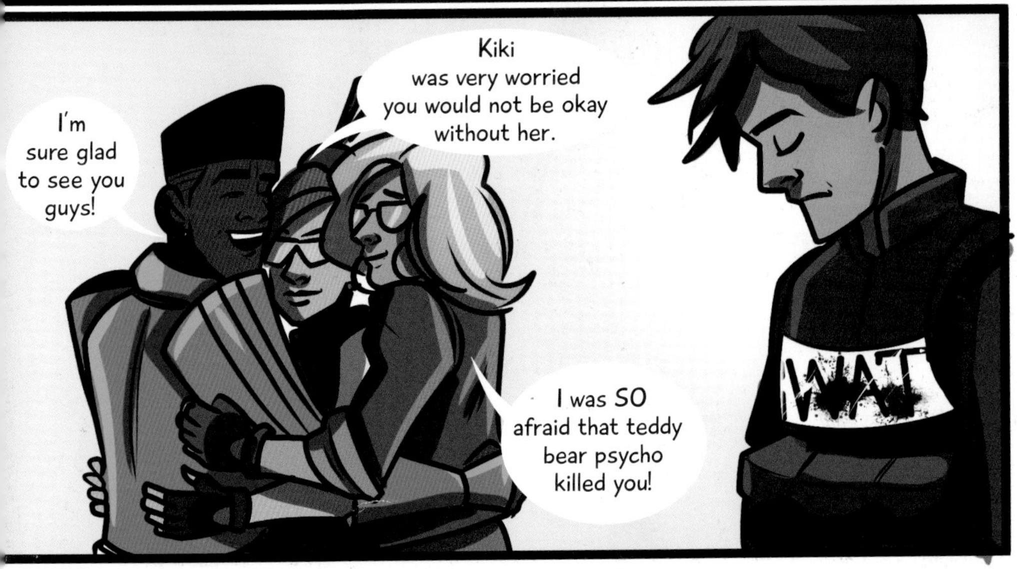
I'm sure glad to see you guys!
Kiki was very worried you would not be okay without her.
I was SO afraid that teddy bear psycho killed you!
WAT

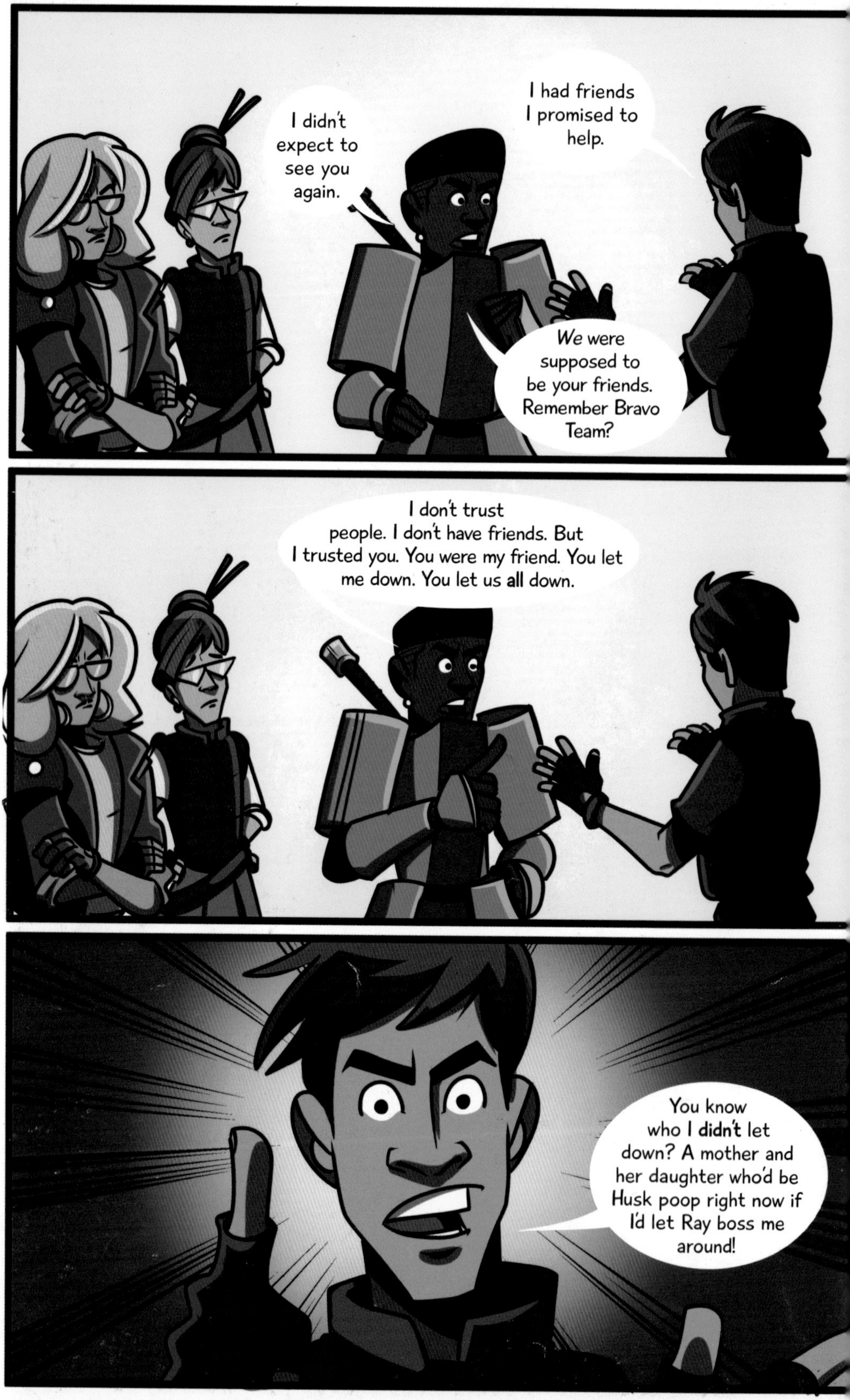
I didn't expect to see you again.
I had friends I promised to help.
We were supposed to be your friends. Remember Bravo Team?
I don't trust people. I don't have friends. But I trusted you. You were my friend. You let me down. You let us **all** down.
You know who I **didn't** let down? A mother and her daughter who'd be Husk poop right now if I'd let Ray boss me around!

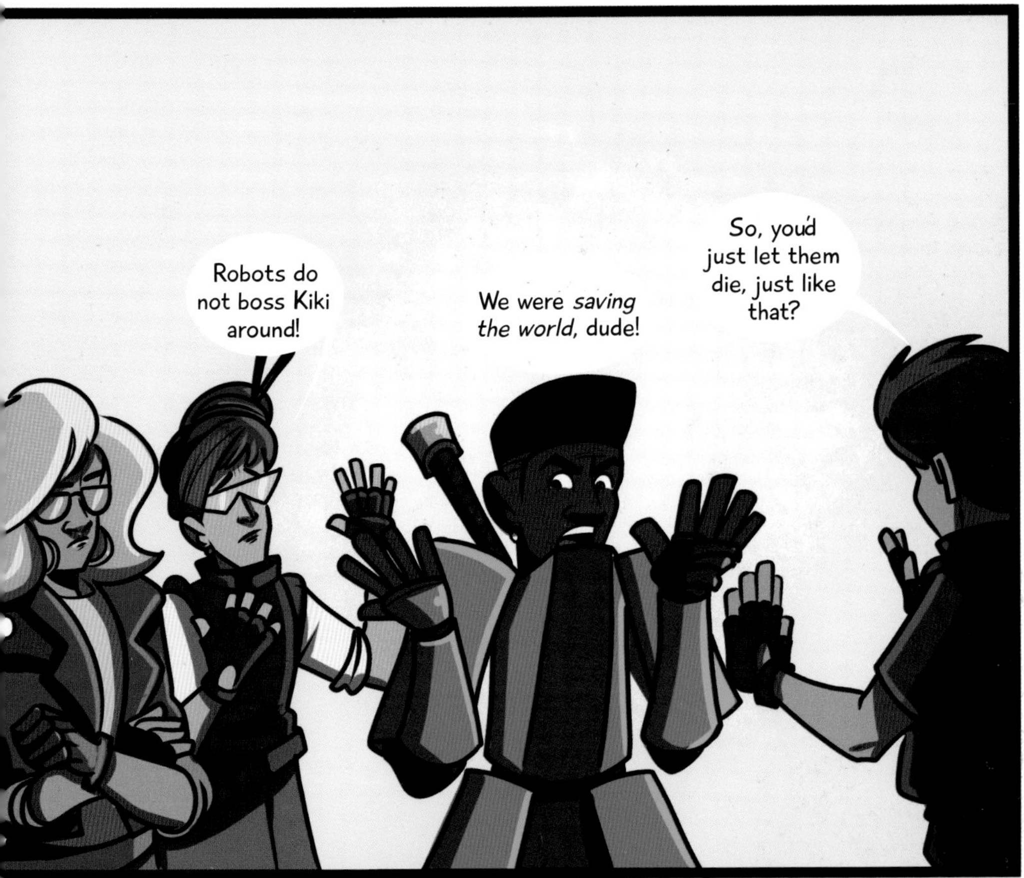
Robots do not boss Kiki around!
We were *saving the world*, dude!
So, you'd just let them die, just like that?

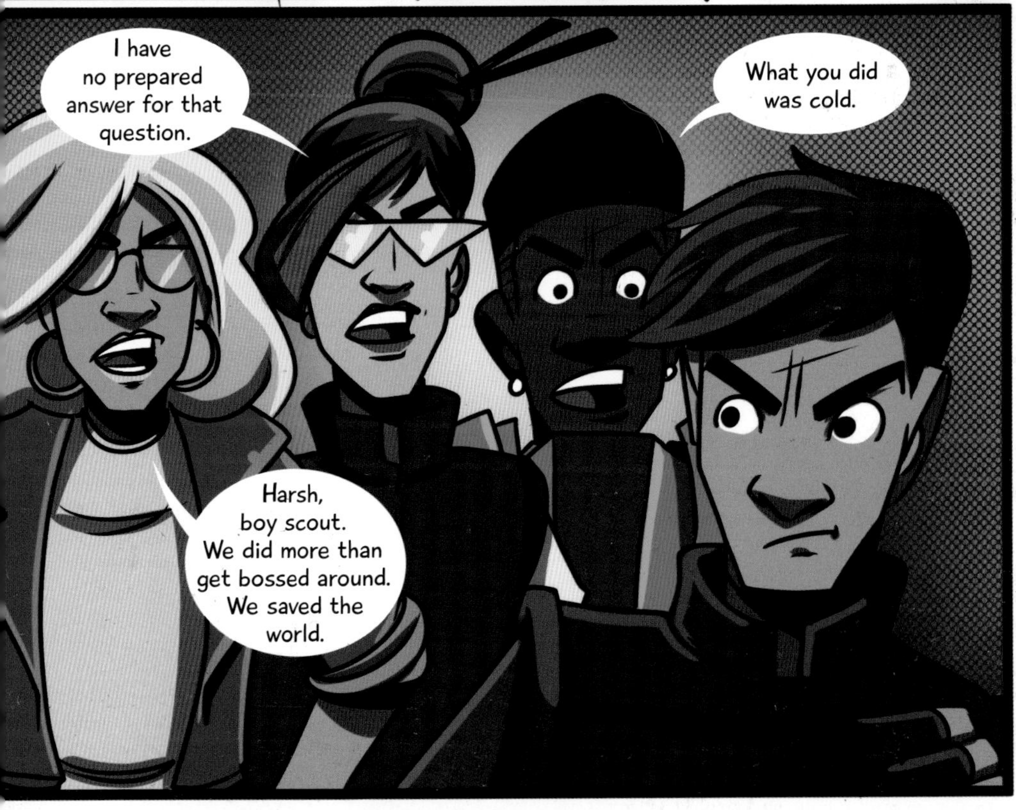
I have no prepared answer for that question.
What you did was cold.
Harsh, boy scout. We did more than get bossed around. We saved the world.

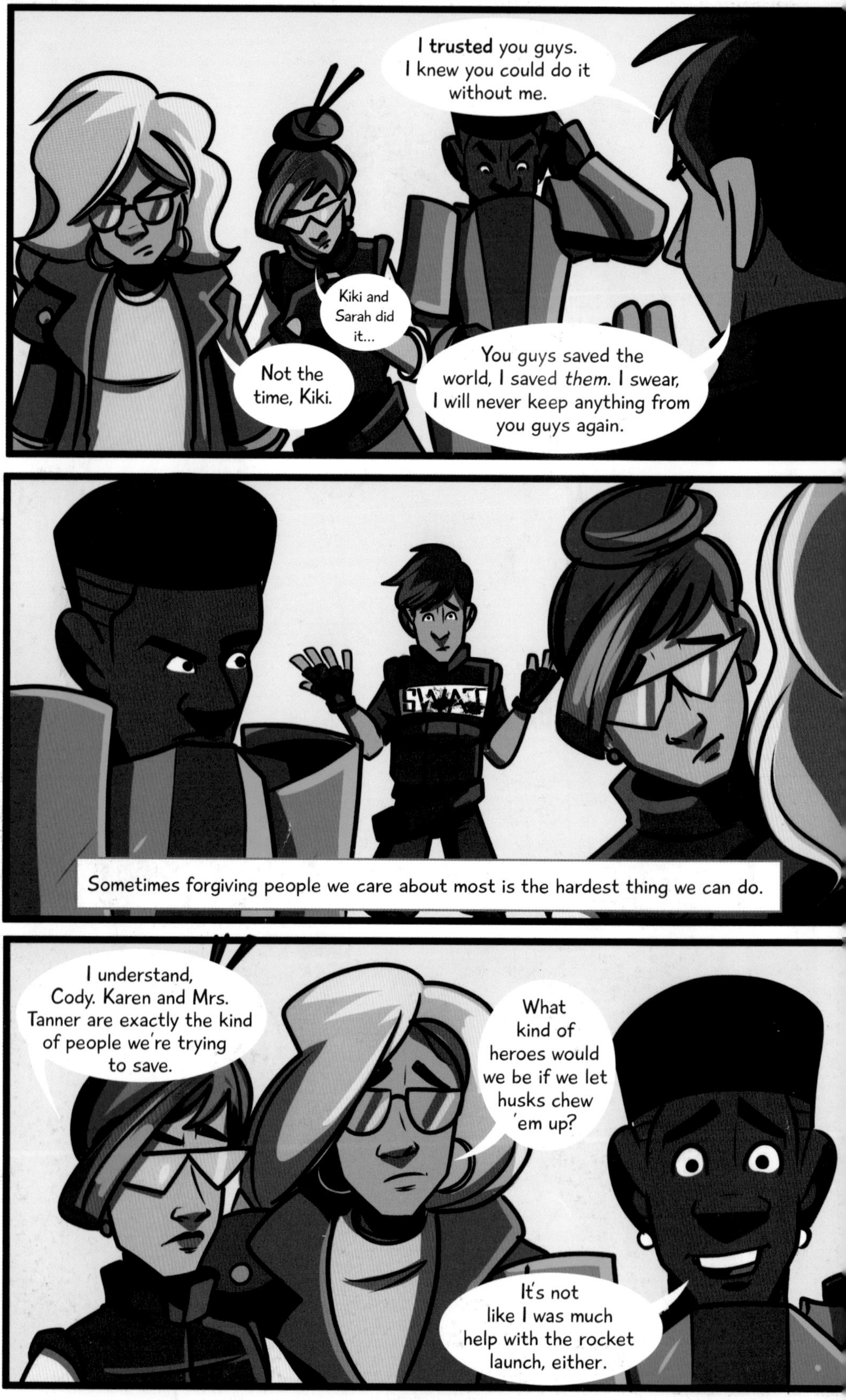
I **trusted** you guys. I knew you could do it without me.
Kiki and Sarah did it...
Not the time, Kiki.
You guys saved the world, I saved *them.* I swear, I will never keep anything from you guys again.
Sometimes forgiving people we care about most is the hardest thing we can do.
I understand, Cody. Karen and Mrs. Tanner are exactly the kind of people we're trying to save.
What kind of heroes would we be if we let husks chew 'em up?
It's not like I was much help with the rocket launch, either.

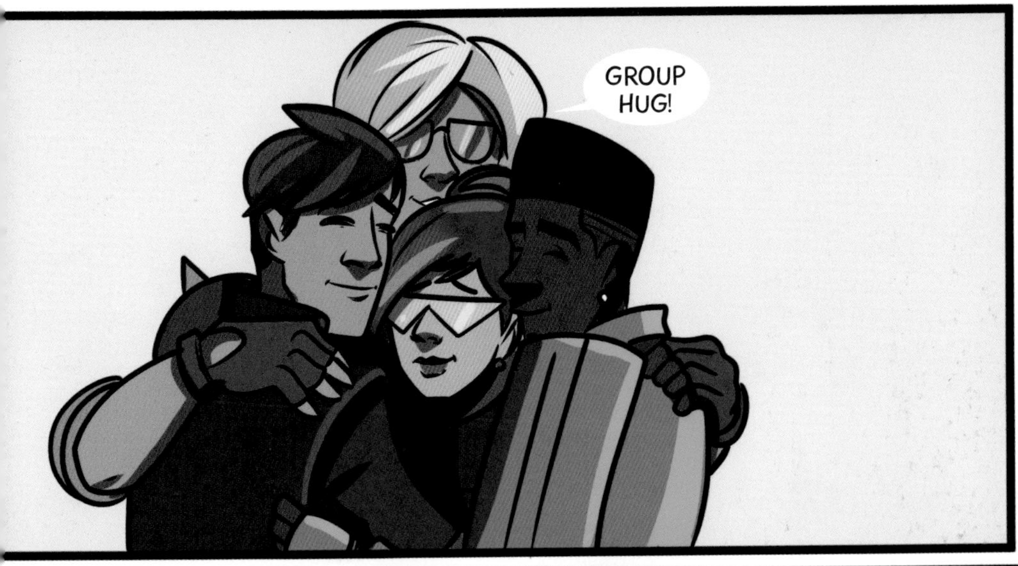
GROUP HUG!

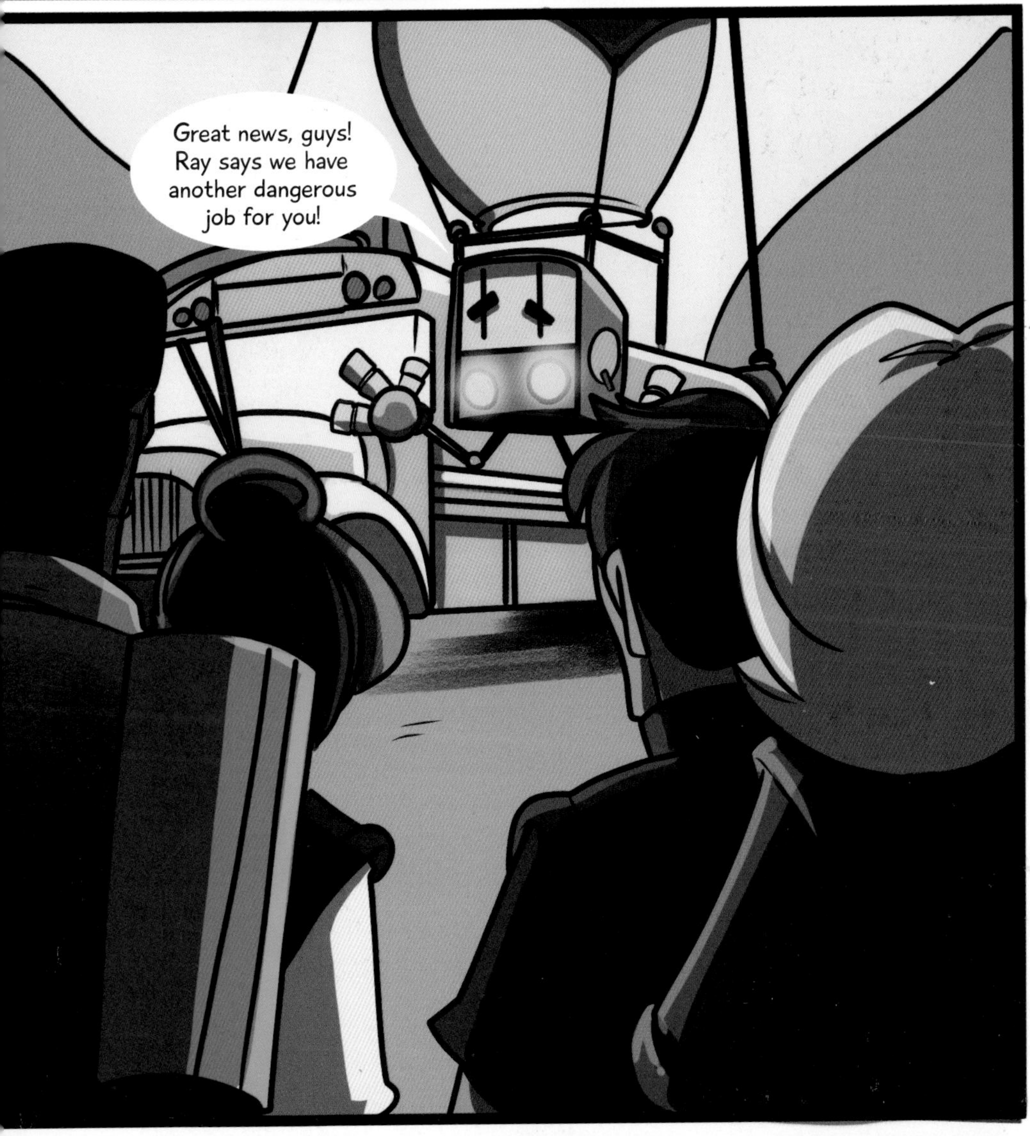
Great news, guys! Ray says we have another dangerous job for you!

CHAPTER 3: DEALT A BAD HAND

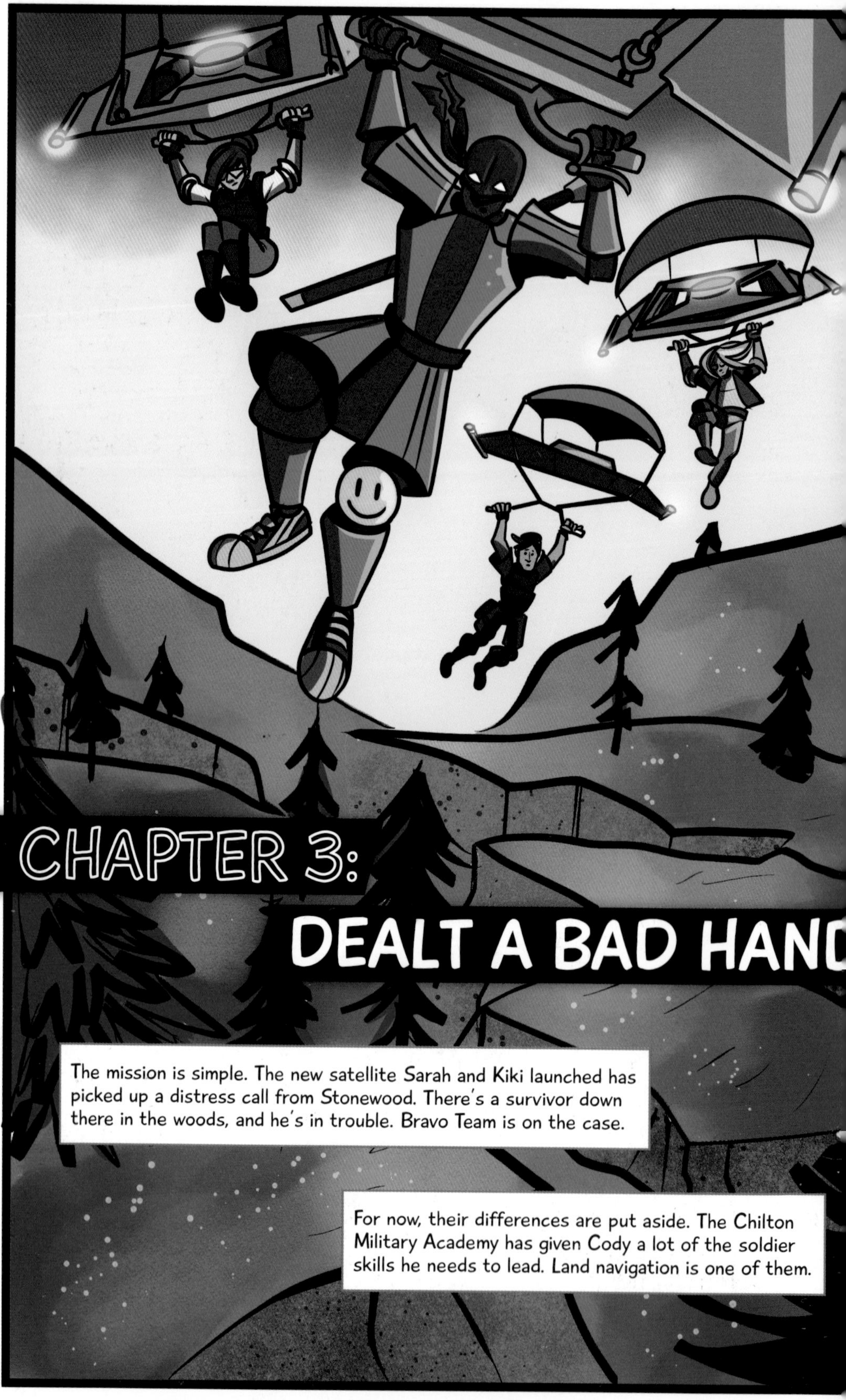
The mission is simple. The new satellite Sarah and Kiki launched has picked up a distress call from Stonewood. There's a survivor down there in the woods, and he's in trouble. Bravo Team is on the case.
For now, their differences are put aside. The Chilton Military Academy has given Cody a lot of the soldier skills he needs to lead. Land navigation is one of them.

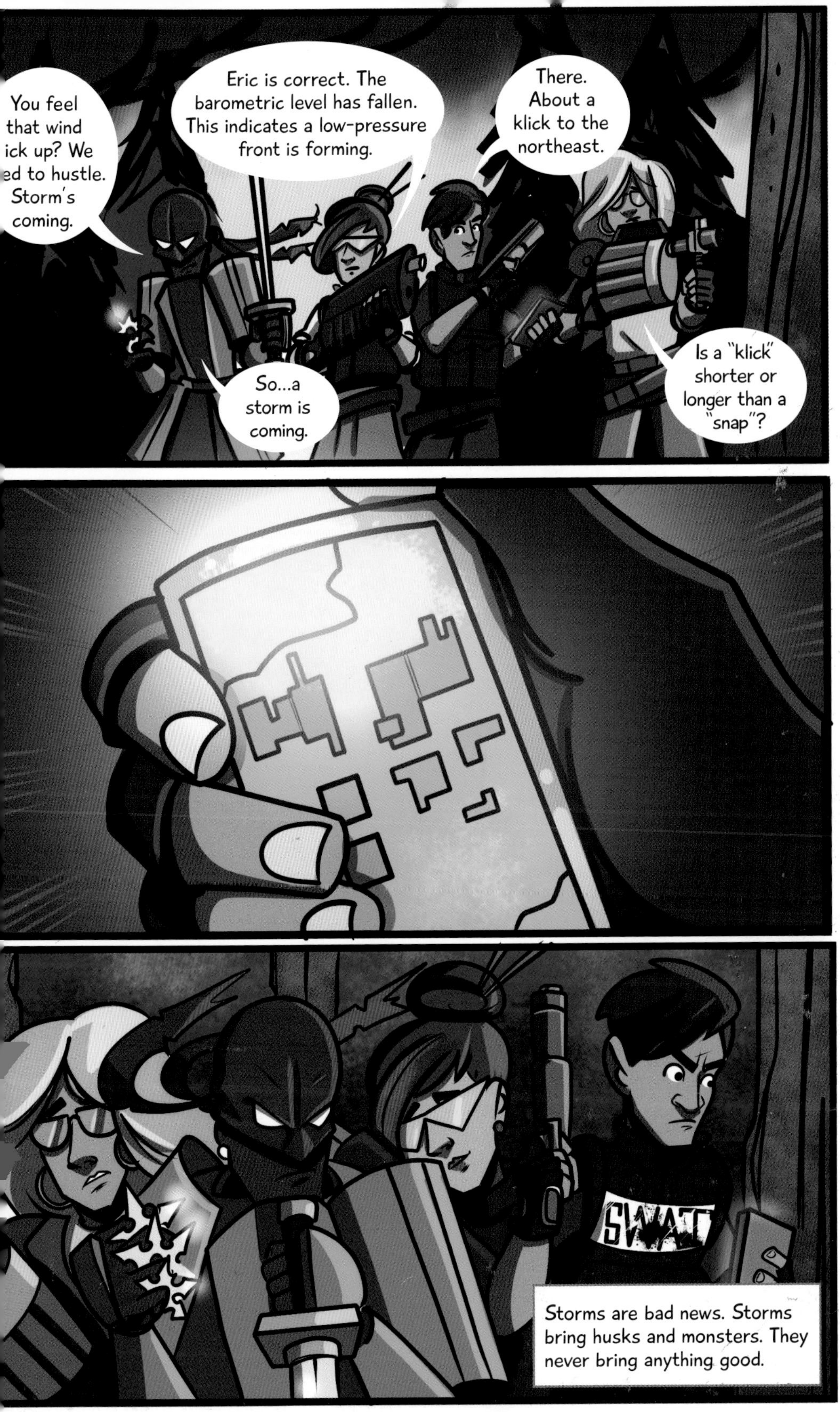
You feel that wind ick up? We ed to hustle. Storm's coming.
Eric is correct. The barometric level has fallen. This indicates a low-pressure front is forming.
There. About a klick to the northeast.
So...a storm is coming.
Is a "klick" shorter or longer than a "snap"?
SWAT
Storms are bad news. Storms bring husks and monsters. They never bring anything good.

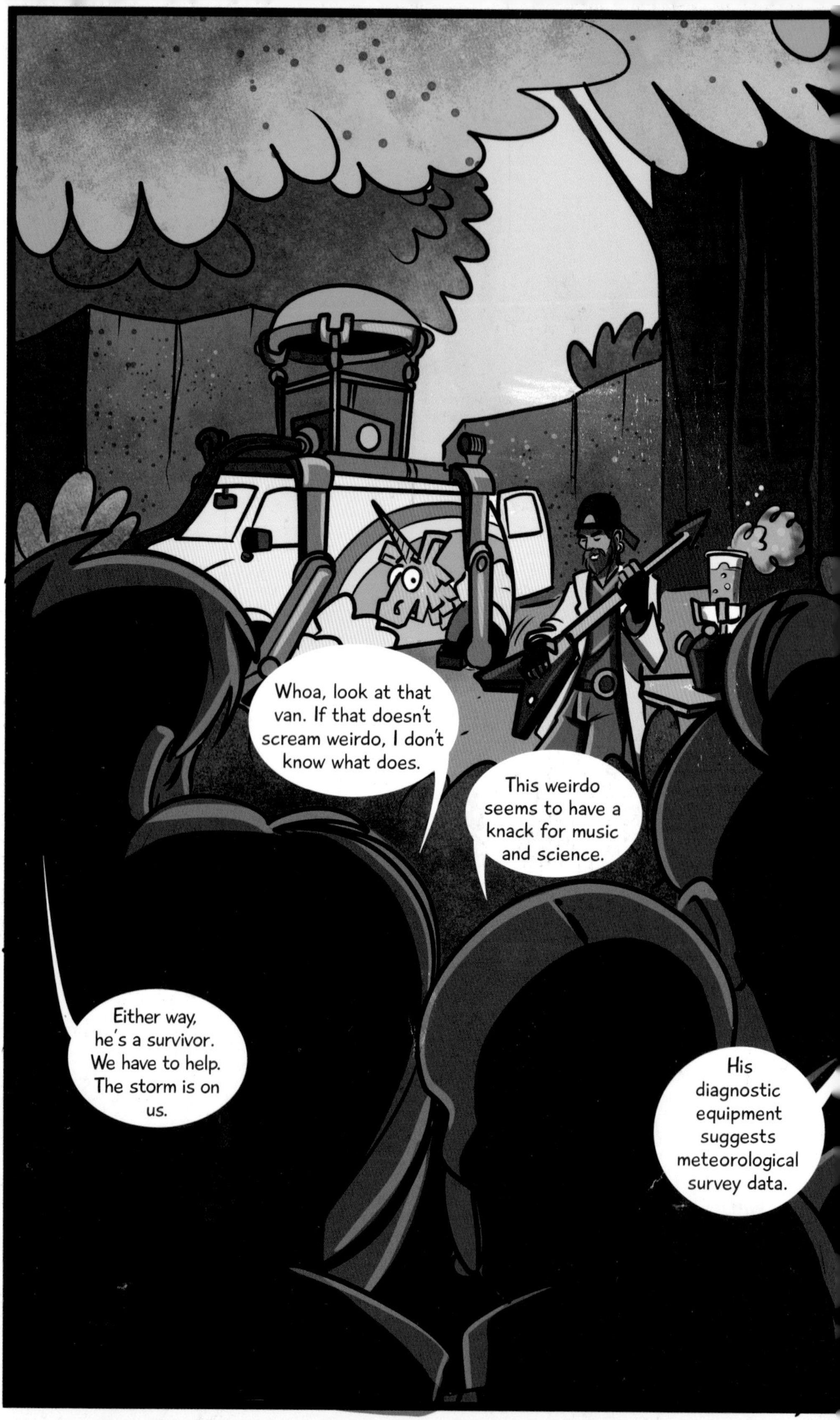

Whoa, look at that van. If that doesn't scream weirdo, I don't know what does.
This weirdo seems to have a knack for music and science.
Either way, he's a survivor. We have to help. The storm is on us.
His diagnostic equipment suggests meteorological survey data.

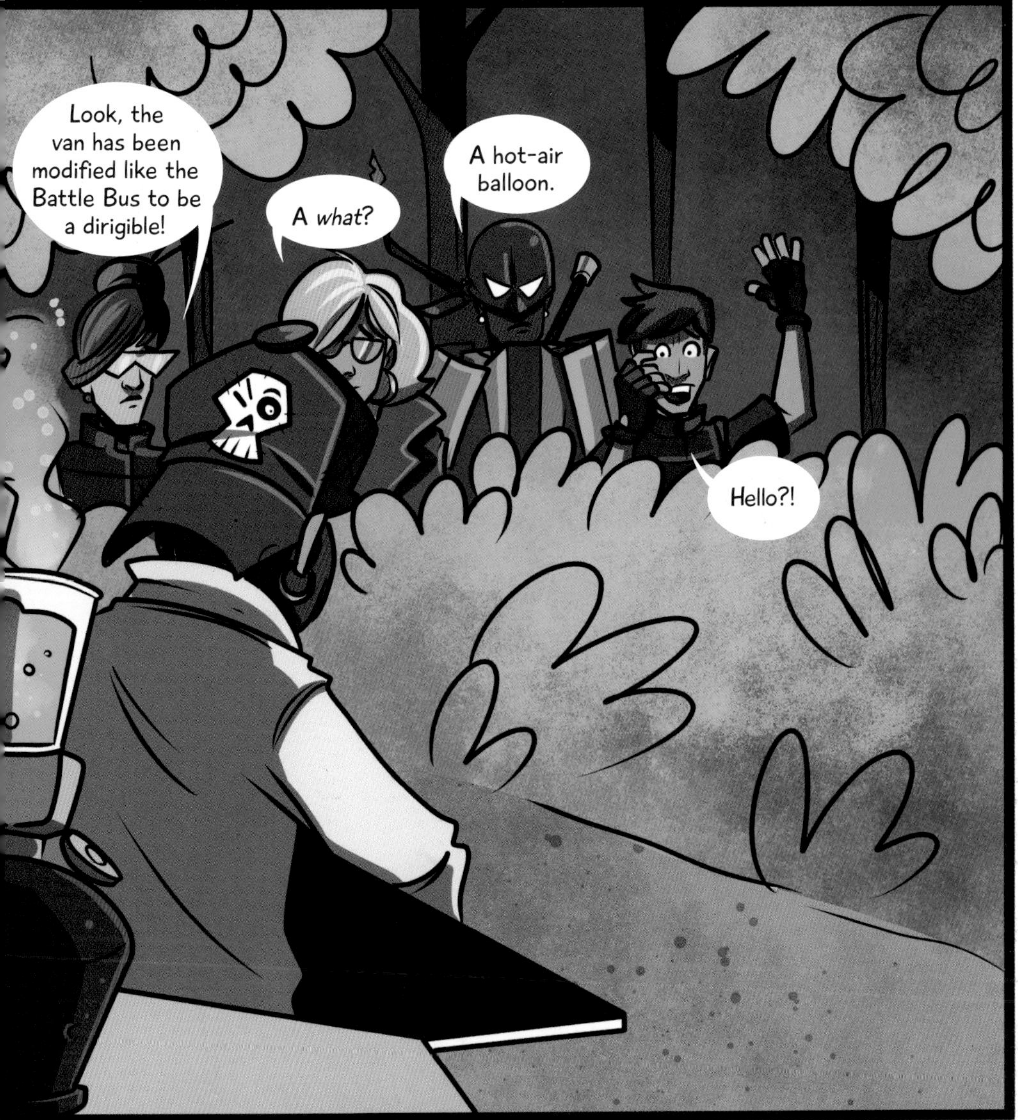
Look, the van has been modified like the Battle Bus to be a dirigible!
A *what*?
A hot-air balloon.
Hello?!
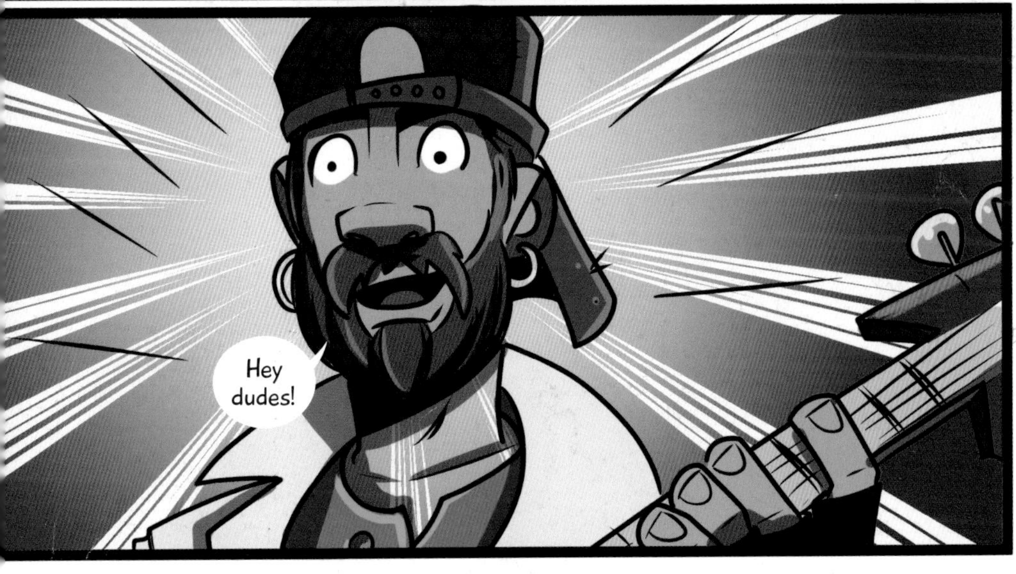
Hey dudes!

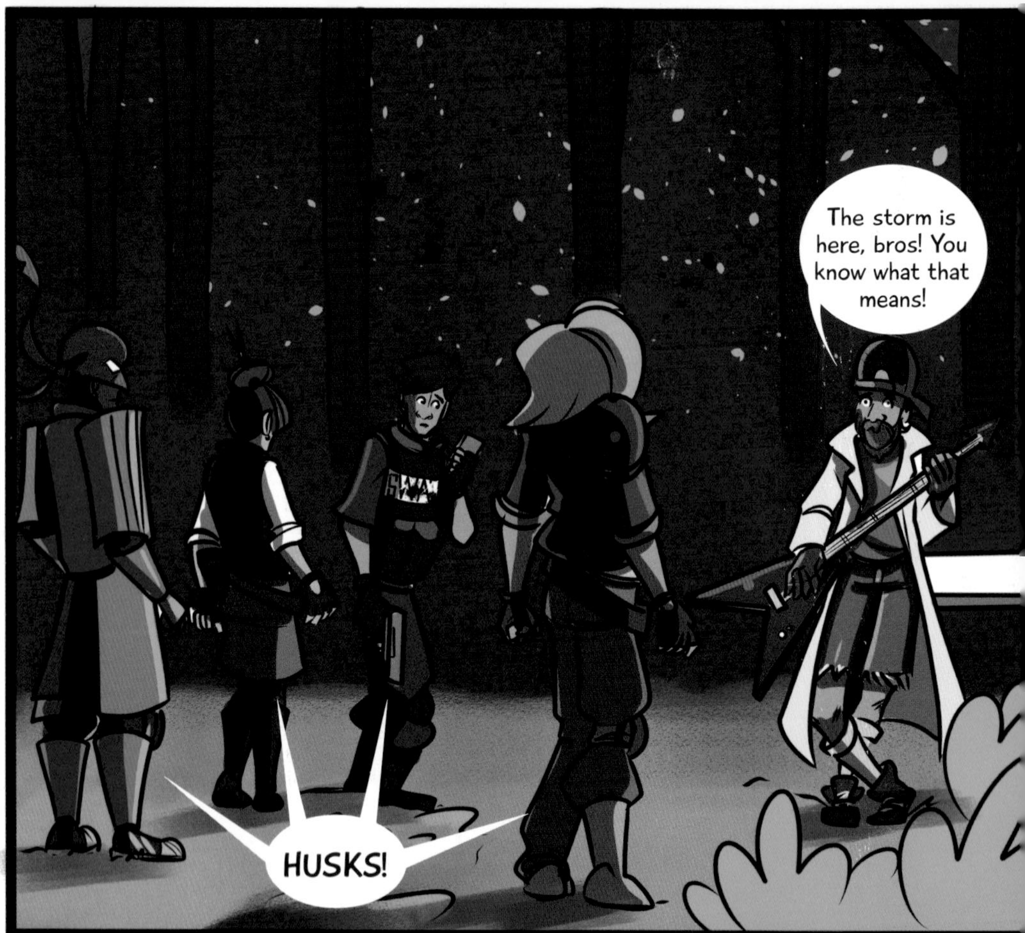
The storm is here, bros! You know what that means!
HUSKS!

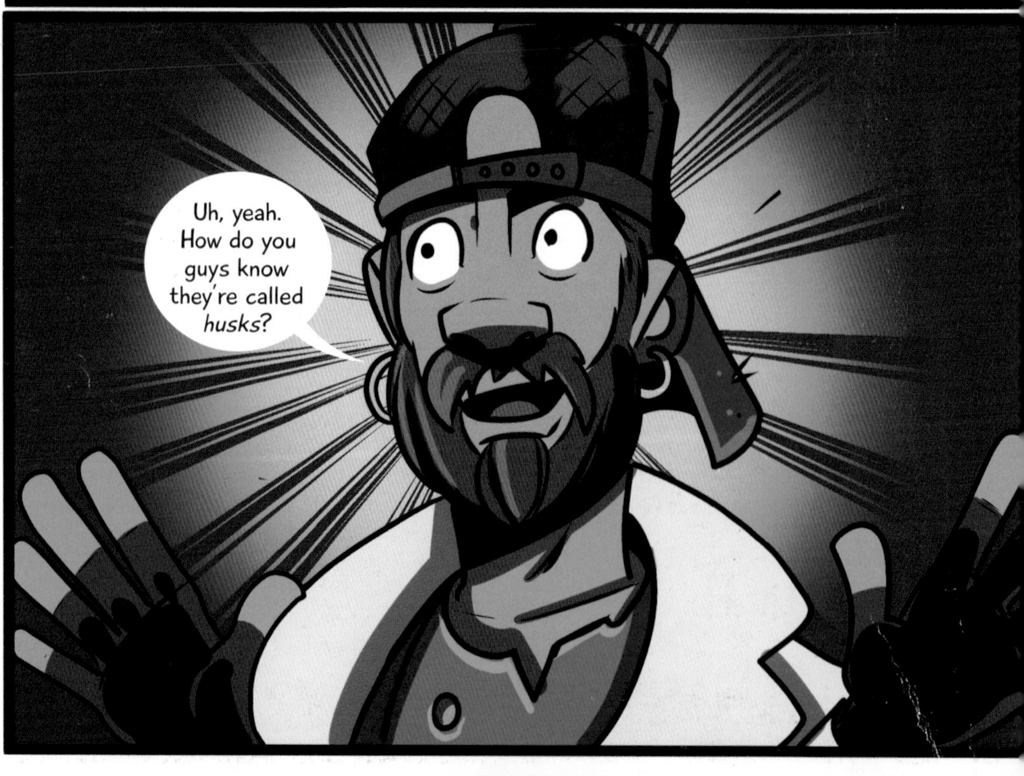
Uh, yeah. How do you guys know they're called *husks*?

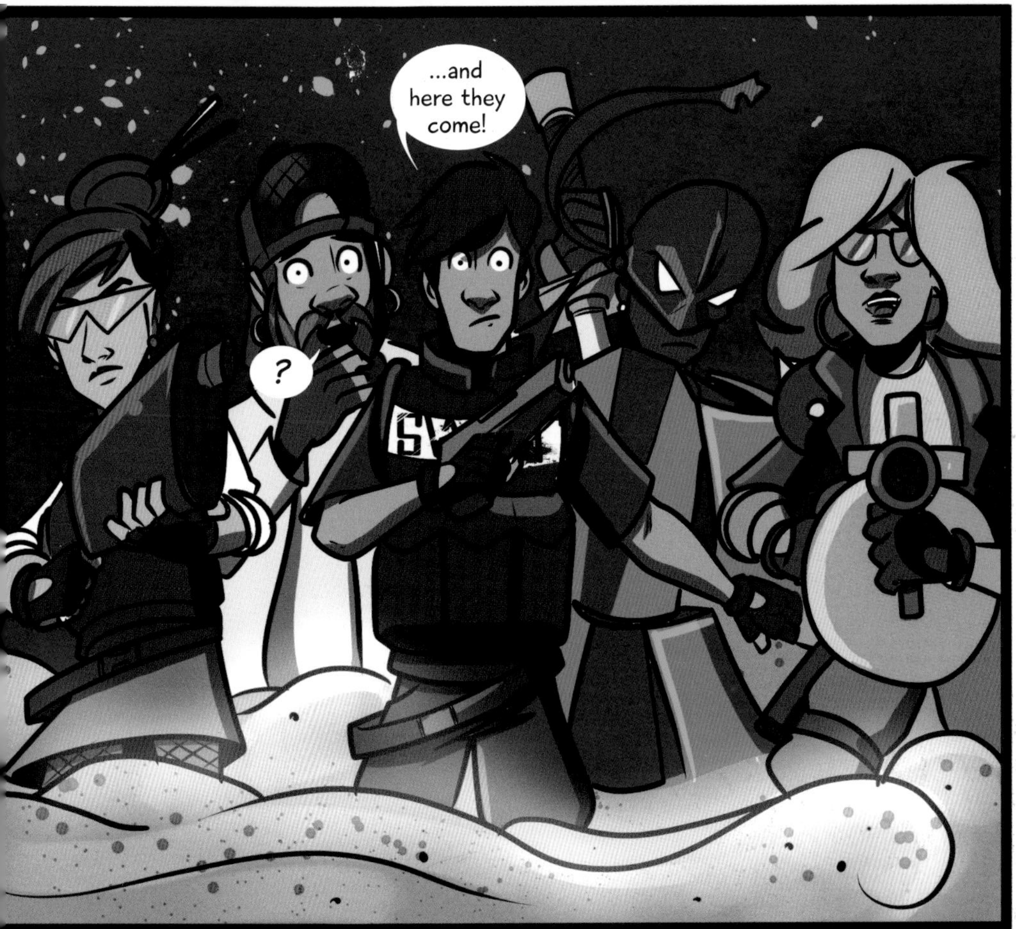
...and here they come!
?

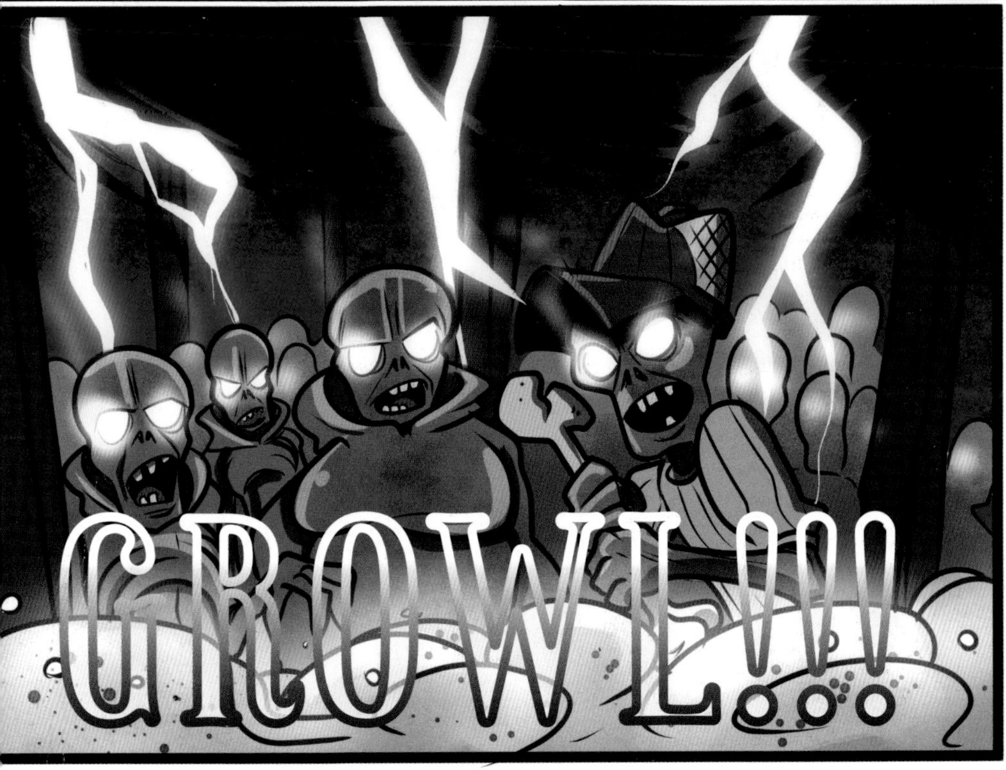
GROWL!!!

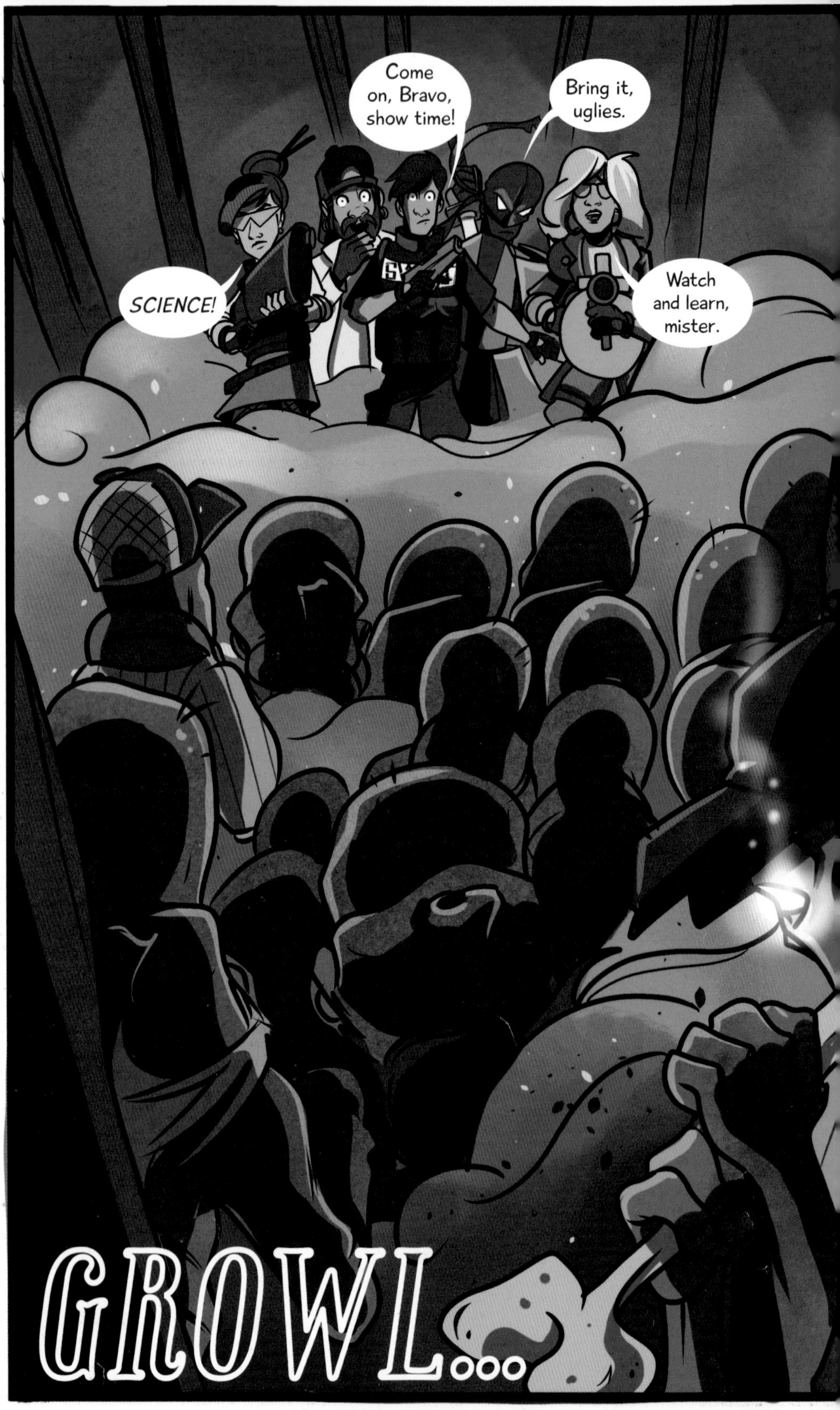

Come on, Bravo, show time!
Bring it, uglies.
SCIENCE!
Watch and learn, mister.
GROWL...

BOOM-BOOM-BOOM!
THUMP!-THUMP!-THUMP!
CRACK-CRACK CRACK-CRACK

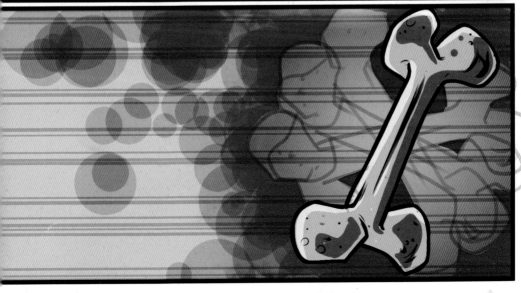

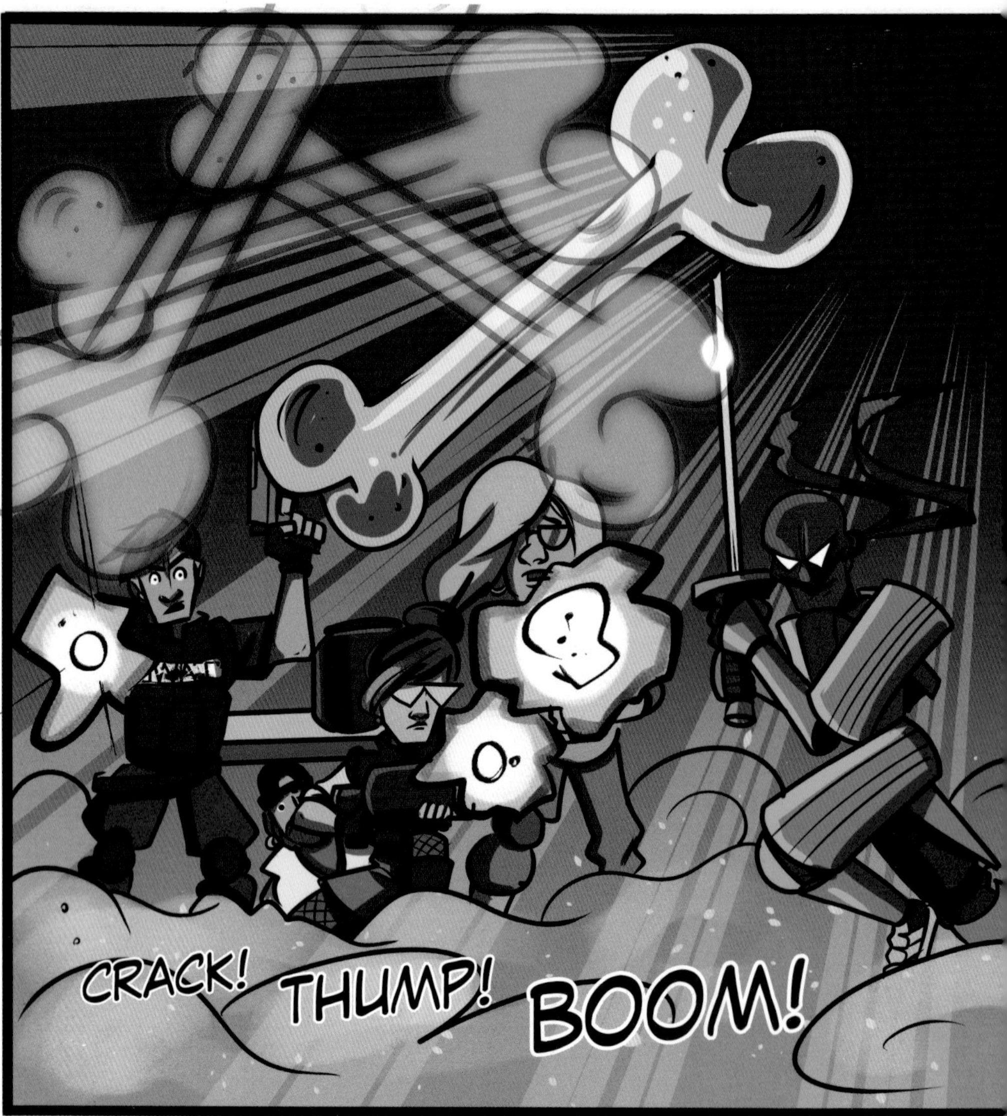
CRACK!
THUMP!
BOOM!

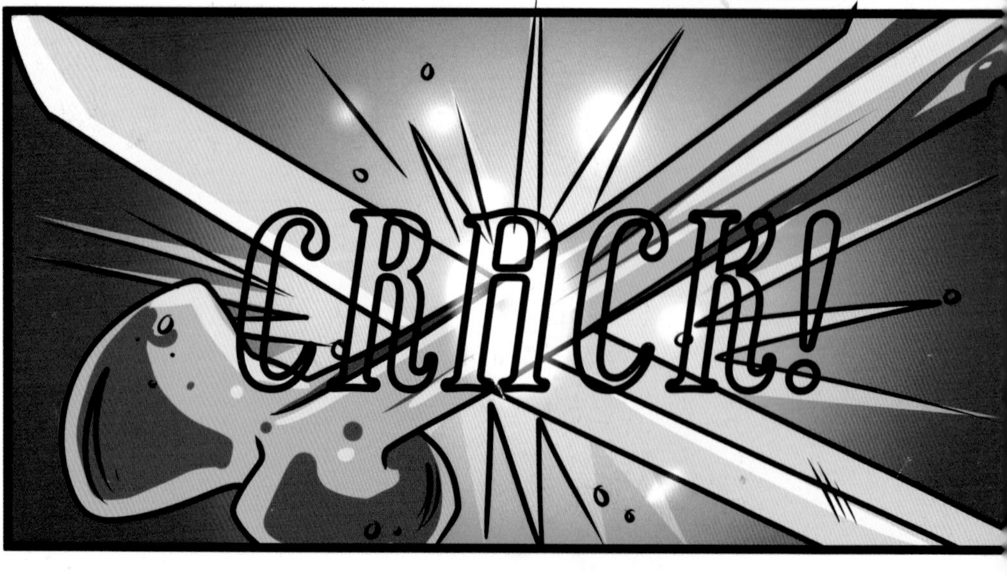
CRACK!

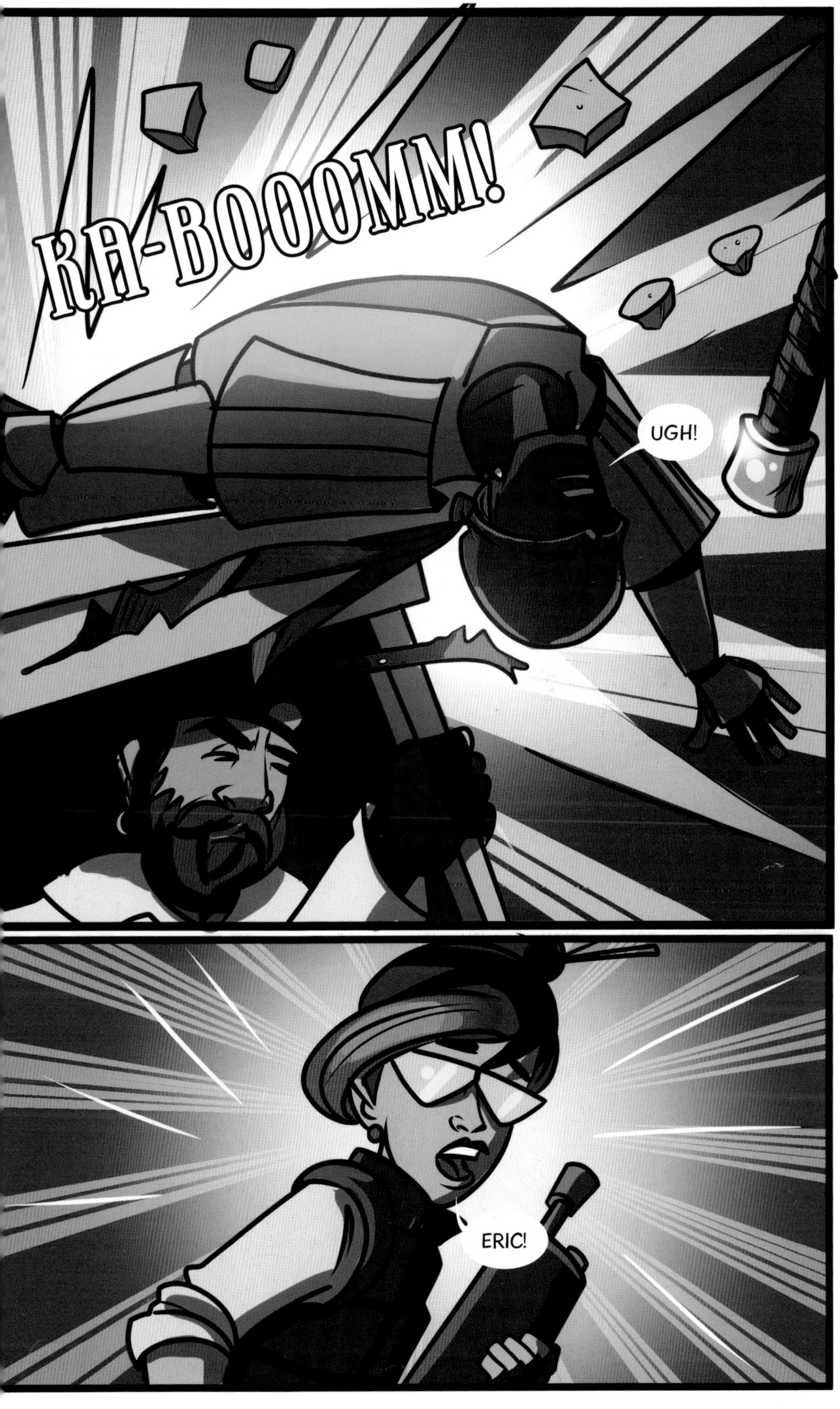
KA-BOOOMM!
UGH!
ERIC!

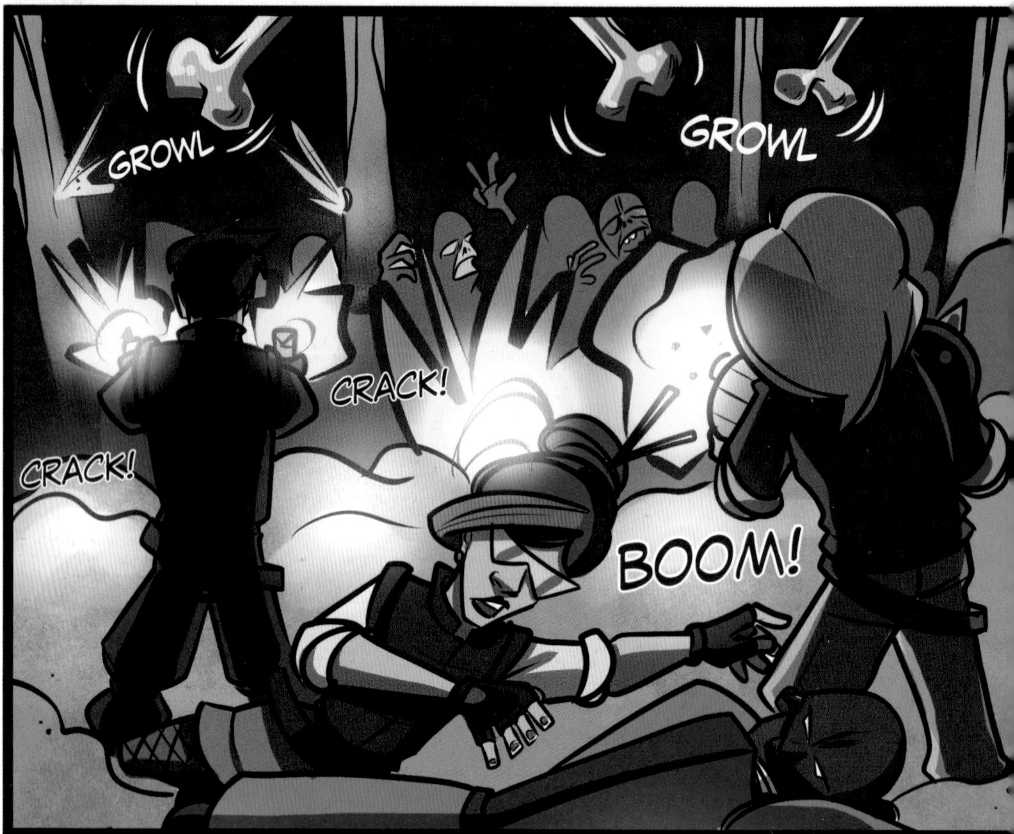
GROWL
GROWL
CRACK!
CRACK!
BOOM!

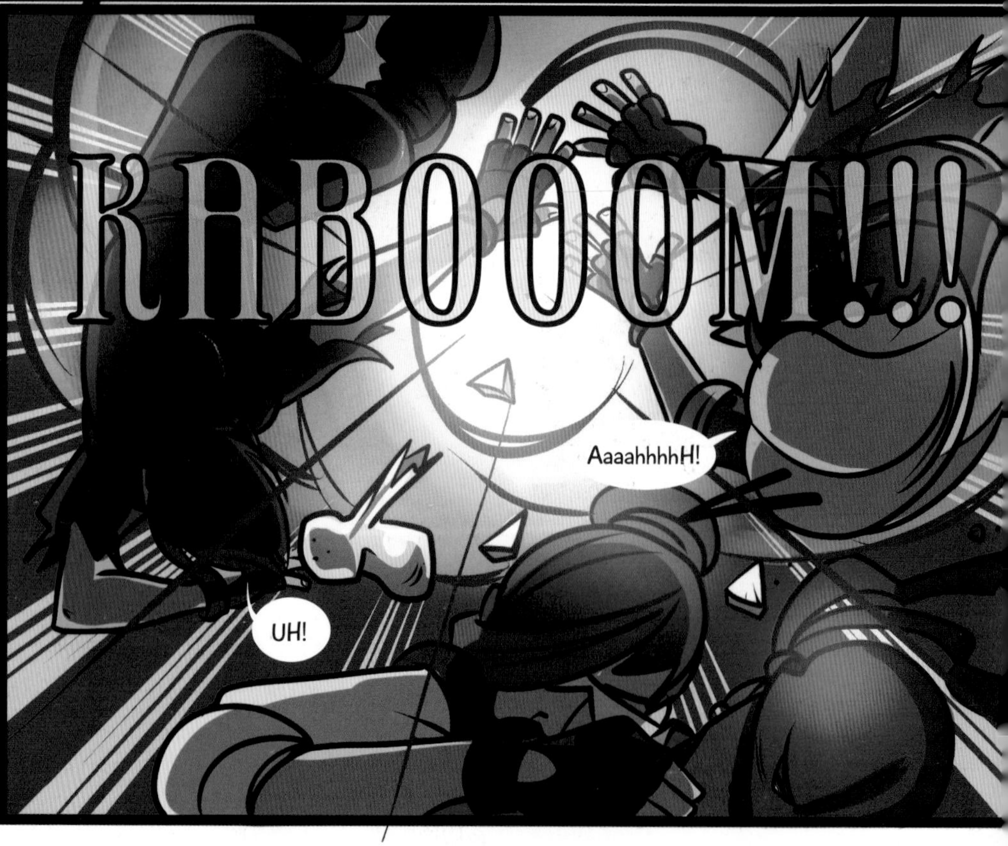
KABOOOM!!!
AaaahhhhH!
UH!

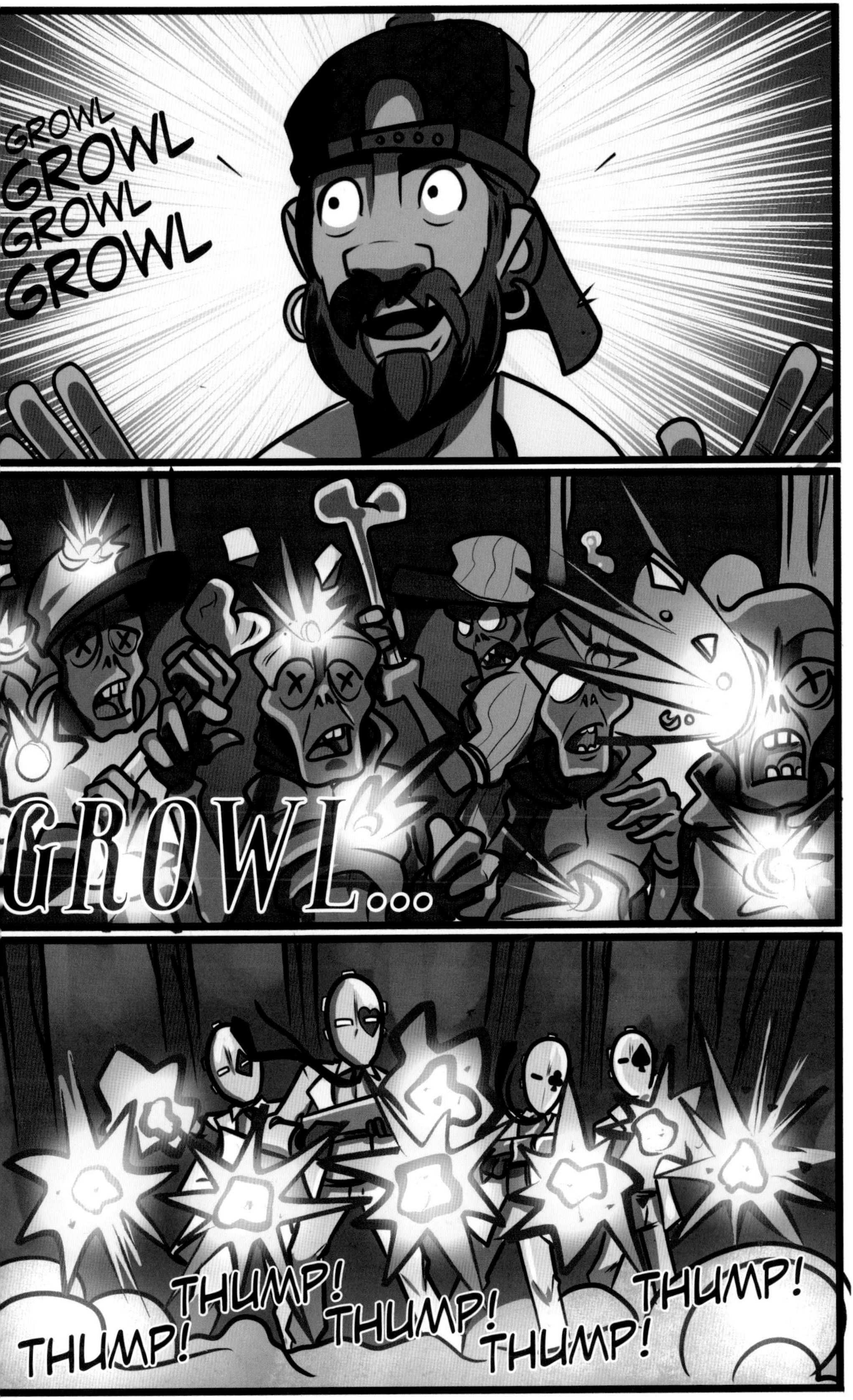
GROWL
GROWL
GROWL
GROWL
GROWL...
THUMP!
THUMP!
THUMP!
THUMP!
THUMP!

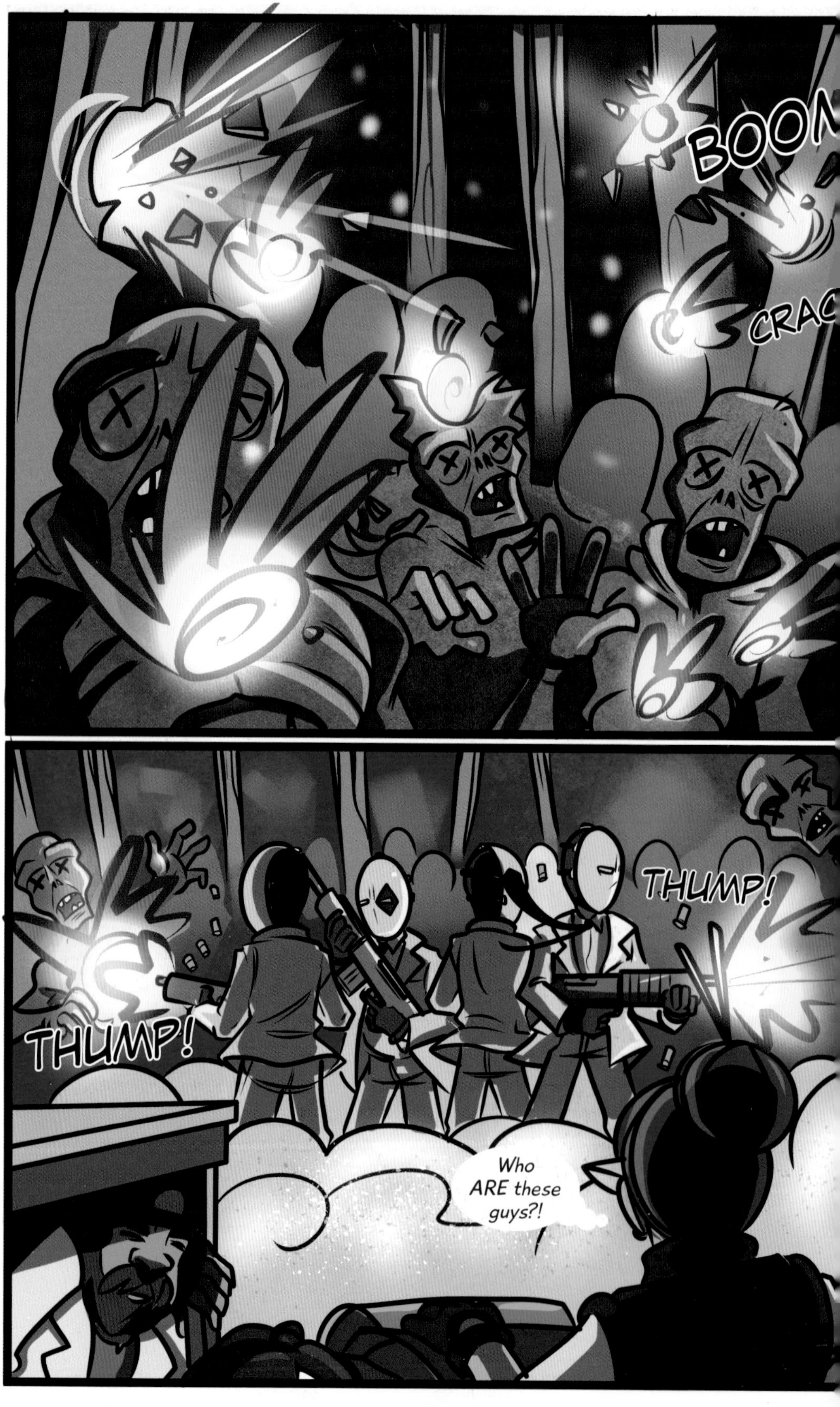
BOO
CRAC
THUMP!
THUMP!
Who ARE these guys?!

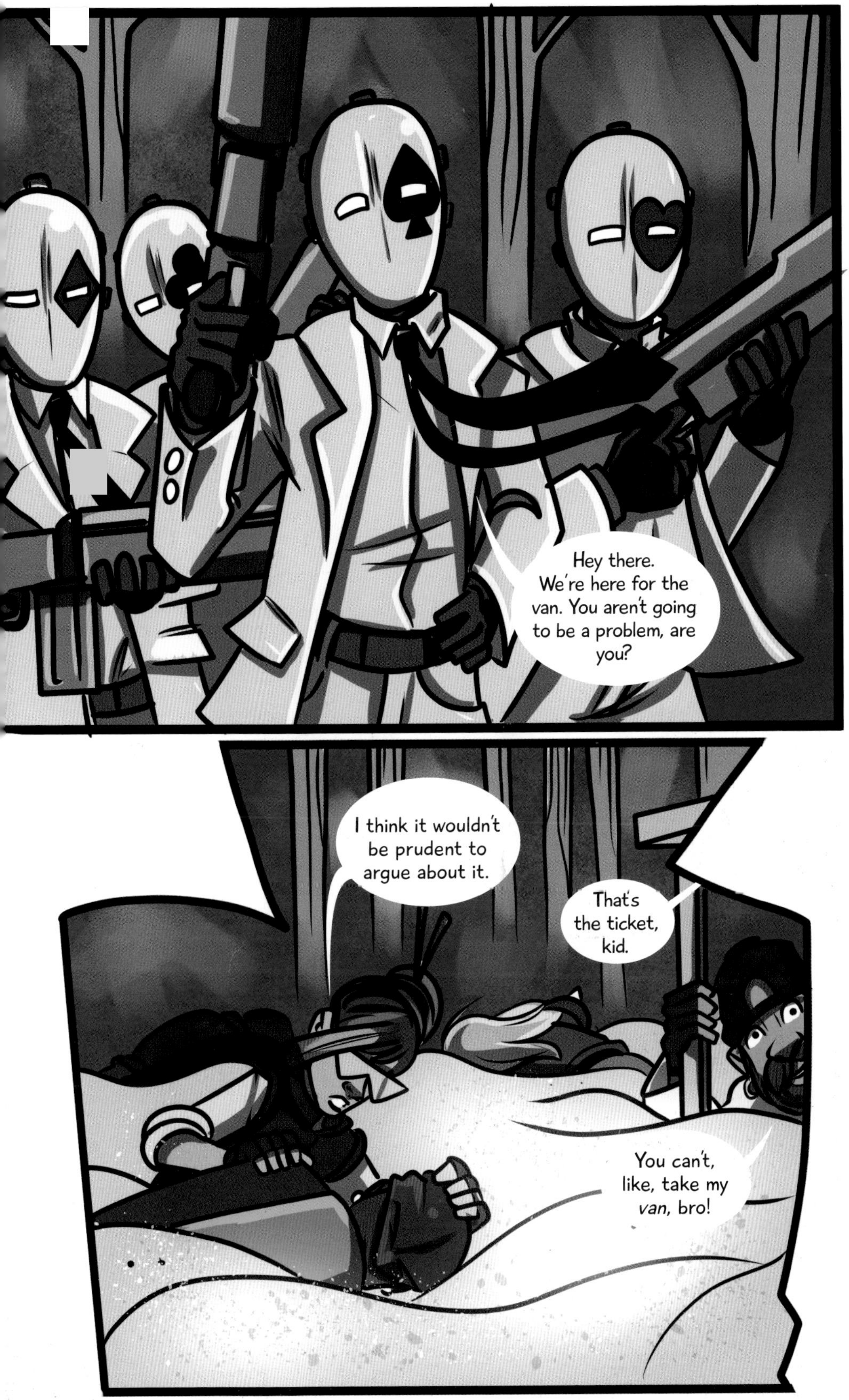
Hey there. We're here for the van. You aren't going to be a problem, are you?
I think it wouldn't be prudent to argue about it.
That's the ticket, kid.
You can't, like, take my *van*, bro!

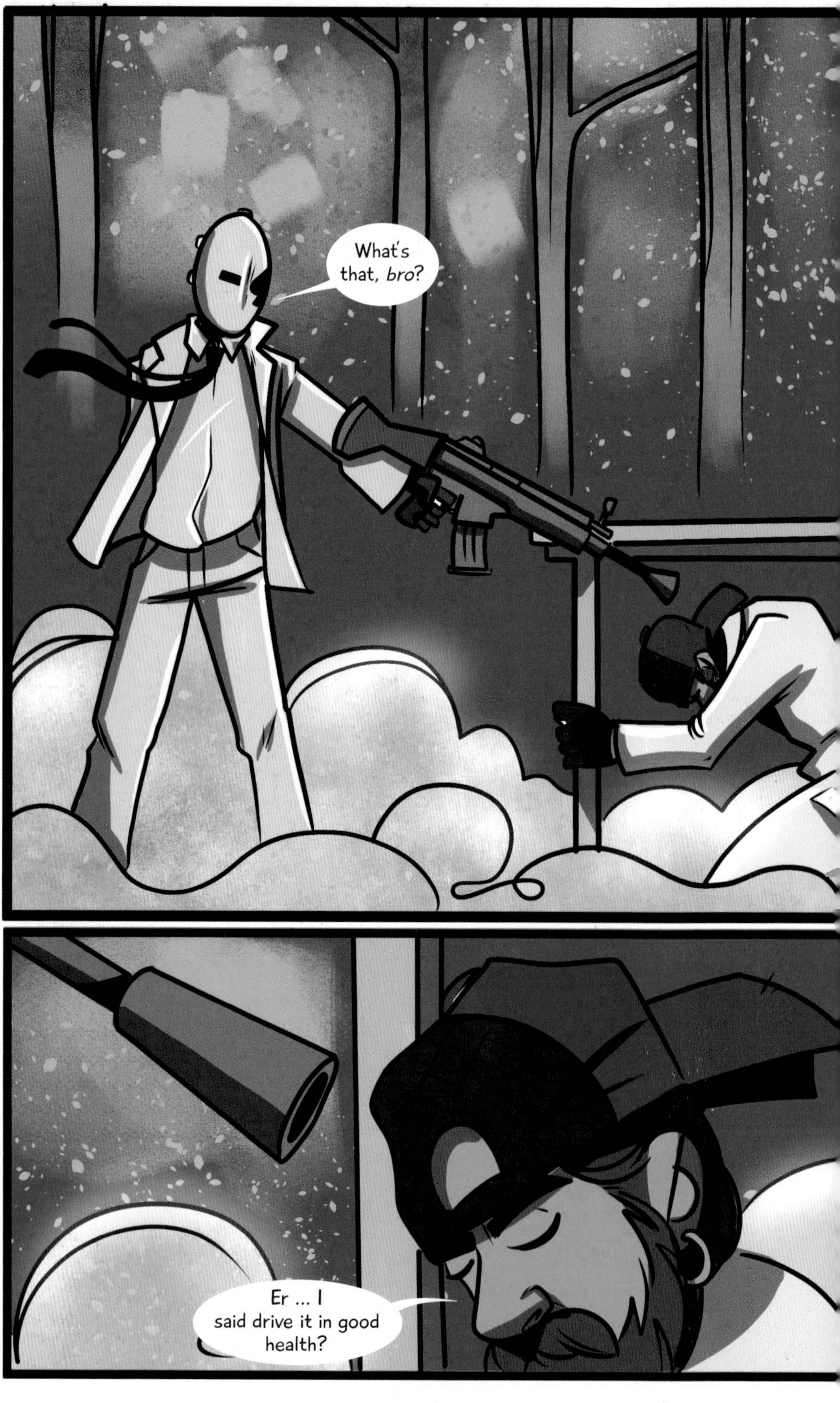
What's that, *bro*?
Er ... I said drive it in good health?

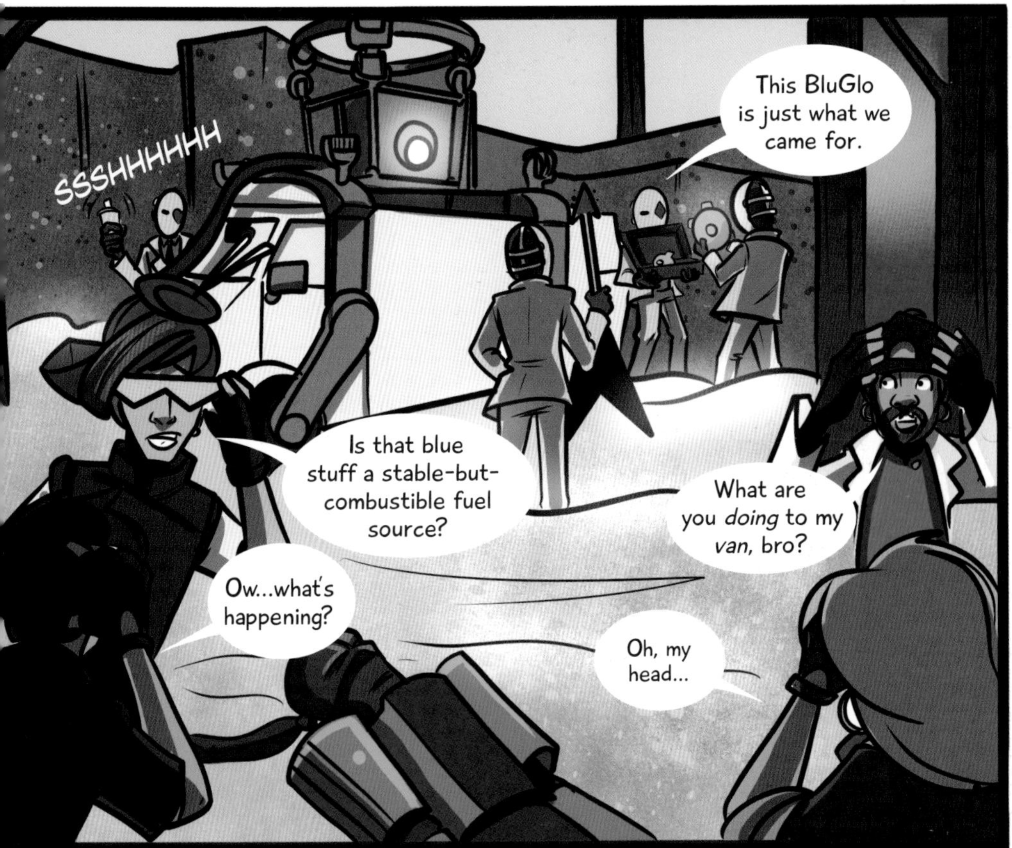
SSSHHHHHH
This BluGlo is just what we came for.
Is that blue stuff a stable-but-combustible fuel source?
What are you *doing* to my *van*, bro?
Ow...what's happening?
Oh, my head...
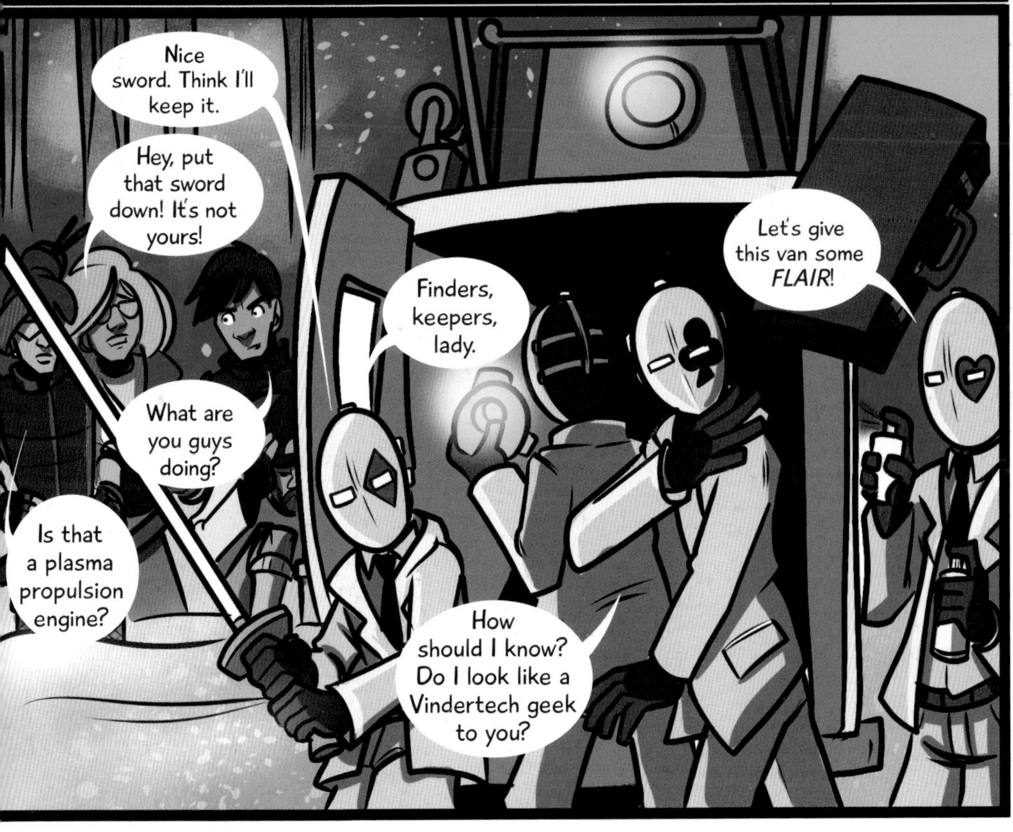
Nice sword. Think I'll keep it.
Hey, put that sword down! It's not yours!
Finders, keepers, lady.
Let's give this van some *FLAIR*!
What are you guys doing?
Is that a plasma propulsion engine?
How should I know? Do I look like a Vindertech geek to you?

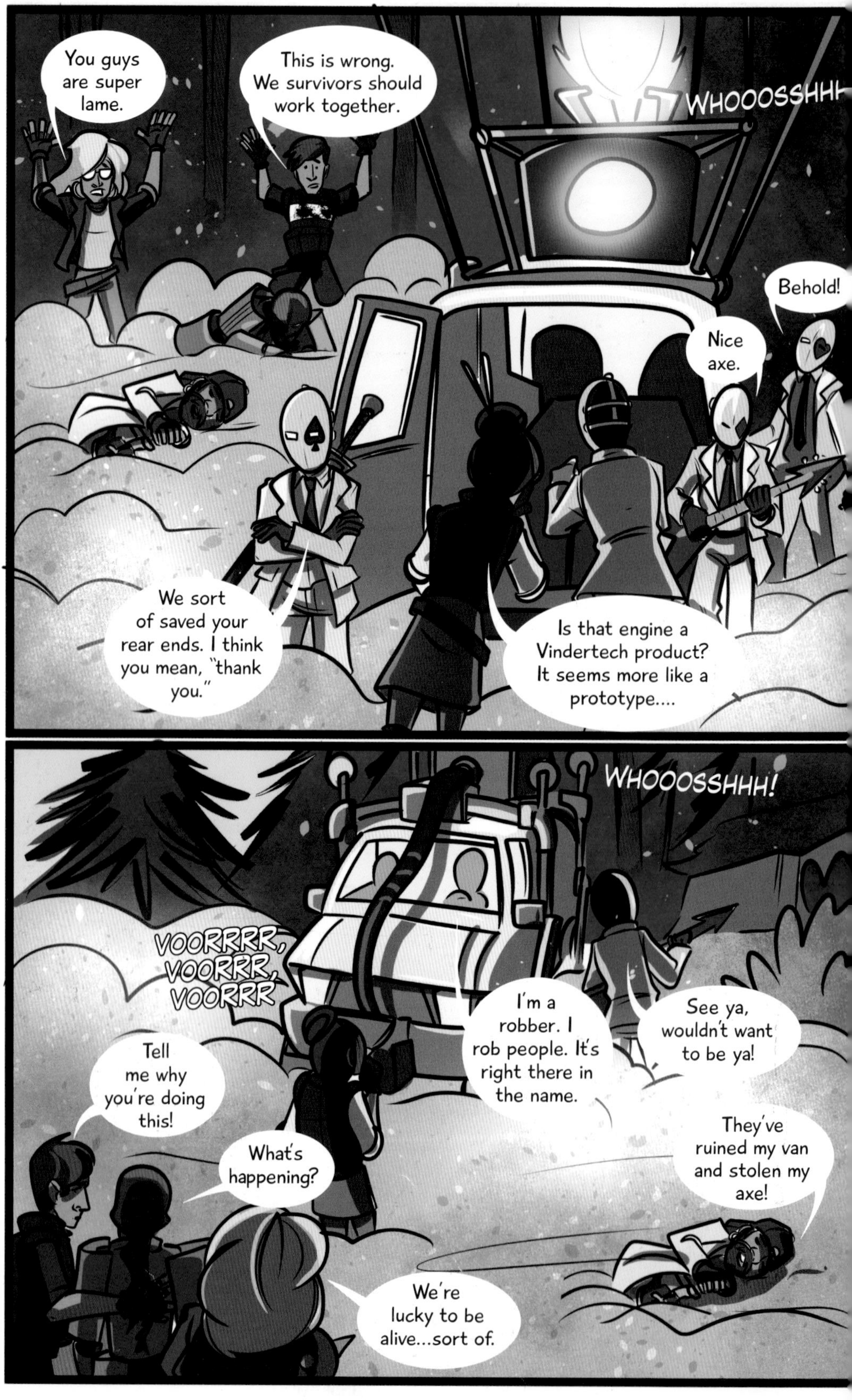
You guys are super lame.
This is wrong. We survivors should work together.
WHOOOSSHHH
Behold!
Nice axe.
We sort of saved your rear ends. I think you mean, "thank you."
Is that engine a Vindertech product? It seems more like a prototype....
WHOOOSSHHH!
VOORRRR, VOORRR, VOORRR
I'm a robber. I rob people. It's right there in the name.
See ya, wouldn't want to be ya!
Tell me why you're doing this!
What's happening?
They've ruined my van and stolen my axe!
We're lucky to be alive...sort of.

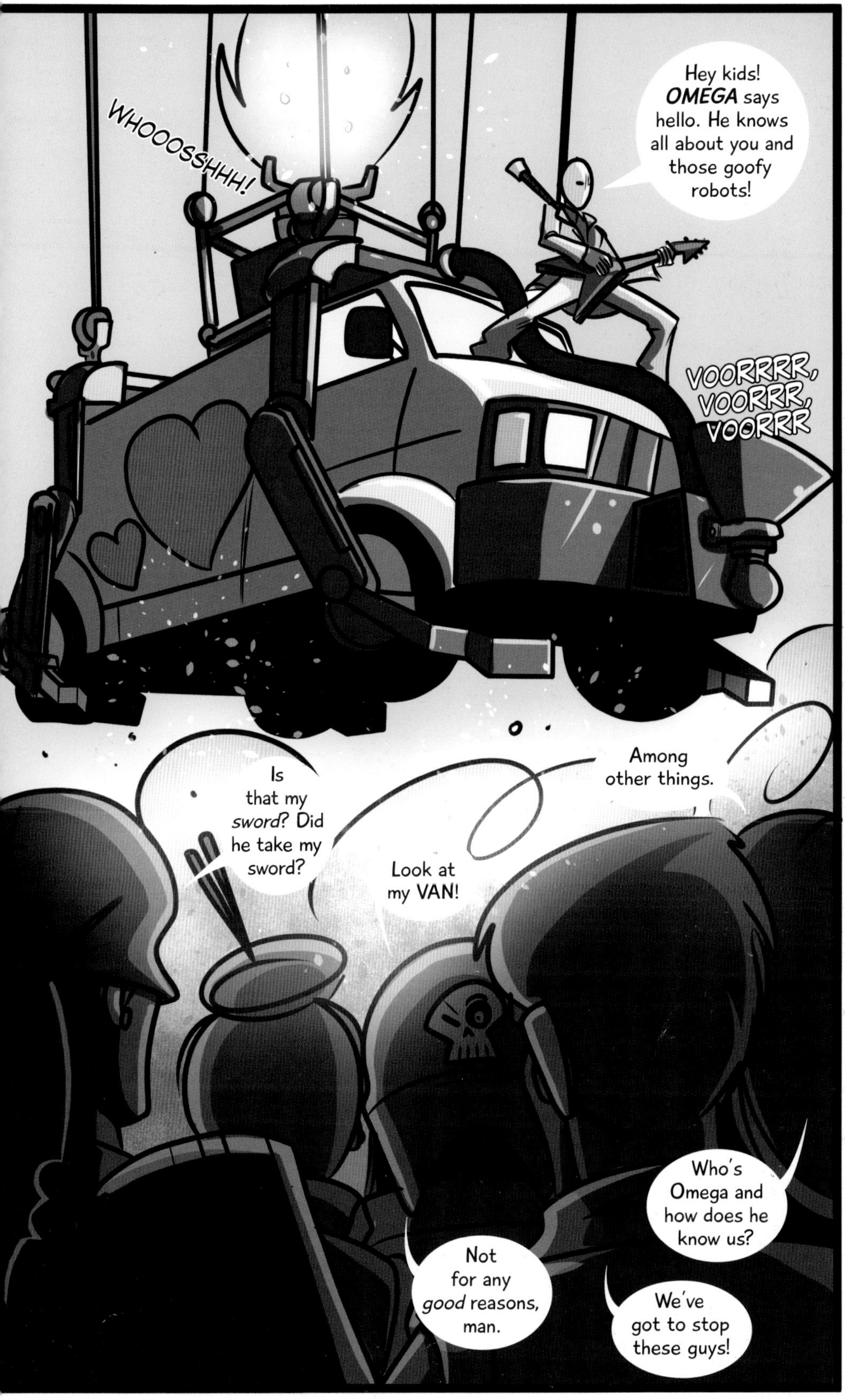
WHOOOSSHHH!
Hey kids! **OMEGA** says hello. He knows all about you and those goofy robots!
VOORRRR, VOORRR, VOORRR
Is that my *sword*? Did he take my sword?
Among other things.
Look at my VAN!
Who's Omega and how does he know us?
Not for any *good* reasons, man.
We've got to stop these guys!

CHAPTER 4: STAND OR FOLD

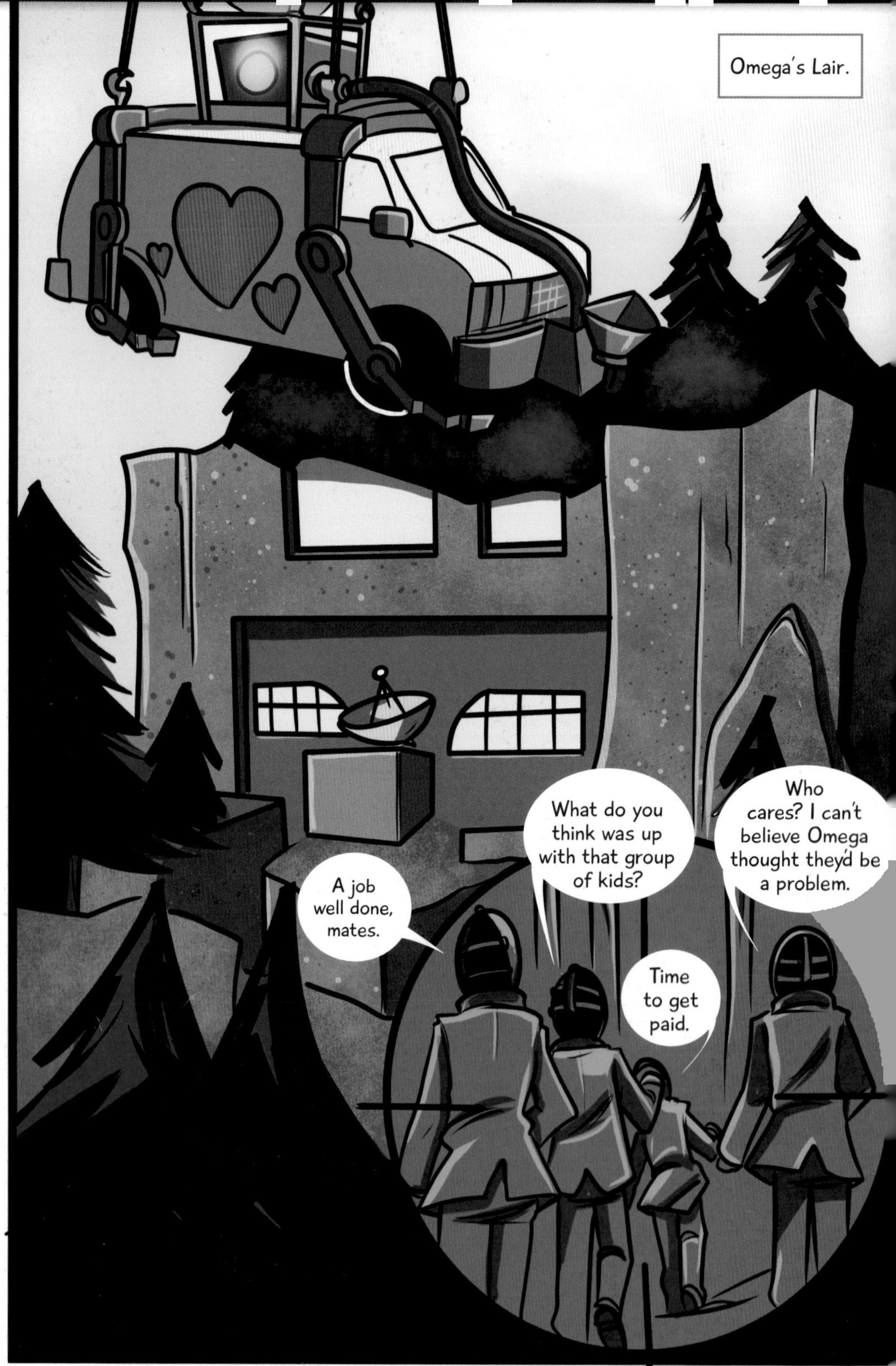

Omega's Lair.
A job well done, mates.
What do you think was up with that group of kids?
Who cares? I can't believe Omega thought they'd be a problem.
Time to get paid.

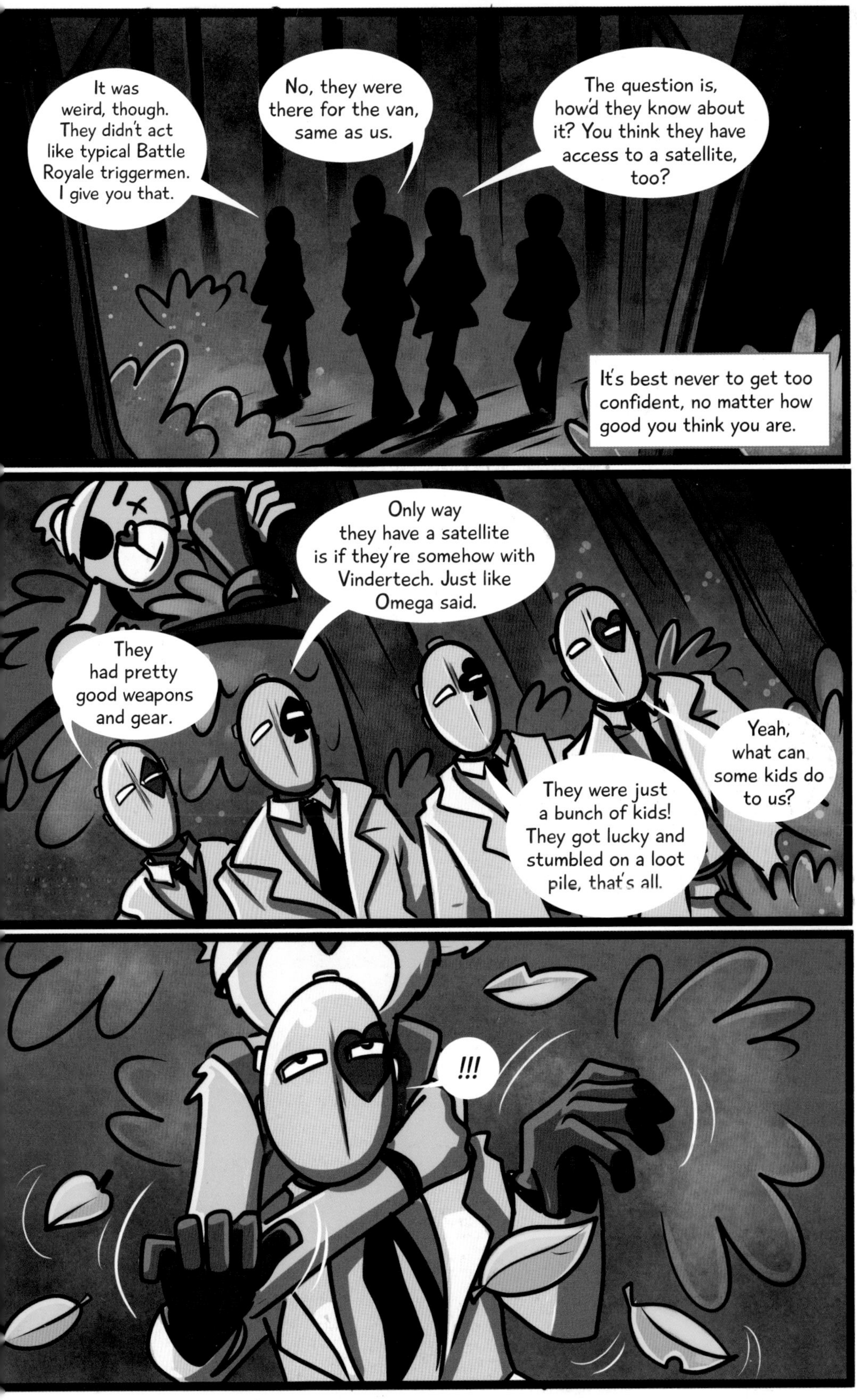
It was weird, though. They didn't act like typical Battle Royale triggermen. I give you that.
No, they were there for the van, same as us.
The question is, how'd they know about it? You think they have access to a satellite, too?
It's best never to get too confident, no matter how good you think you are.
Only way they have a satellite is if they're somehow with Vindertech. Just like Omega said.
They had pretty good weapons and gear.
They were just a bunch of kids! They got lucky and stumbled on a loot pile, that's all.
Yeah, what can some kids do to us?
!!!

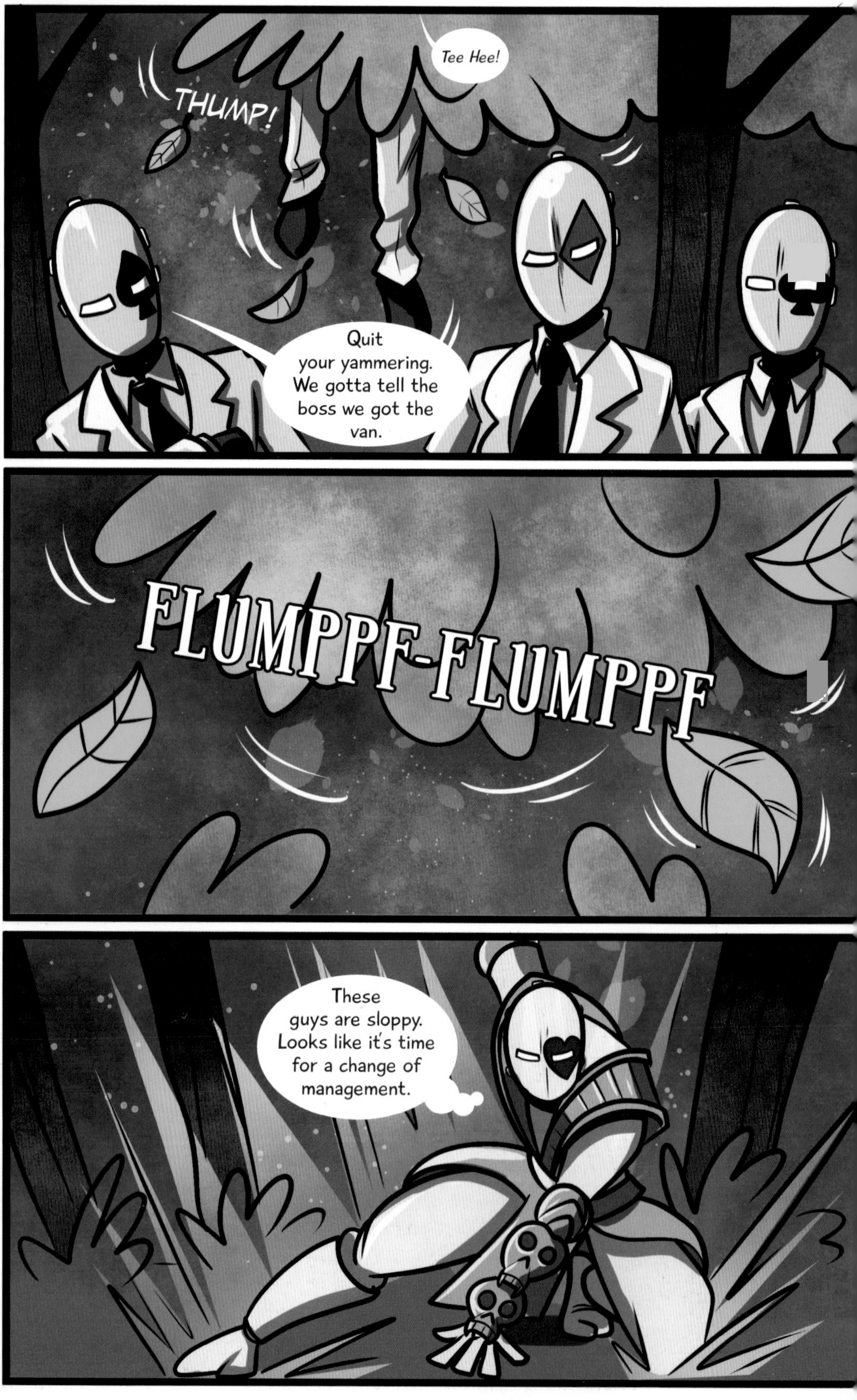
Tee Hee!
THUMP!
Quit your yammering. We gotta tell the boss we got the van.
FLUMPPF-FLUMPPF
These guys are sloppy. Looks like it's time for a change of management.

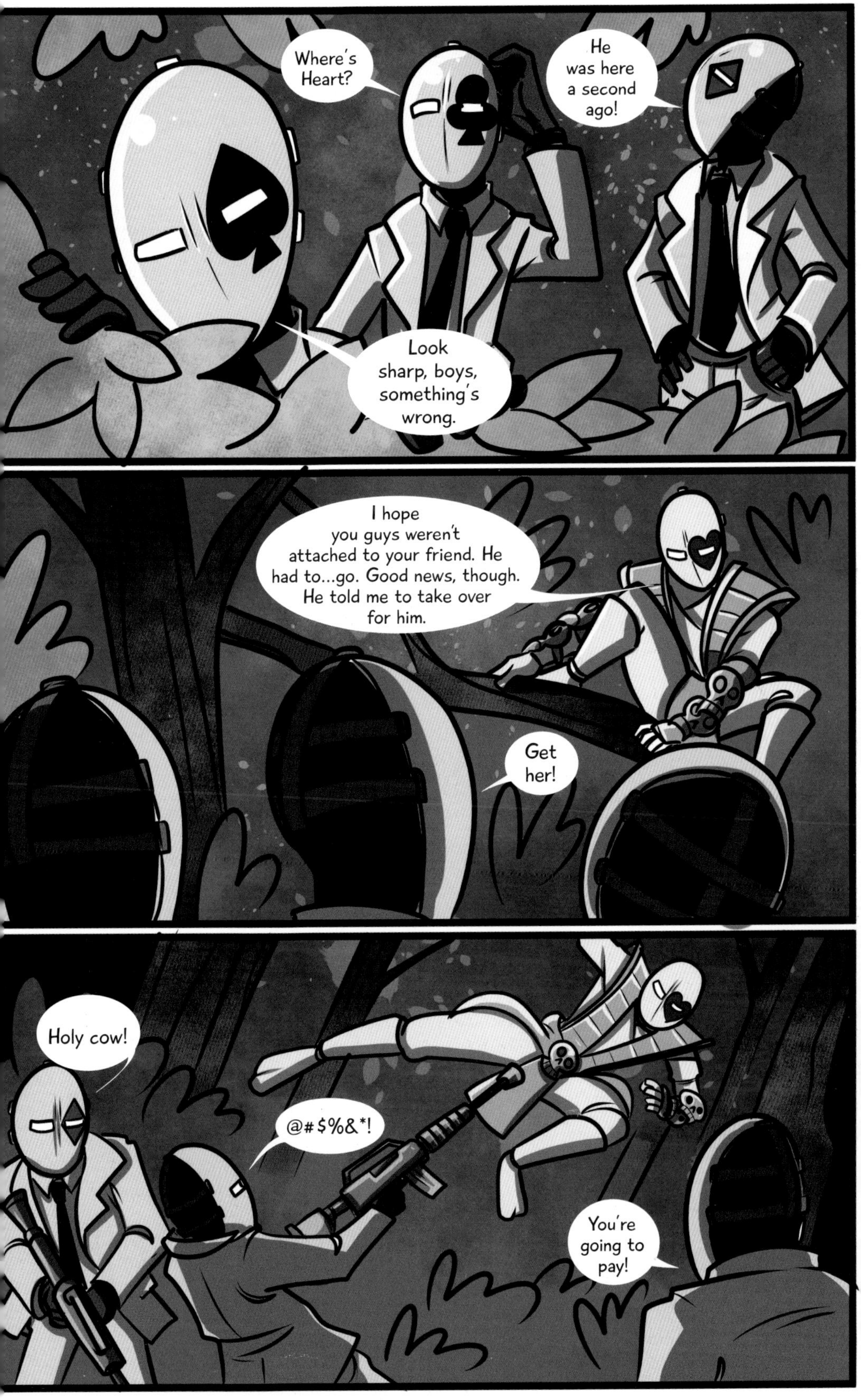
Where's Heart?
He was here a second ago!
Look sharp, boys, something's wrong.
I hope you guys weren't attached to your friend. He had to...go. Good news, though. He told me to take over for him.
Get her!
Holy cow!
@#$%&*!
You're going to pay!

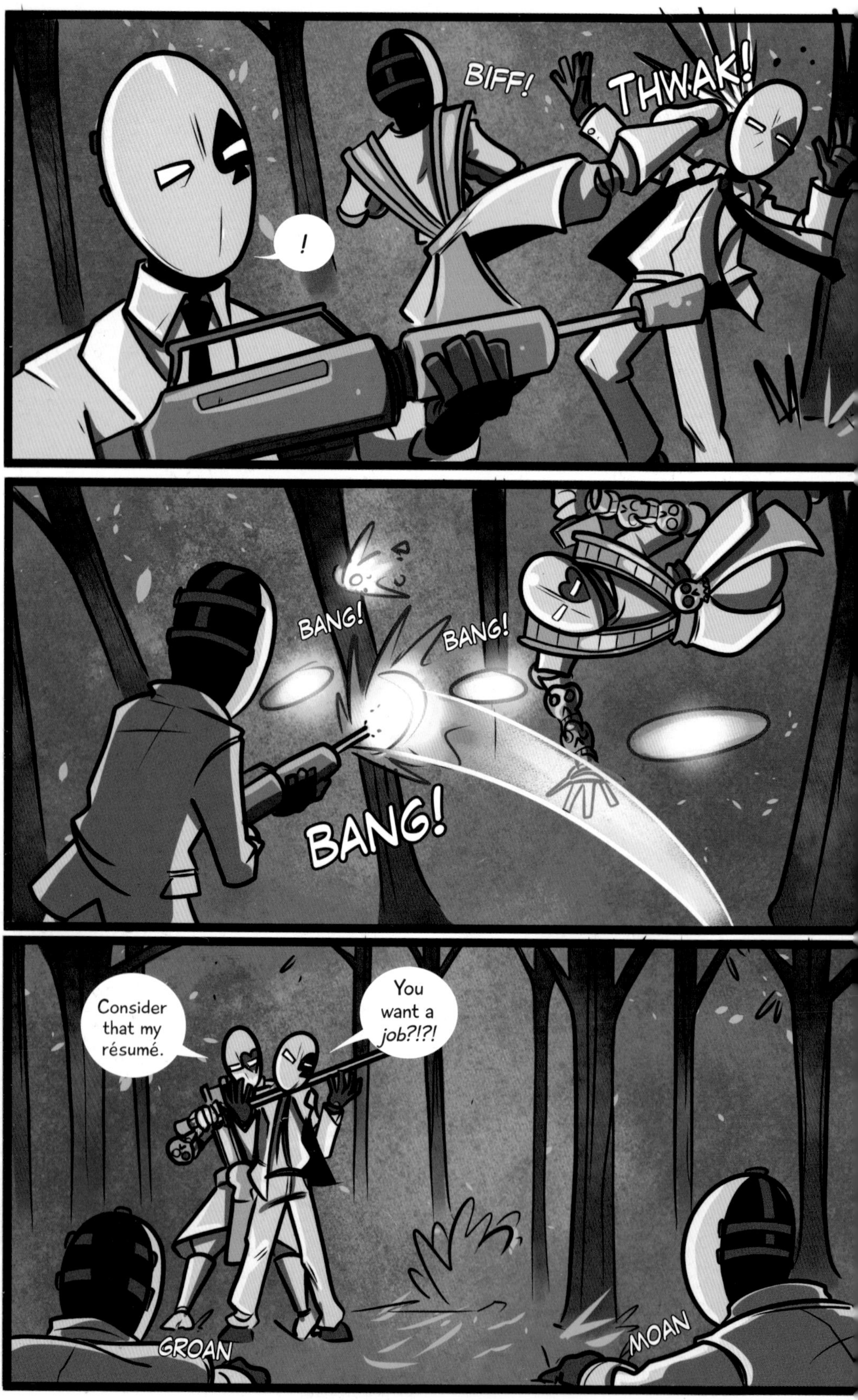
BIFF!
THWAK!
!
BANG!
BANG!
BANG!
Consider that my résumé.
You want a job?!?!
GROAN
MOAN

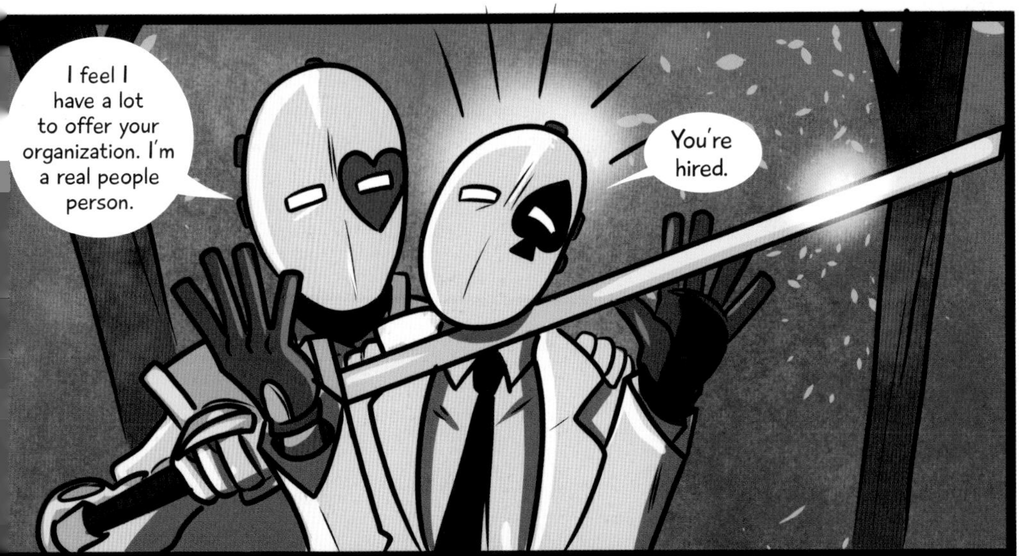
I feel I have a lot to offer your organization. I'm a real people person.
You're hired.

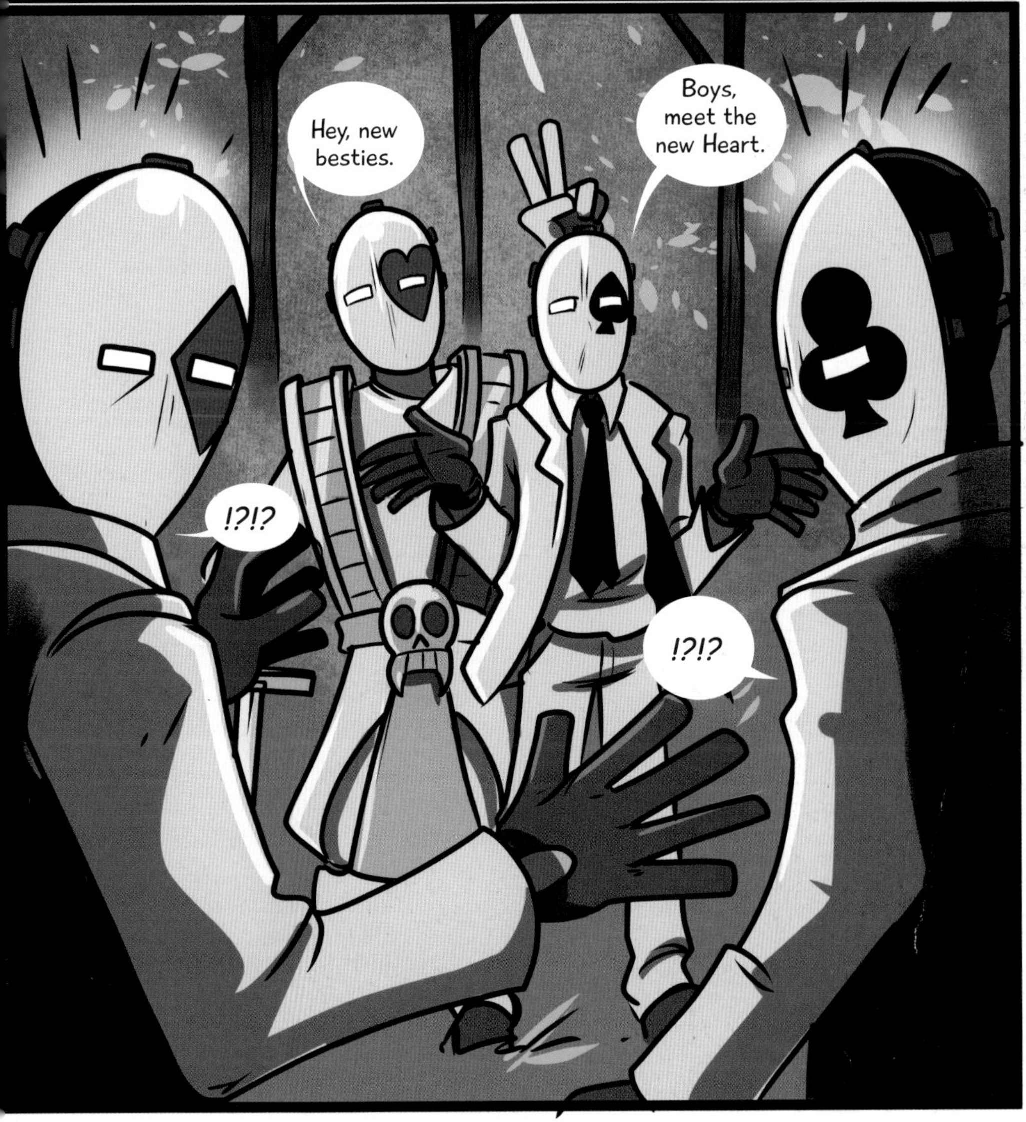
Hey, new besties.
Boys, meet the new Heart.
!?!?
!?!?

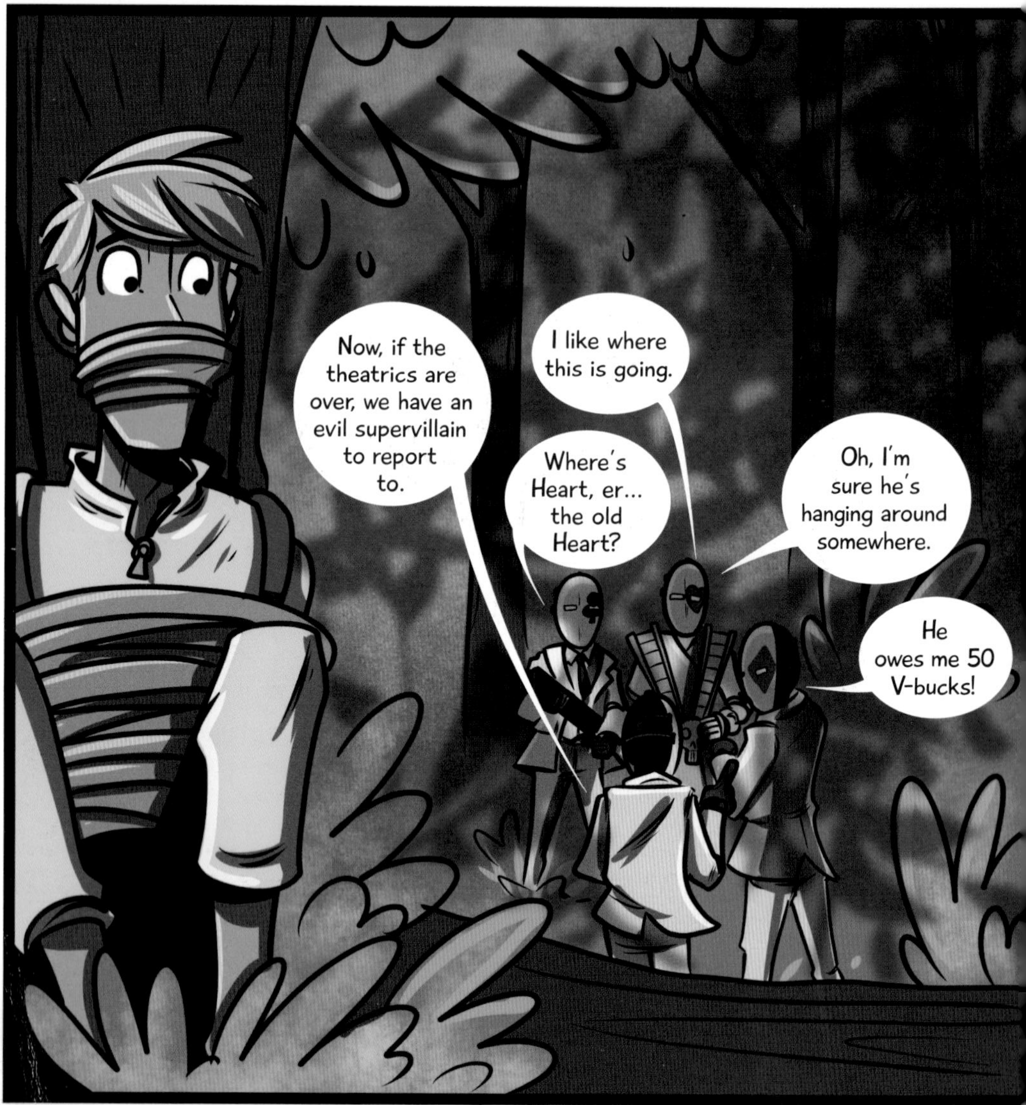
Now, if the theatrics are over, we have an evil supervillain to report to.
I like where this is going.
Where's Heart, er... the old Heart?
Oh, I'm sure he's hanging around somewhere.
He owes me 50 V-bucks!

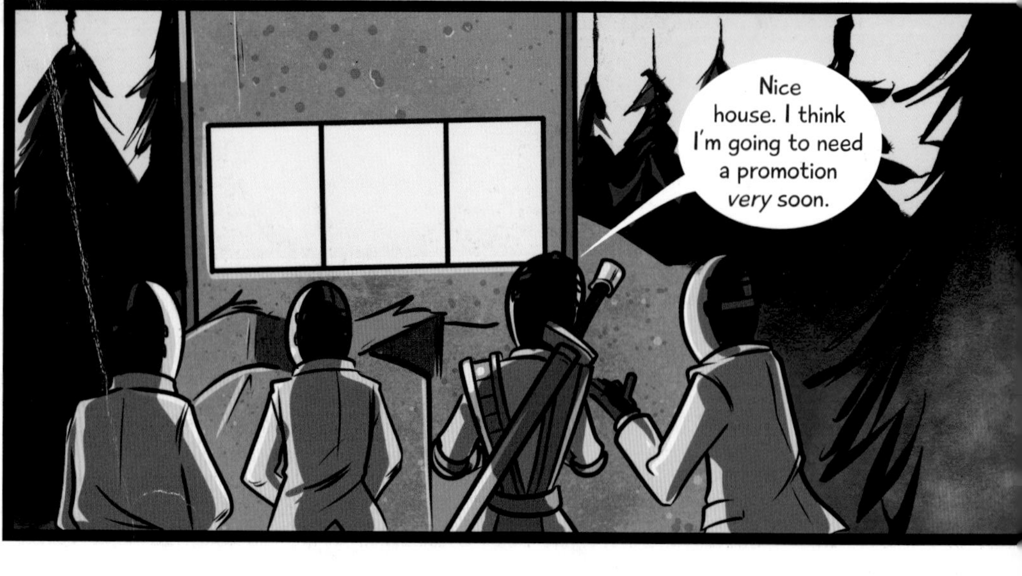
Nice house. I think I'm going to need a promotion *very* soon.

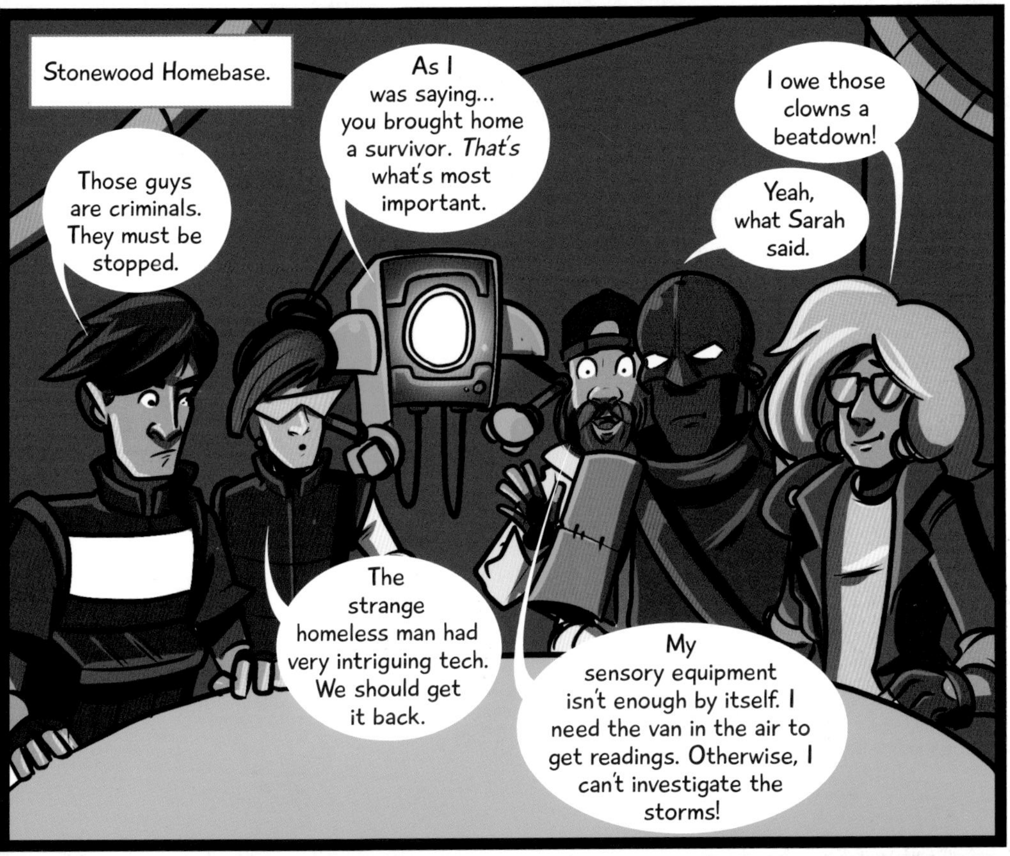
Stonewood Homebase.
Those guys are criminals. They must be stopped.
As I was saying... you brought home a survivor. *That's* what's most important.
I owe those clowns a beatdown!
Yeah, what Sarah said.
The strange homeless man had very intriguing tech. We should get it back.
My sensory equipment isn't enough by itself. I need the van in the air to get readings. Otherwise, I can't investigate the storms!

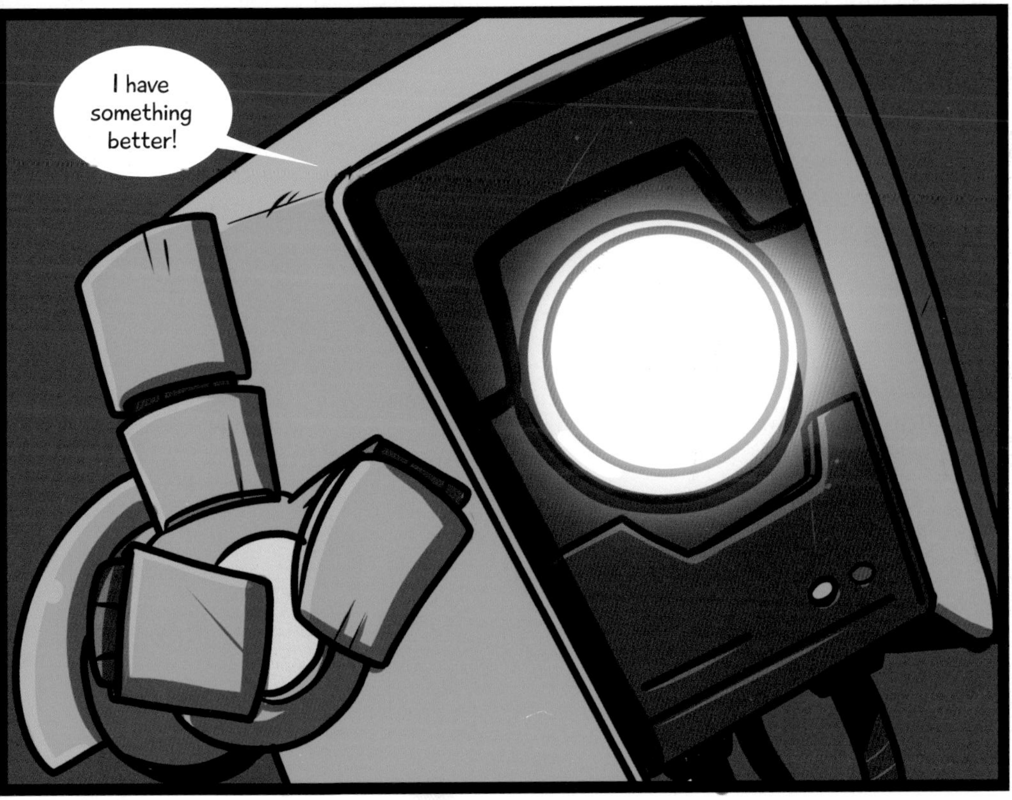
I have something better!

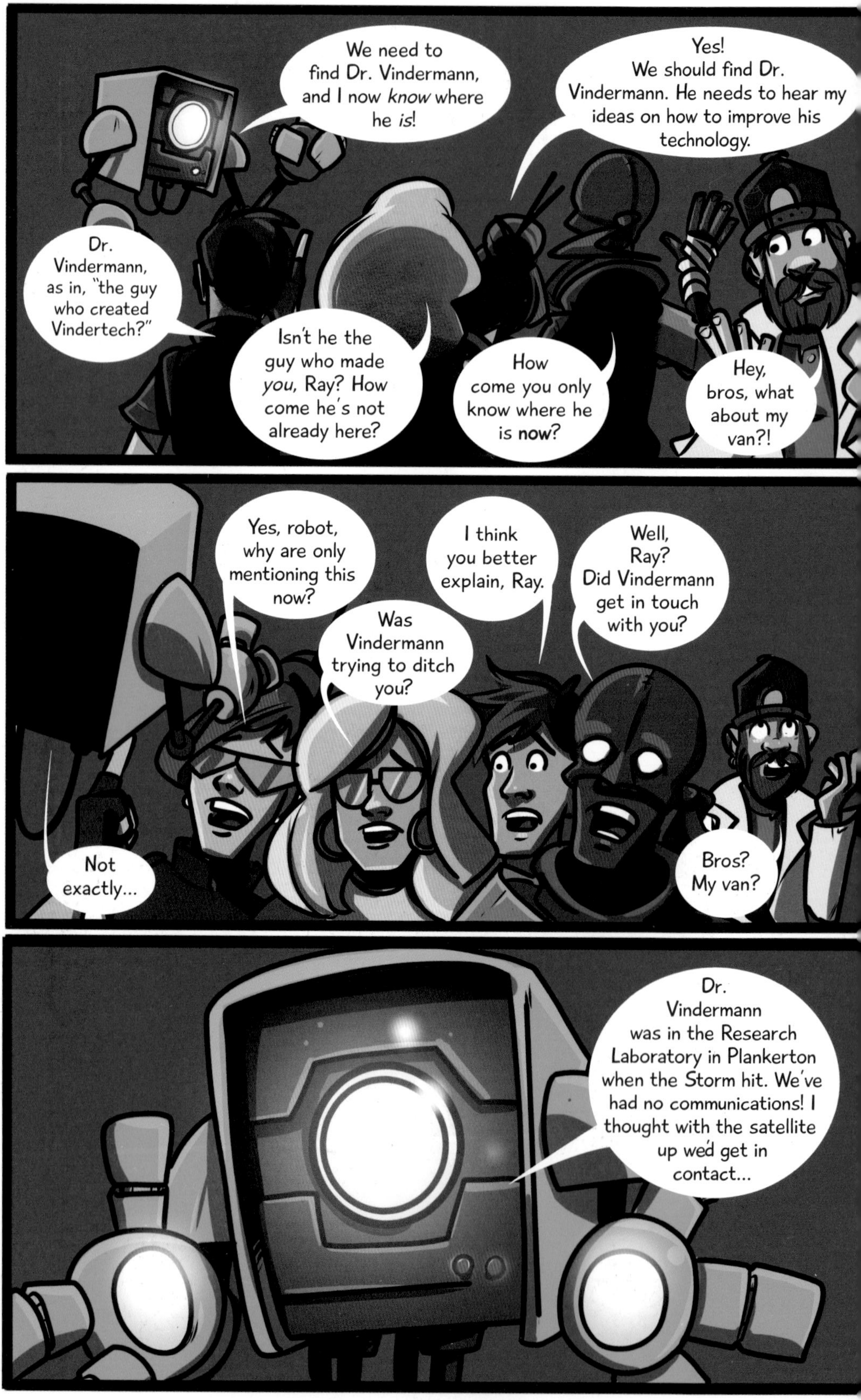
We need to find Dr. Vindermann, and I now *know* where he *is*!
Yes! We should find Dr. Vindermann. He needs to hear my ideas on how to improve his technology.
Dr. Vindermann, as in, "the guy who created Vindertech?"
Isn't he the guy who made *you*, Ray? How come he's not already here?
How come you only know where he is **now**?
Hey, bros, what about my van?!
Yes, robot, why are only mentioning this now?
I think you better explain, Ray.
Well, Ray? Did Vindermann get in touch with you?
Was Vindermann trying to ditch you?
Not exactly...
Bros? My van?
Dr. Vindermann was in the Research Laboratory in Plankerton when the Storm hit. We've had no communications! I thought with the satellite up we'd get in contact...

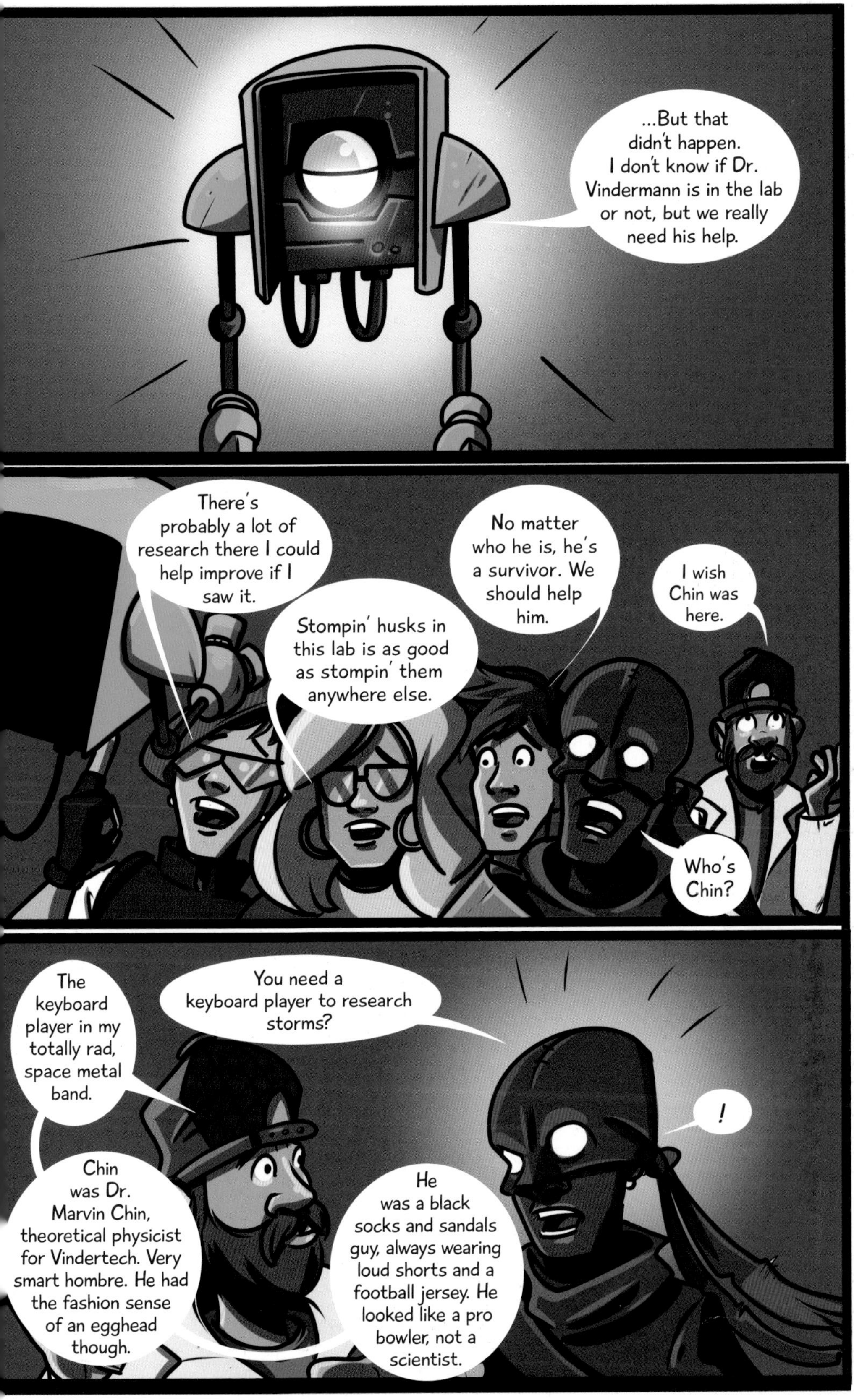
...But that didn't happen. I don't know if Dr. Vindermann is in the lab or not, but we really need his help.
There's probably a lot of research there I could help improve if I saw it.
Stompin' husks in this lab is as good as stompin' them anywhere else.
No matter who he is, he's a survivor. We should help him.
I wish Chin was here.
Who's Chin?
The keyboard player in my totally rad, space metal band.
You need a keyboard player to research storms?
!
Chin was Dr. Marvin Chin, theoretical physicist for Vindertech. Very smart hombre. He had the fashion sense of an egghead though.
He was a black socks and sandals guy, always wearing loud shorts and a football jersey. He looked like a pro bowler, not a scientist.

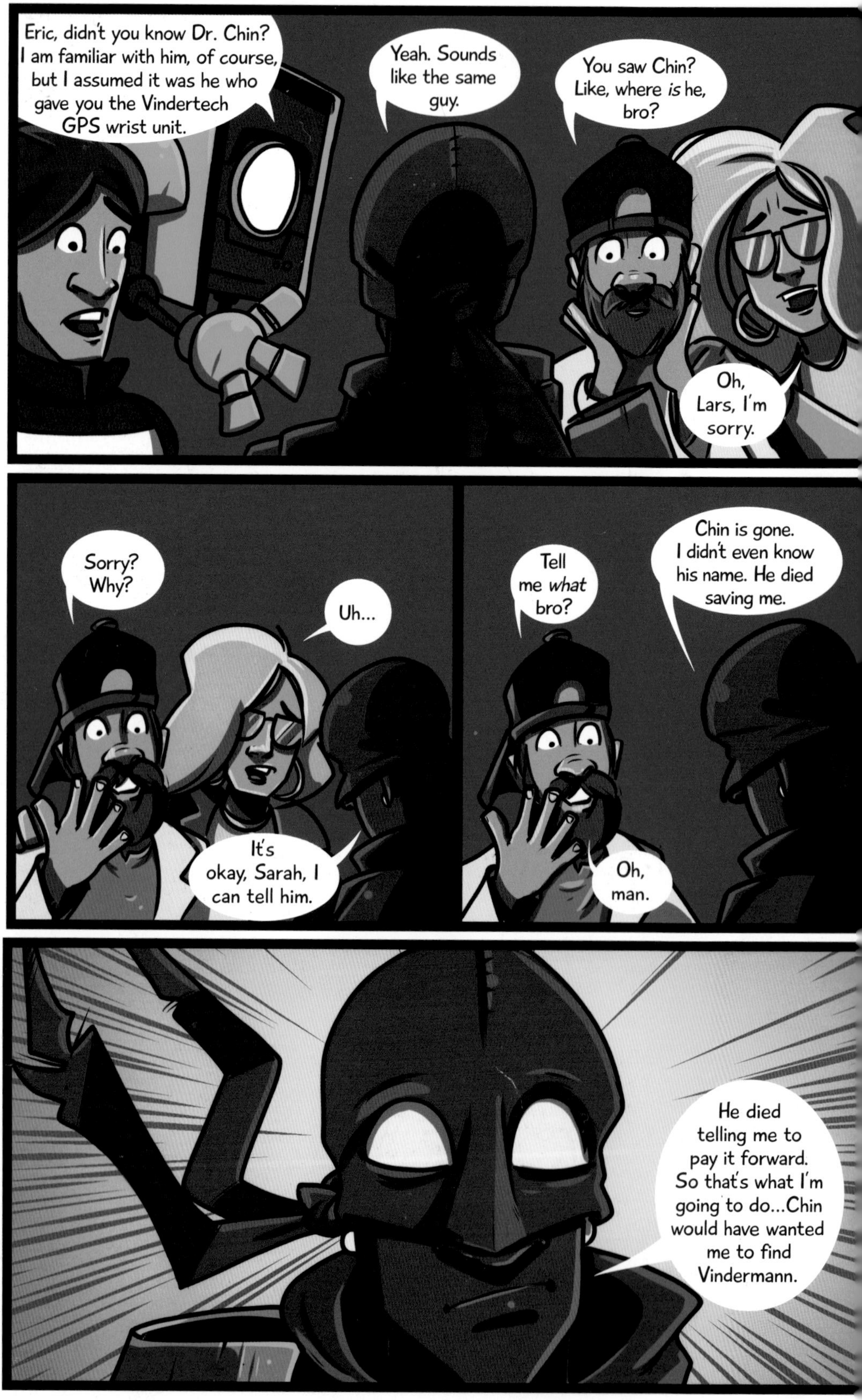
Eric, didn't you know Dr. Chin? I am familiar with him, of course, but I assumed it was he who gave you the Vindertech GPS wrist unit.
Yeah. Sounds like the same guy.
You saw Chin? Like, where *is* he, bro?
Oh, Lars, I'm sorry.
Sorry? Why?
Uh...
It's okay, Sarah, I can tell him.
Tell me *what* bro?
Chin is gone. I didn't even know his name. He died saving me.
Oh, man.
He died telling me to pay it forward. So that's what I'm going to do...Chin would have wanted me to find Vindermann.

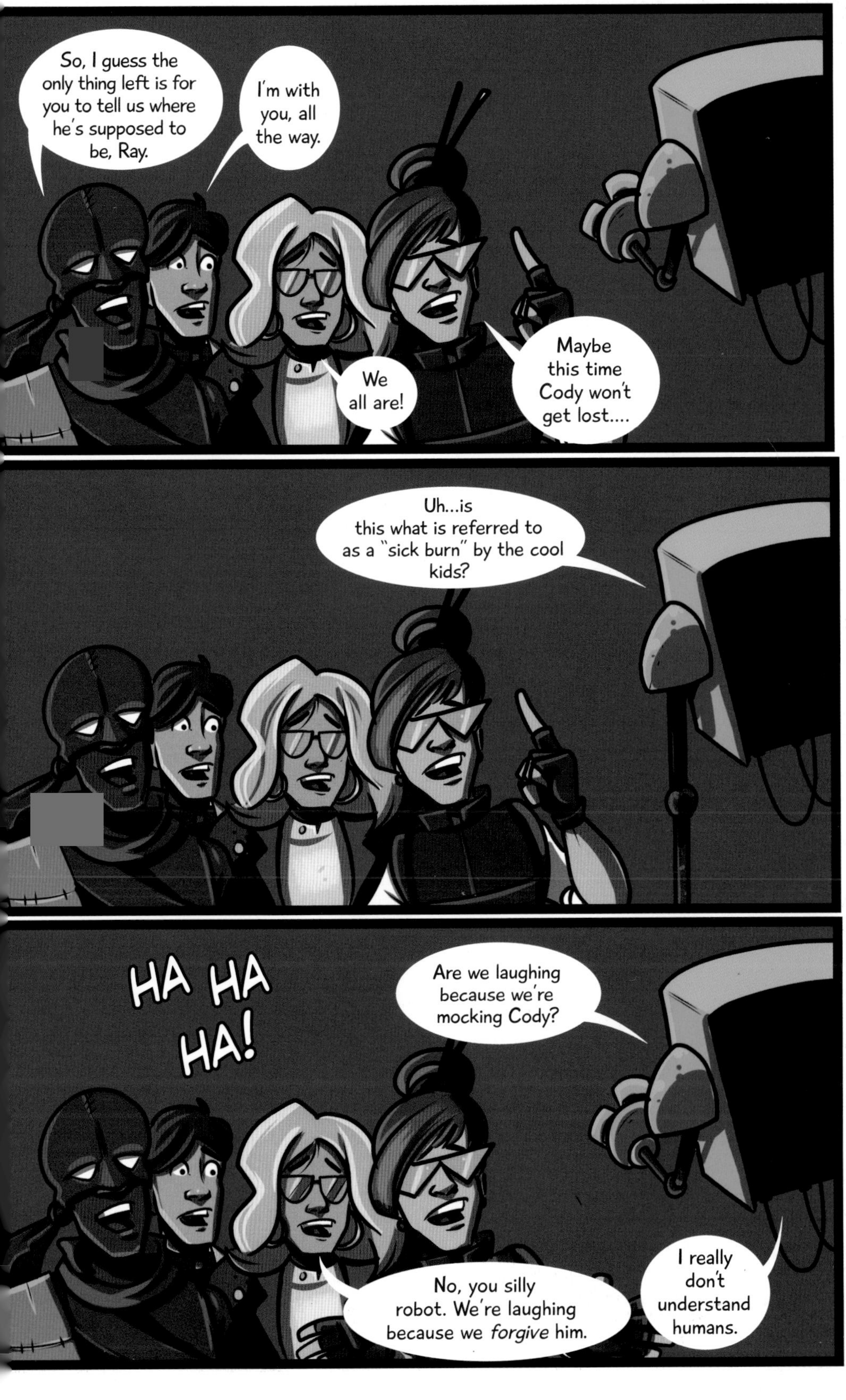
So, I guess the only thing left is for you to tell us where he's supposed to be, Ray.
I'm with you, all the way.
We all are!
Maybe this time Cody won't get lost....
Uh...is this what is referred to as a "sick burn" by the cool kids?
HA HA HA!
Are we laughing because we're mocking Cody?
No, you silly robot. We're laughing because we *forgive* him.
I really don't understand humans.

CHAPTER 5: UP THE ANTE

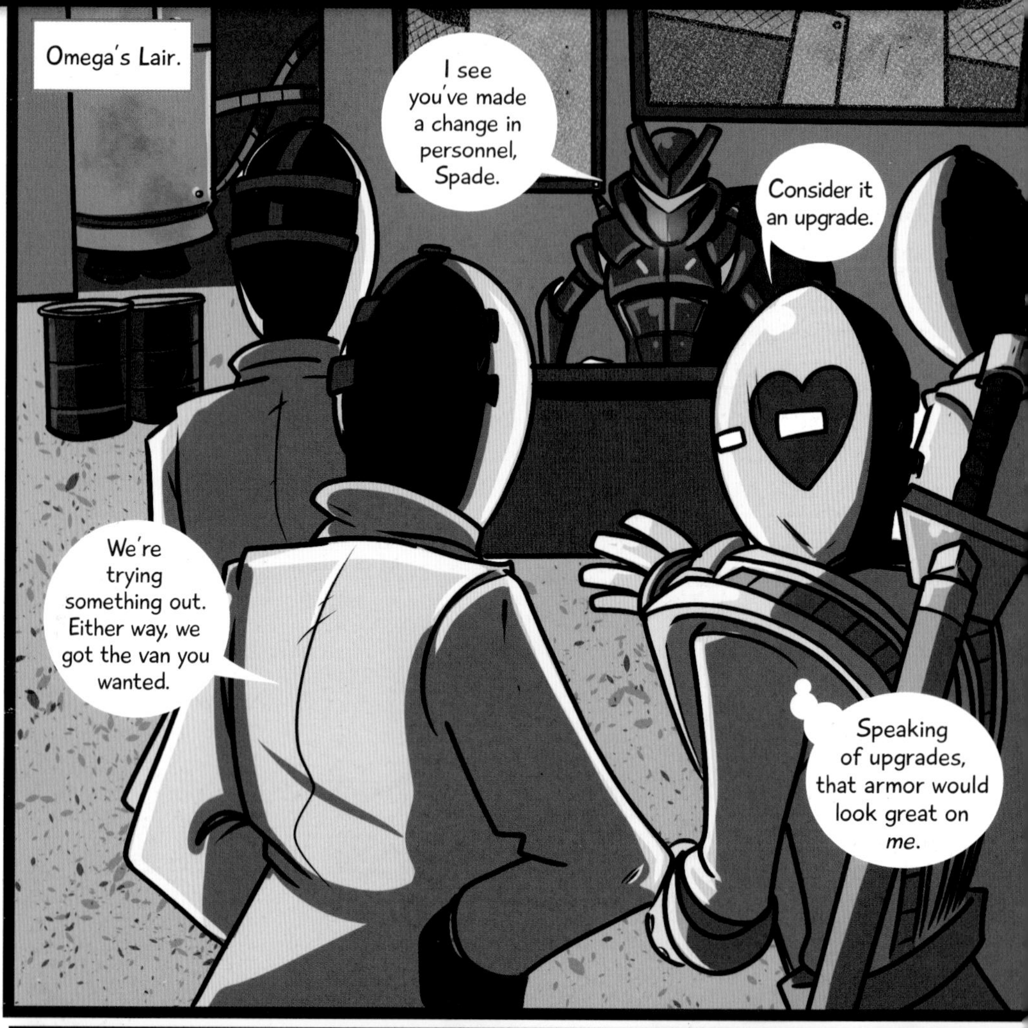
Omega's Lair.
I see you've made a change in personnel, Spade.
Consider it an upgrade.
We're trying something out. Either way, we got the van you wanted.
Speaking of upgrades, that armor would look great on *me*.

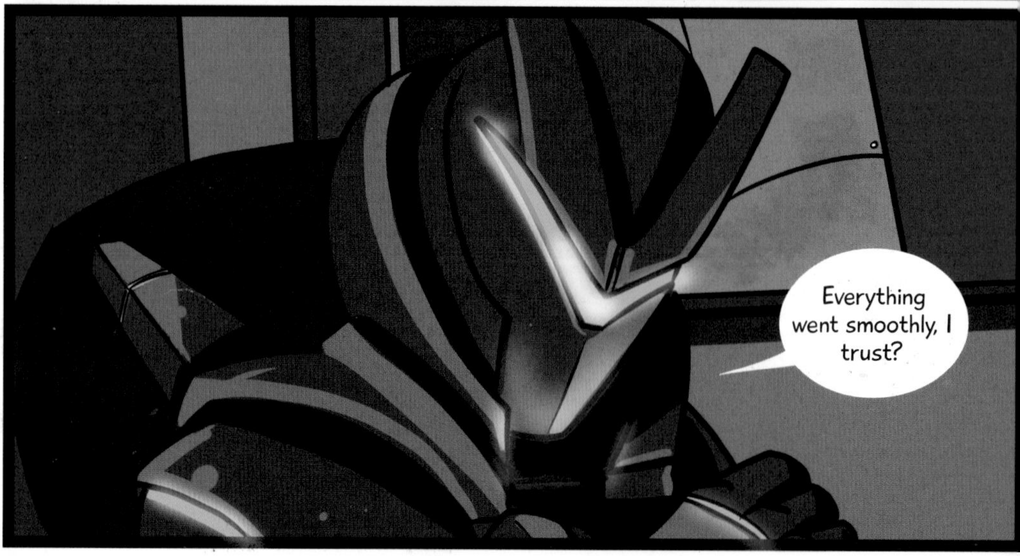
Everything went smoothly, I trust?

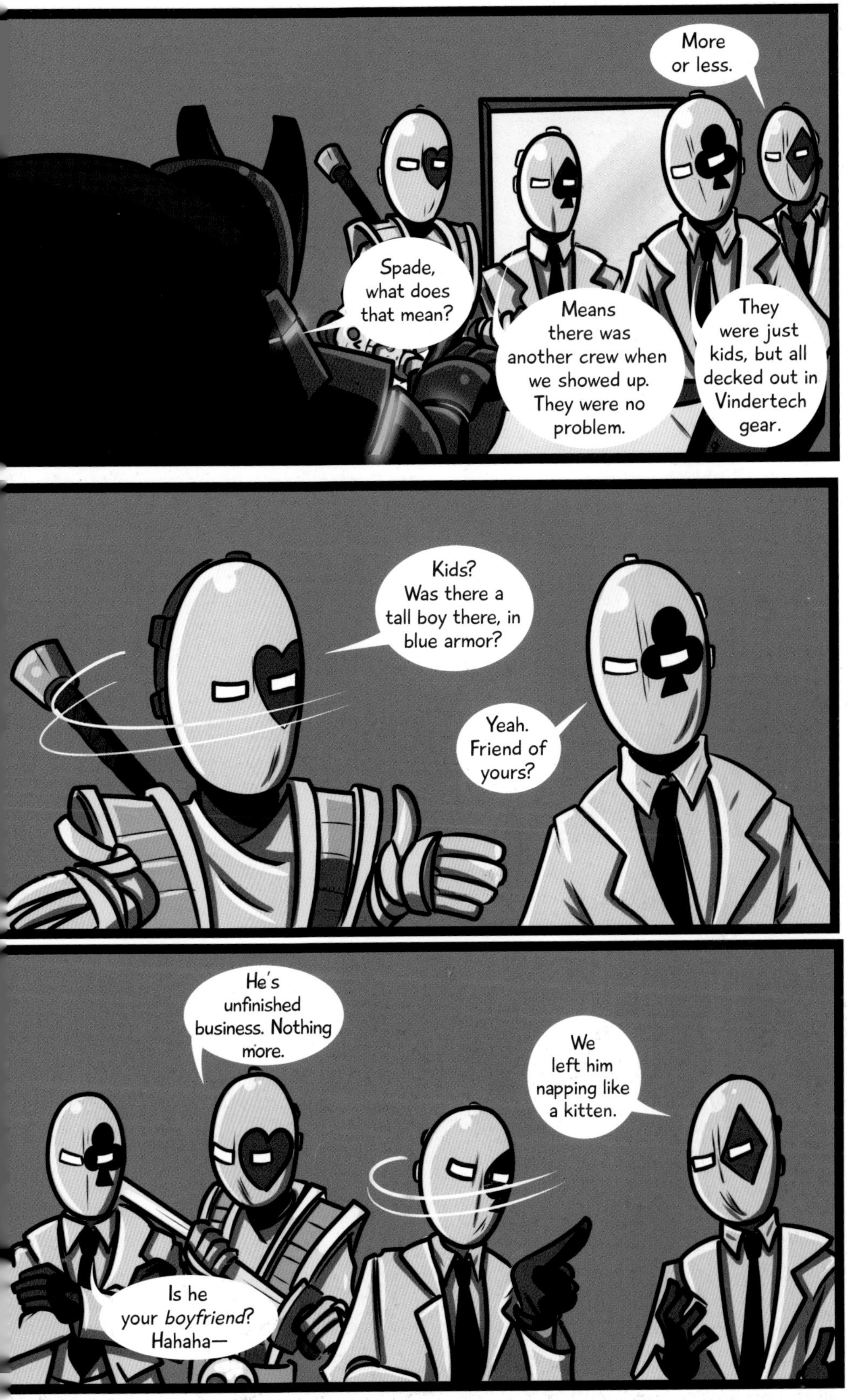

More or less.
Spade, what does that mean?
Means there was another crew when we showed up. They were no problem.
They were just kids, but all decked out in Vindertech gear.
Kids? Was there a tall boy there, in blue armor?
Yeah. Friend of yours?
He's unfinished business. Nothing more.
We left him napping like a kitten.
Is he your *boyfriend*? Hahaha—

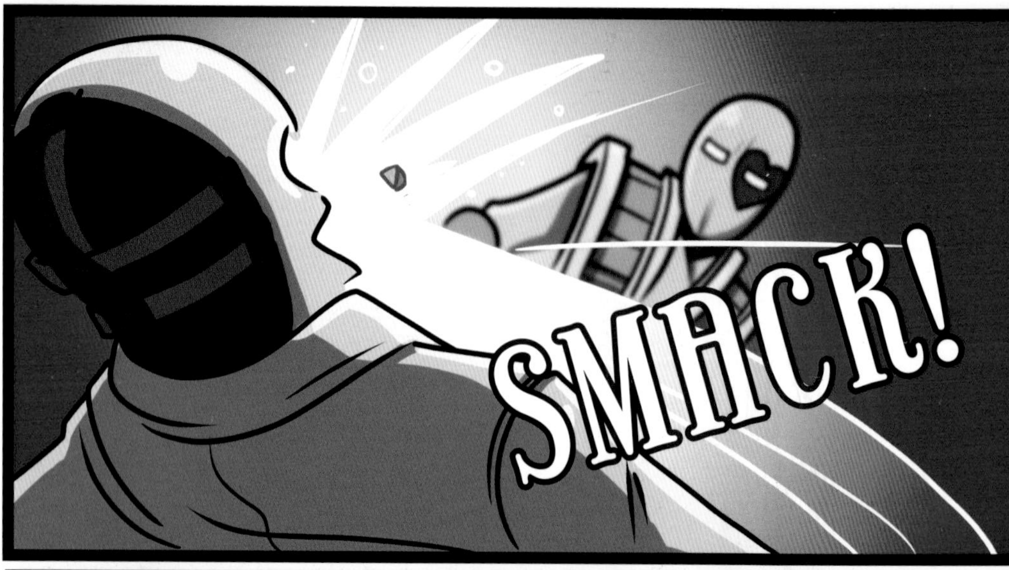
SMACK!

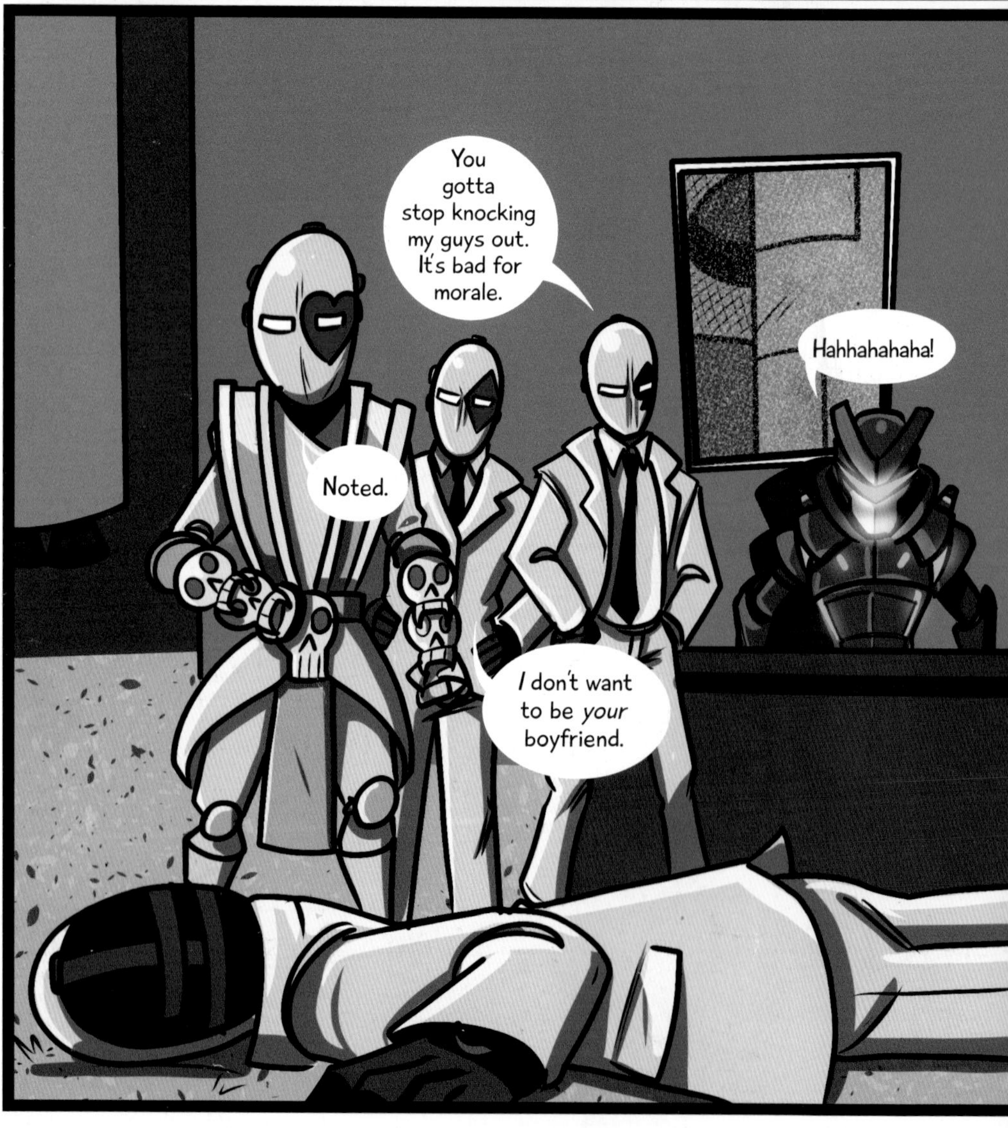
You gotta stop knocking my guys out. It's bad for morale.
Noted.
Hahhahahaha!
I don't want to be *your* boyfriend.

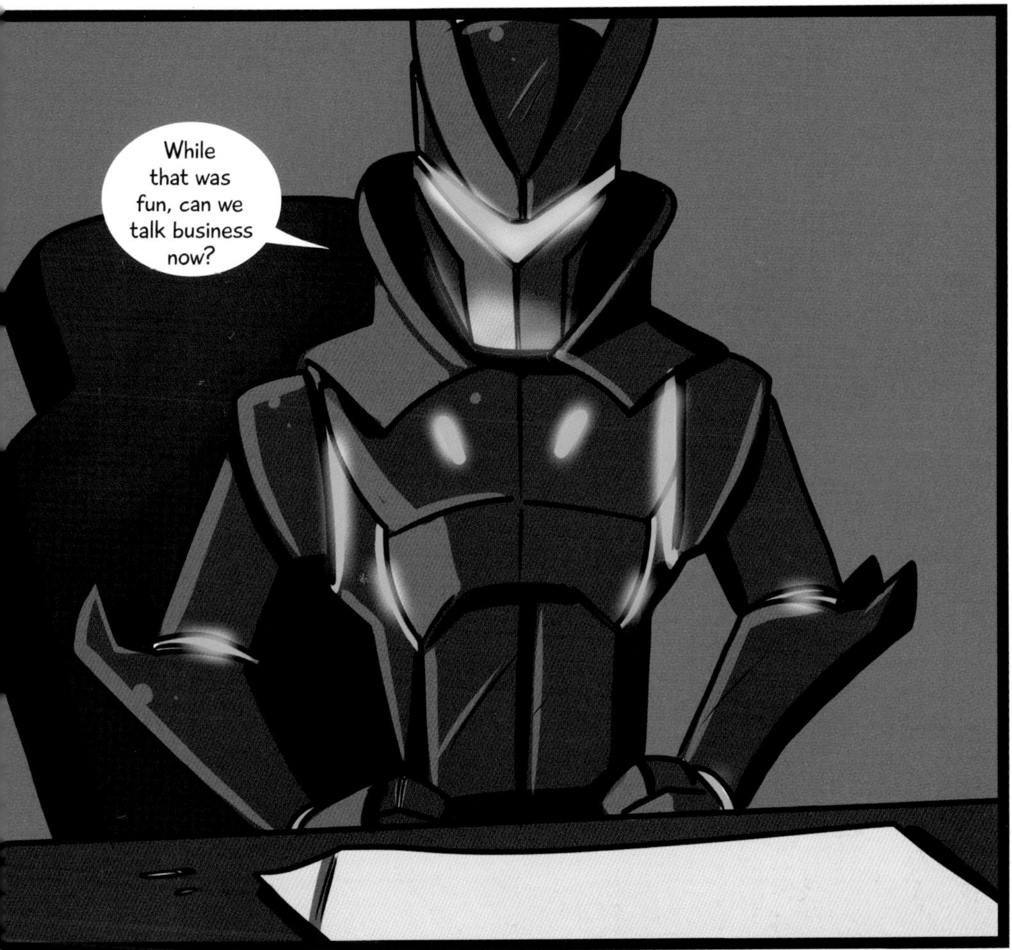
While that was fun, can we talk business now?

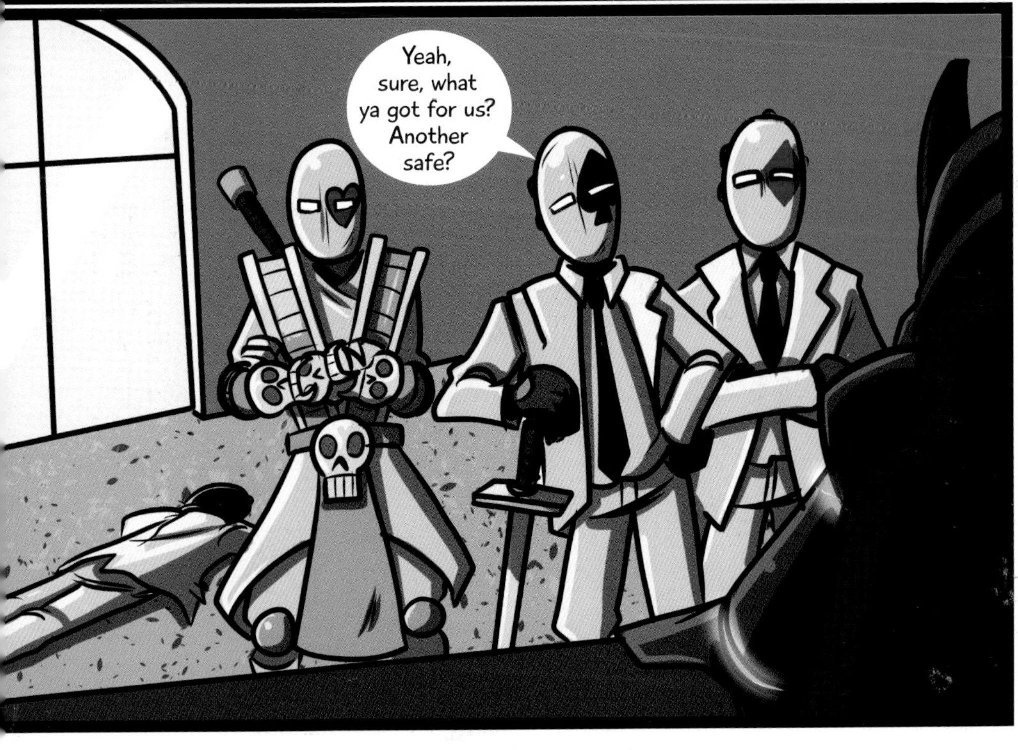
Yeah, sure, what ya got for us? Another safe?

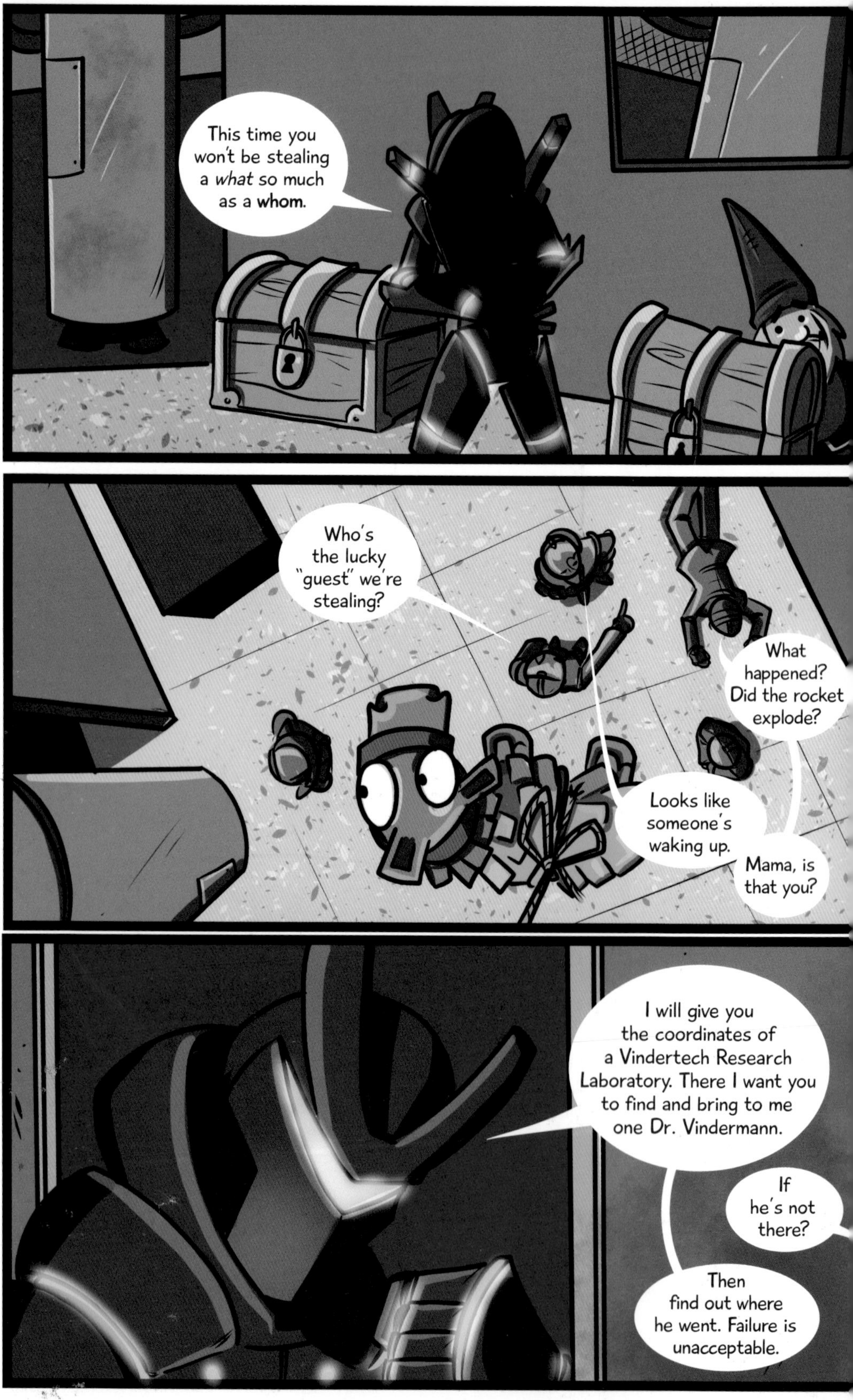
This time you won't be stealing a *what* so much as a **whom**.
Who's the lucky "guest" we're stealing?
What happened? Did the rocket explode?
Looks like someone's waking up.
Mama, is that you?
I will give you the coordinates of a Vindertech Research Laboratory. There I want you to find and bring to me one Dr. Vindermann.
If he's not there?
Then find out where he went. Failure is unacceptable.

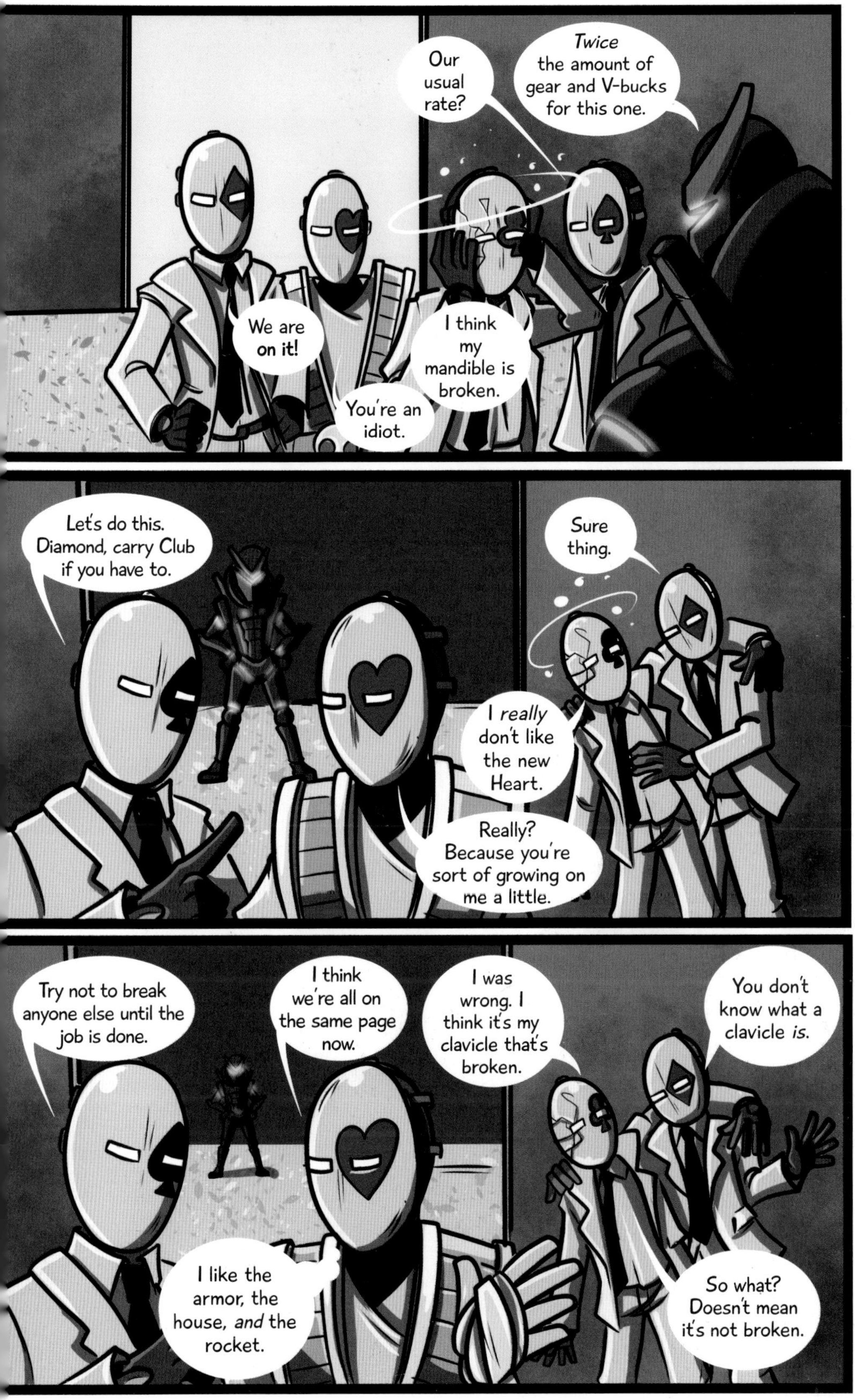
Our usual rate?
Twice the amount of gear and V-bucks for this one.
We are **on it!**
I think my mandible is broken.
You're an idiot.
Let's do this. Diamond, carry Club if you have to.
Sure thing.
I *really* don't like the new Heart.
Really? Because you're sort of growing on me a little.
Try not to break anyone else until the job is done.
I think we're all on the same page now.
I was wrong. I think it's my clavicle that's broken.
You don't know what a clavicle *is*.
I like the armor, the house, *and* the rocket.
So what? Doesn't mean it's not broken.

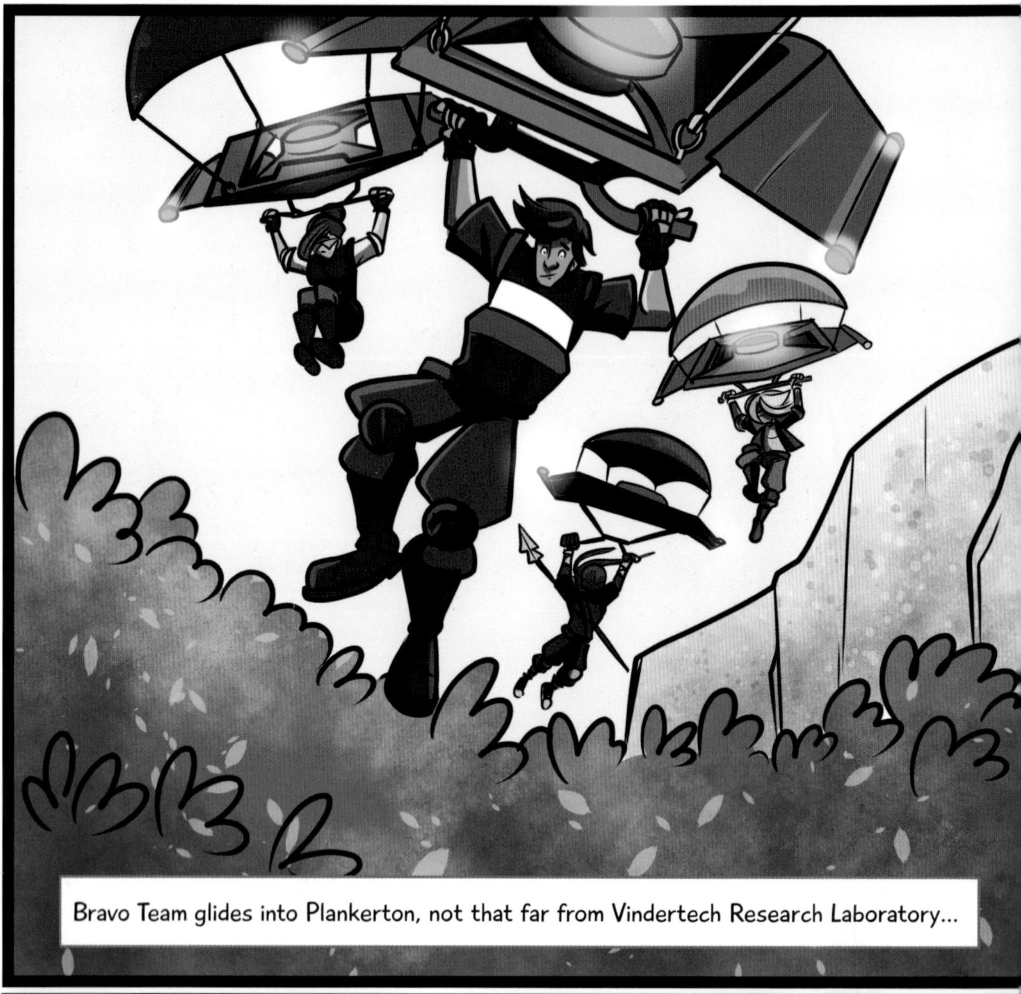
Bravo Team glides into Plankerton, not that far from Vindertech Research Laboratory...

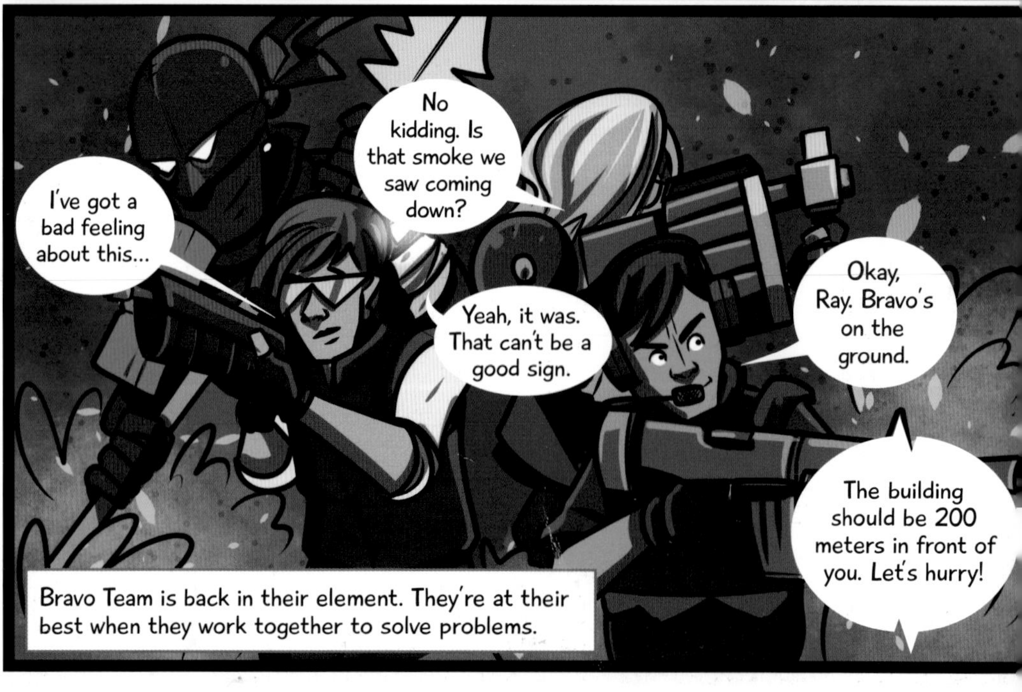
I've got a bad feeling about this...
No kidding. Is that smoke we saw coming down?
Yeah, it was. That can't be a good sign.
Okay, Ray. Bravo's on the ground.
The building should be 200 meters in front of you. Let's hurry!
Bravo Team is back in their element. They're at their best when they work together to solve problems.

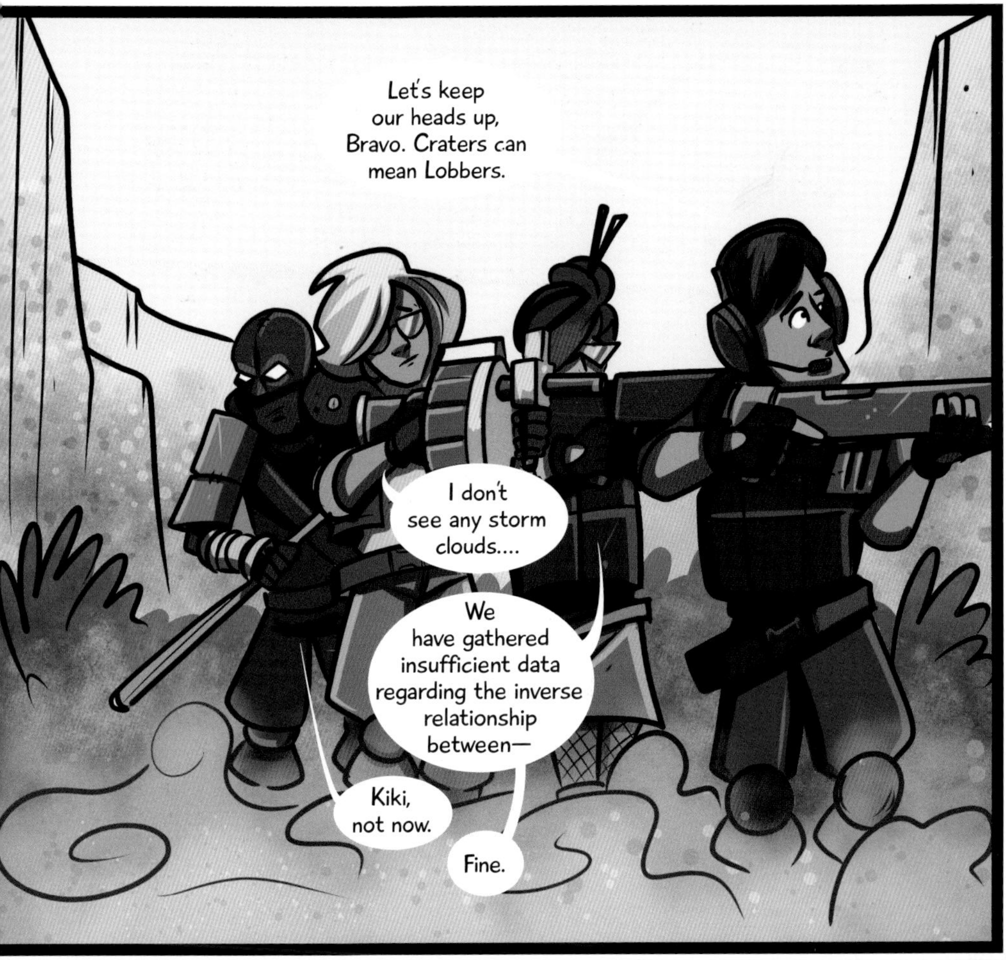
Let's keep our heads up, Bravo. Craters can mean Lobbers.
I don't see any storm clouds....
We have gathered insufficient data regarding the inverse relationship between—
Kiki, not now.
Fine.

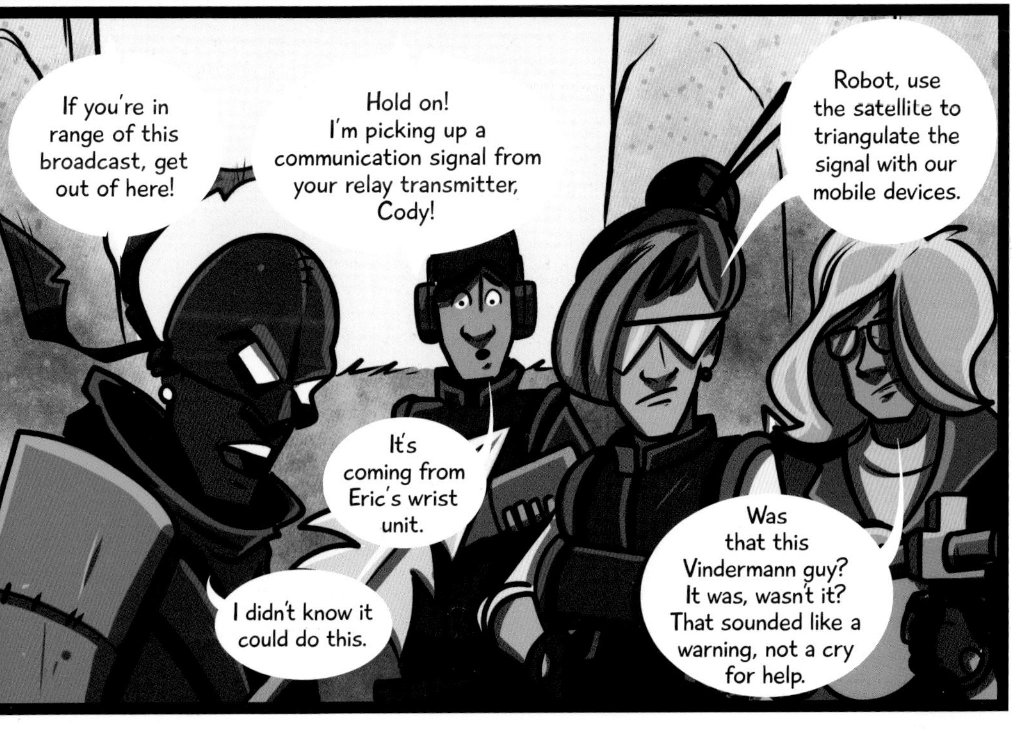
If you're in range of this broadcast, get out of here!
Hold on! I'm picking up a communication signal from your relay transmitter, Cody!
Robot, use the satellite to triangulate the signal with our mobile devices.
It's coming from Eric's wrist unit.
I didn't know it could do this.
Was that this Vindermann guy? It was, wasn't it? That sounded like a warning, not a cry for help.

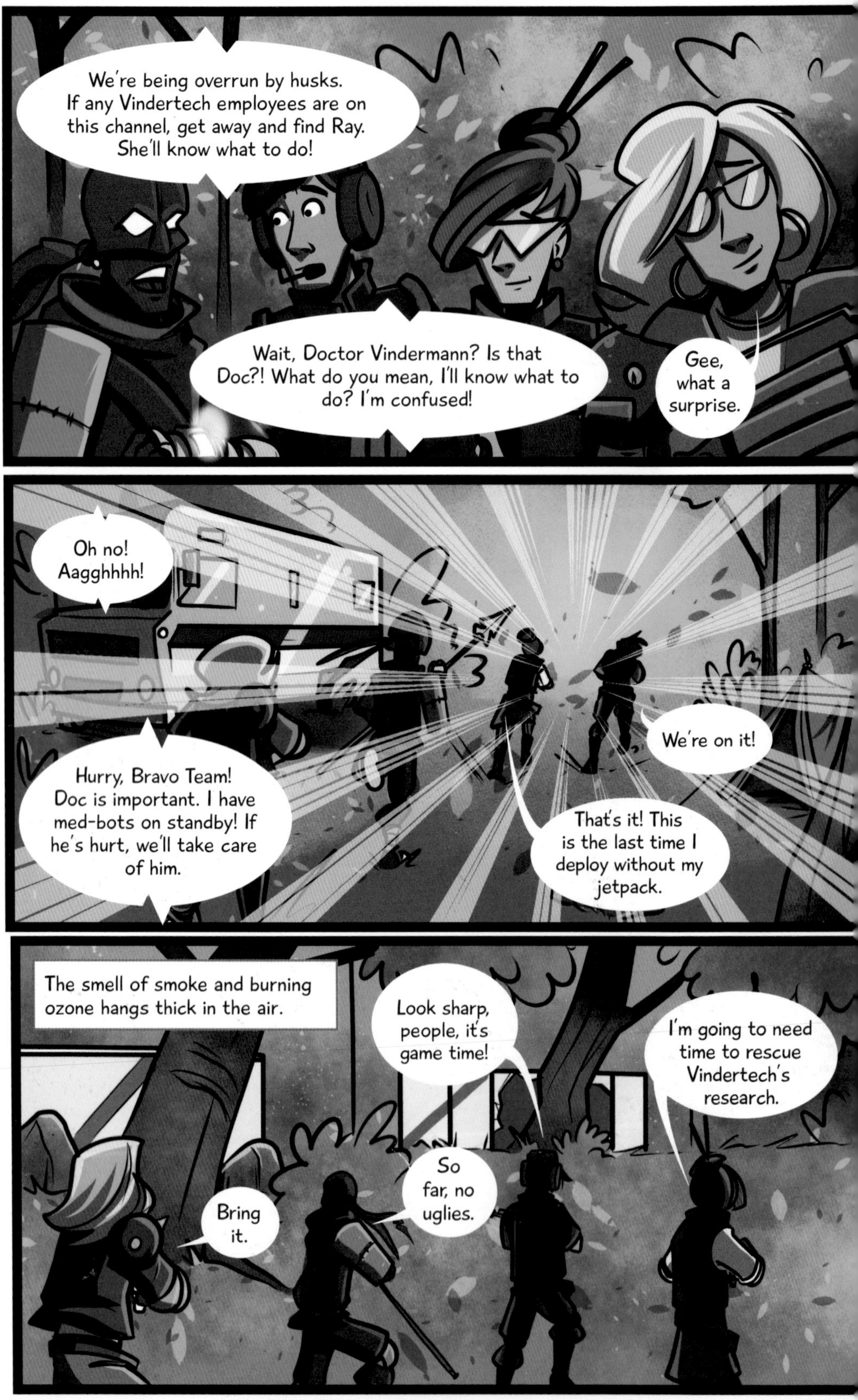
We're being overrun by husks. If any Vindertech employees are on this channel, get away and find Ray. She'll know what to do!
Wait, Doctor Vindermann? Is that Doc?! What do you mean, I'll know what to do? I'm confused!
Gee, what a surprise.
Oh no! Aagghhhh!
Hurry, Bravo Team! Doc is important. I have med-bots on standby! If he's hurt, we'll take care of him.
We're on it!
That's it! This is the last time I deploy without my jetpack.
The smell of smoke and burning ozone hangs thick in the air.
Look sharp, people, it's game time!
I'm going to need time to rescue Vindertech's research.
Bring it.
So far, no uglies.

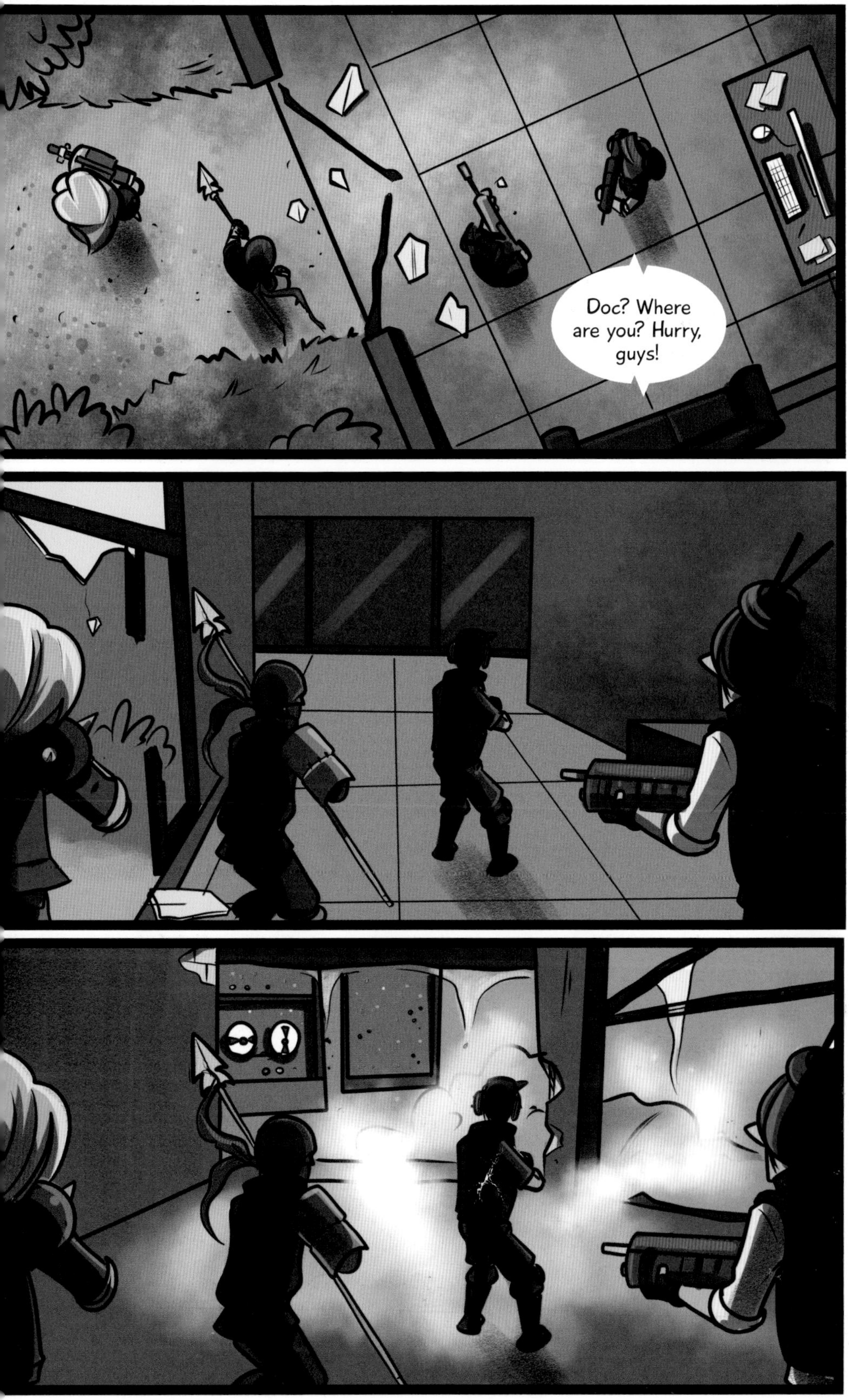
Doc? Where are you? Hurry, guys!

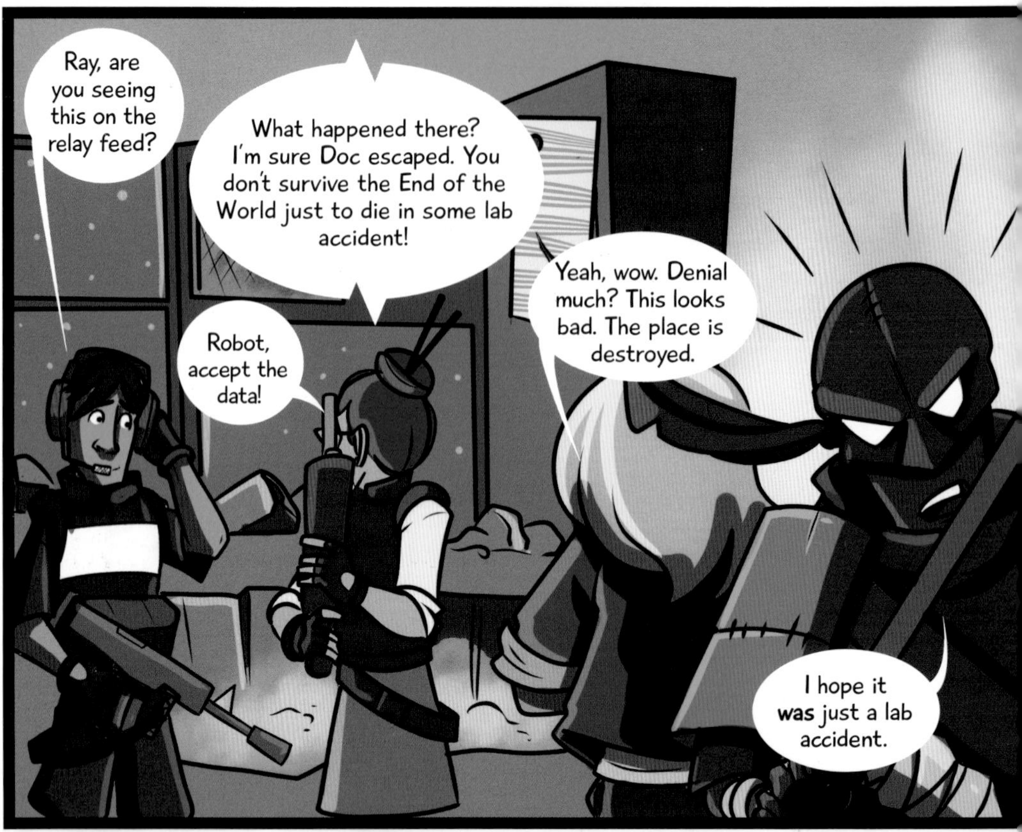
Ray, are you seeing this on the relay feed?
What happened there? I'm sure Doc escaped. You don't survive the End of the World just to die in some lab accident!
Robot, accept the data!
Yeah, wow. Denial much? This looks bad. The place is destroyed.
I hope it **was** just a lab accident.

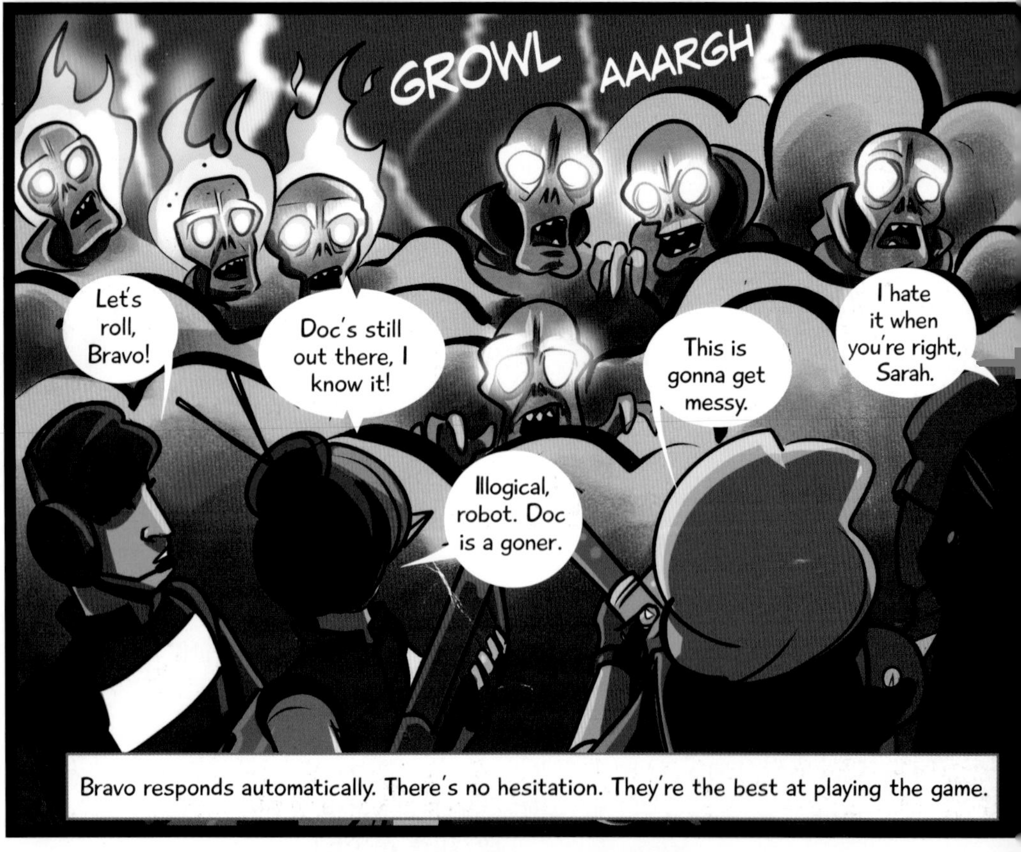
GROWL
AAARGH
Let's roll, Bravo!
Doc's still out there, I know it!
Illogical, robot. Doc is a goner.
This is gonna get messy.
I hate it when you're right, Sarah.
Bravo responds automatically. There's no hesitation. They're the best at playing the game.

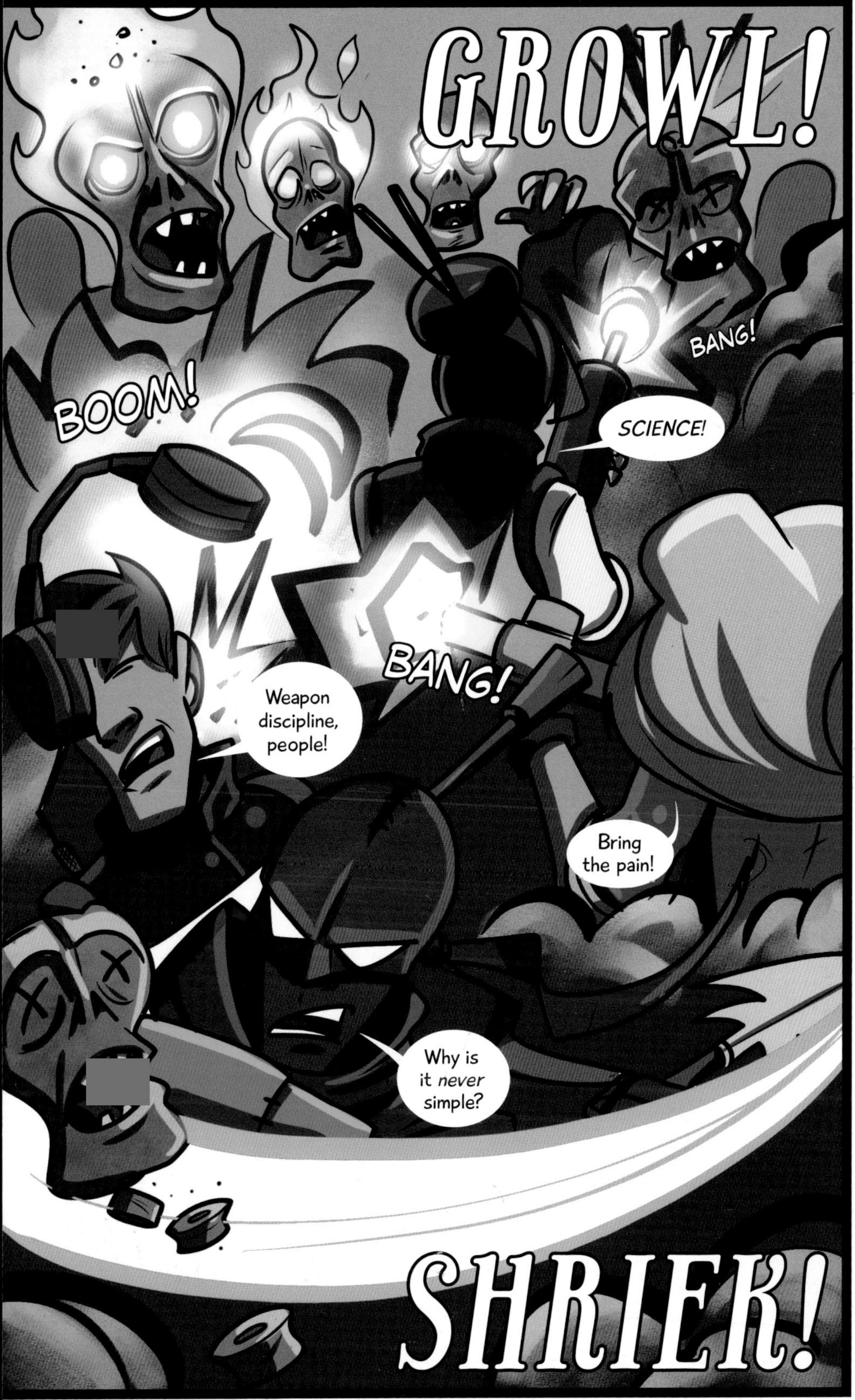
GROWL!
BOOM!
BANG!
SCIENCE!
BANG!
Weapon discipline, people!
Bring the pain!
Why is it *never* simple?
SHRIEK!

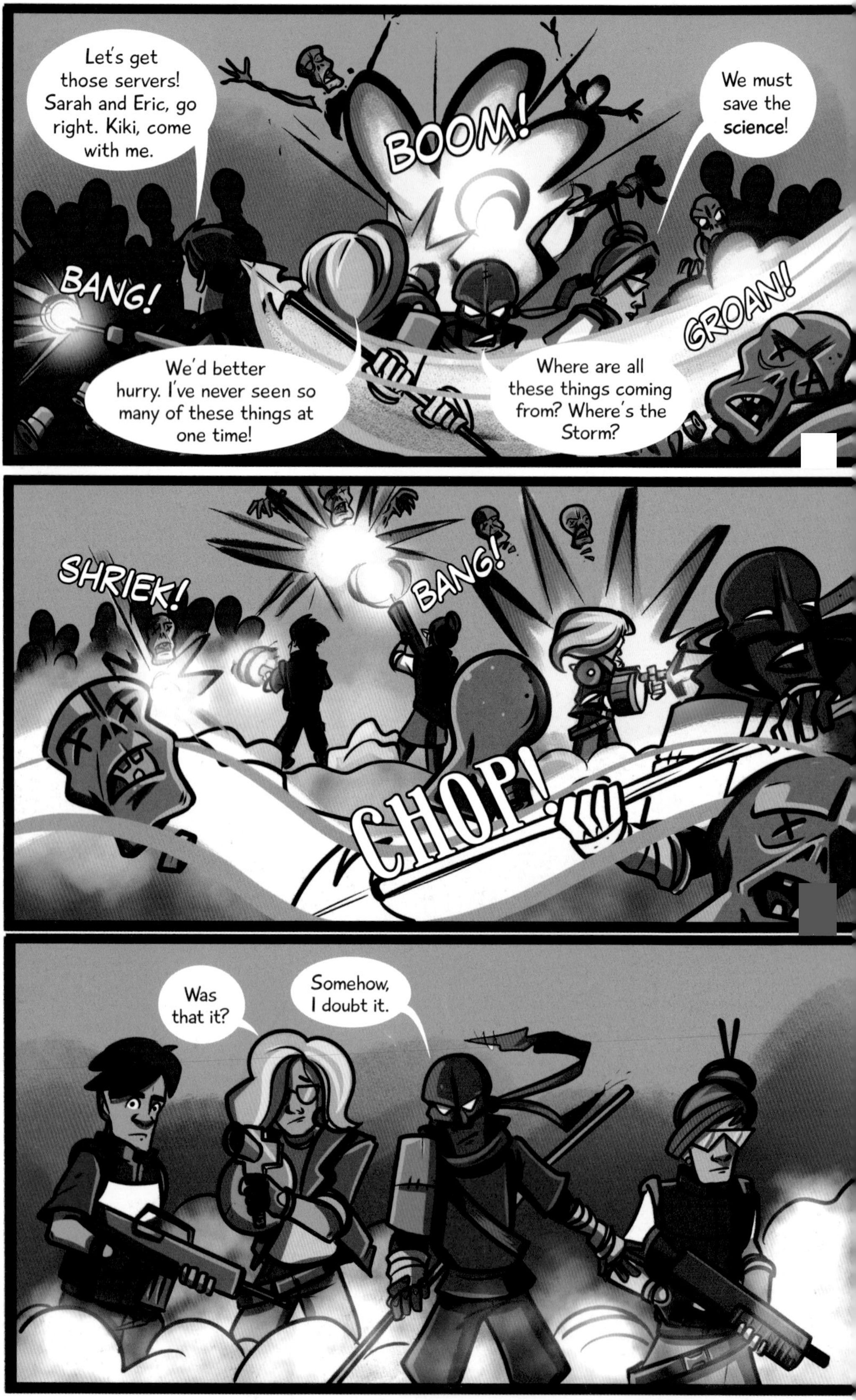
Let's get those servers! Sarah and Eric, go right. Kiki, come with me.
BOOM!
We must save the **science**!
BANG!
GROAN!
We'd better hurry. I've never seen so many of these things at one time!
Where are all these things coming from? Where's the Storm?
SHRIEK!
BANG!
CHOP!
Was that it?
Somehow, I doubt it.

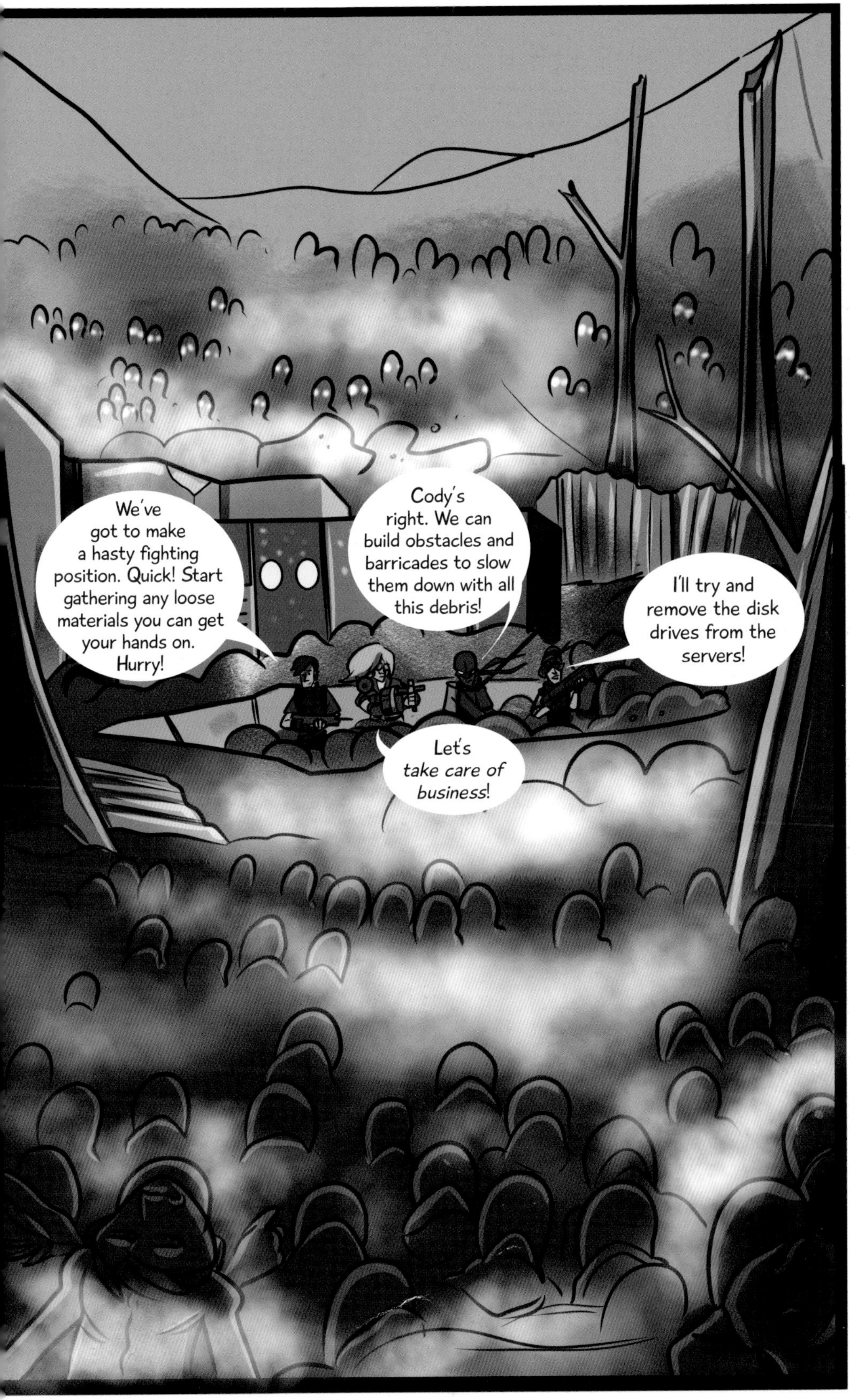
We've got to make a hasty fighting position. Quick! Start gathering any loose materials you can get your hands on. Hurry!
Cody's right. We can build obstacles and barricades to slow them down with all this debris!
I'll try and remove the disk drives from the servers!
Let's *take care of business*!

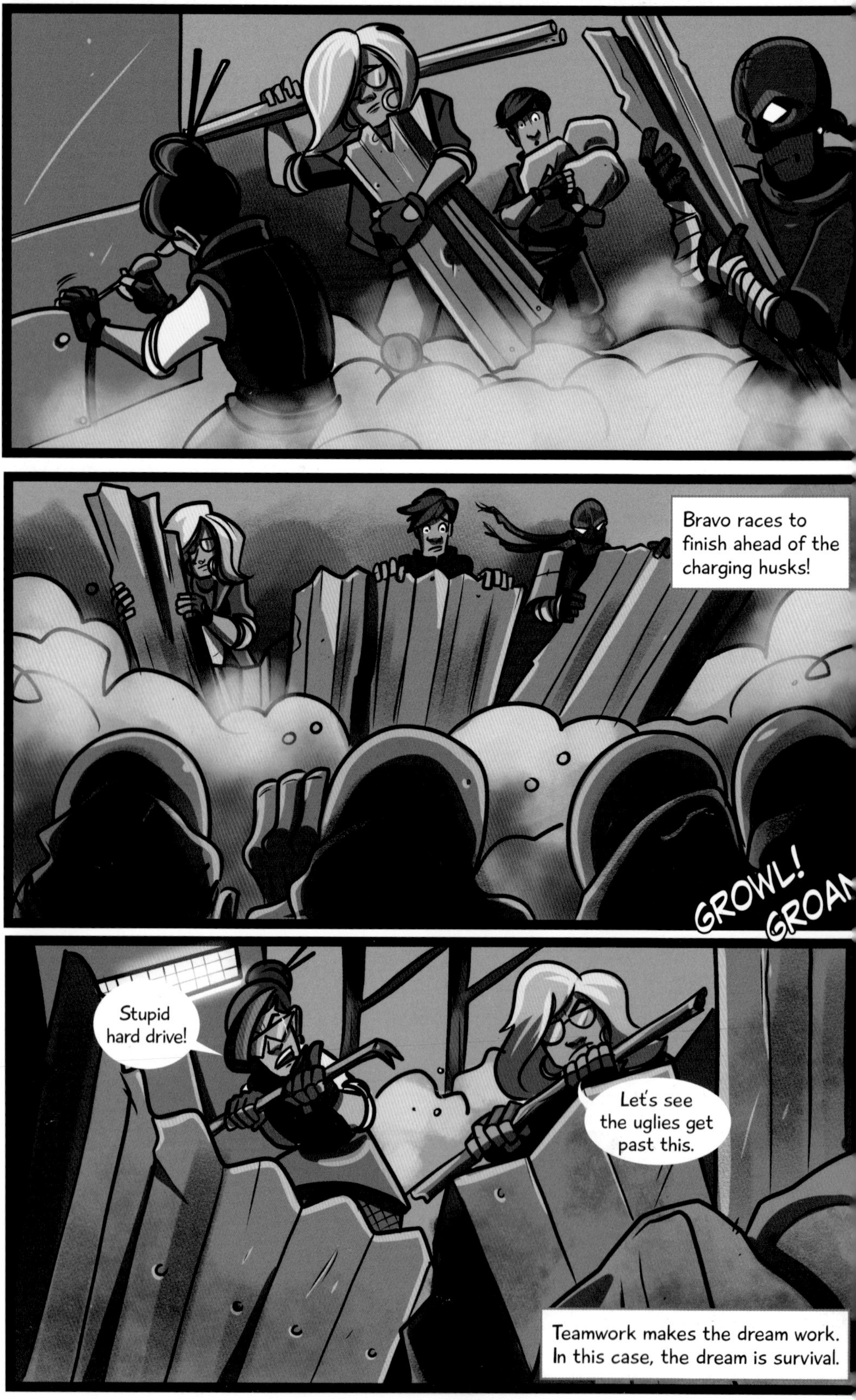

Bravo races to finish ahead of the charging husks!
GROWL!
GROA
Stupid hard drive!
Let's see the uglies get past this.
Teamwork makes the dream work. In this case, the dream is survival.

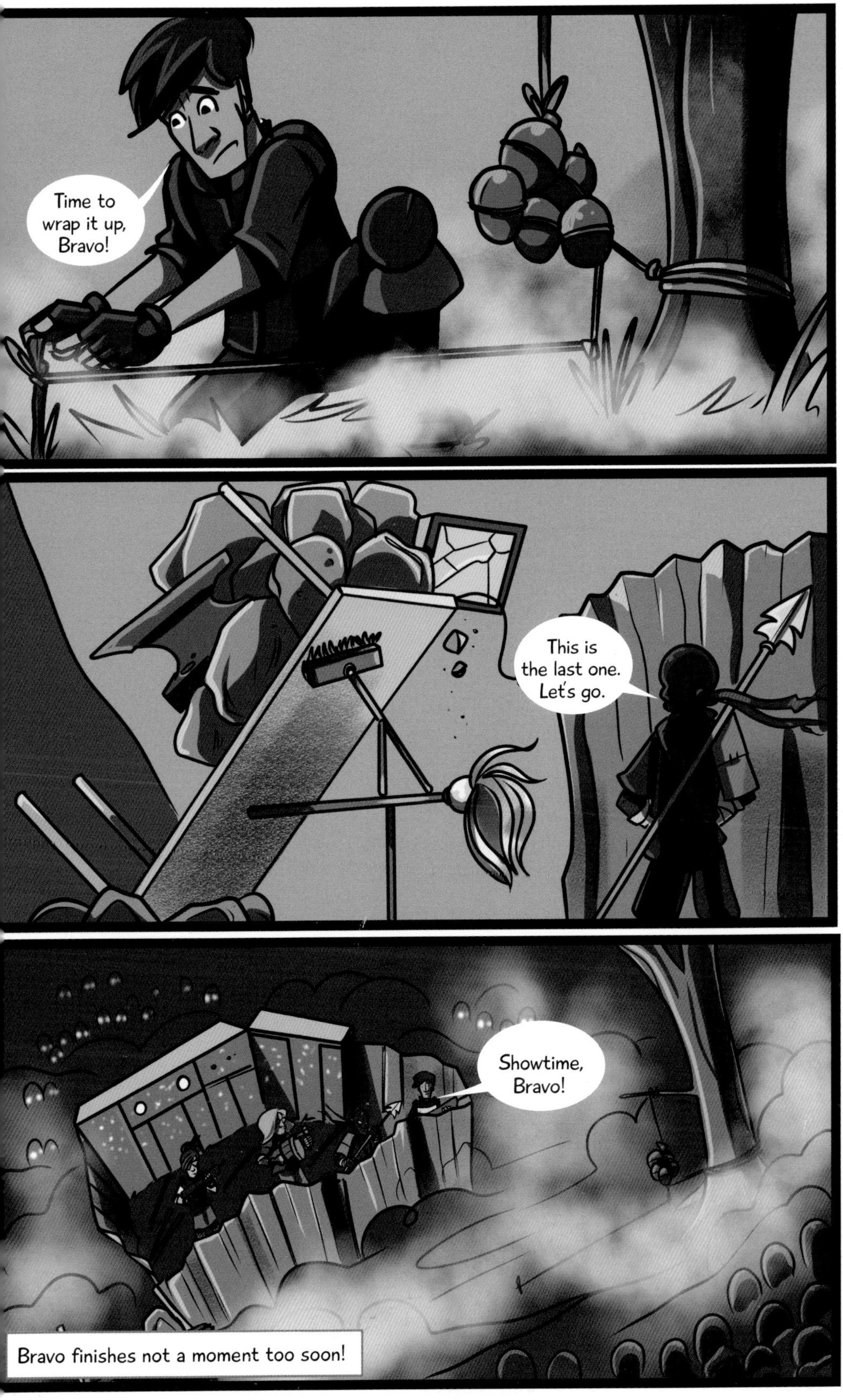
Time to wrap it up, Bravo!
This is the last one. Let's go.
Showtime, Bravo!
Bravo finishes not a moment too soon!

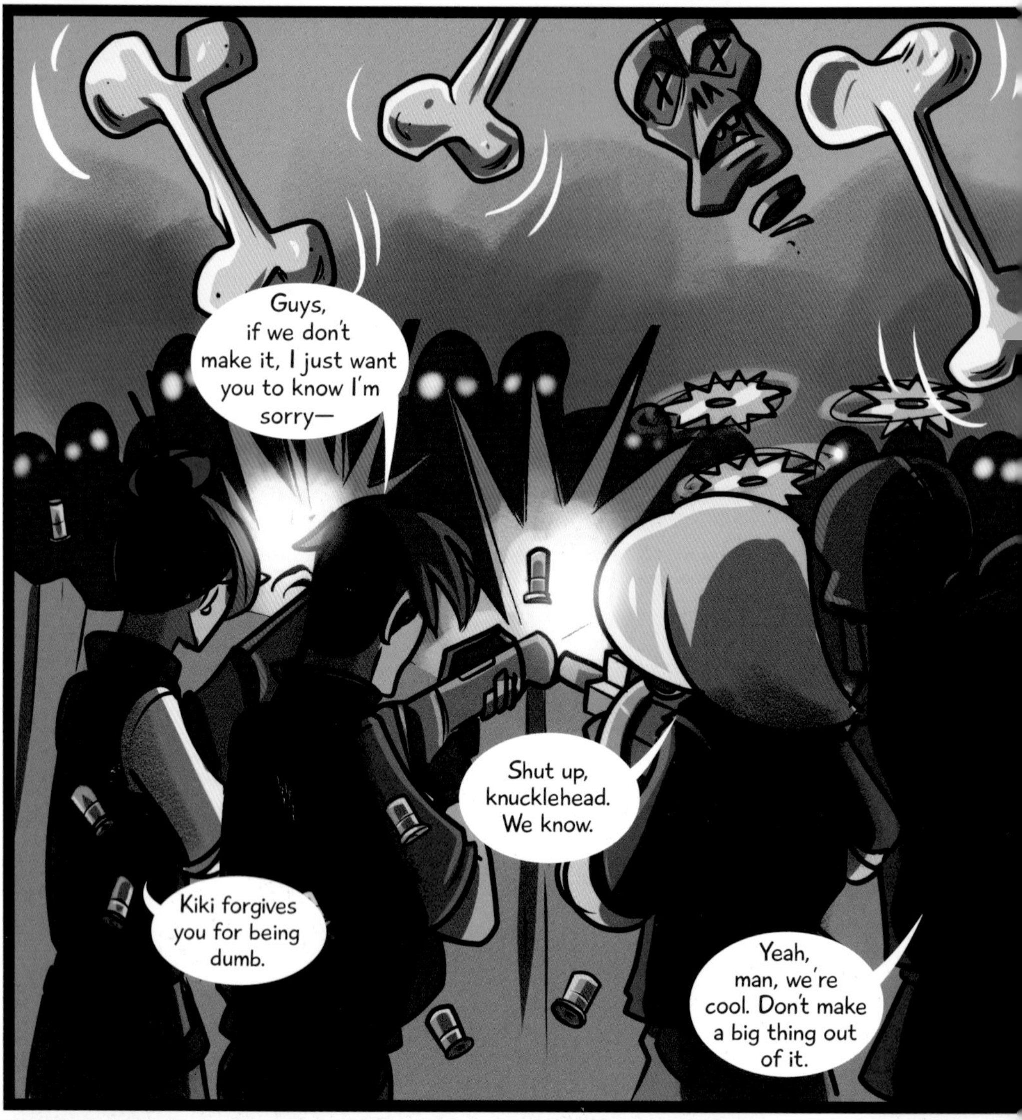
Guys, if we don't make it, I just want you to know I'm sorry—
Kiki forgives you for being dumb.
Shut up, knucklehead. We know.
Yeah, man, we're cool. Don't make a big thing out of it.

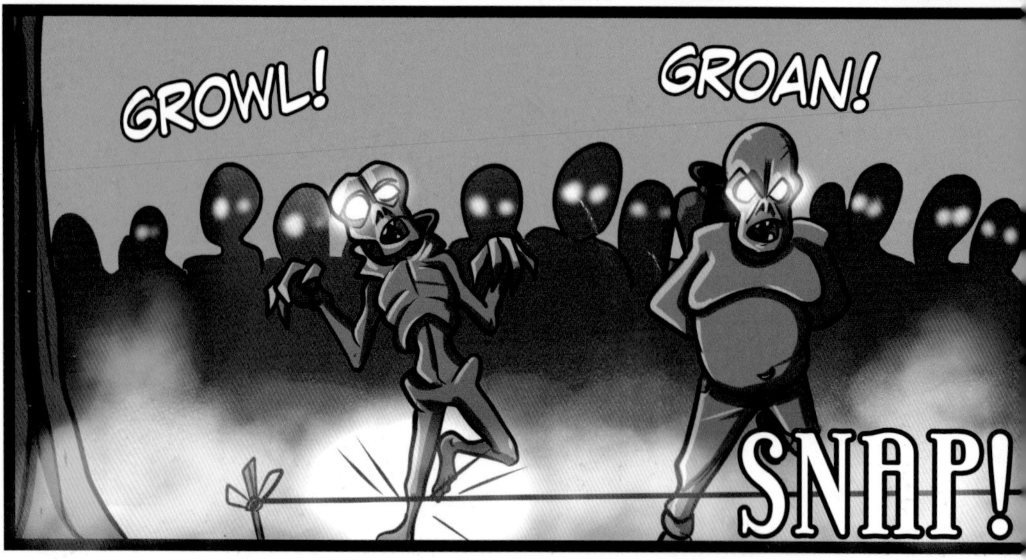
GROWL!
GROAN!
SNAP!

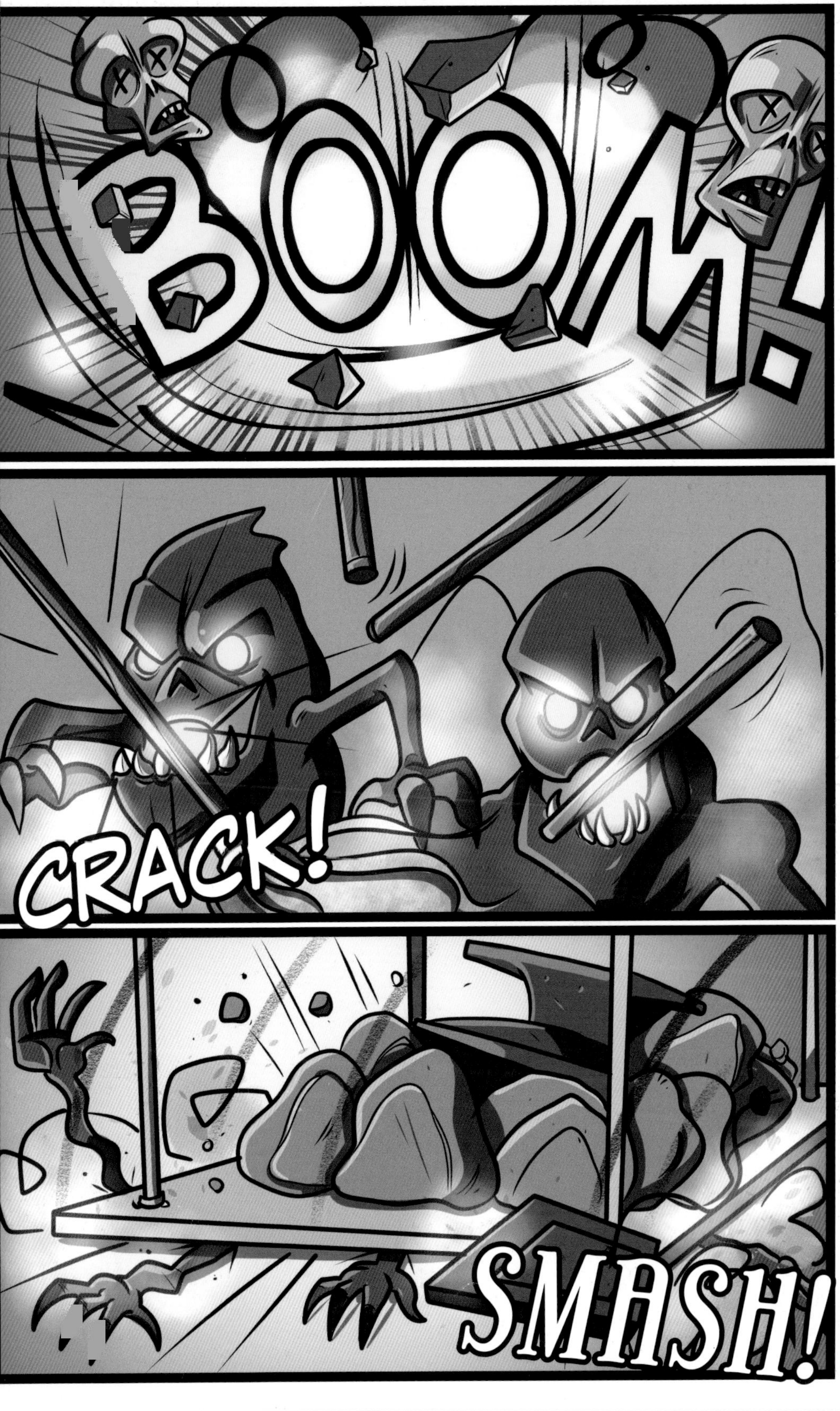
BOOM!
CRACK!
SMASH!

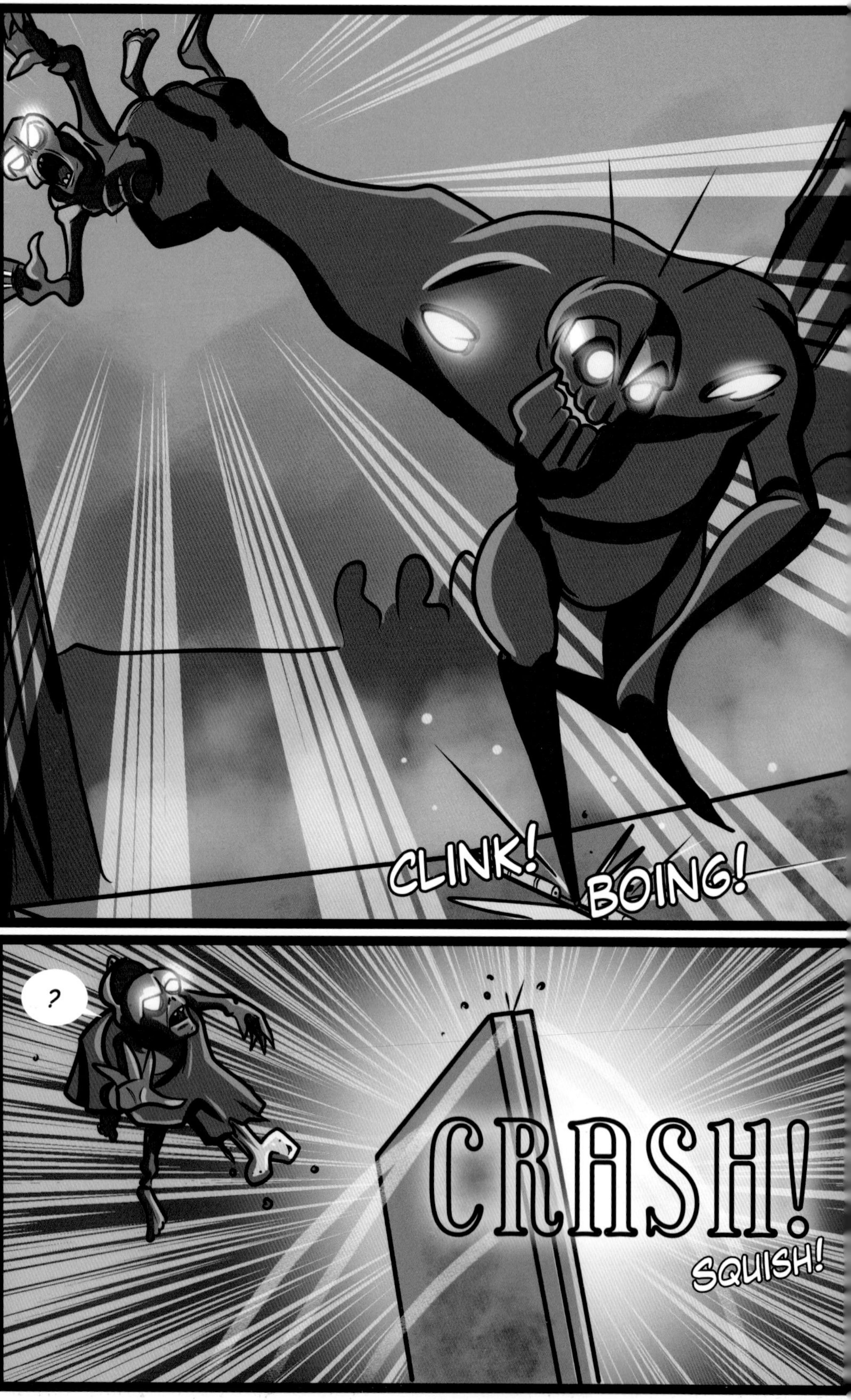
CLINK!
BOING!
?
CRASH!
SQUISH!

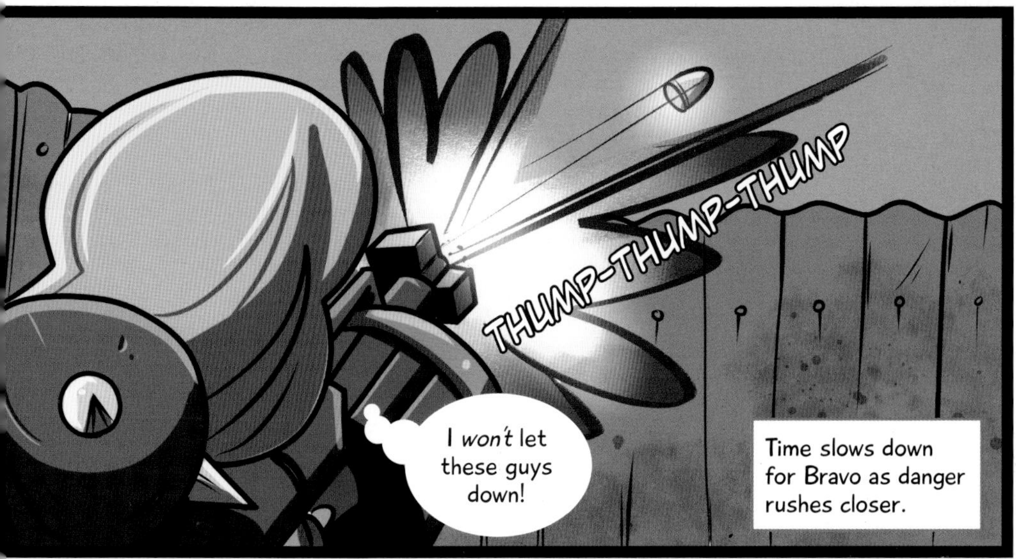
THUMP-THUMP-THUMP-THUMP
I *won't* let these guys down!
Time slows down for Bravo as danger rushes closer.

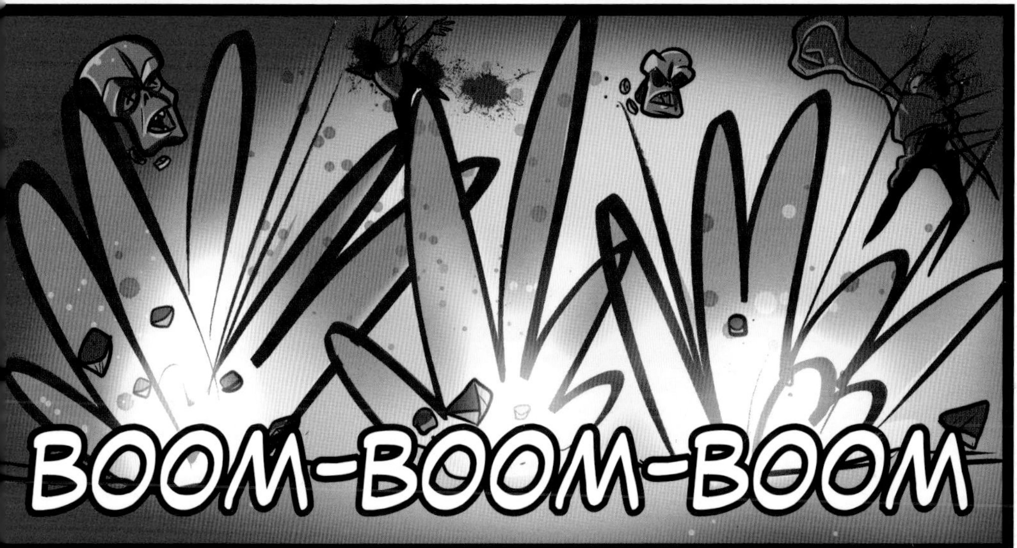
BOOM-BOOM-BOOM

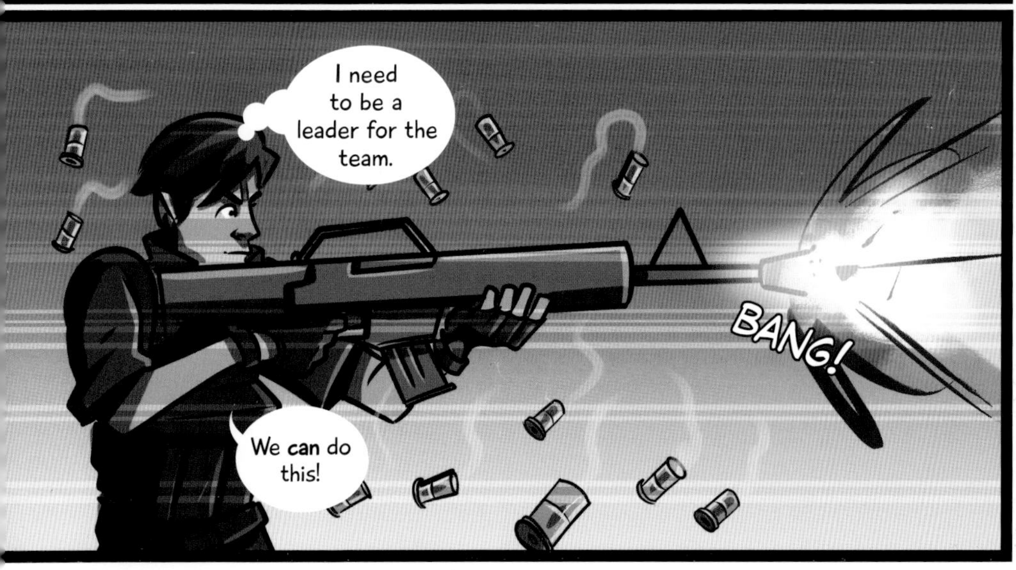
I need to be a leader for the team.
BANG!
We **can** do this!

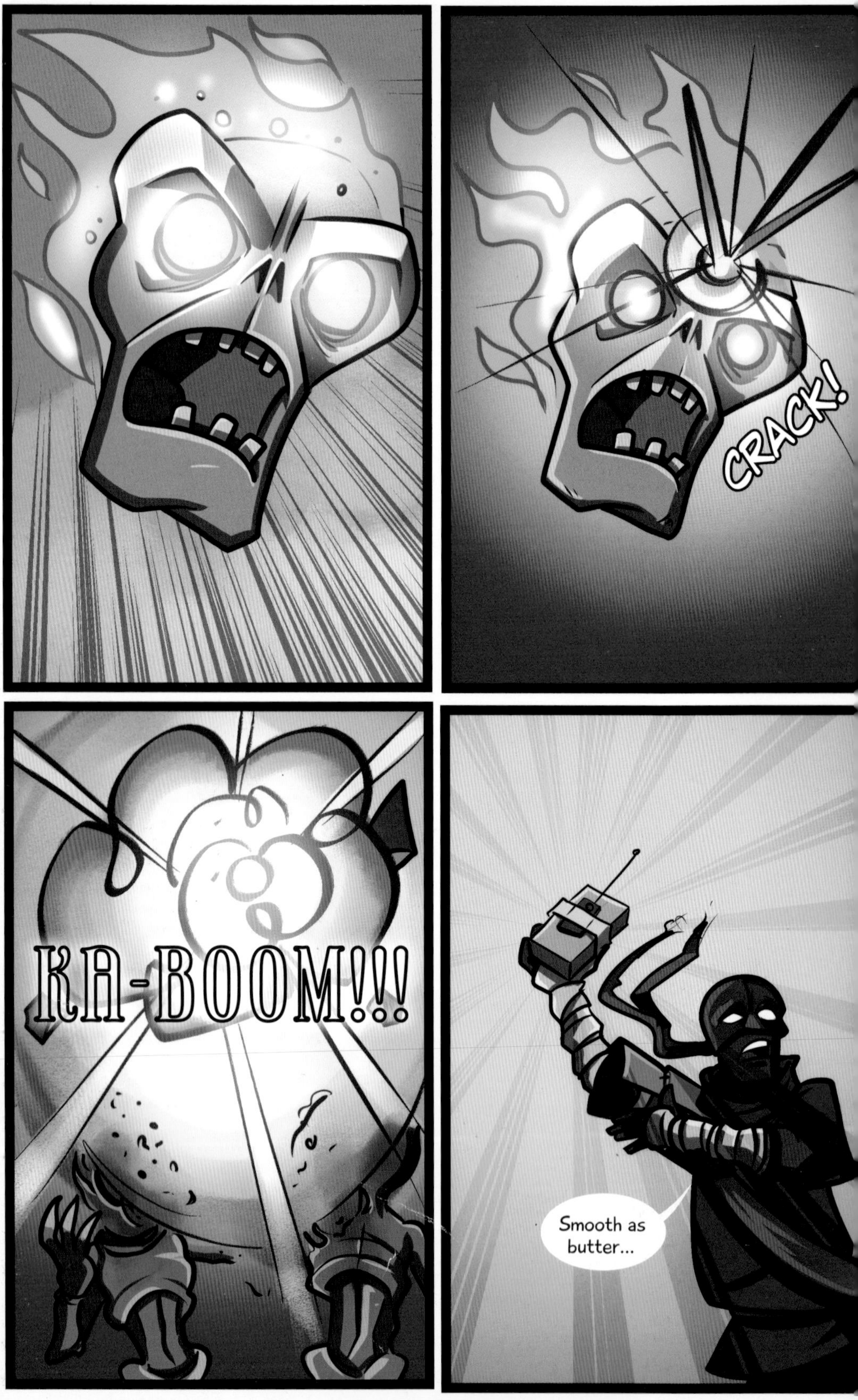
CRACK!
KA-BOOM!!!
Smooth as butter...

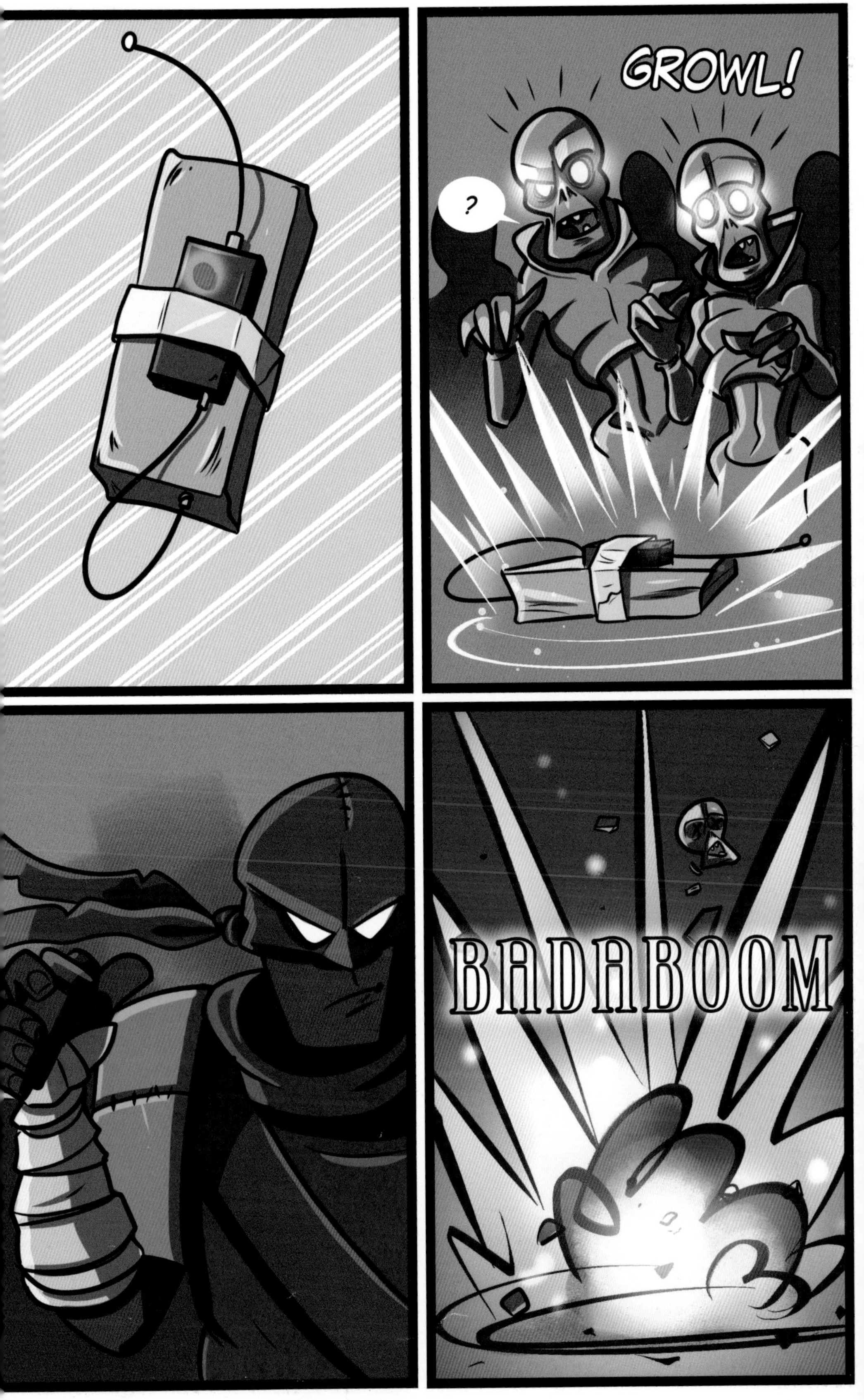
GROWL!
?
BADABOOM

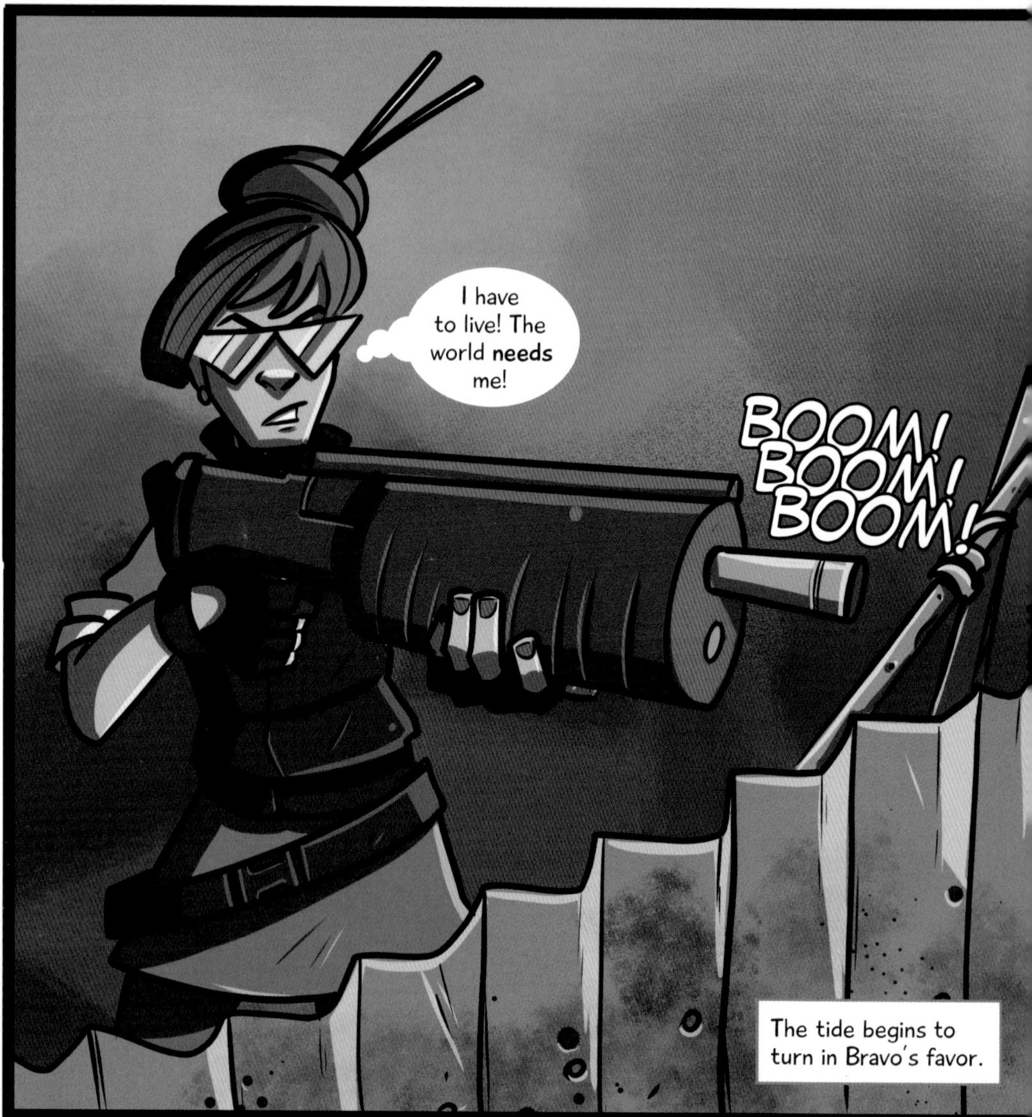
I have to live! The world **needs** me!
BOOM! BOOM! BOOM!
The tide begins to turn in Bravo's favor.

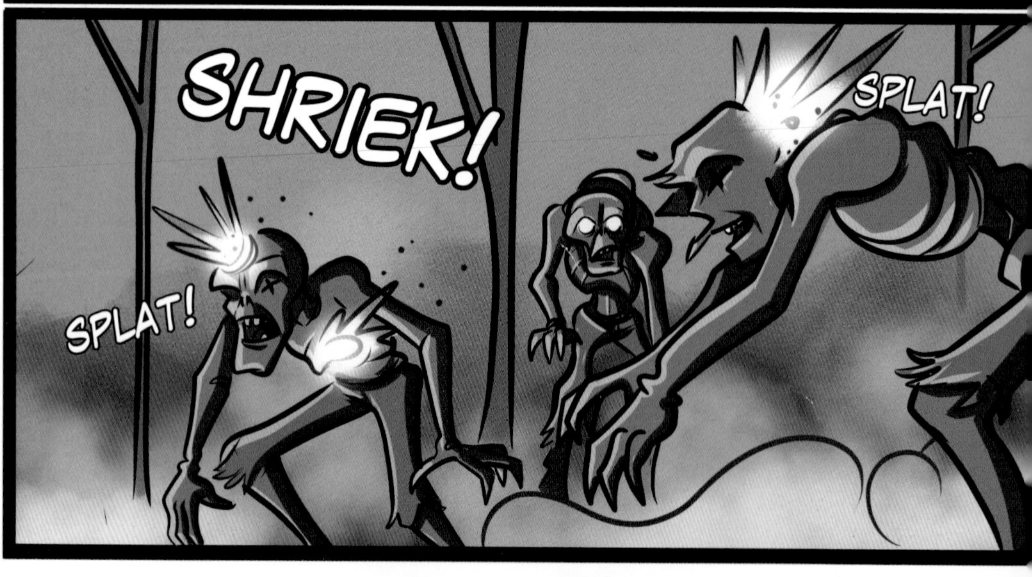
SHRIEK!
SPLAT!
SPLAT!

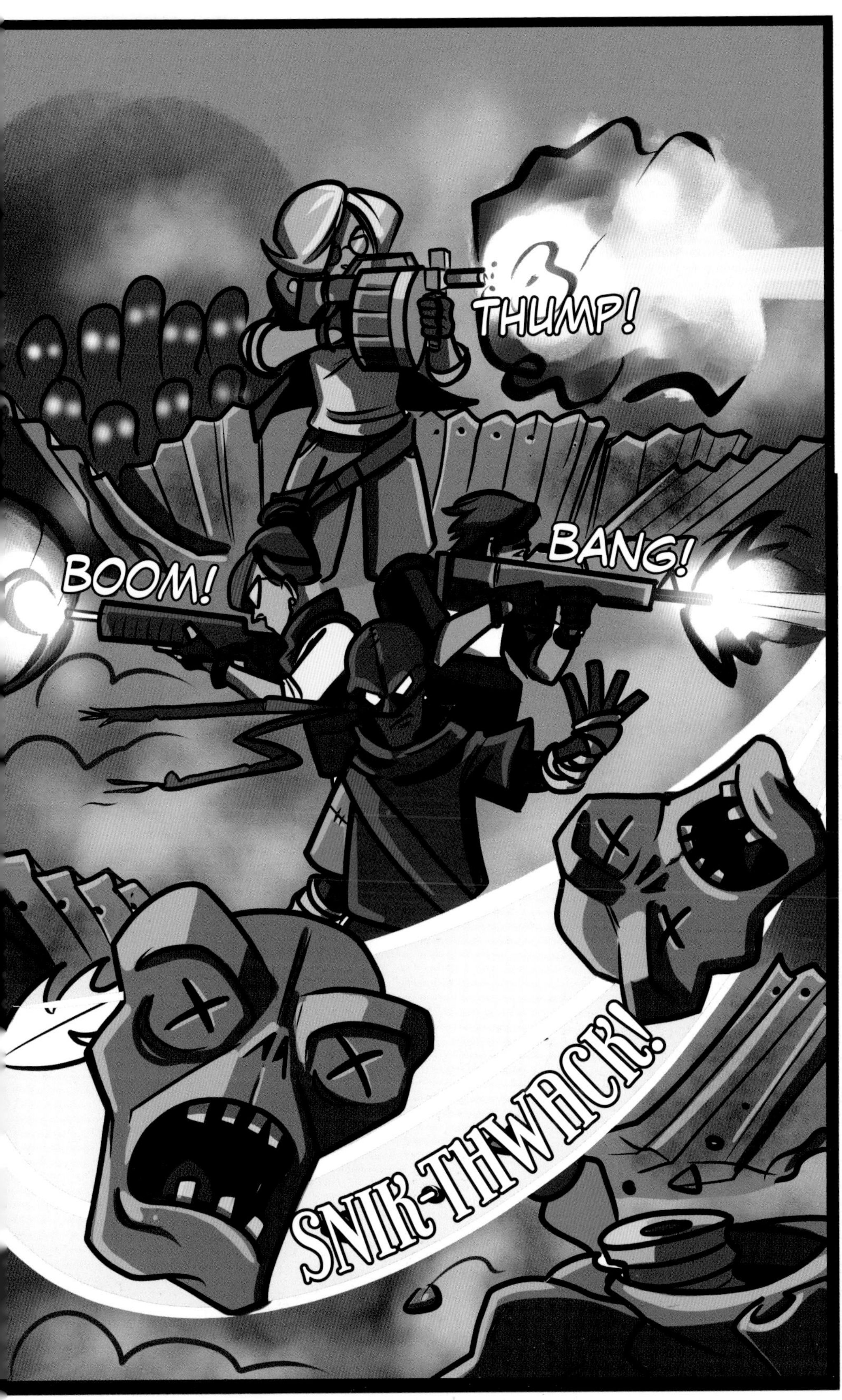
THUMP!
BOOM!
BANG!
SNIK-THWACK!

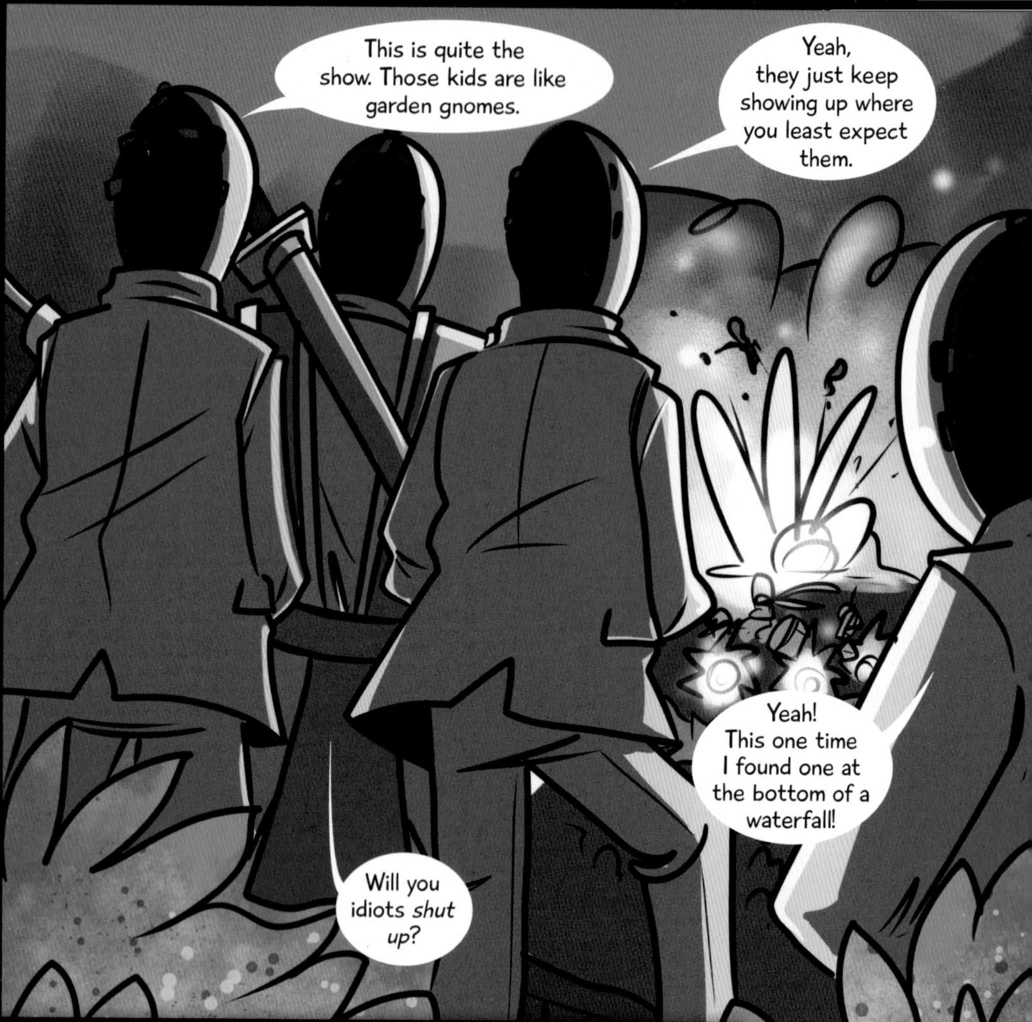
This is quite the show. Those kids are like garden gnomes.
Yeah, they just keep showing up where you least expect them.
Yeah! This one time I found one at the bottom of a waterfall!
Will you idiots *shut up*?

CHAPTER 6: ALL IN

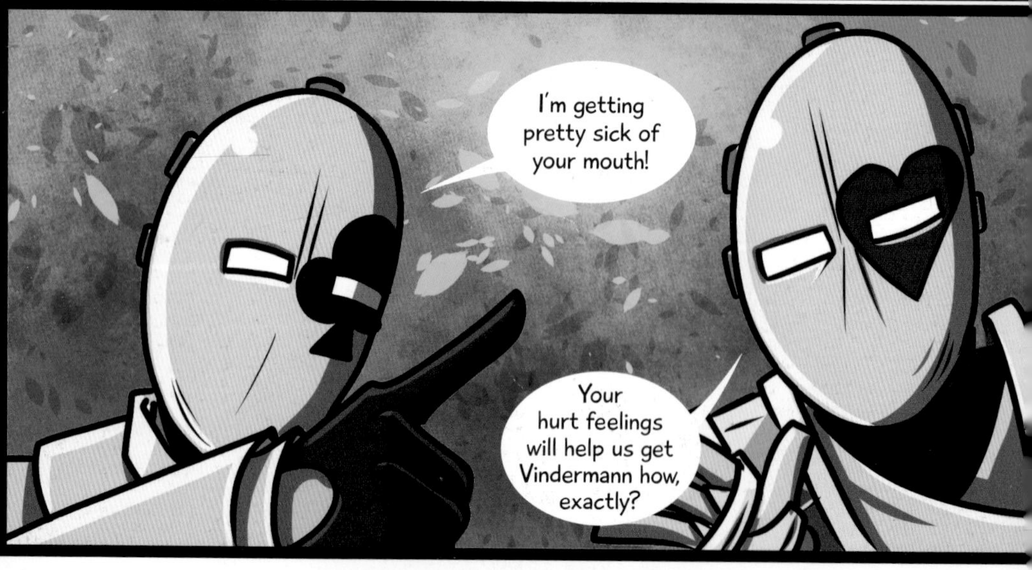
I'm getting pretty sick of your mouth!
Your hurt feelings will help us get Vindermann how, exactly?

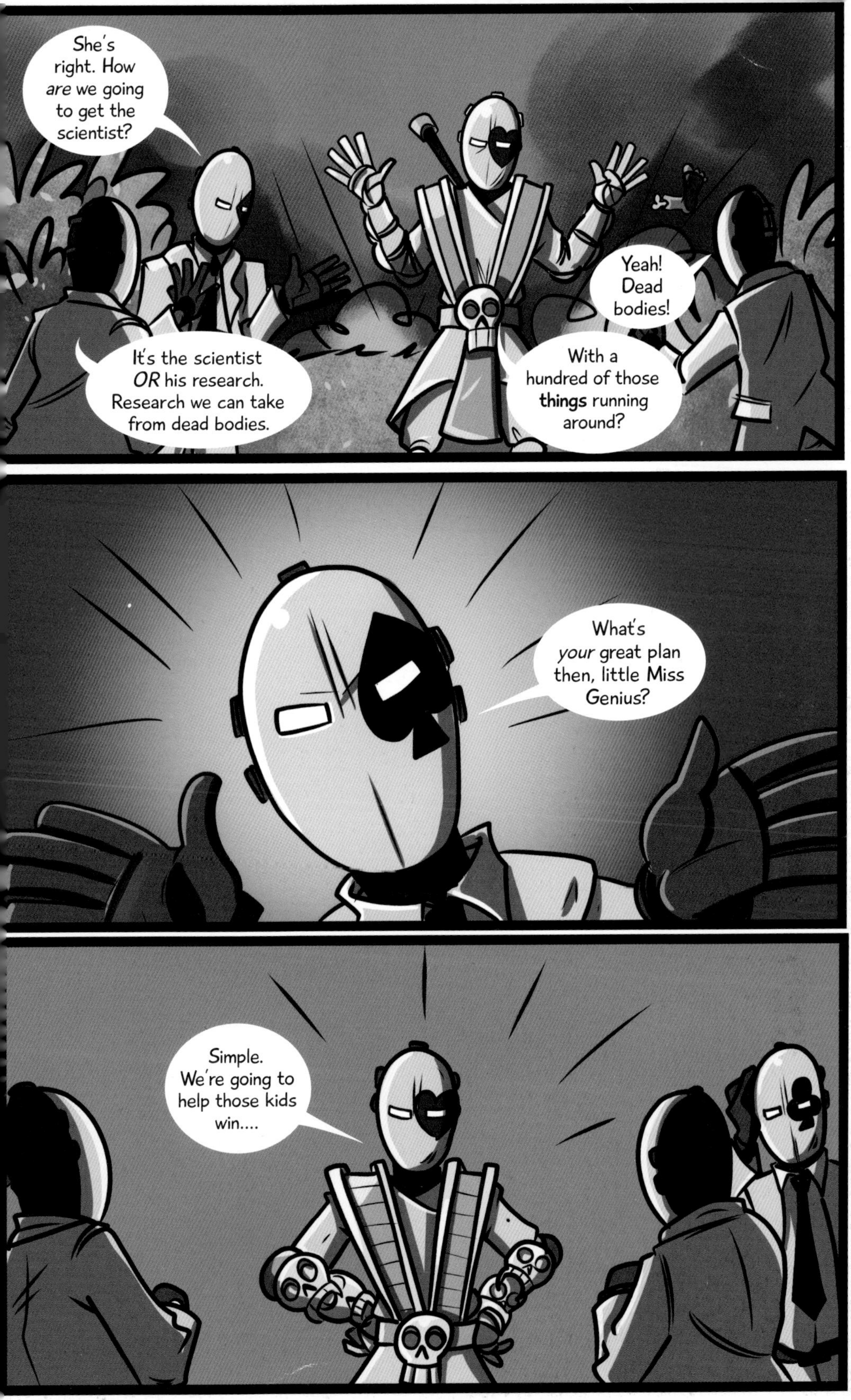
She's right. How *are* we going to get the scientist?
It's the scientist *OR* his research. Research we can take from dead bodies.
Yeah! Dead bodies!
With a hundred of those **things** running around?
What's *your* great plan then, little Miss Genius?
Simple. We're going to help those kids win....

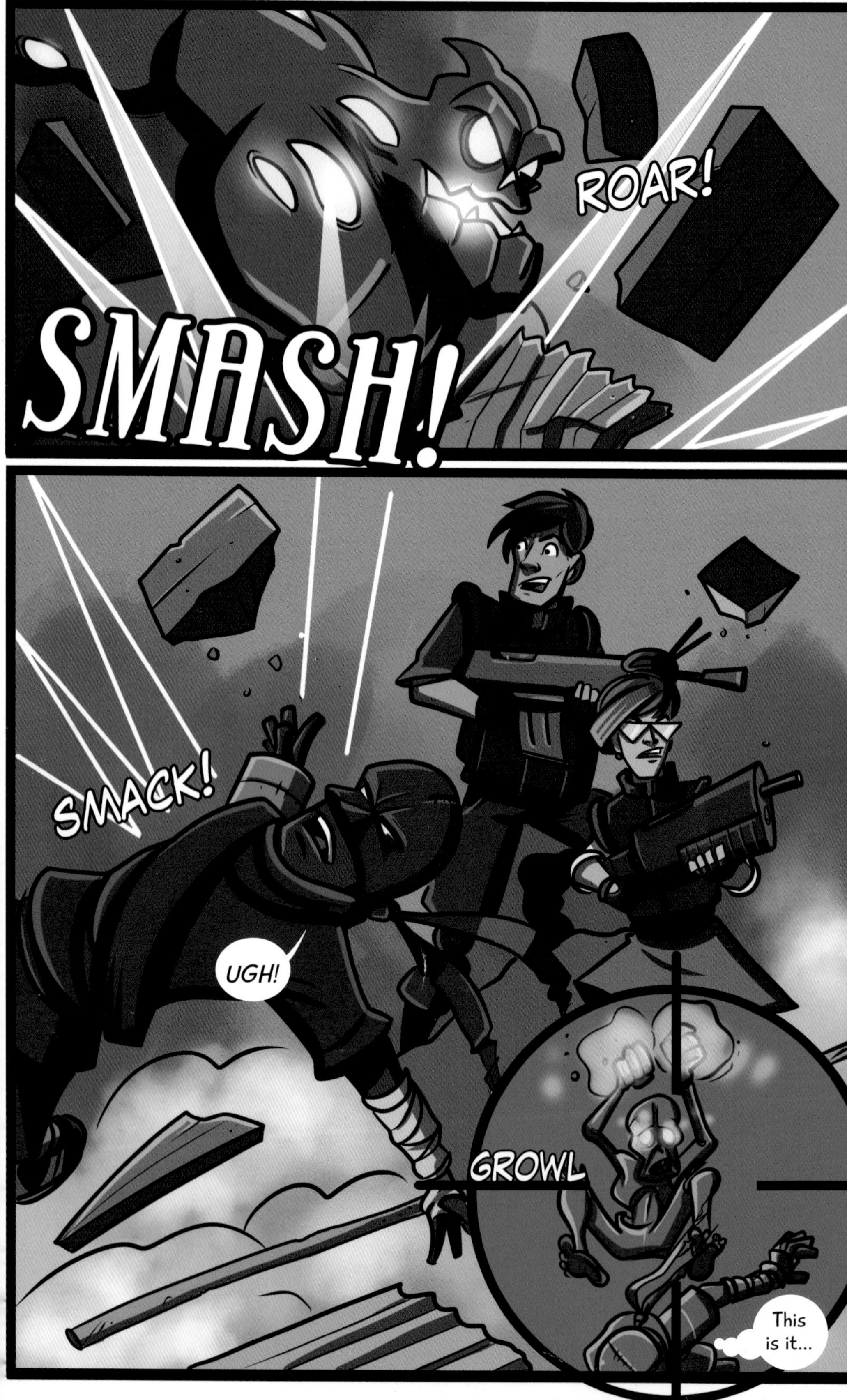
ROAR!
SMASH!
SMACK!
UGH!
GROWL
This is it...

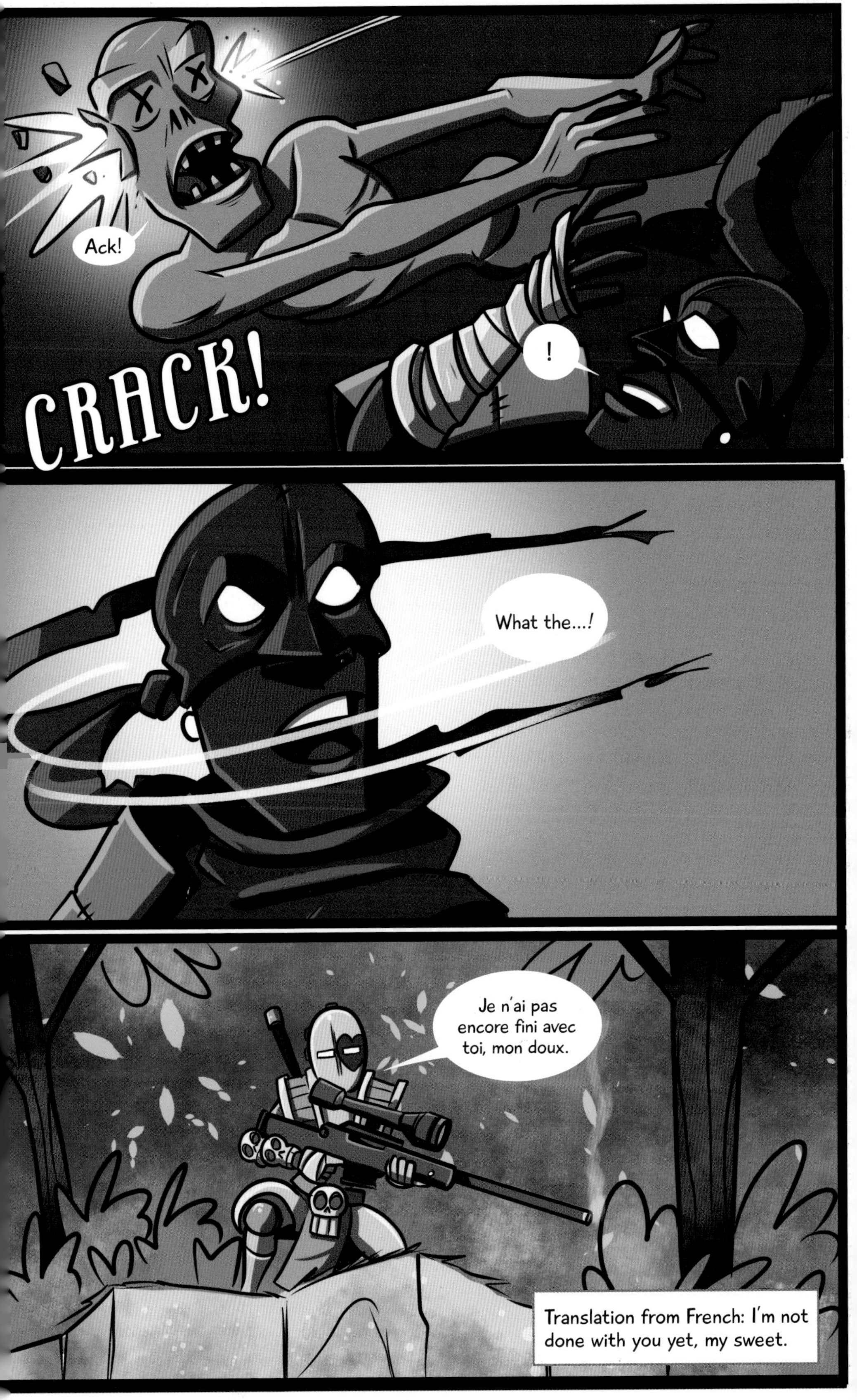
Ack!
CRACK!
!
What the...!
Je n'ai pas encore fini avec toi, mon doux.
Translation from French: I'm not done with you yet, my sweet.

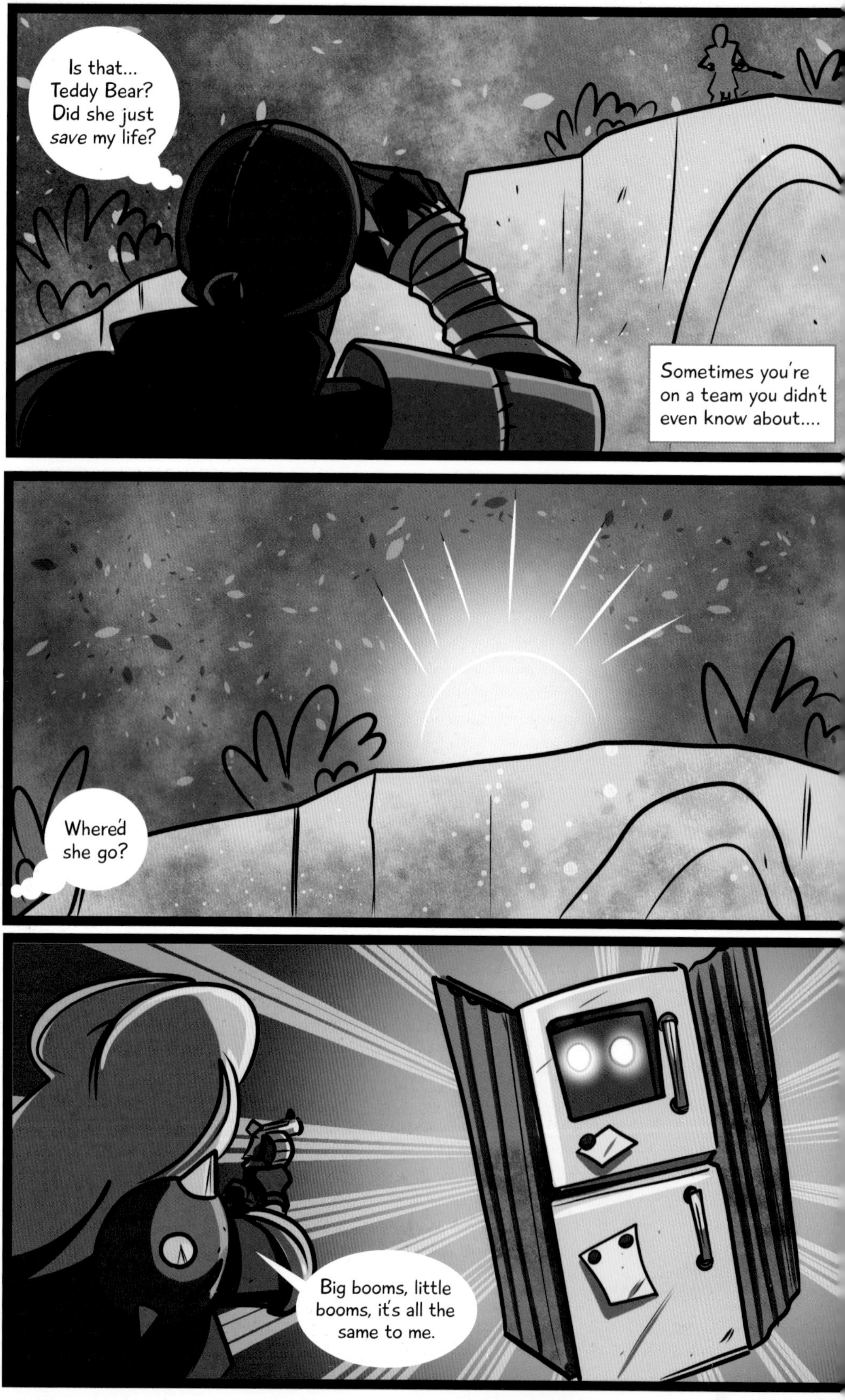
Is that... Teddy Bear? Did she just *save* my life?
Sometimes you're on a team you didn't even know about....
Where'd she go?
Big booms, little booms, it's all the same to me.

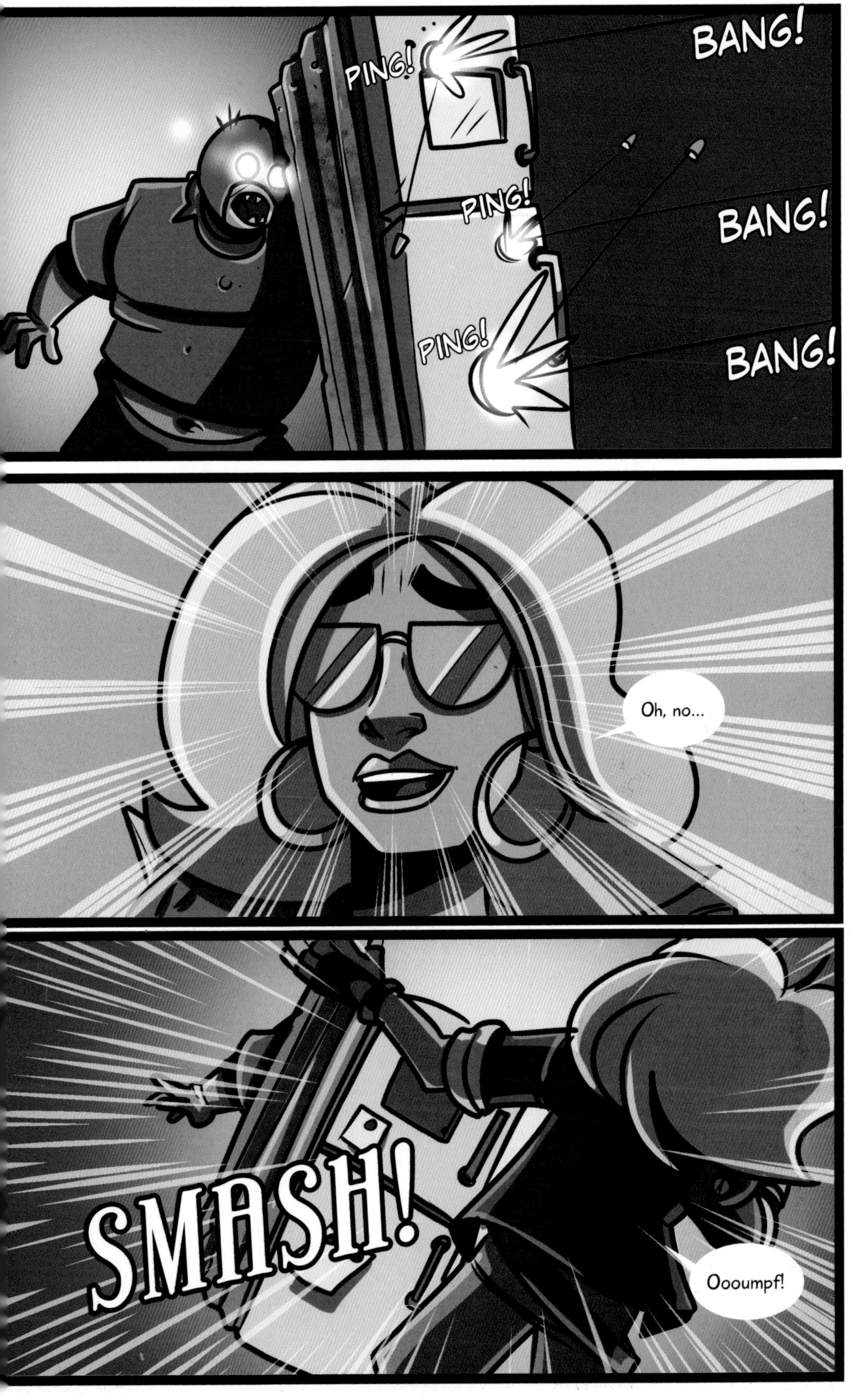
BANG!
PING!
PING!
BANG!
PING!
BANG!
Oh, no...
SMASH!
Oooumpf!

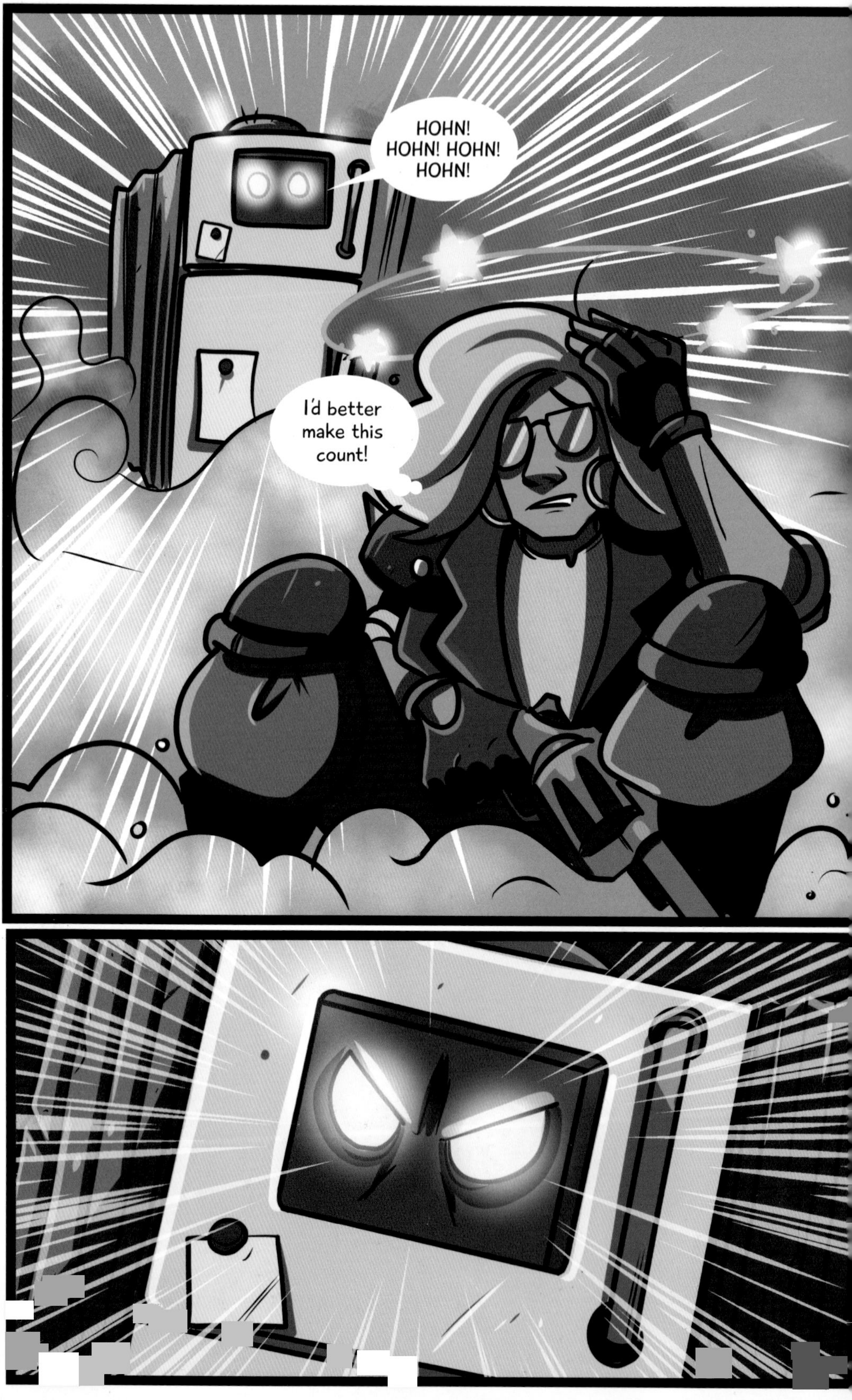
HOHN!
HOHN! HOHN!
HOHN!
I'd better make this count!

GROAN

BANG!

If there's one thing Sarah's gotten good at, it's making things count.

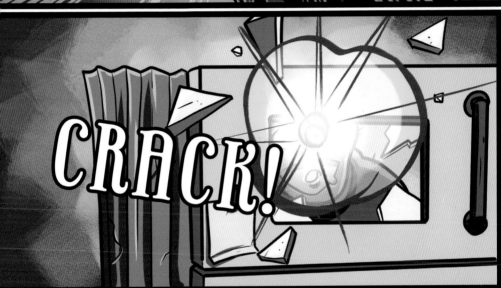

CRACK!

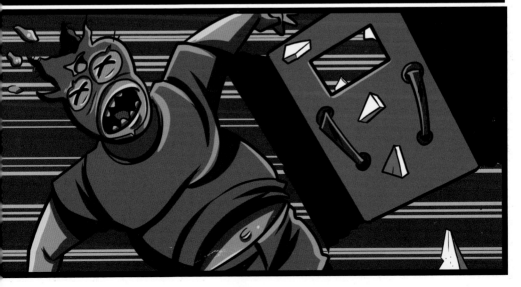

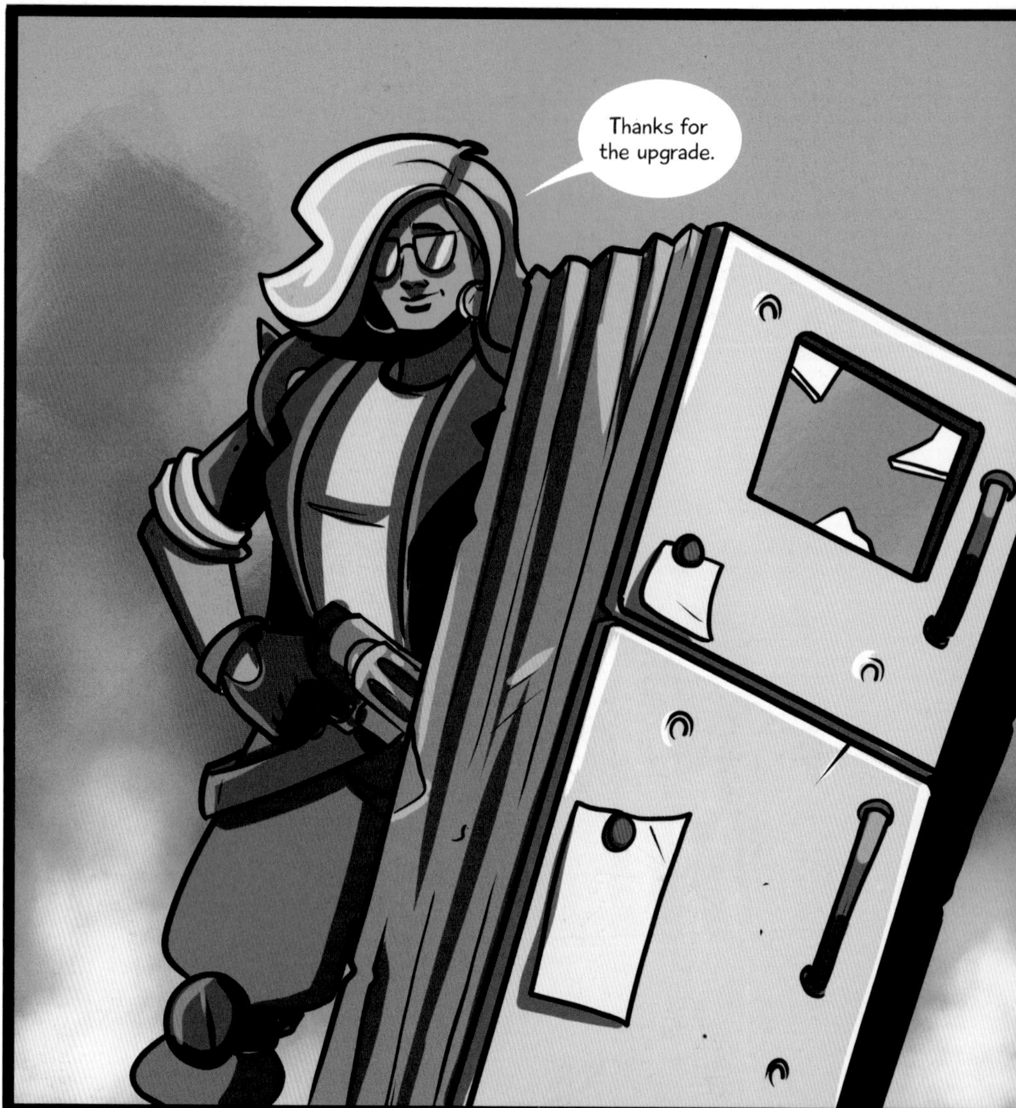
Thanks for the upgrade.

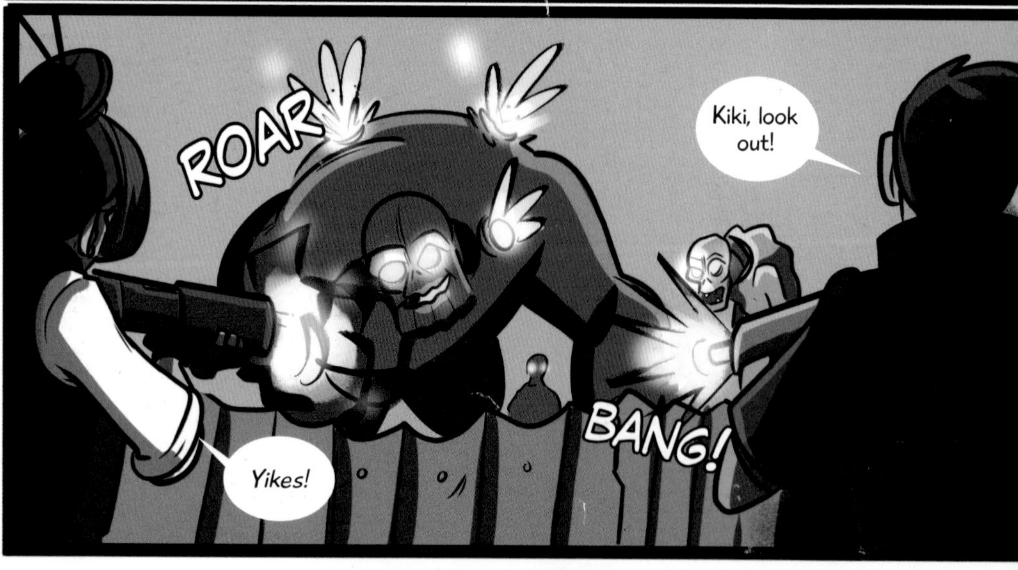
ROAR
Kiki, look out!
BANG!
Yikes!

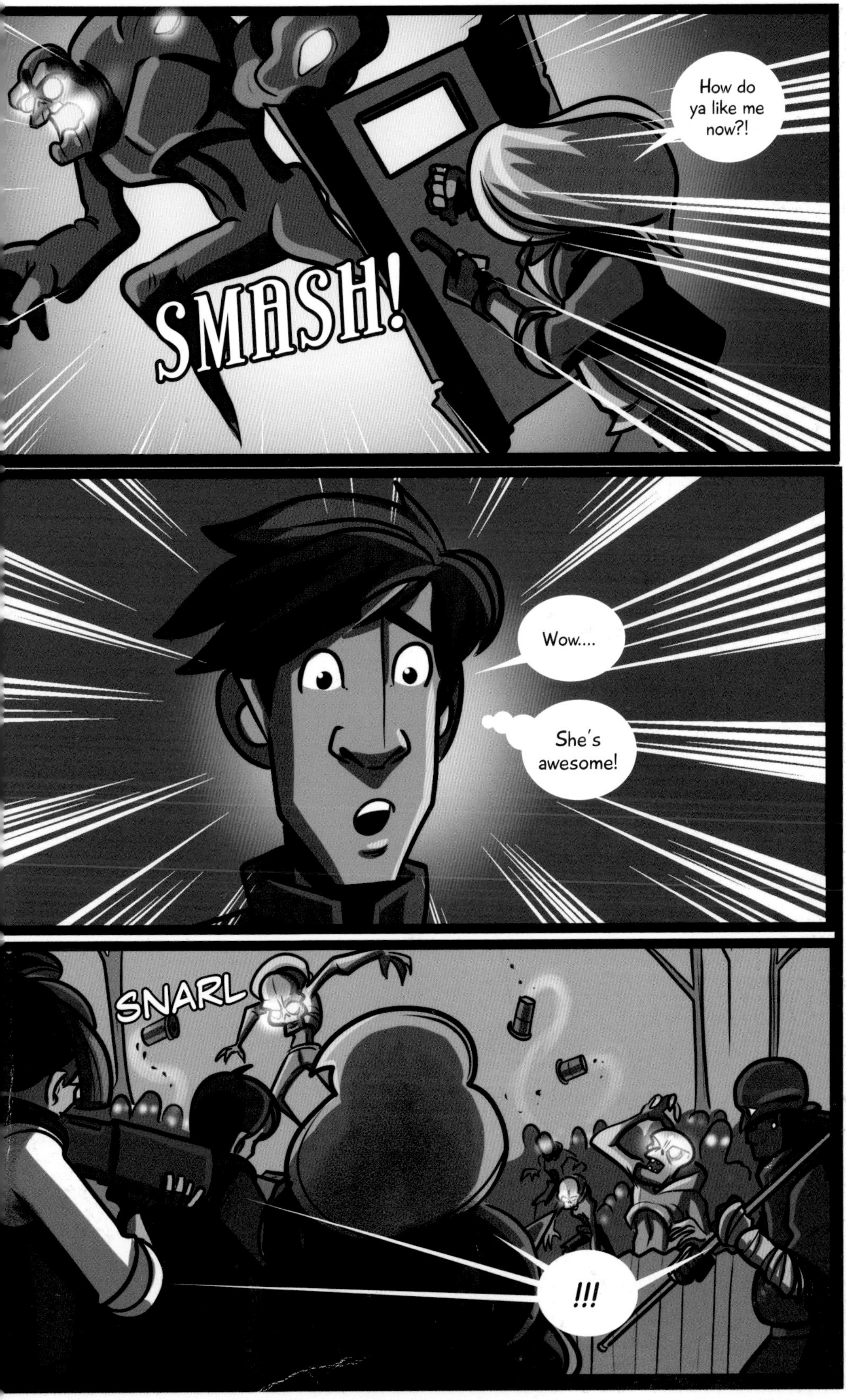
How do ya like me now?!
SMASH!
Wow....
She's awesome!
SNARL
!!!

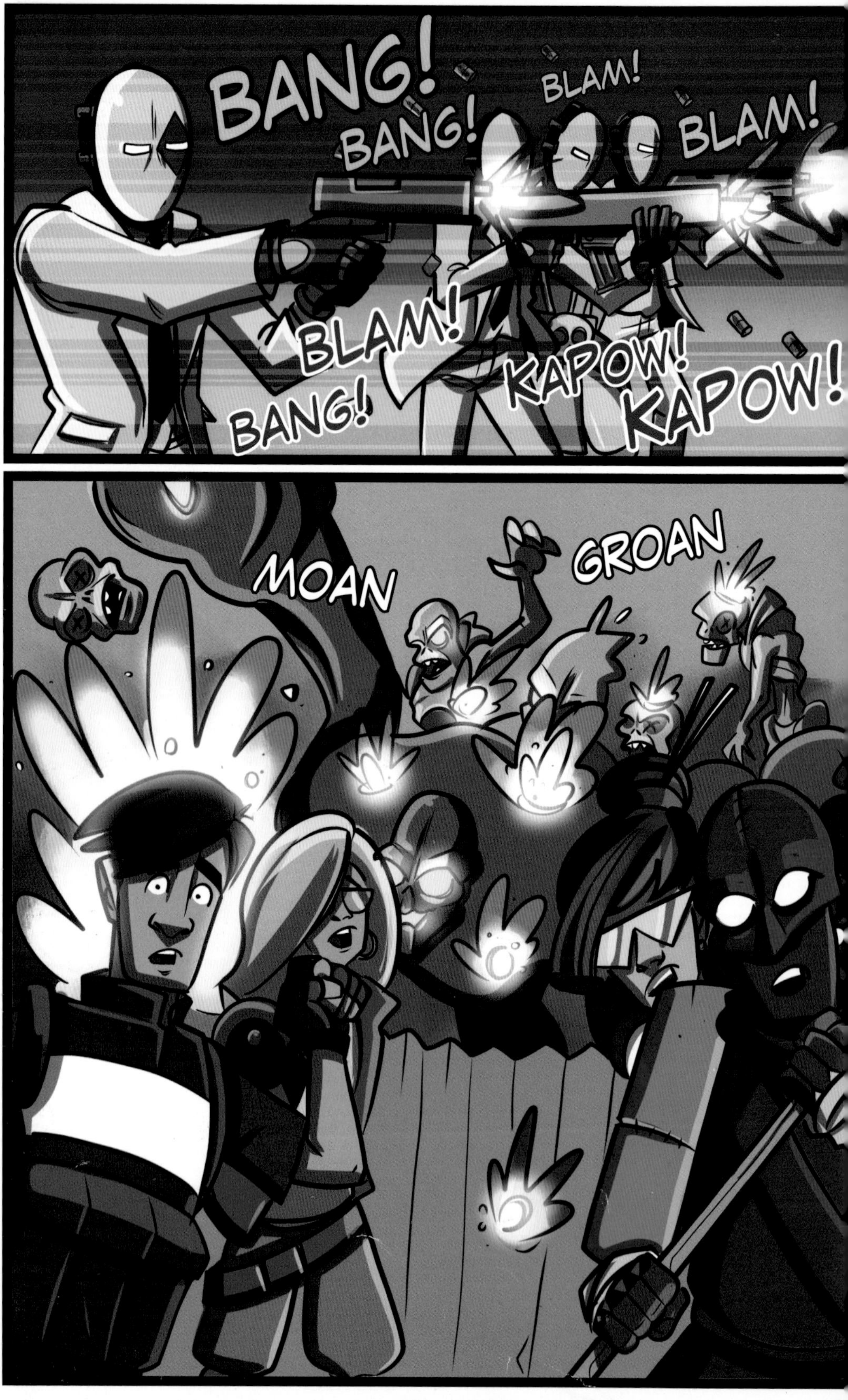
BANG!
BANG!
BLAM!
BLAM!
BLAM!
BANG!
KAPOW!
KAPOW!
MOAN
GROAN

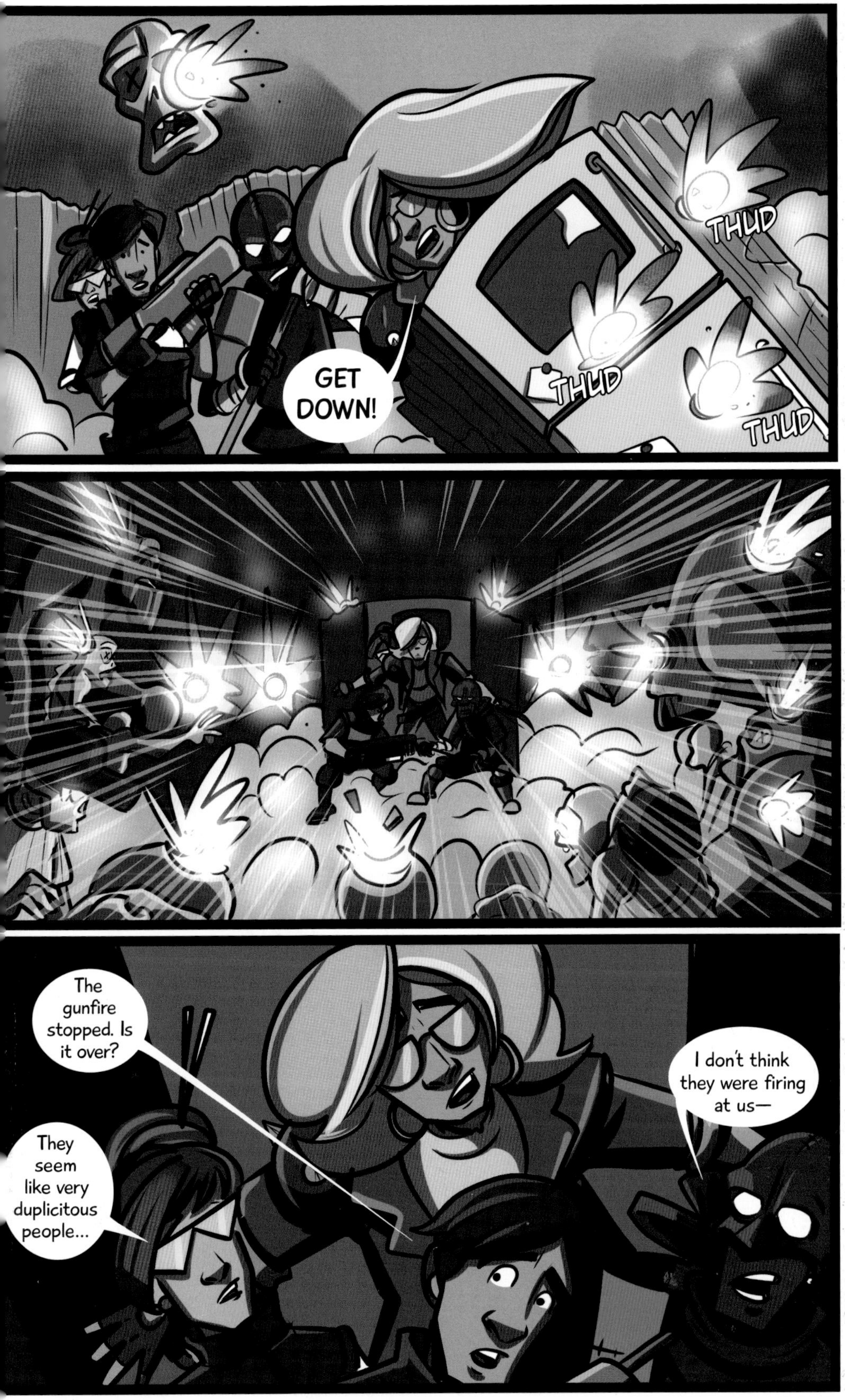
GET DOWN!
THUD
THUD
THUD
The gunfire stopped. Is it over?
I don't think they were firing at us—
They seem like very duplicitous people...

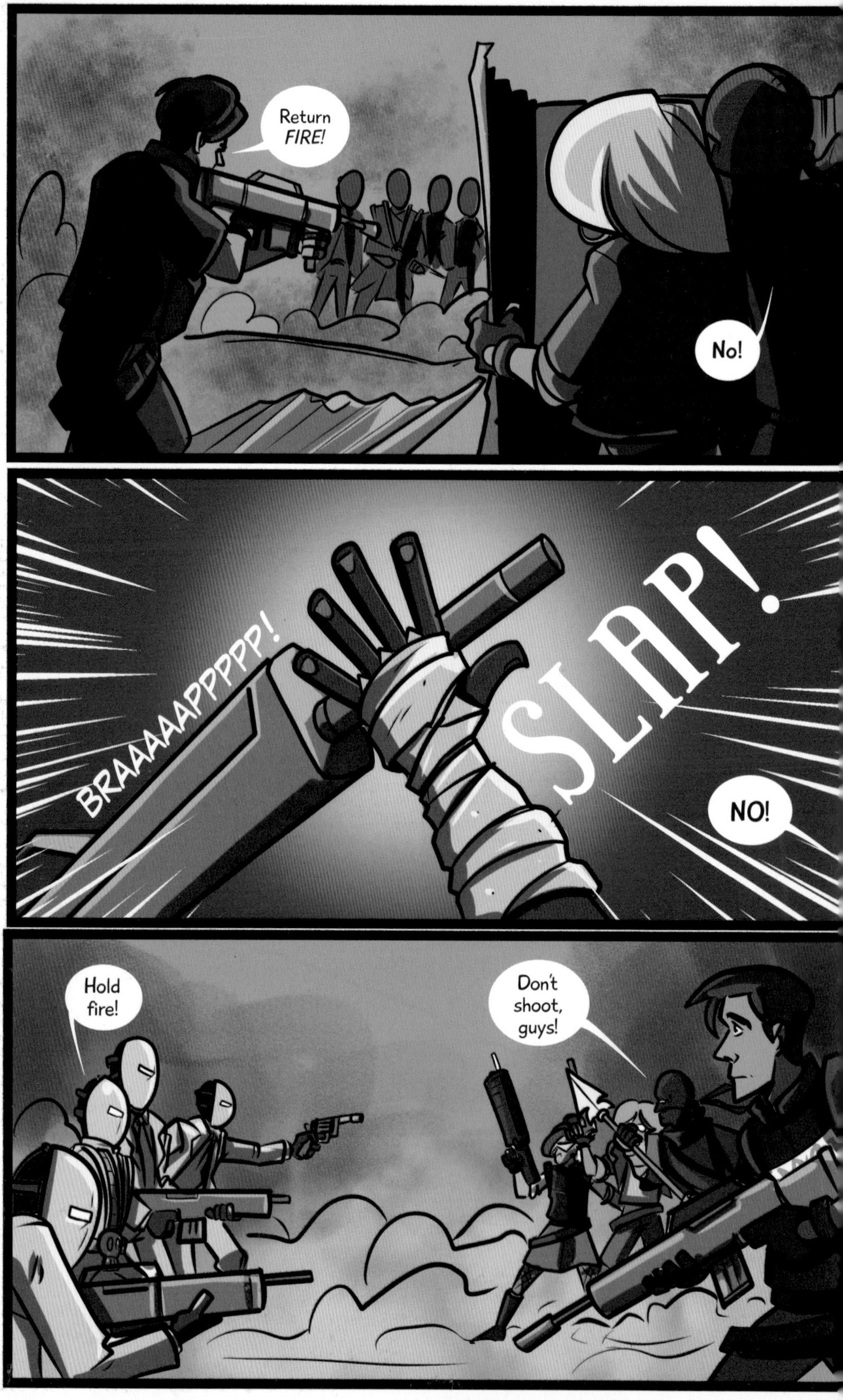
Return FIRE!
No!
BRAAAAAPPPPP!
SLAP!
NO!
Hold fire!
Don't shoot, guys!

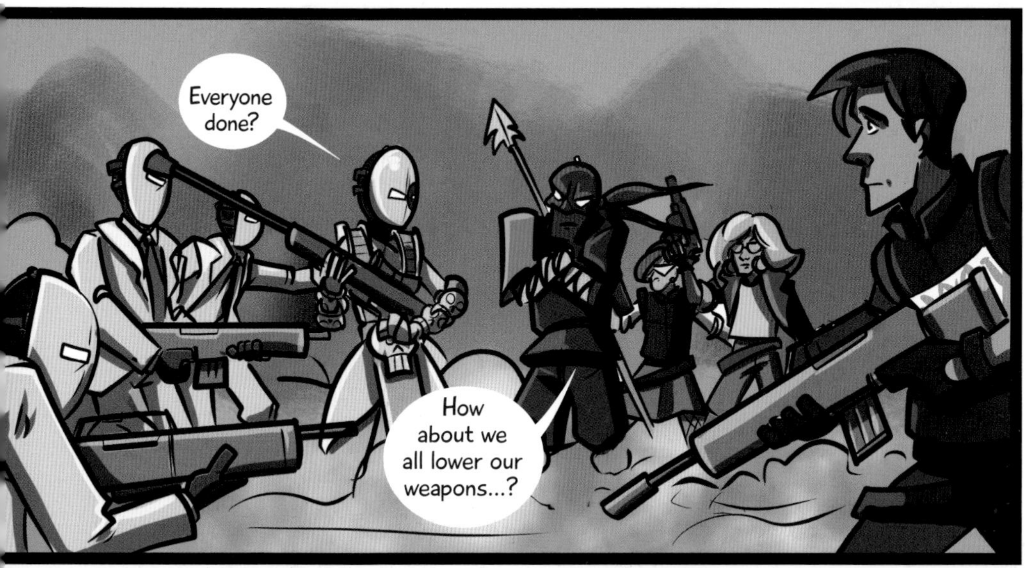
Everyone done?
How about we all lower our weapons...?

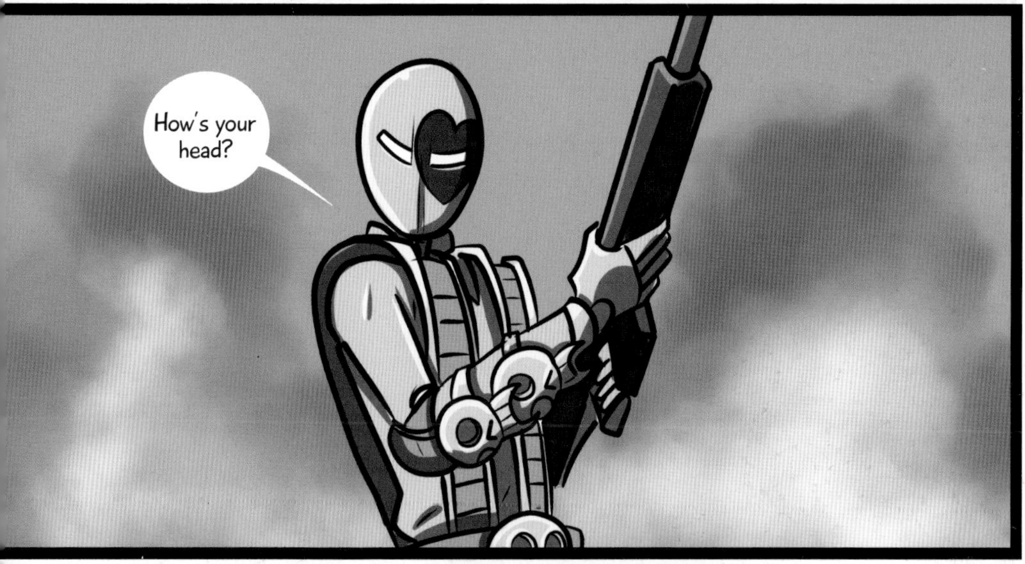
How's your head?

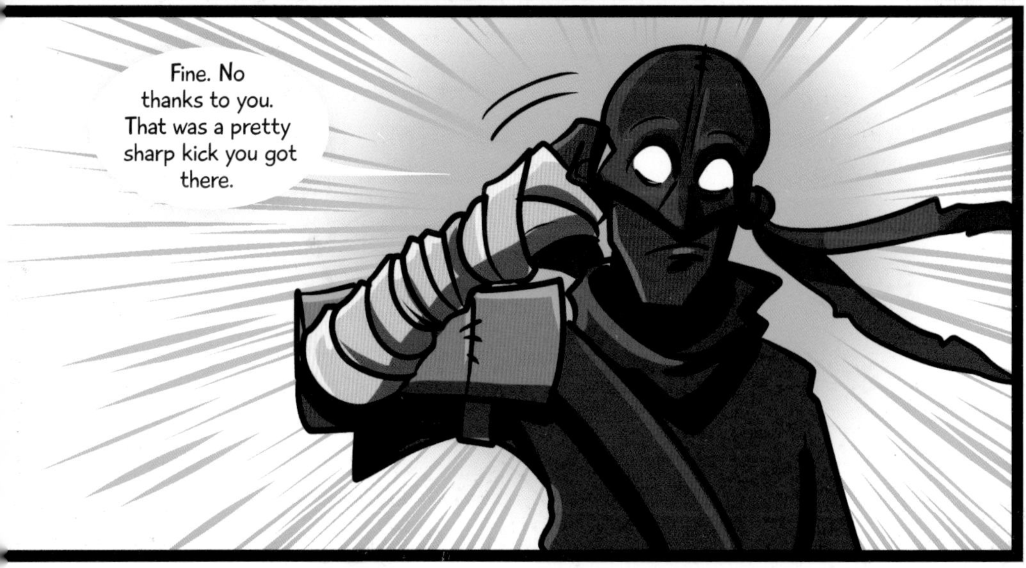
Fine. No thanks to you. That was a pretty sharp kick you got there.

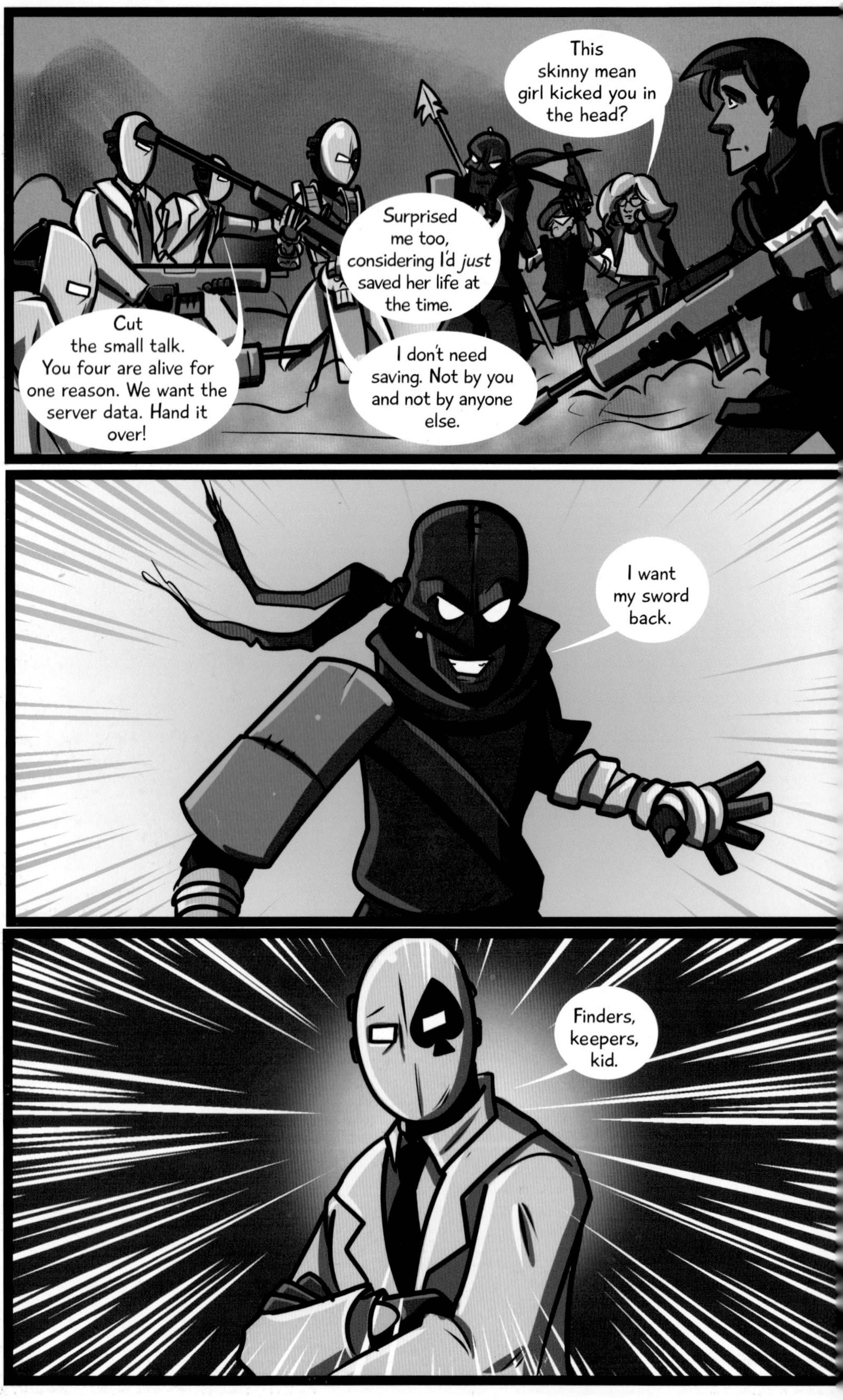
This skinny mean girl kicked you in the head?
Surprised me too, considering I'd *just* saved her life at the time.
I don't need saving. Not by you and not by anyone else.
Cut the small talk. You four are alive for one reason. We want the server data. Hand it over!
I want my sword back.
Finders, keepers, kid.

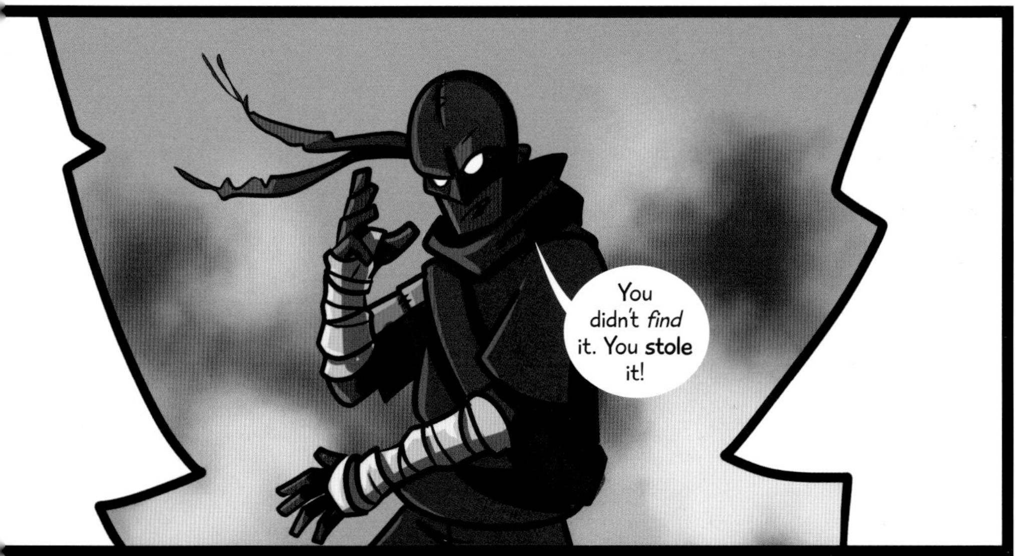
You didn't *find* it. You **stole** it!

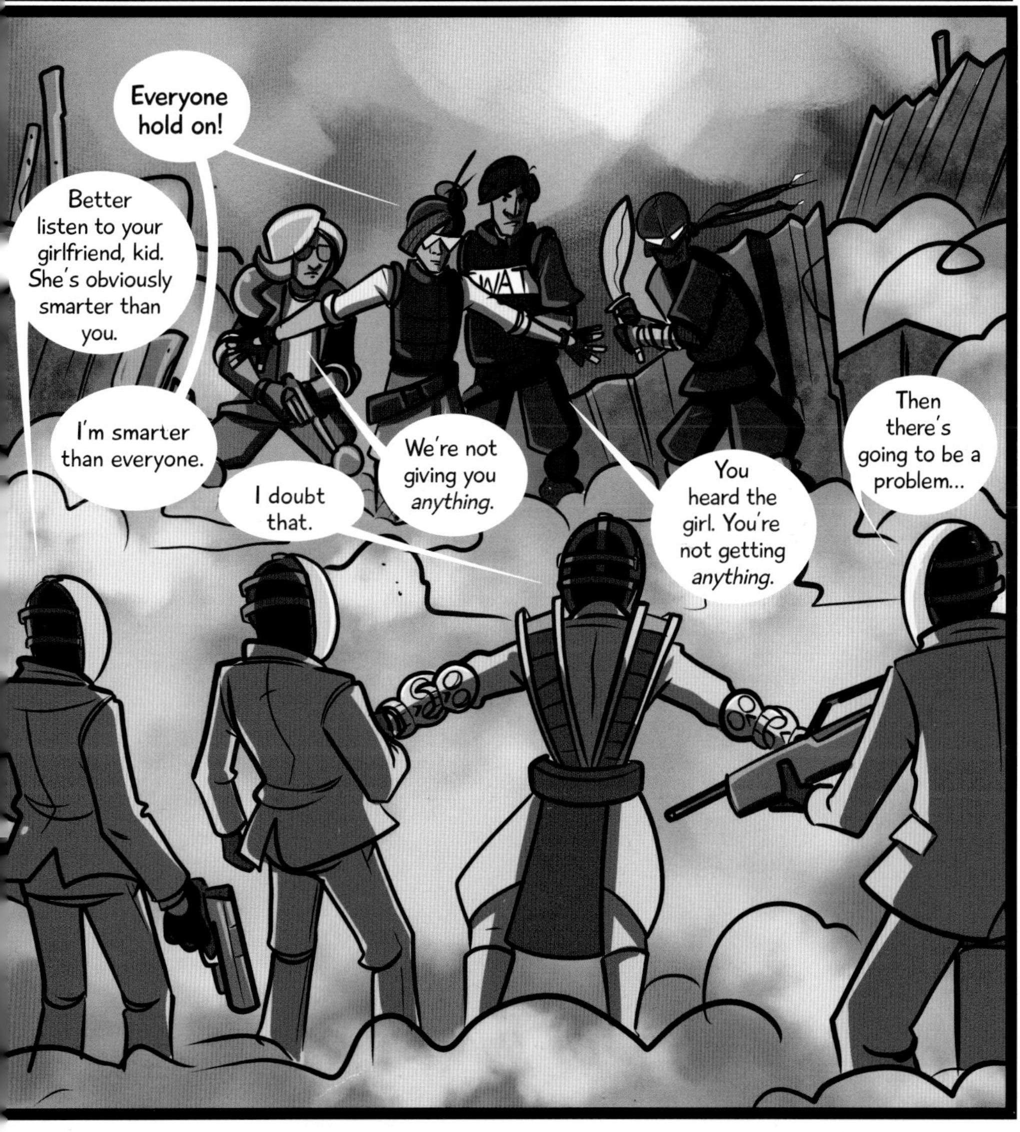
Everyone hold on!
Better listen to your girlfriend, kid. She's obviously smarter than you.
I'm smarter than everyone.
I doubt that.
We're not giving you *anything*.
You heard the girl. You're not getting *anything*.
Then there's going to be a problem...

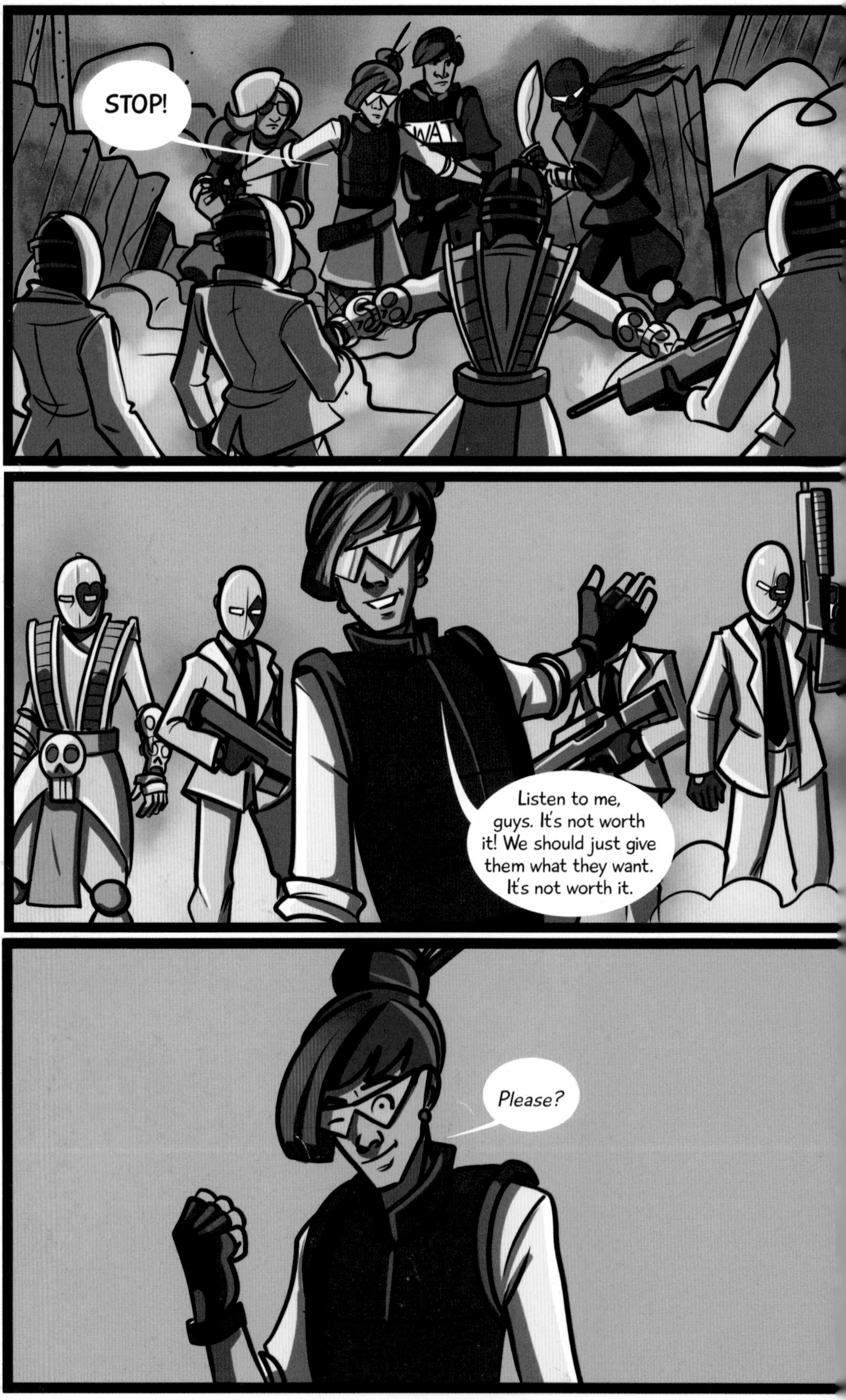
STOP!
SWAT
Listen to me, guys. It's not worth it! We should just give them what they want. It's not worth it.
Please?

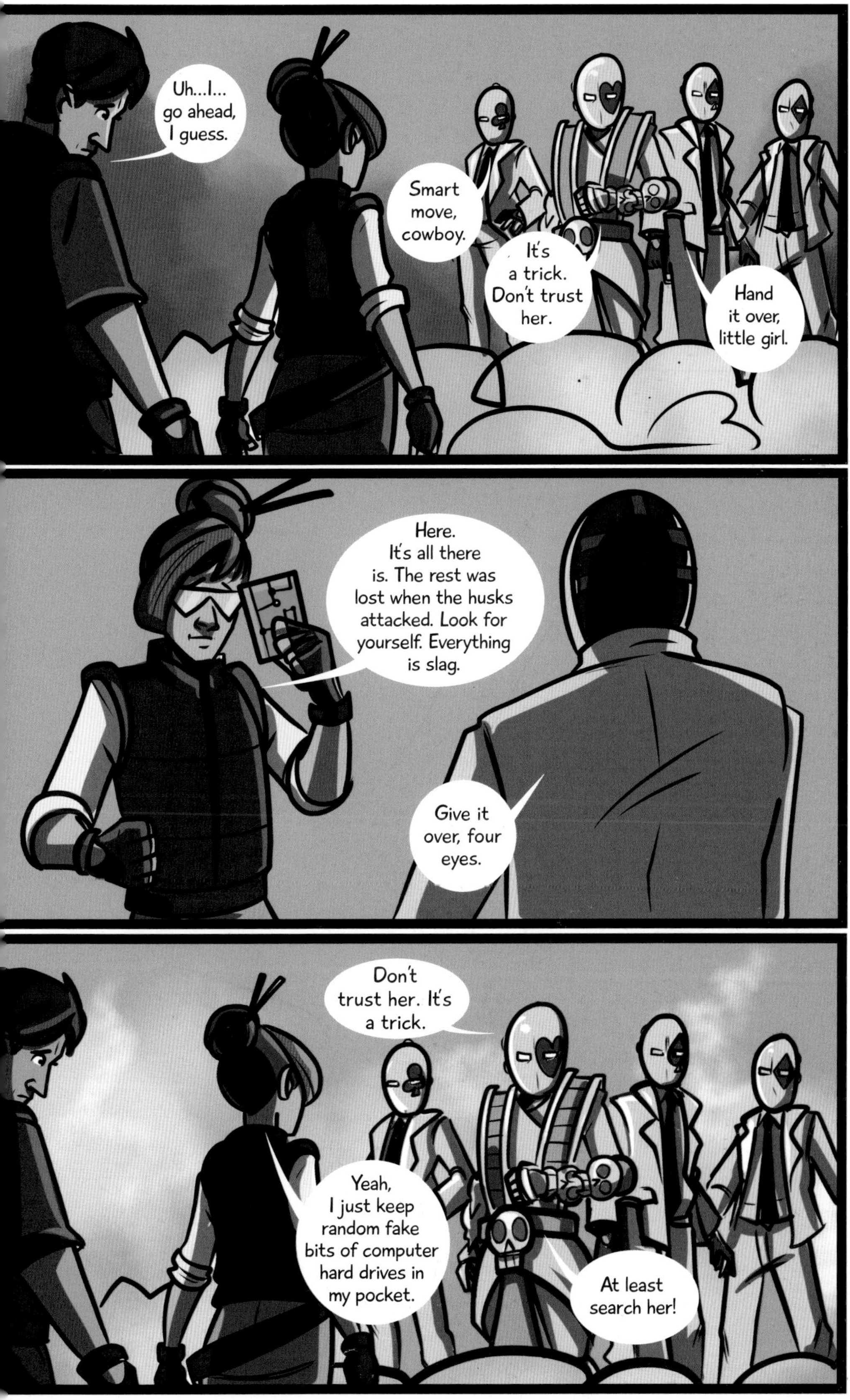
Uh...I... go ahead, I guess.
Smart move, cowboy.
It's a trick. Don't trust her.
Hand it over, little girl.
Here. It's all there is. The rest was lost when the husks attacked. Look for yourself. Everything is slag.
Give it over, four eyes.
Don't trust her. It's a trick.
Yeah, I just keep random fake bits of computer hard drives in my pocket.
At least search her!

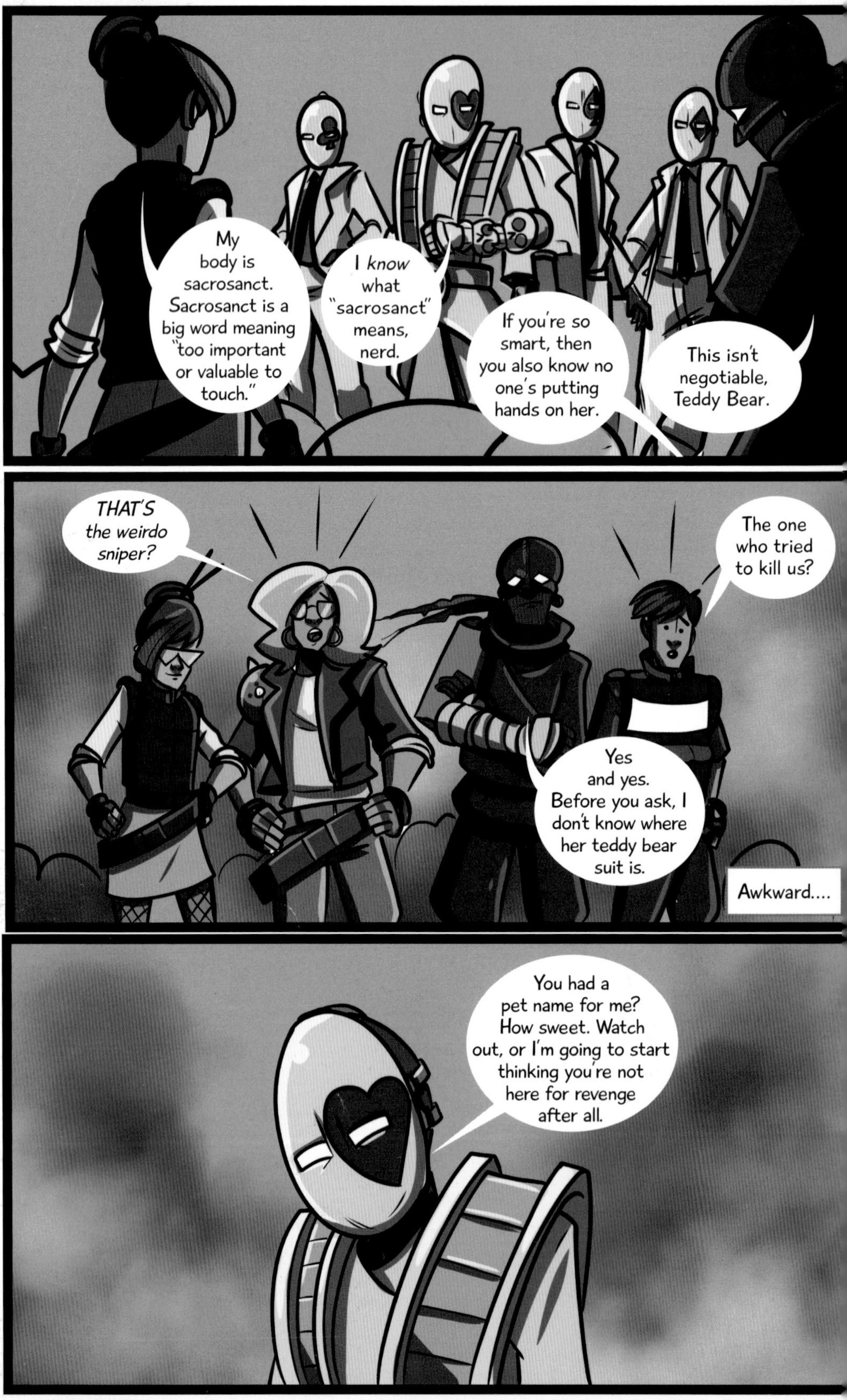
My body is sacrosanct. Sacrosanct is a big word meaning "too important or valuable to touch."
I *know* what "sacrosanct" means, nerd.
If you're so smart, then you also know no one's putting hands on her.
This isn't negotiable, Teddy Bear.
THAT'S the weirdo sniper?
The one who tried to kill us?
Yes and yes. Before you ask, I don't know where her teddy bear suit is.
Awkward....
You had a pet name for me? How sweet. Watch out, or I'm going to start thinking you're not here for revenge after all.

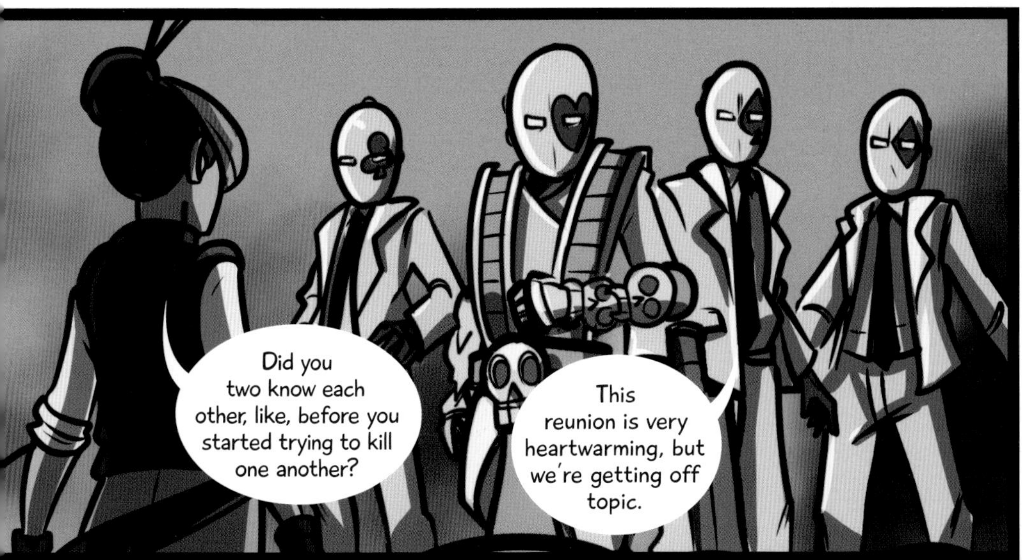
Did you two know each other, like, before you started trying to kill one another?
This reunion is very heartwarming, but we're getting off topic.

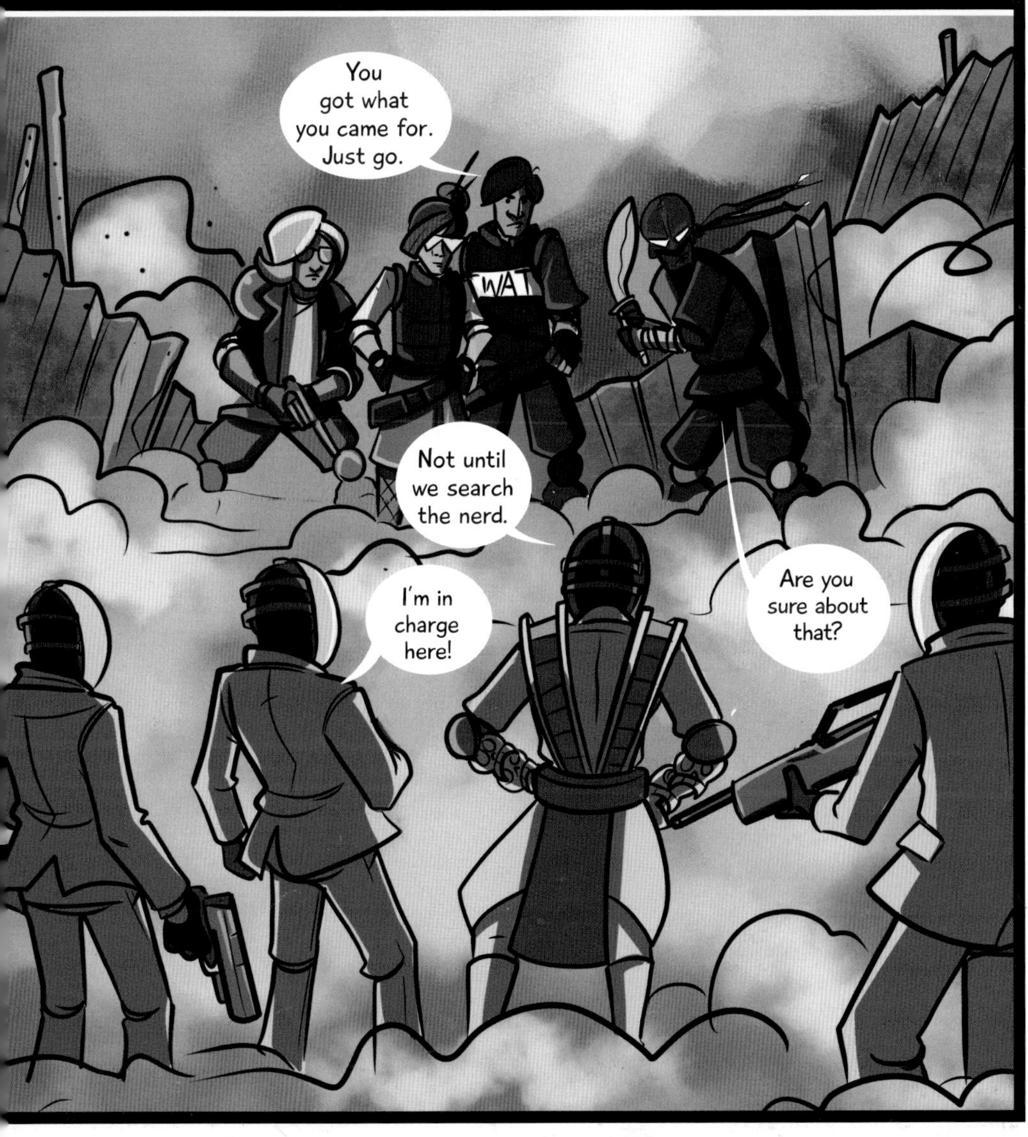
You got what you came for. Just go.
Not until we search the nerd.
I'm in charge here!
Are you sure about that?

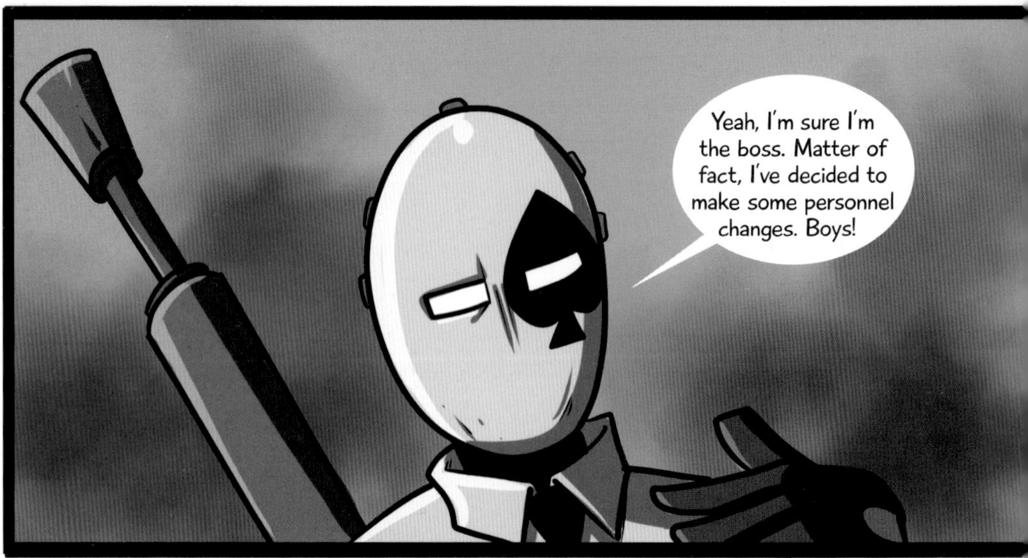
Yeah, I'm sure I'm the boss. Matter of fact, I've decided to make some personnel changes. Boys!

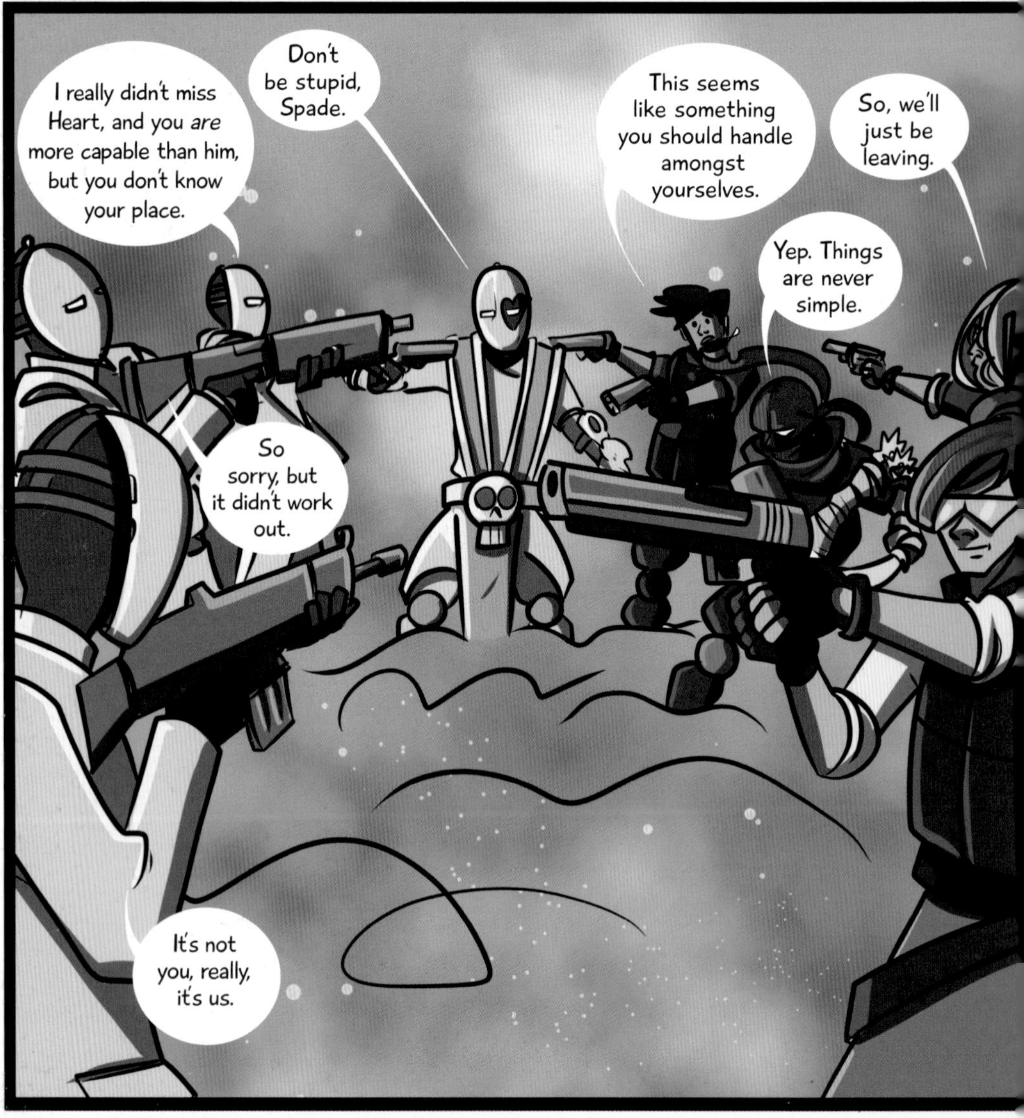
I really didn't miss Heart, and you *are* more capable than him, but you don't know your place.
Don't be stupid, Spade.
This seems like something you should handle amongst yourselves.
So, we'll just be leaving.
Yep. Things are never simple.
So sorry, but it didn't work out.
It's not you, really, it's us.

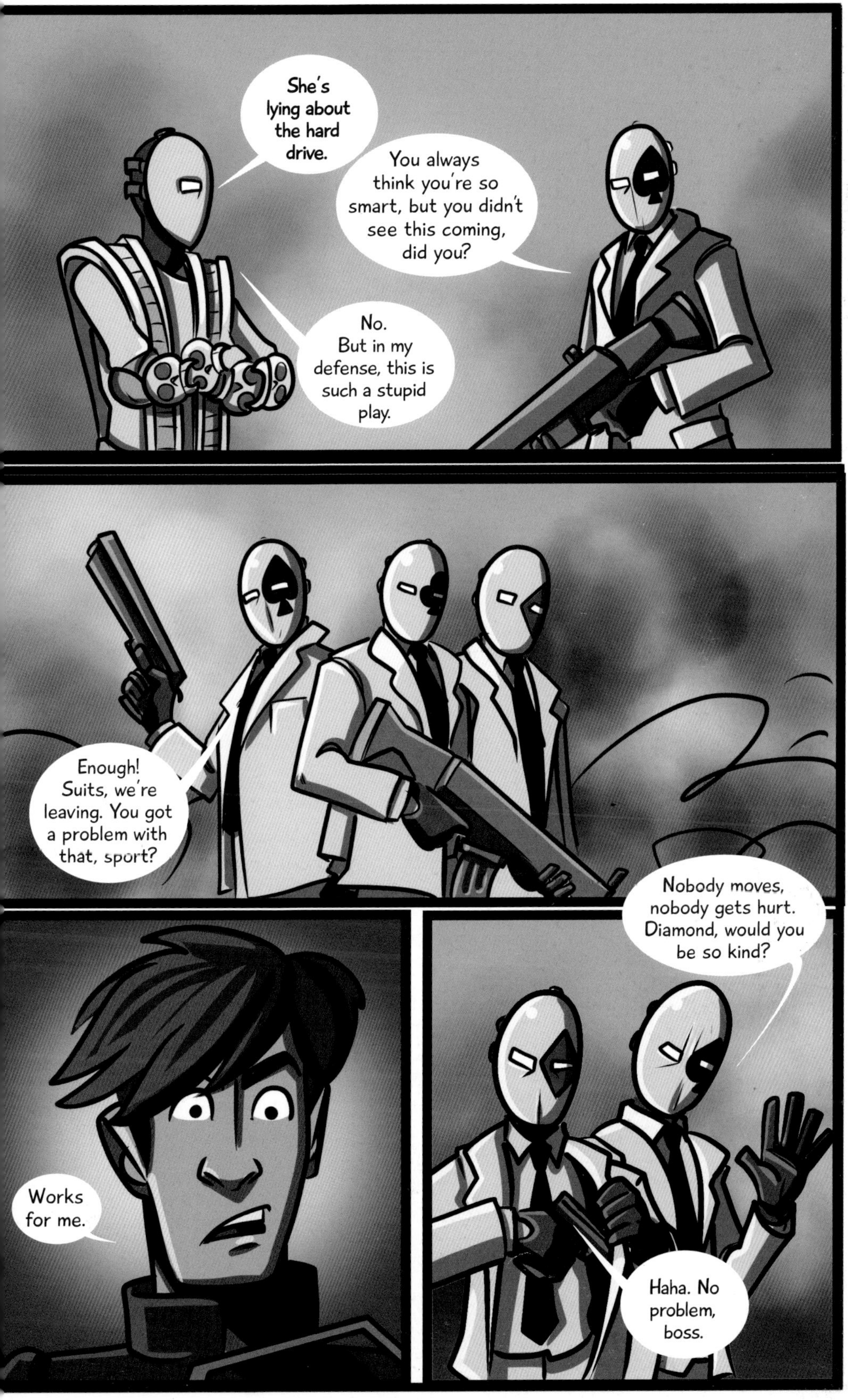
She's lying about the hard drive.
You always think you're so smart, but you didn't see this coming, did you?
No. But in my defense, this is such a stupid play.
Enough! Suits, we're leaving. You got a problem with that, sport?
Works for me.
Nobody moves, nobody gets hurt. Diamond, would you be so kind?
Haha. No problem, boss.

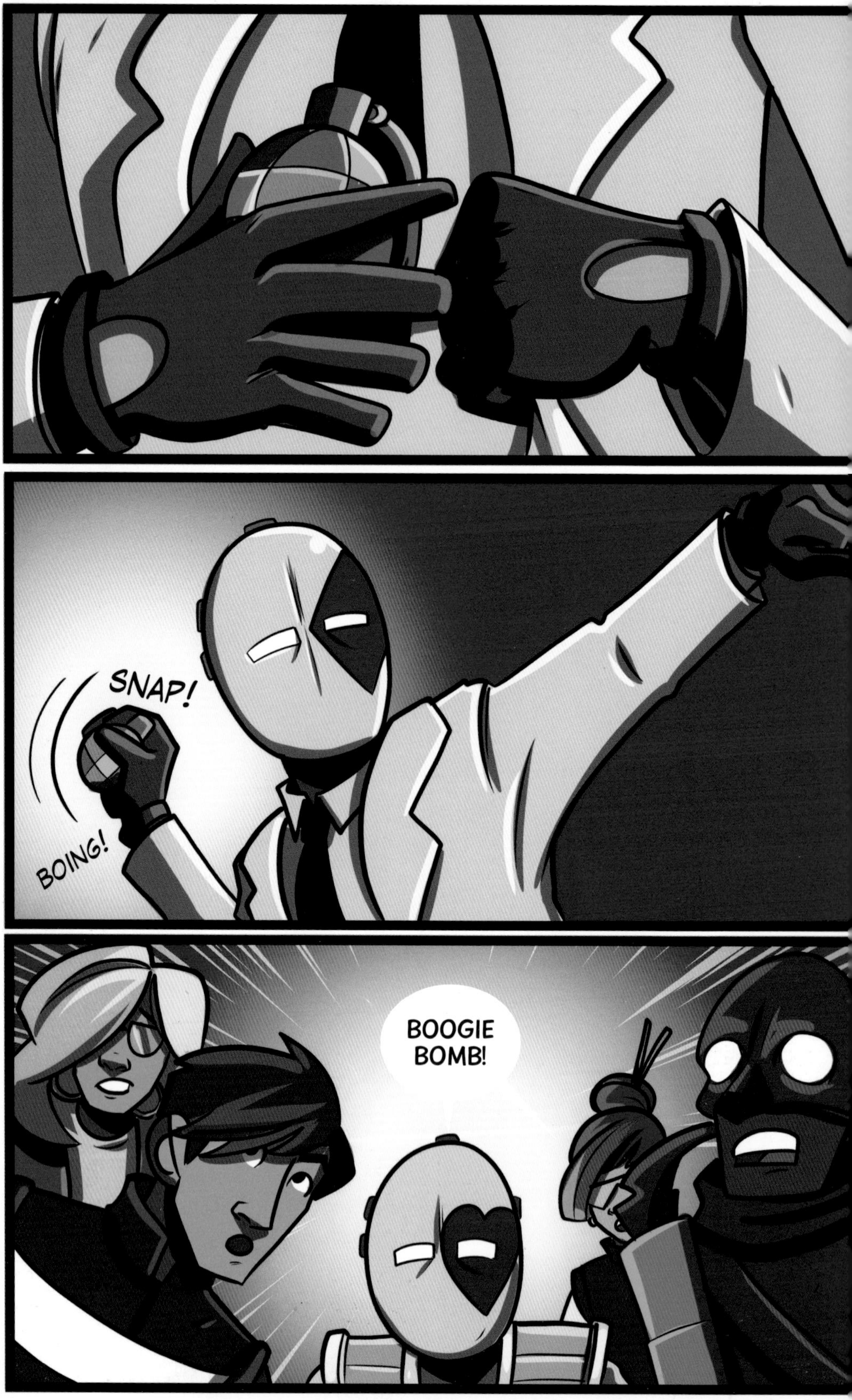
SNAP!
BOING!
BOOGIE BOMB!

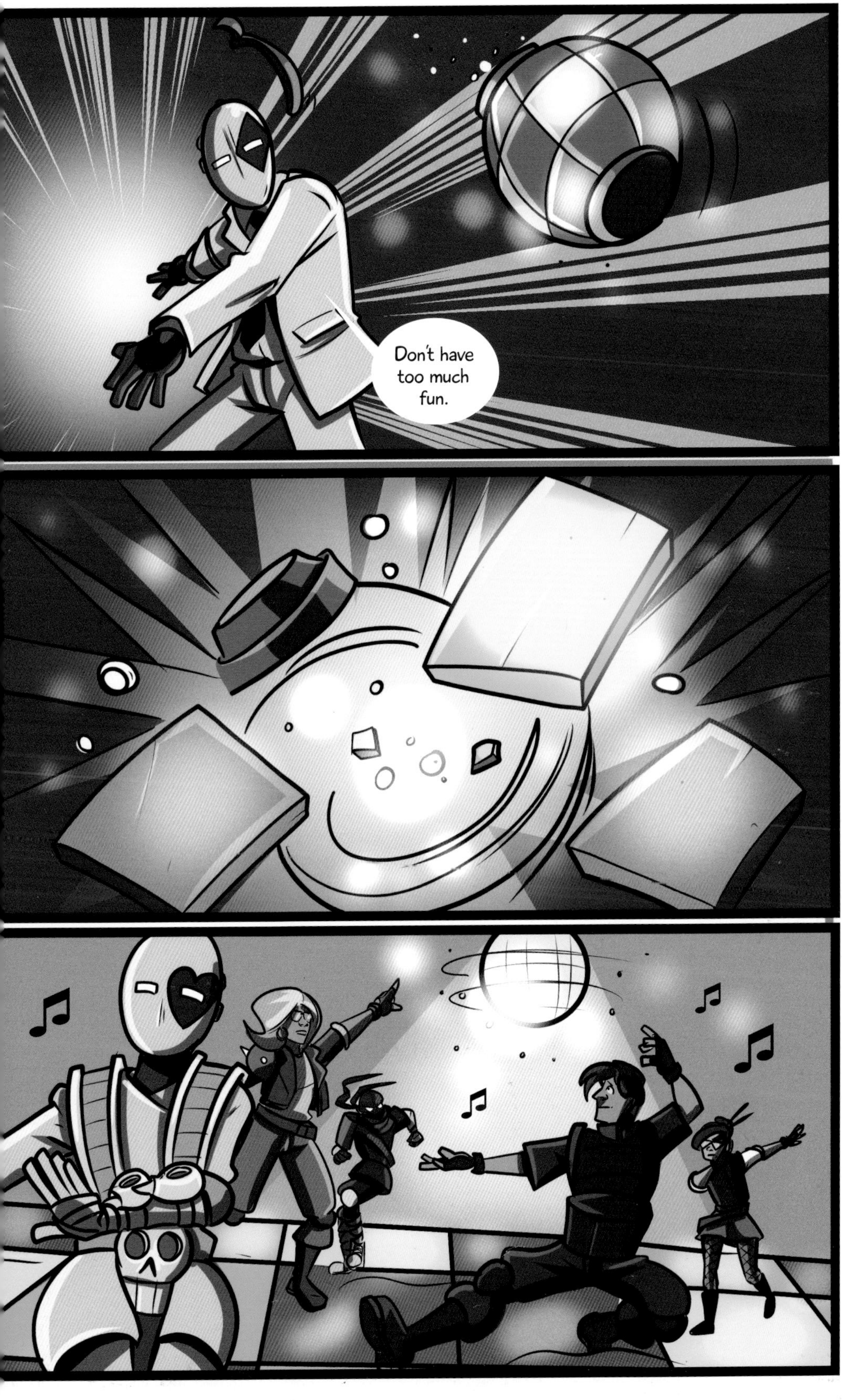
Don't have too much fun.

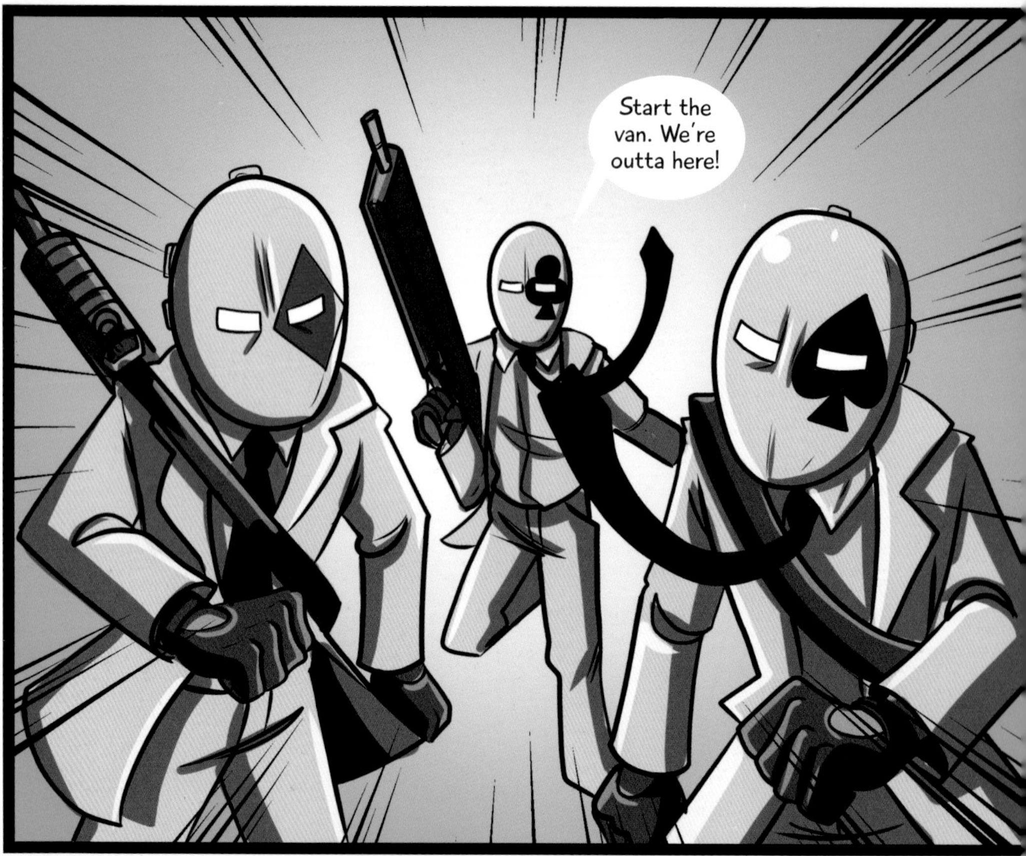
Start the van. We're outta here!

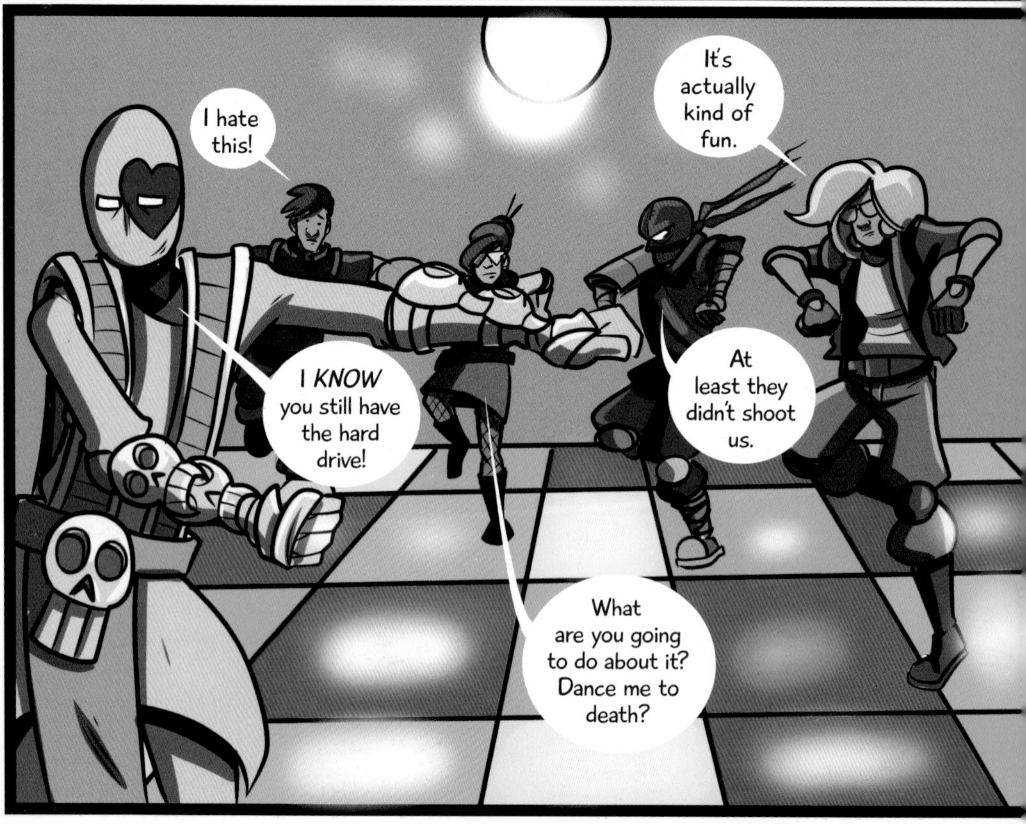
I hate this!
It's actually kind of fun.
I *KNOW* you still have the hard drive!
At least they didn't shoot us.
What are you going to do about it? Dance me to death?

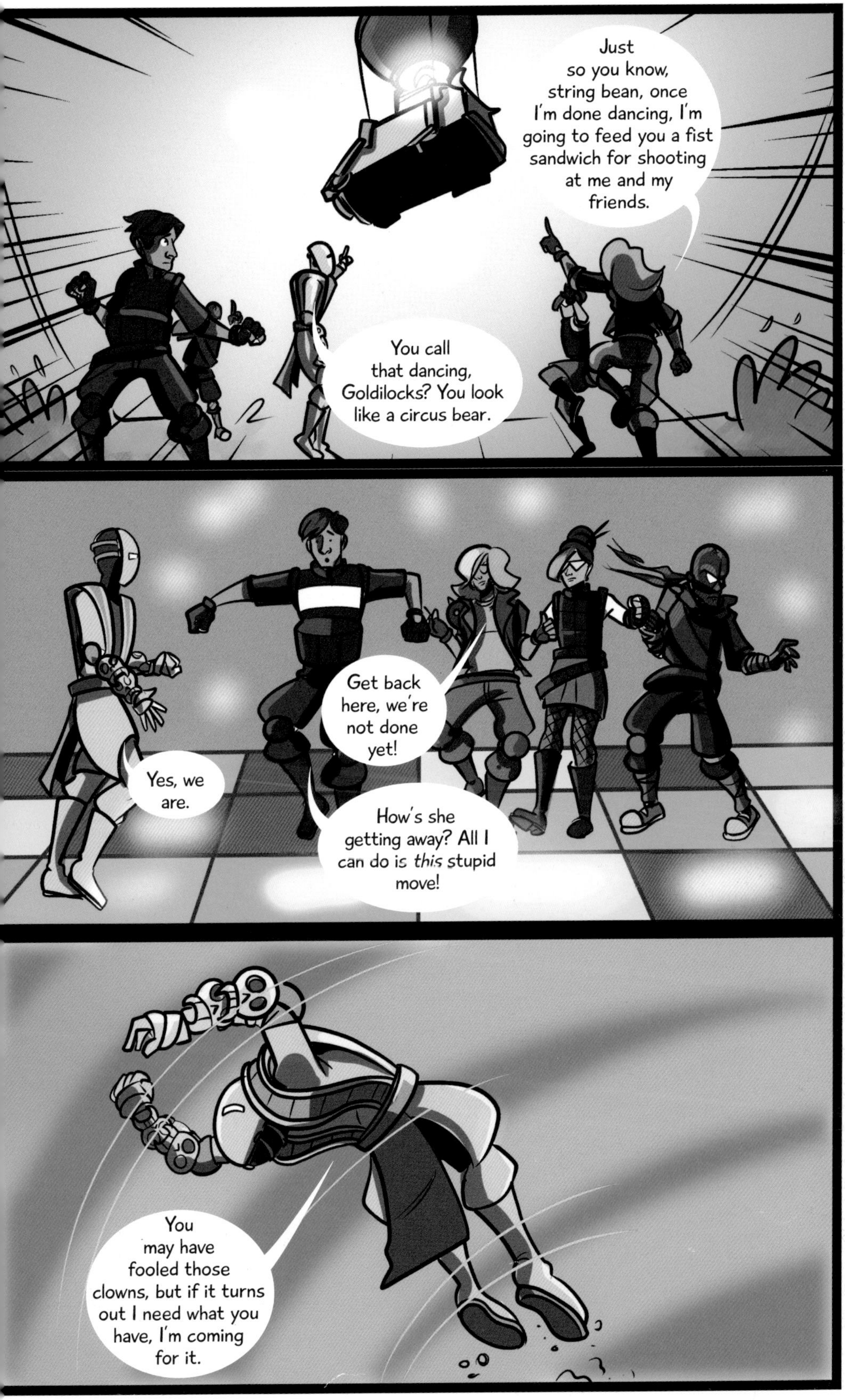
Just so you know, string bean, once I'm done dancing, I'm going to feed you a fist sandwich for shooting at me and my friends.
You call that dancing, Goldilocks? You look like a circus bear.
Get back here, we're not done yet!
Yes, we are.
How's she getting away? All I can do is *this* stupid move!
You may have fooled those clowns, but if it turns out I need what you have, I'm coming for it.

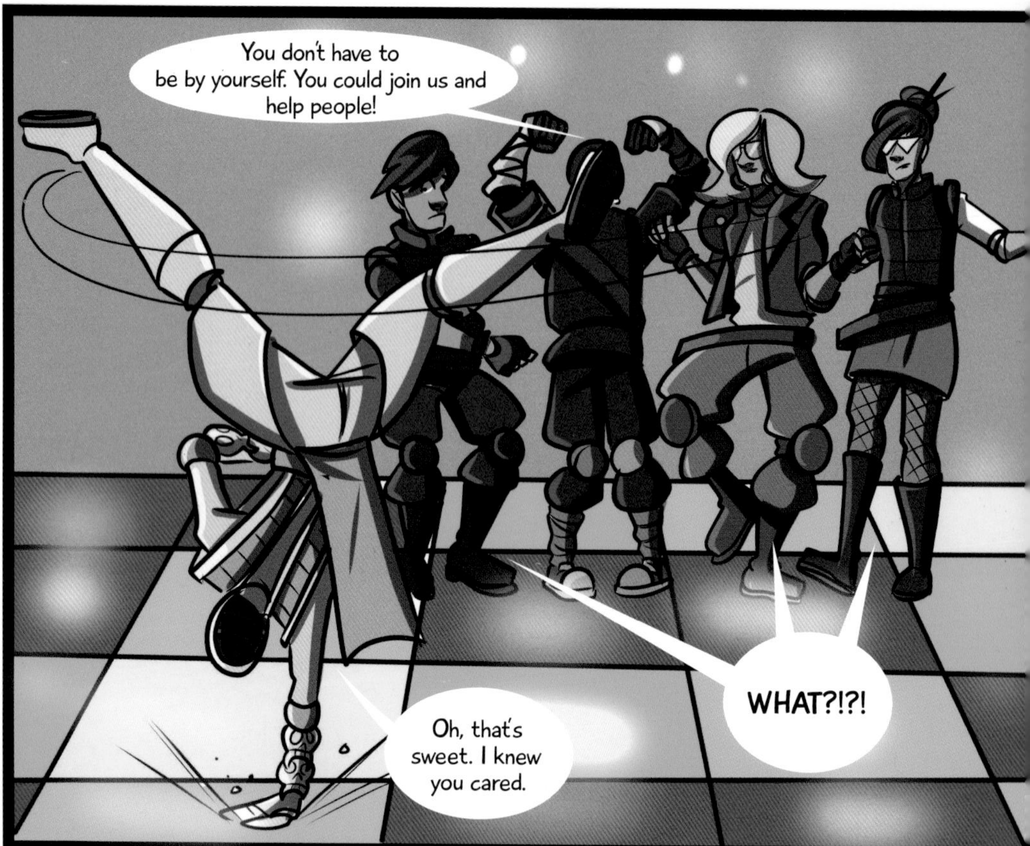

You don't have to be by yourself. You could join us and help people!
WHAT?!?!
Oh, that's sweet. I knew you cared.

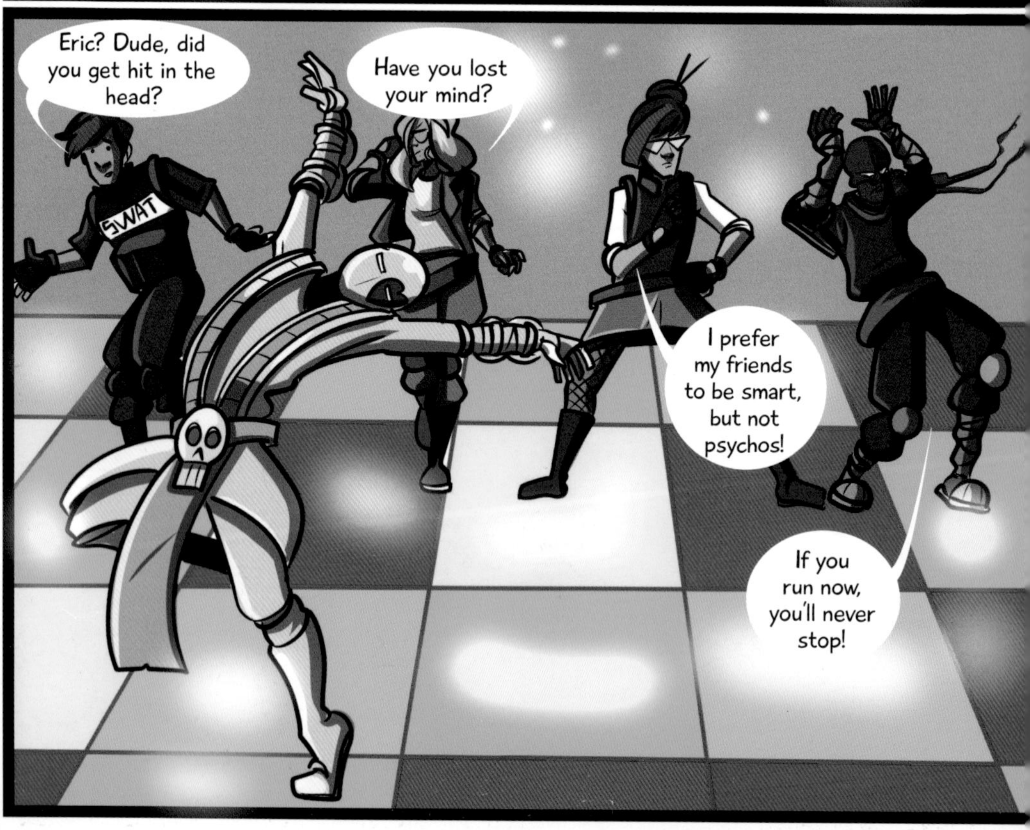

Eric? Dude, did you get hit in the head?
SWAT
Have you lost your mind?
I prefer my friends to be smart, but not psychos!
If you run now, you'll never stop!

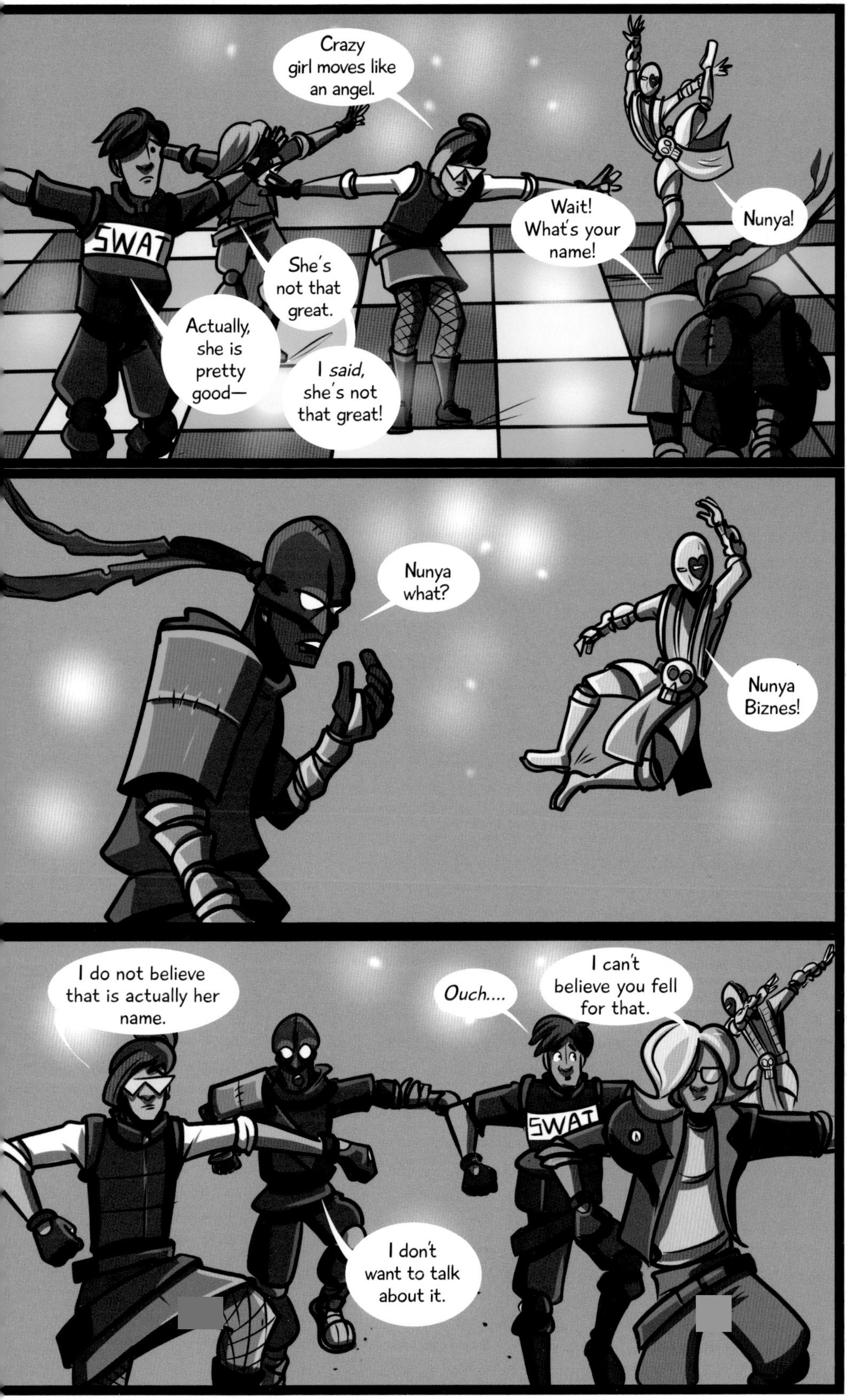

Crazy girl moves like an angel.
Actually, she is pretty good—
She's not that great.
I *said*, she's not that great!
Wait! What's your name!
Nunya!
Nunya what?
Nunya Biznes!
I do not believe that is actually her name.
Ouch....
I can't believe you fell for that.
I don't want to talk about it.

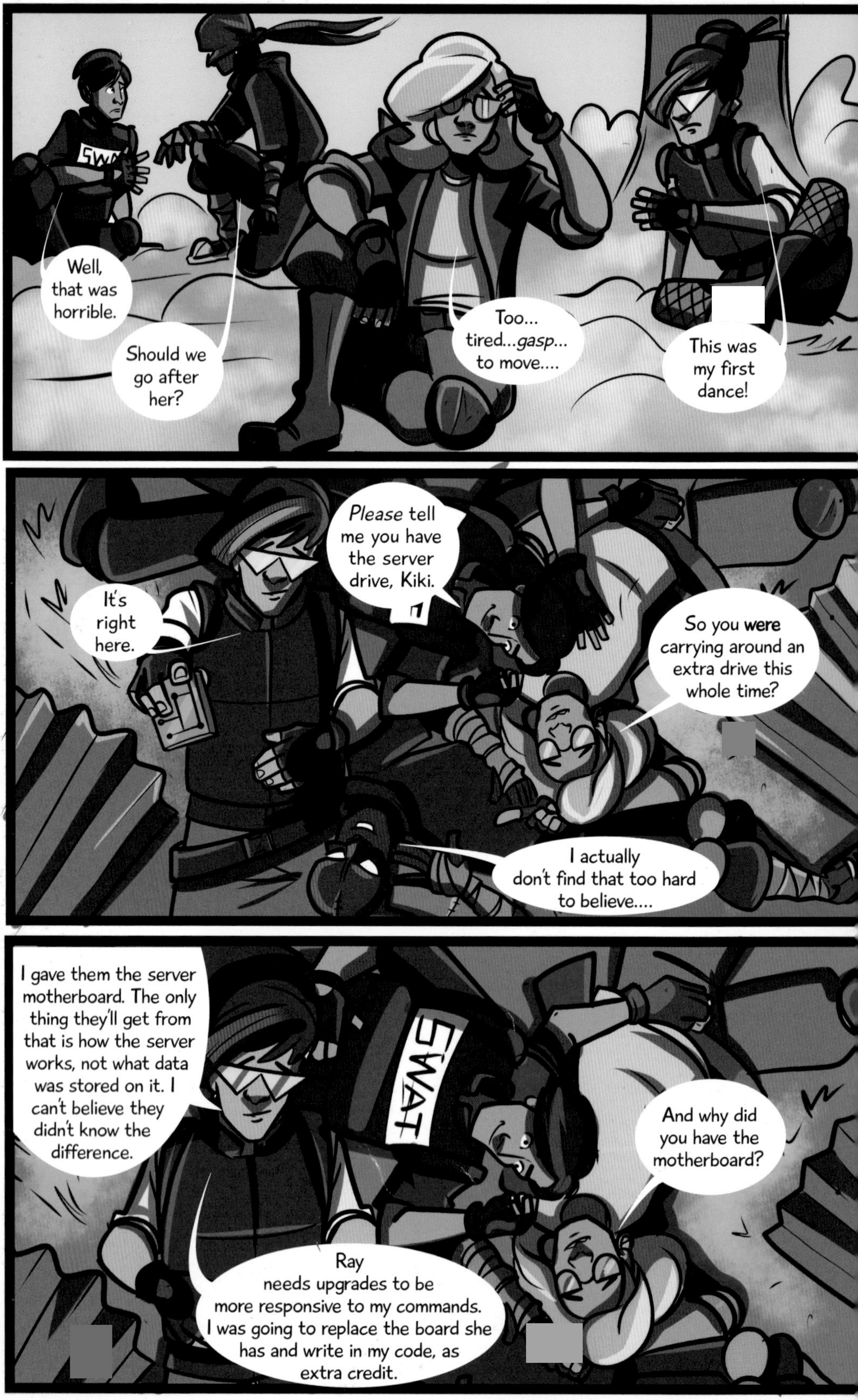
Well, that was horrible.
Should we go after her?
Too... tired...*gasp*... to move....
This was my first dance!
Please tell me you have the server drive, Kiki.
It's right here.
So you **were** carrying around an extra drive this whole time?
I actually don't find that too hard to believe....
I gave them the server motherboard. The only thing they'll get from that is how the server works, not what data was stored on it. I can't believe they didn't know the difference.
And why did you have the motherboard?
Ray needs upgrades to be more responsive to my commands. I was going to replace the board she has and write in my code, as extra credit.

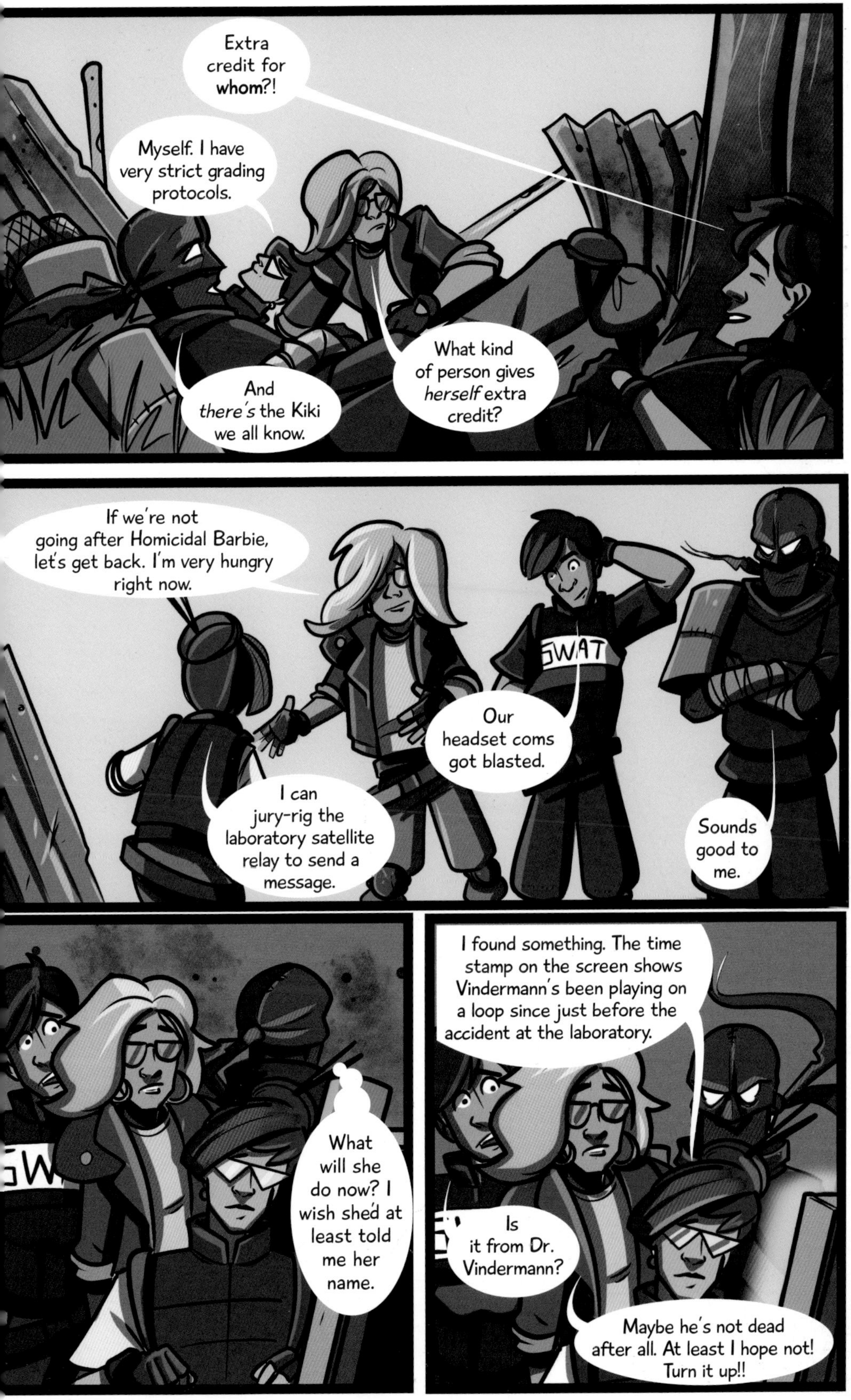
Extra credit for **whom**?!
Myself. I have very strict grading protocols.
And *there's* the Kiki we all know.
What kind of person gives *herself* extra credit?
If we're not going after Homicidal Barbie, let's get back. I'm very hungry right now.
SWAT
Our headset coms got blasted.
I can jury-rig the laboratory satellite relay to send a message.
Sounds good to me.
What will she do now? I wish she'd at least told me her name.
I found something. The time stamp on the screen shows Vindermann's been playing on a loop since just before the accident at the laboratory.
Is it from Dr. Vindermann?
Maybe he's not dead after all. At least I hope not! Turn it up!!

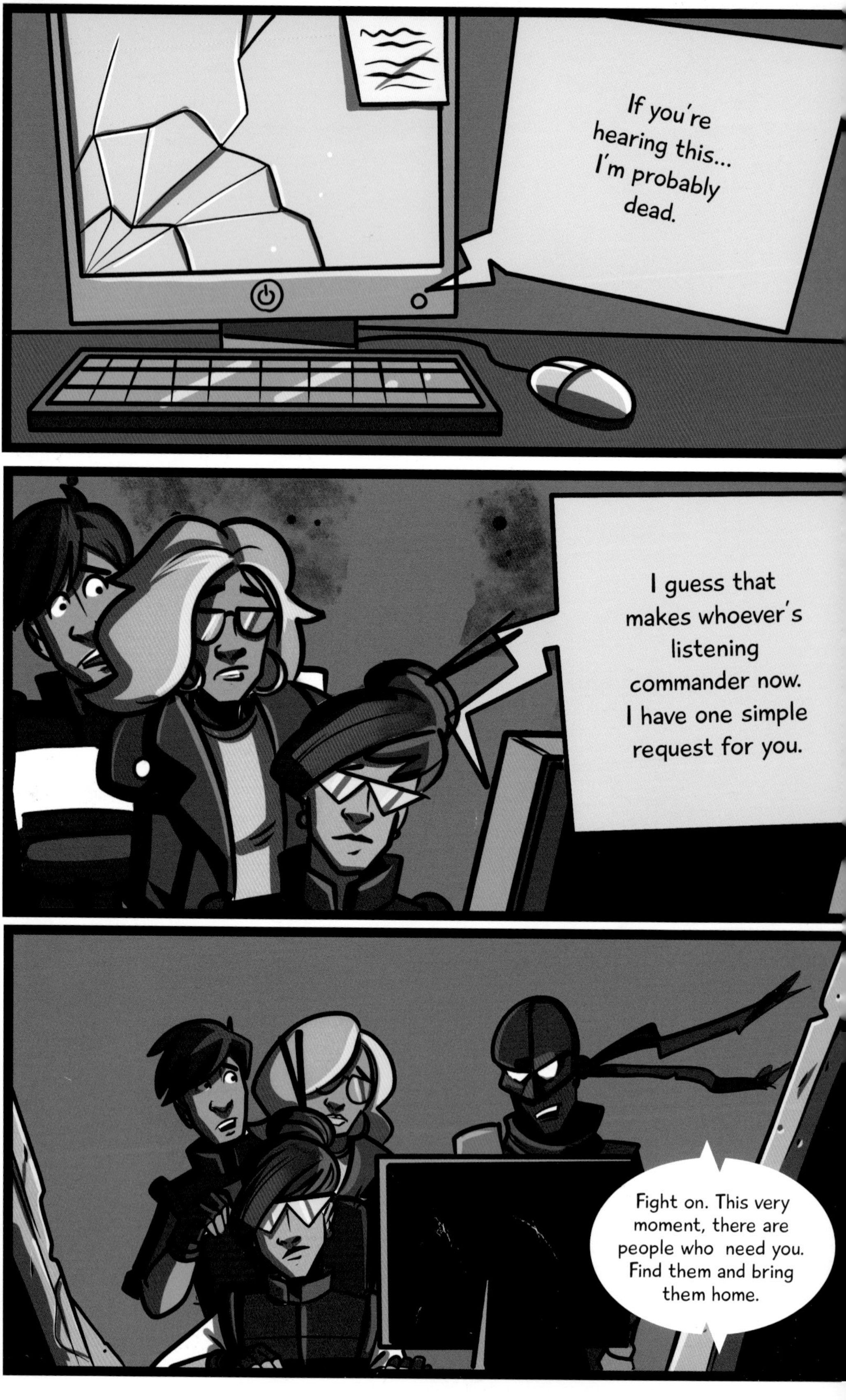

If you're hearing this... I'm probably dead.
I guess that makes whoever's listening commander now. I have one simple request for you.
Fight on. This very moment, there are people who need you. Find them and bring them home.

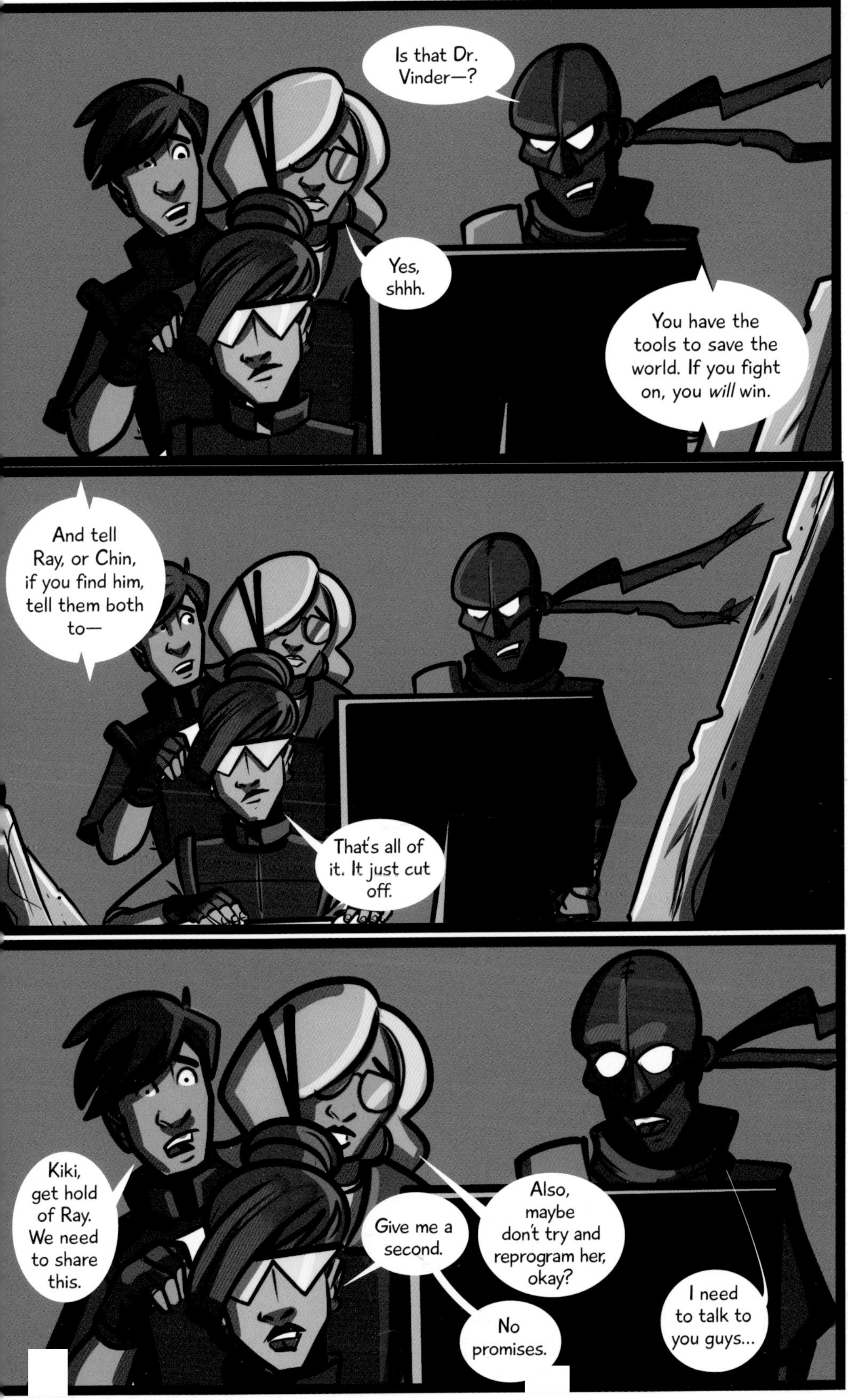
Is that Dr. Vinder—?
Yes, shhh.
You have the tools to save the world. If you fight on, you *will* win.
And tell Ray, or Chin, if you find him, tell them both to—
That's all of it. It just cut off.
Kiki, get hold of Ray. We need to share this.
Give me a second.
Also, maybe don't try and reprogram her, okay?
No promises.
I need to talk to you guys...

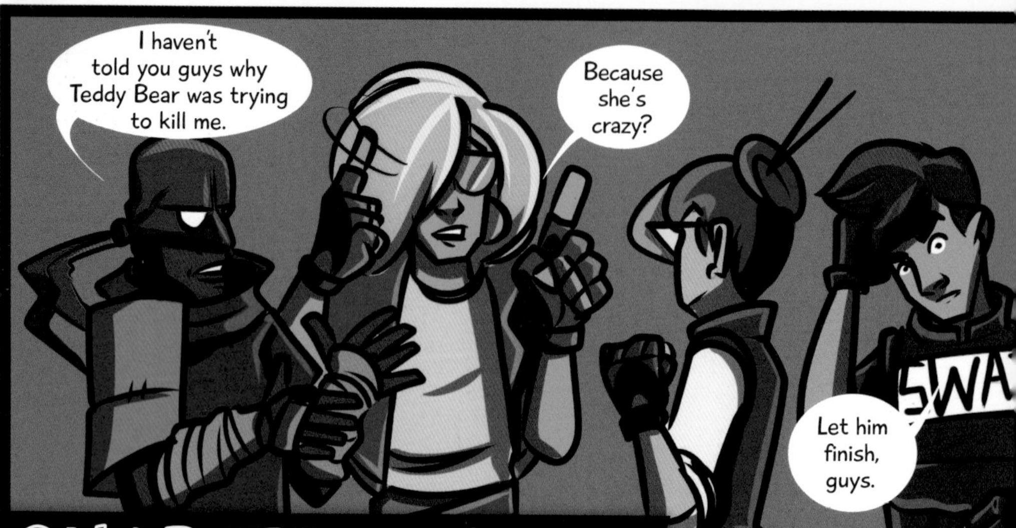
I haven't told you guys why Teddy Bear was trying to kill me.
Because she's crazy?
Let him finish, guys.

CHAPTER 7: CALL

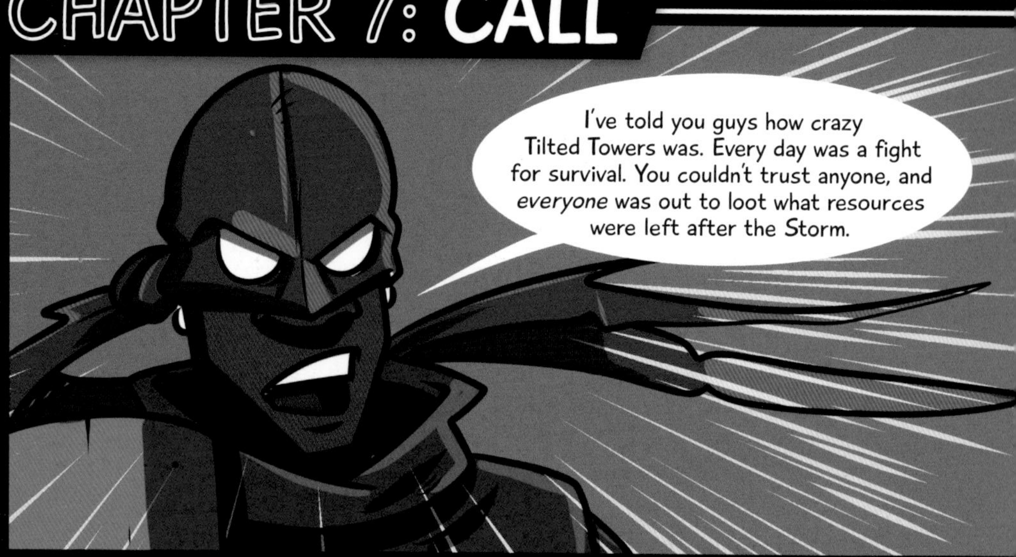
I've told you guys how crazy Tilted Towers was. Every day was a fight for survival. You couldn't trust anyone, and *everyone* was out to loot what resources were left after the Storm.

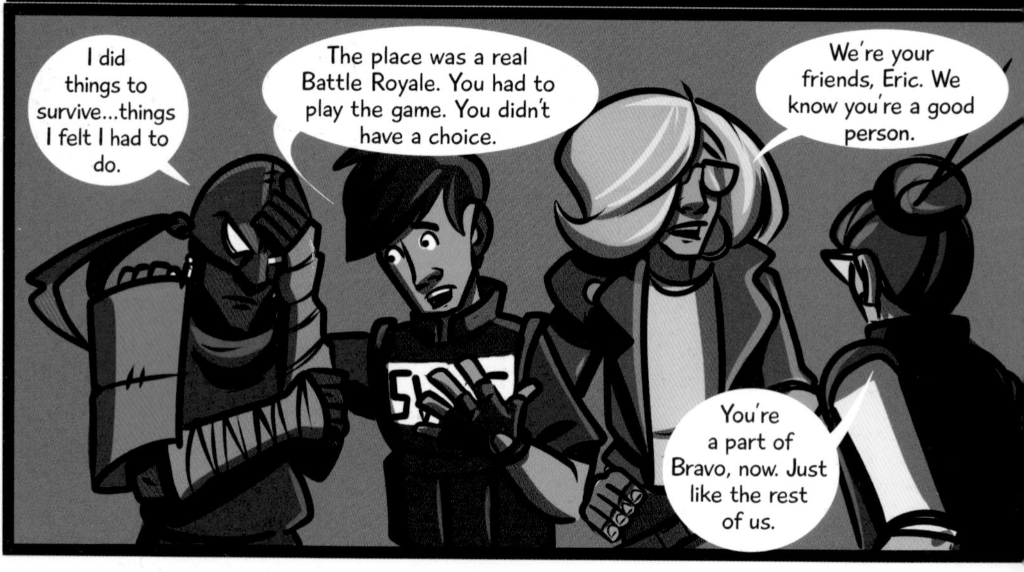
I did things to survive...things I felt I had to do.
The place was a real Battle Royale. You had to play the game. You didn't have a choice.
We're your friends, Eric. We know you're a good person.
You're a part of Bravo, now. Just like the rest of us.

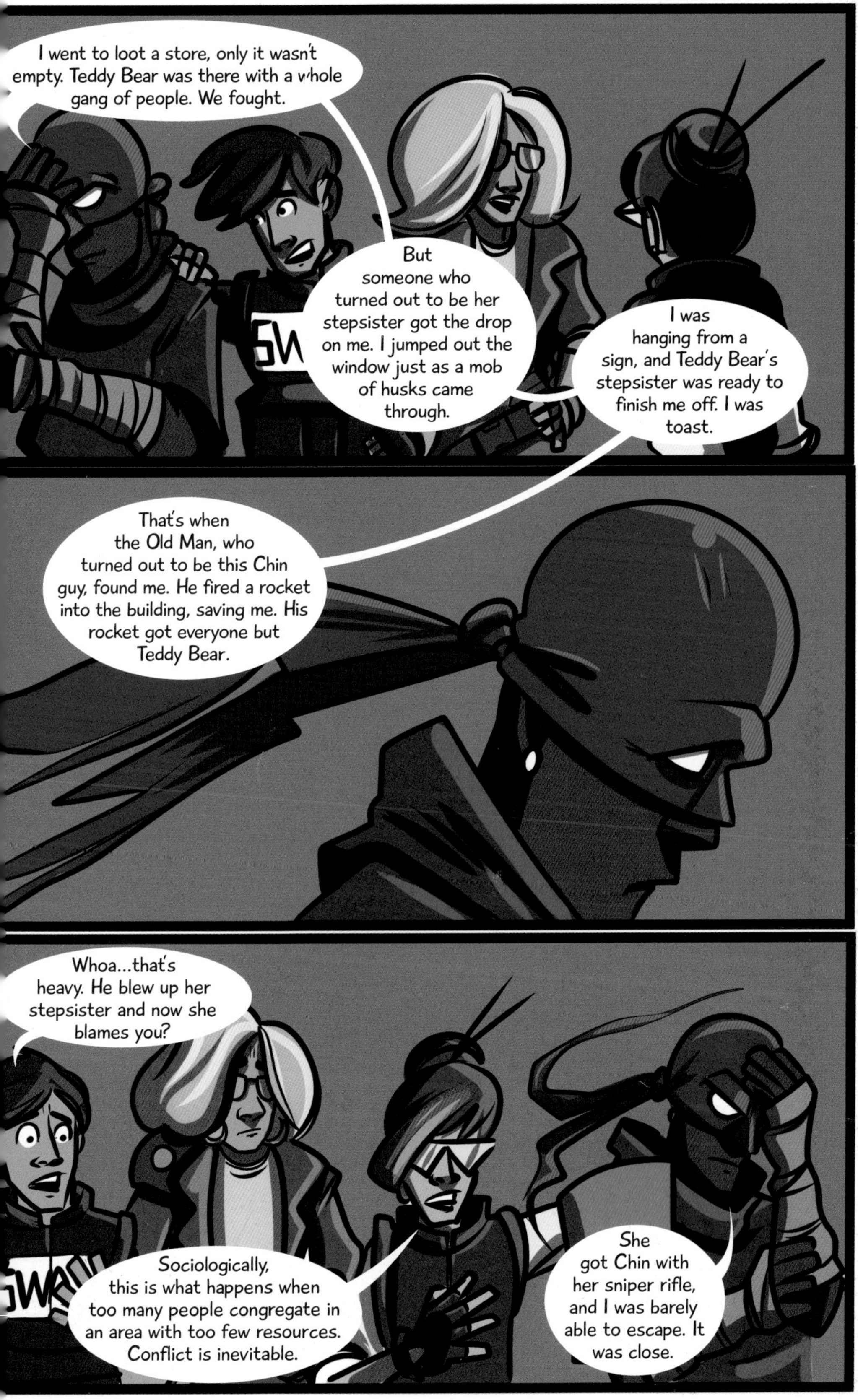
I went to loot a store, only it wasn't empty. Teddy Bear was there with a whole gang of people. We fought.
But someone who turned out to be her stepsister got the drop on me. I jumped out the window just as a mob of husks came through.
I was hanging from a sign, and Teddy Bear's stepsister was ready to finish me off. I was toast.
That's when the Old Man, who turned out to be this Chin guy, found me. He fired a rocket into the building, saving me. His rocket got everyone but Teddy Bear.
Whoa...that's heavy. He blew up her stepsister and now she blames you?
Sociologically, this is what happens when too many people congregate in an area with too few resources. Conflict is inevitable.
She got Chin with her sniper rifle, and I was barely able to escape. It was close.

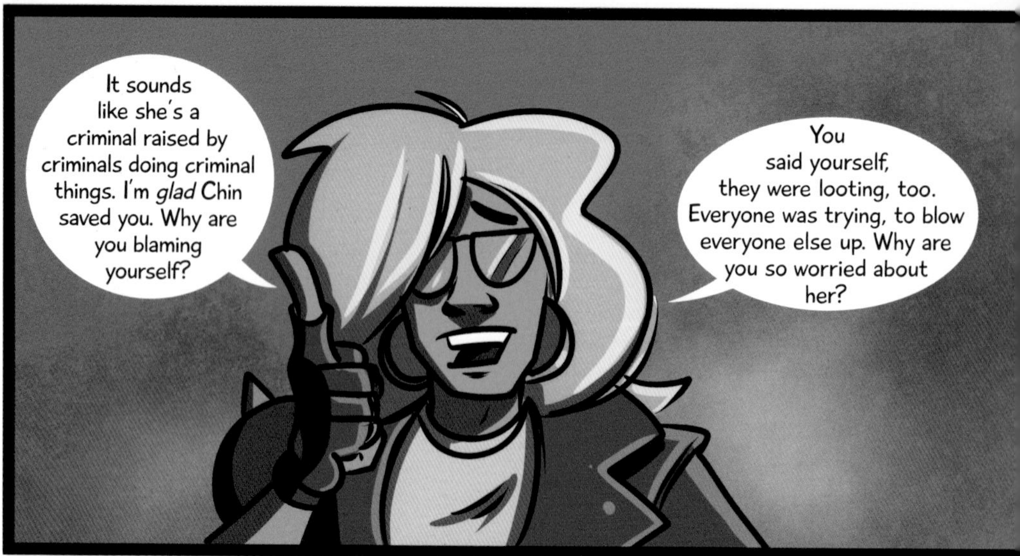
It sounds like she's a criminal raised by criminals doing criminal things. I'm *glad* Chin saved you. Why are you blaming yourself?
You said yourself, they were looting, too. Everyone was trying, to blow everyone else up. Why are you so worried about her?

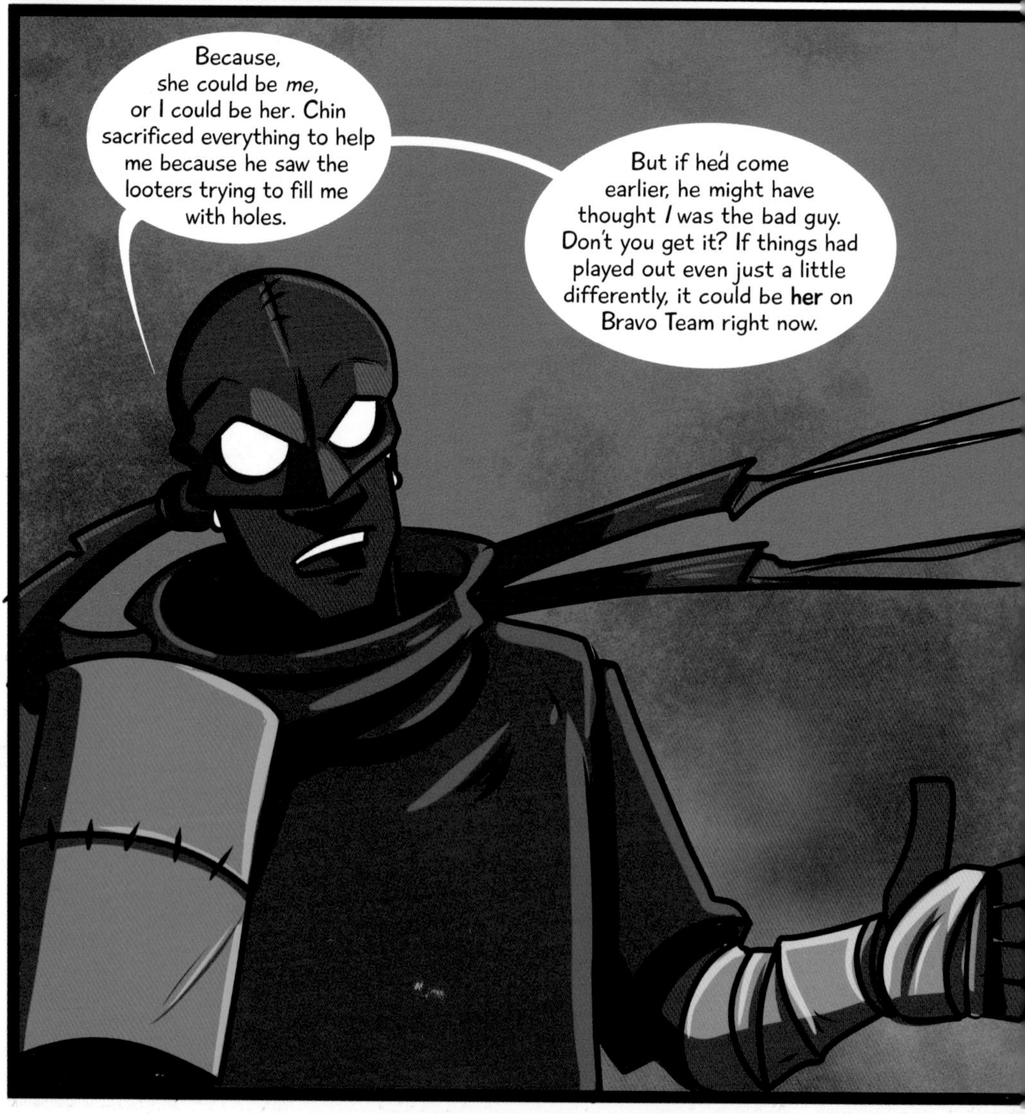
Because, she could be *me*, or I could be her. Chin sacrificed everything to help me because he saw the looters trying to fill me with holes.
But if he'd come earlier, he might have thought *I* was the bad guy. Don't you get it? If things had played out even just a little differently, it could be **her** on Bravo Team right now.

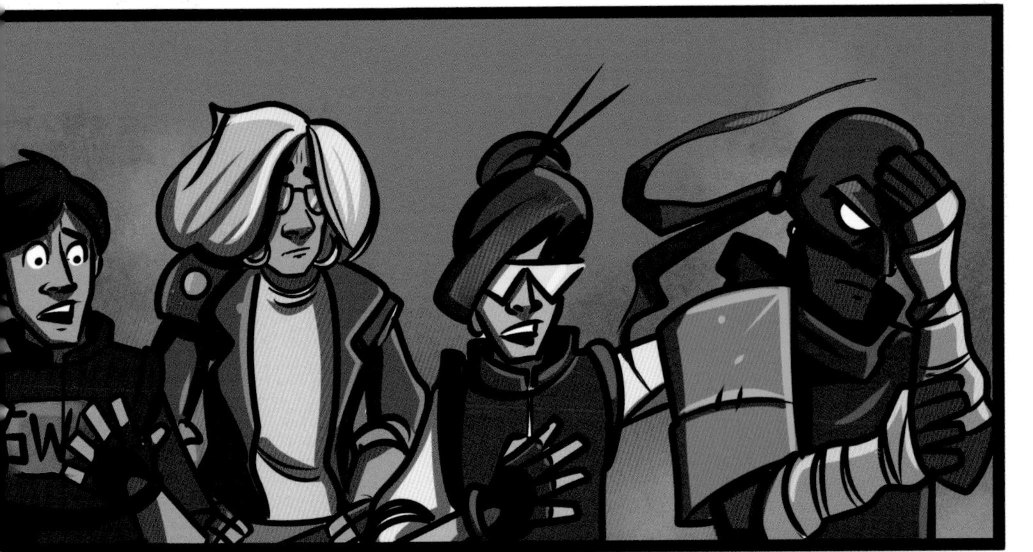

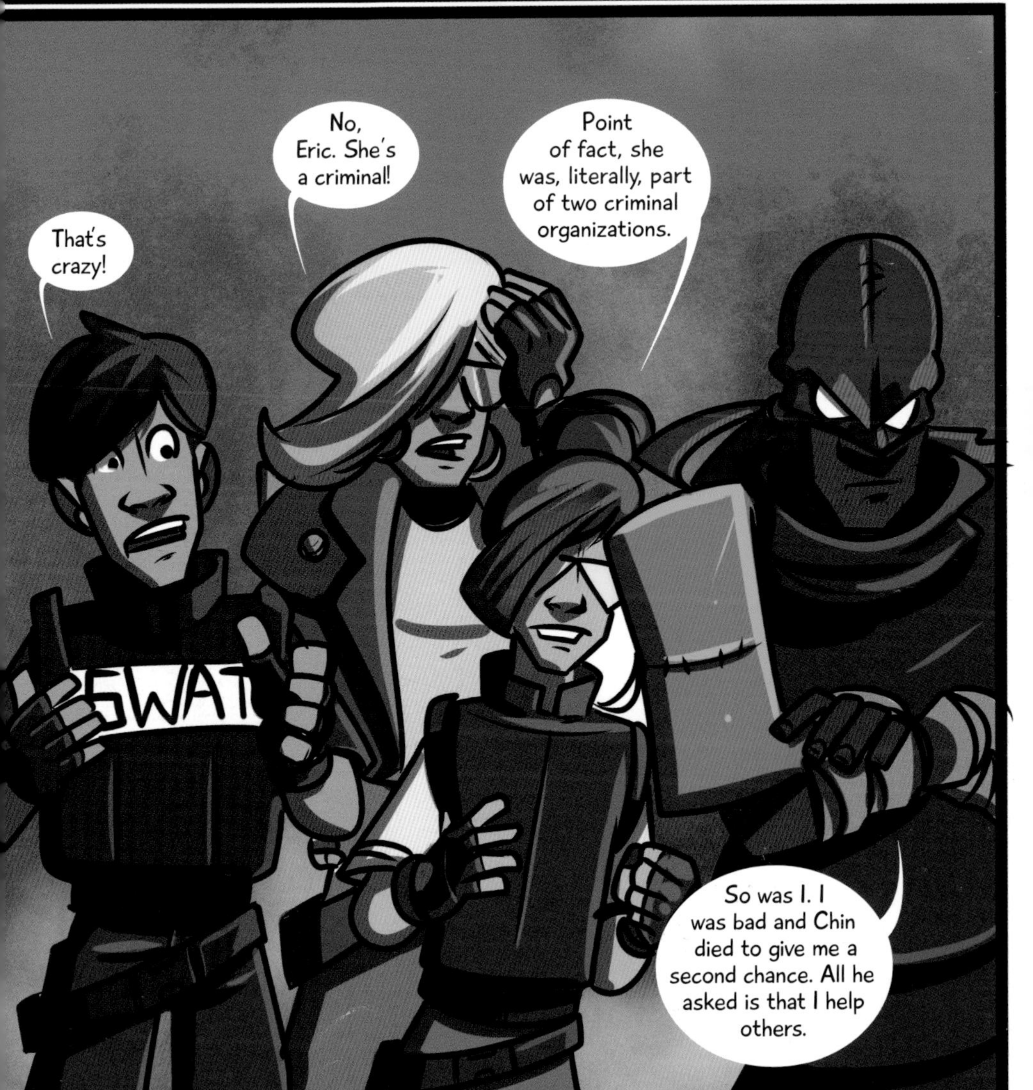

That's crazy!
No, Eric. She's a criminal!
Point of fact, she was, literally, part of two criminal organizations.
So was I. I was bad and Chin died to give me a second chance. All he asked is that I help others.
SWAT

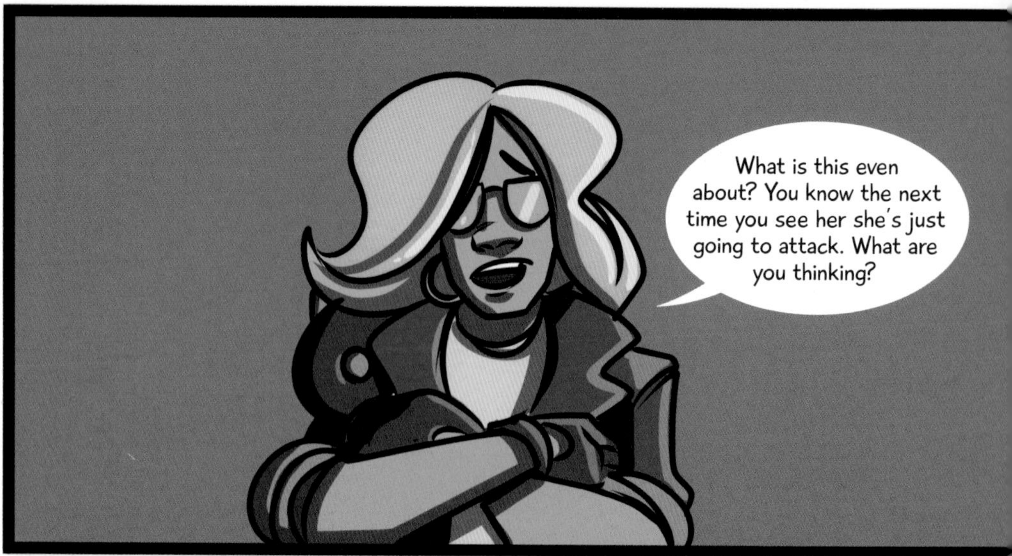
What is this even about? You know the next time you see her she's just going to attack. What are you thinking?

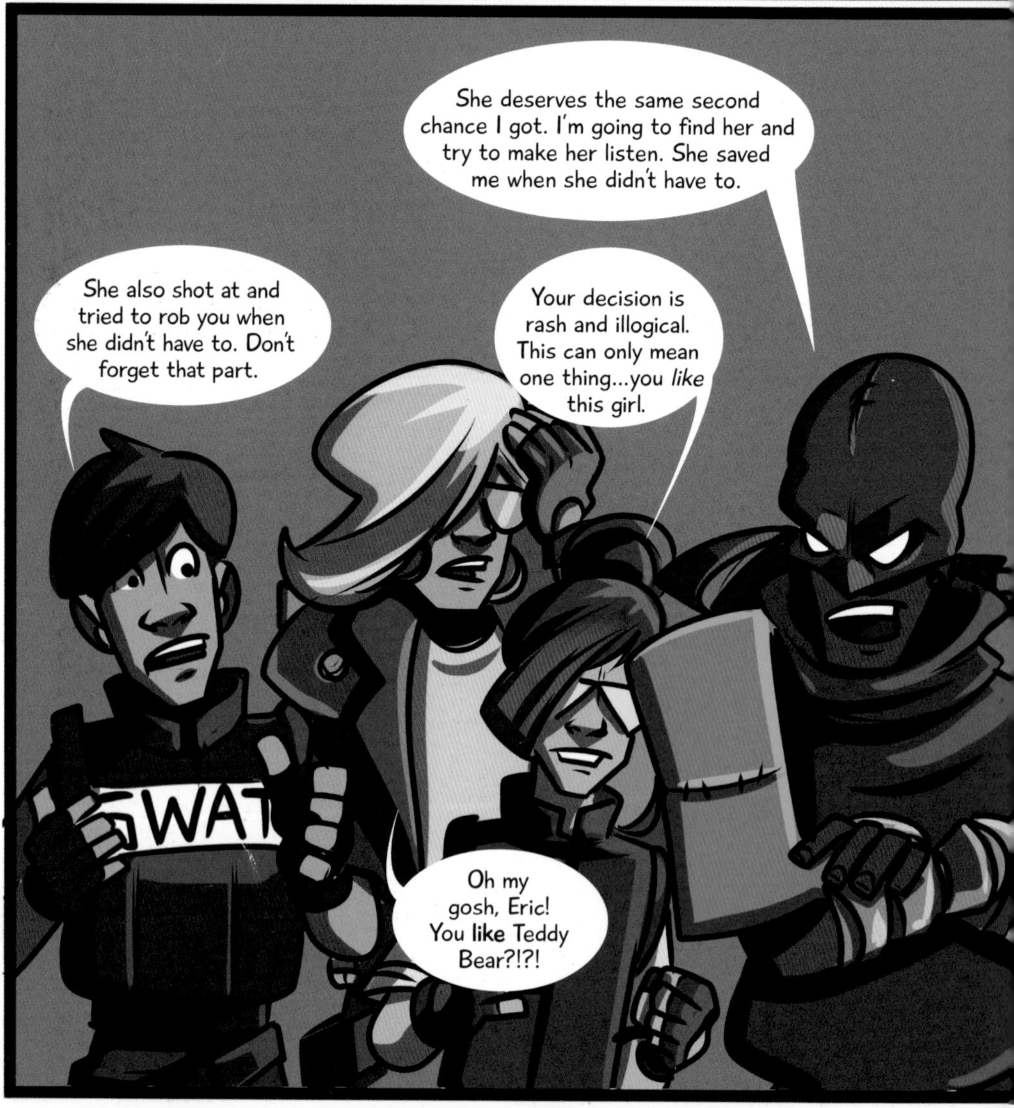
She deserves the same second chance I got. I'm going to find her and try to make her listen. She saved me when she didn't have to.
She also shot at and tried to rob you when she didn't have to. Don't forget that part.
Your decision is rash and illogical. This can only mean one thing...you *like* this girl.
SWAT
Oh my gosh, Eric! You **like** Teddy Bear?!?!

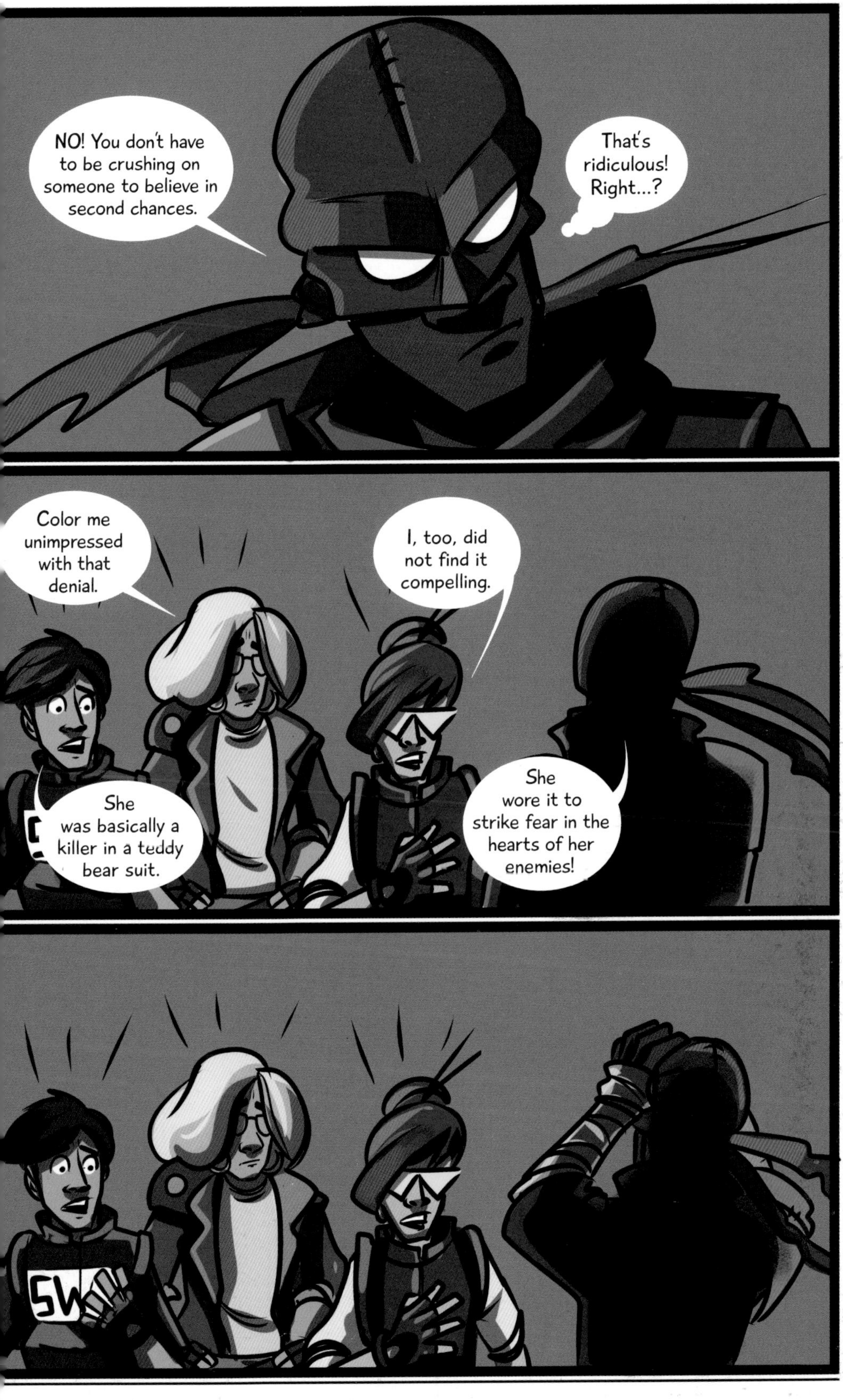
NO! You don't have to be crushing on someone to believe in second chances.
That's ridiculous! Right...?
Color me unimpressed with that denial.
I, too, did not find it compelling.
She was basically a killer in a teddy bear suit.
She wore it to strike fear in the hearts of her enemies!

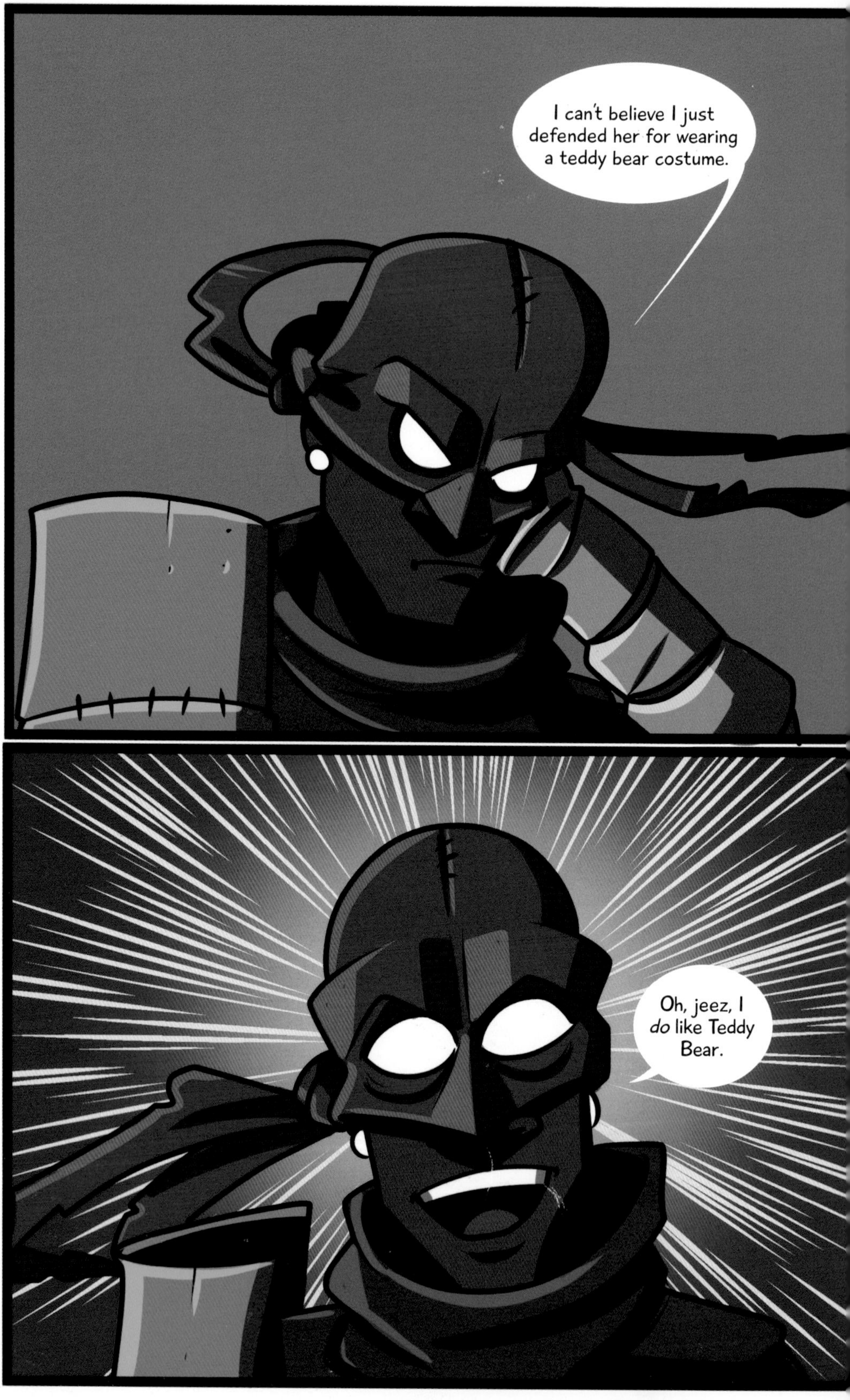
I can't believe I just defended her for wearing a teddy bear costume.
Oh, jeez, I *do* like Teddy Bear.

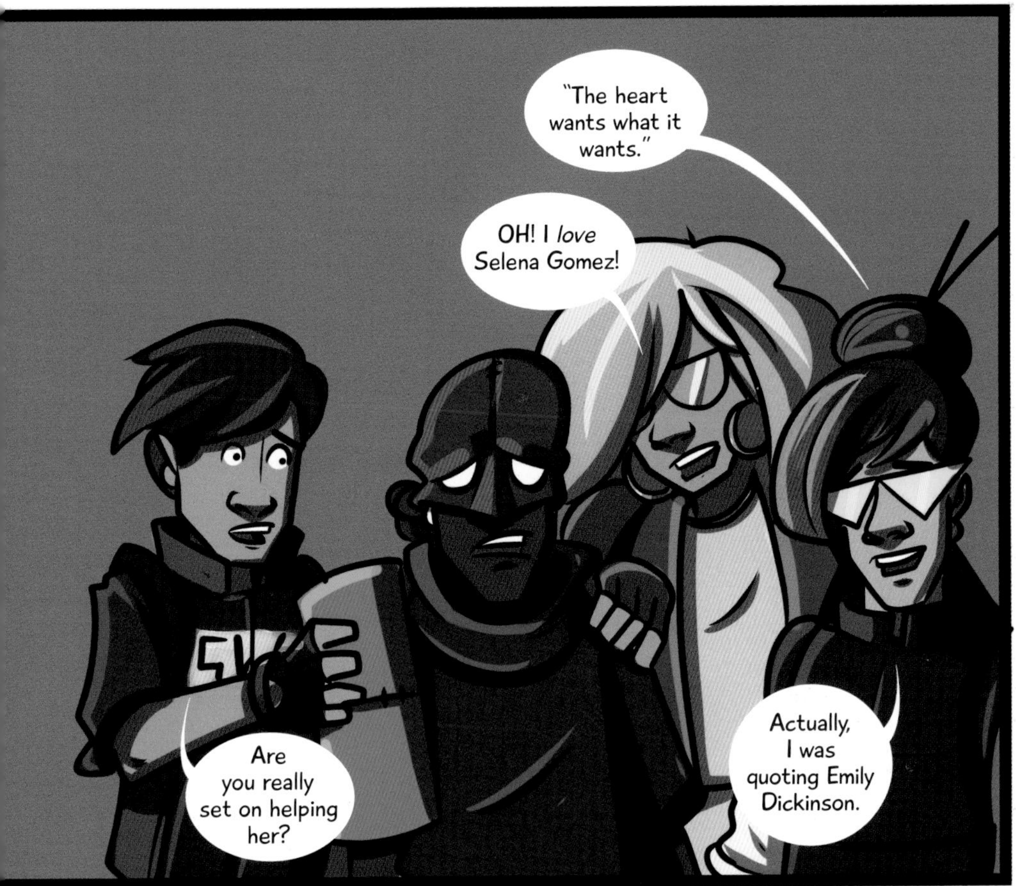
"The heart wants what it wants."
OH! I *love* Selena Gomez!
Are you really set on helping her?
Actually, I was quoting Emily Dickinson.

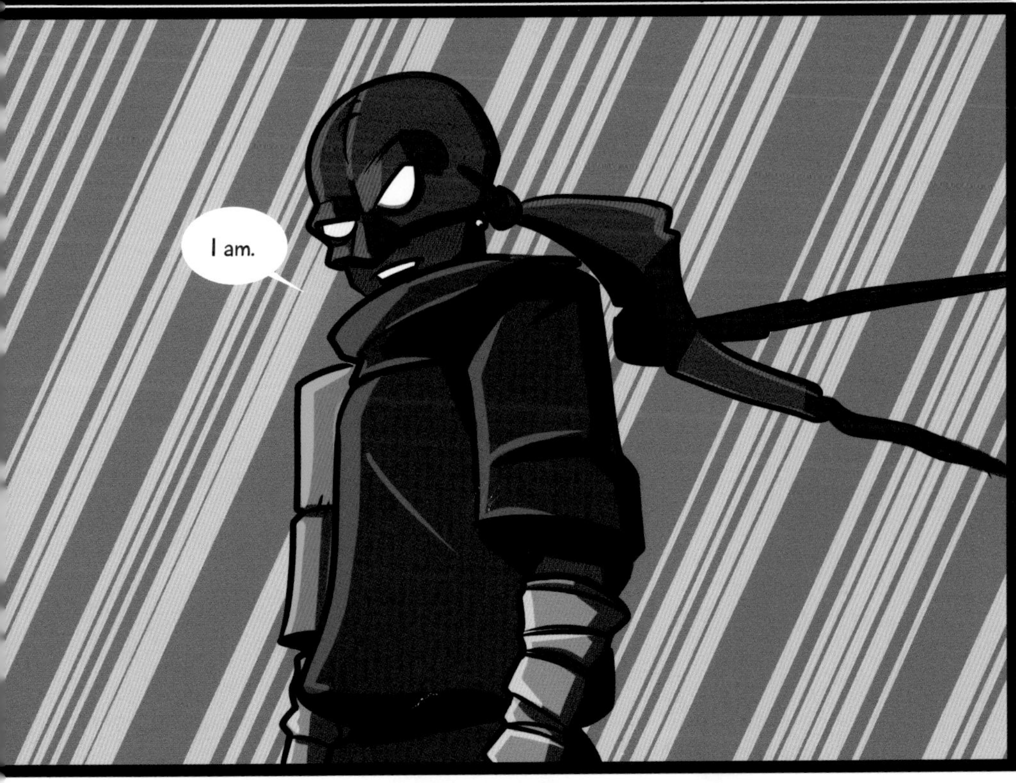
I am.

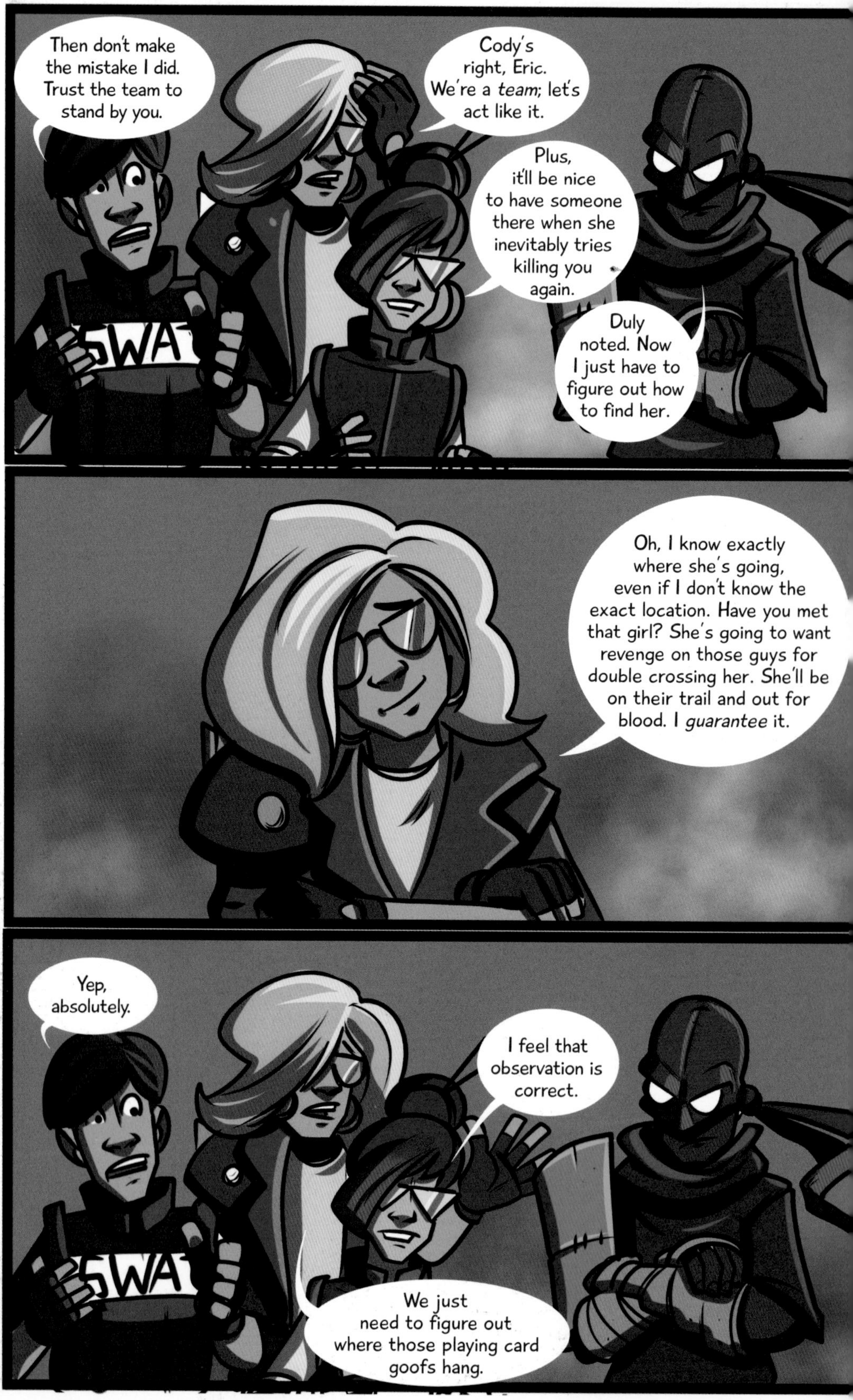
Then don't make the mistake I did. Trust the team to stand by you.
Cody's right, Eric. We're a *team*; let's act like it.
Plus, it'll be nice to have someone there when she inevitably tries killing you again.
Duly noted. Now I just have to figure out how to find her.
SWAT
Oh, I know exactly where she's going, even if I don't know the exact location. Have you met that girl? She's going to want revenge on those guys for double crossing her. She'll be on their trail and out for blood. I *guarantee* it.
Yep, absolutely.
I feel that observation is correct.
We just need to figure out where those playing card goofs hang.
SWAT

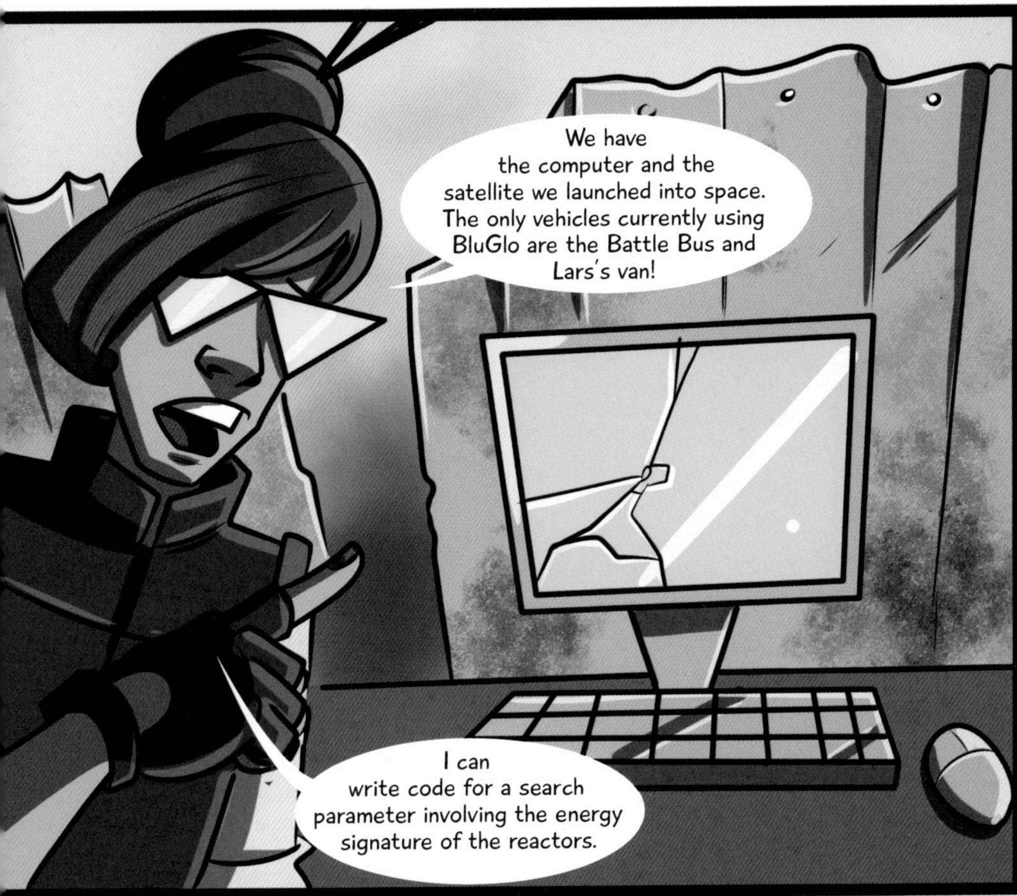
We have the computer and the satellite we launched into space. The only vehicles currently using BluGlo are the Battle Bus and Lars's van!
I can write code for a search parameter involving the energy signature of the reactors.

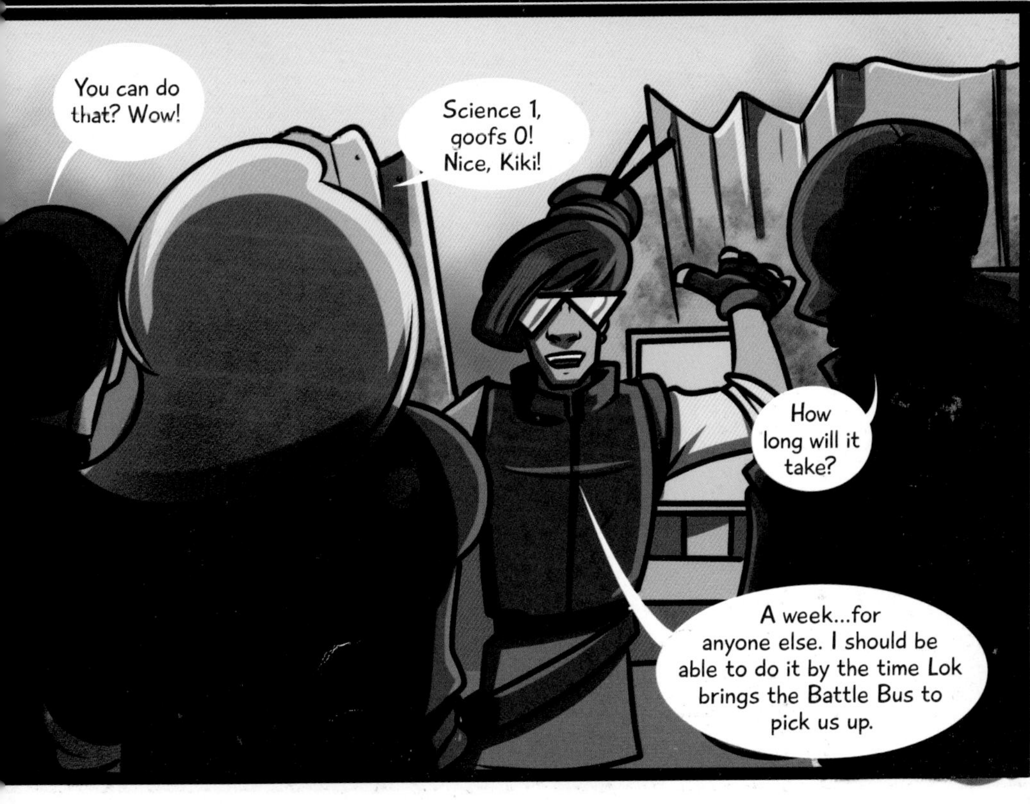
You can do that? Wow!
Science 1, goofs 0! Nice, Kiki!
How long will it take?
A week...for anyone else. I should be able to do it by the time Lok brings the Battle Bus to pick us up.

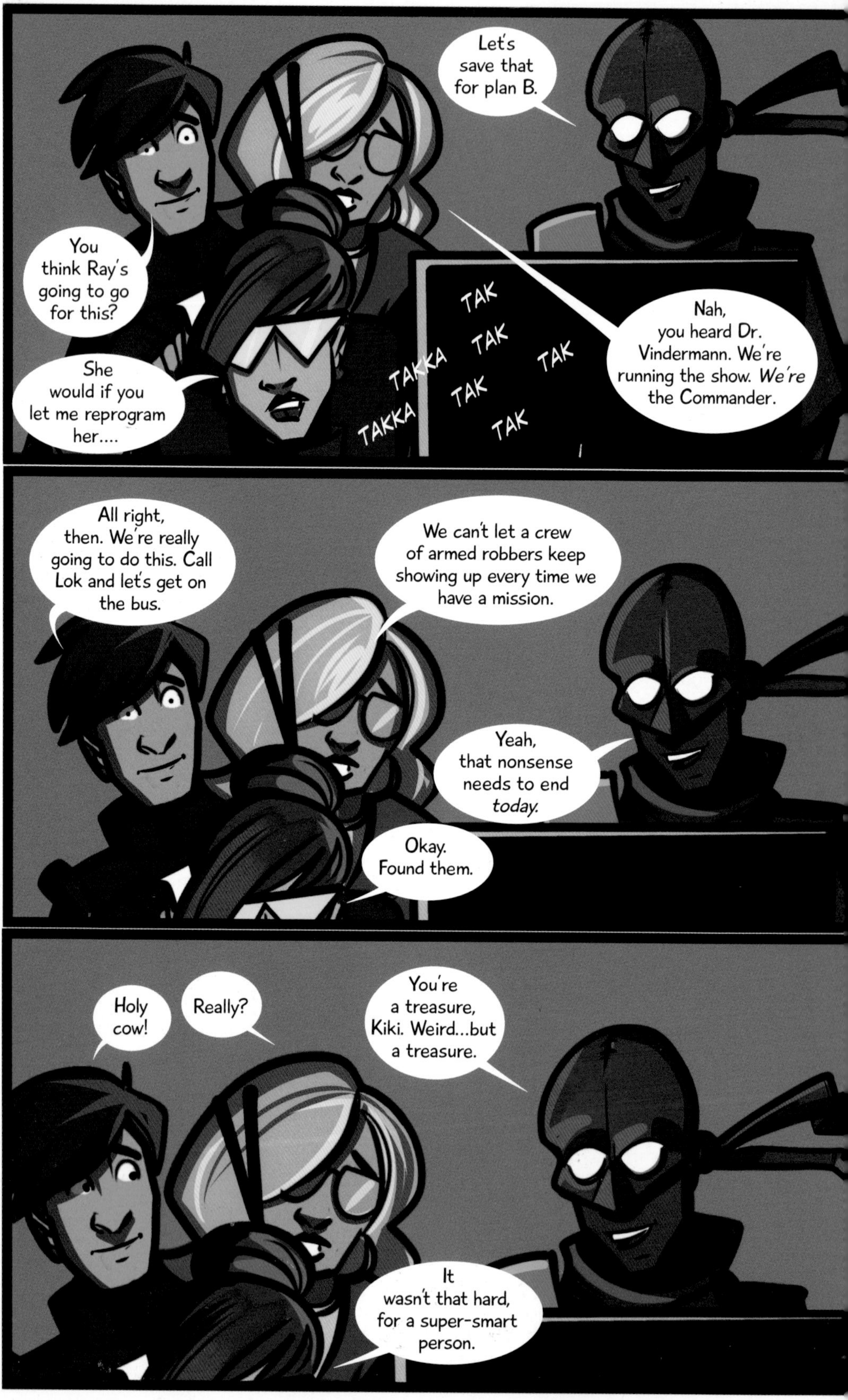
Let's save that for plan B.
You think Ray's going to go for this?
She would if you let me reprogram her....
TAK
TAK
TAK
TAKKA
TAK
TAKKA
TAK
Nah, you heard Dr. Vindermann. We're running the show. *We're* the Commander.
All right, then. We're really going to do this. Call Lok and let's get on the bus.
We can't let a crew of armed robbers keep showing up every time we have a mission.
Yeah, that nonsense needs to end *today.*
Okay. Found them.
Holy cow!
Really?
You're a treasure, Kiki. Weird...but a treasure.
It wasn't that hard, for a super-smart person.

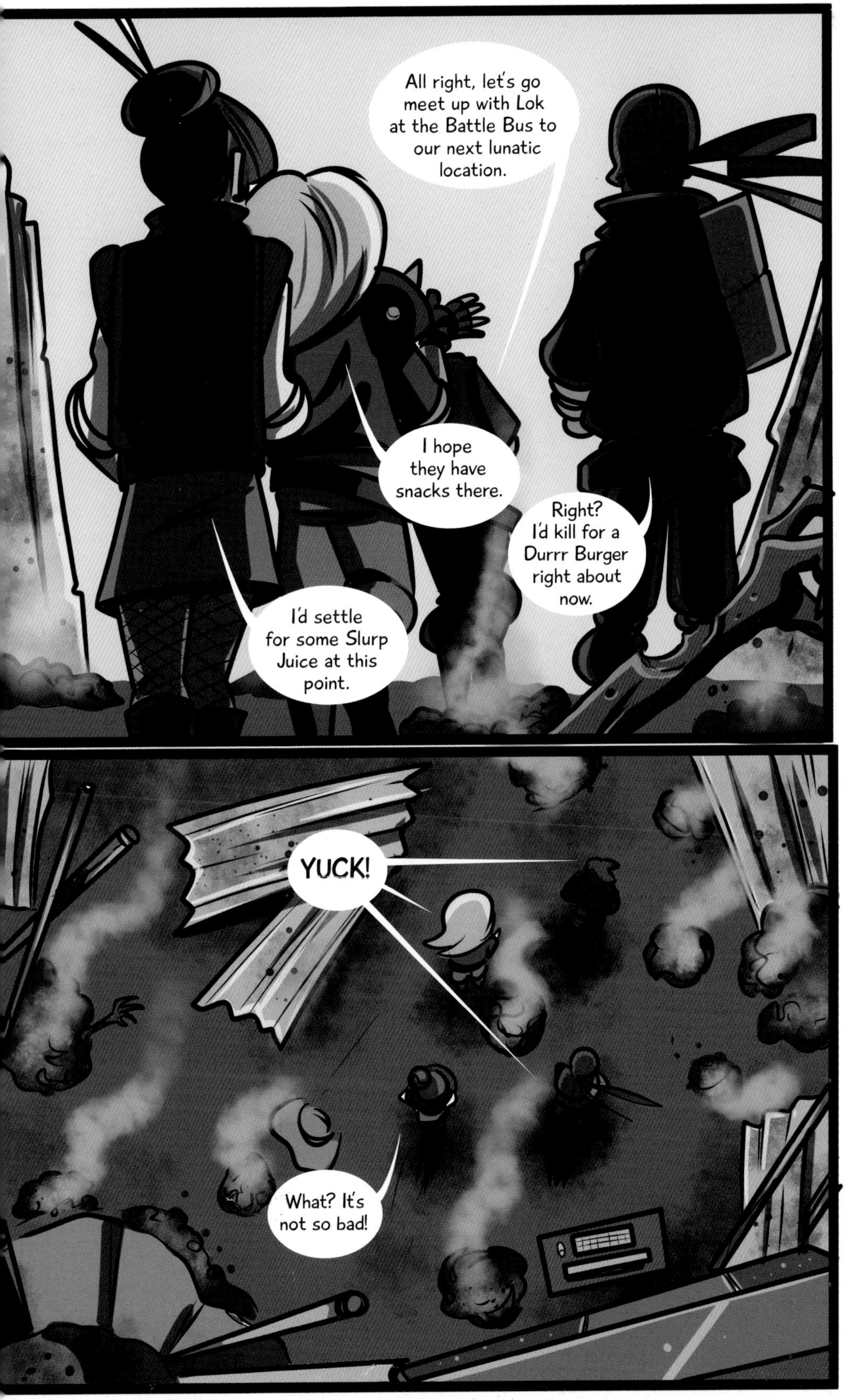
All right, let's go meet up with Lok at the Battle Bus to our next lunatic location.
I hope they have snacks there.
Right? I'd kill for a Durrr Burger right about now.
I'd settle for some Slurp Juice at this point.
YUCK!
What? It's not so bad!

CHAPTER 8: SHOW YOUR CARDS

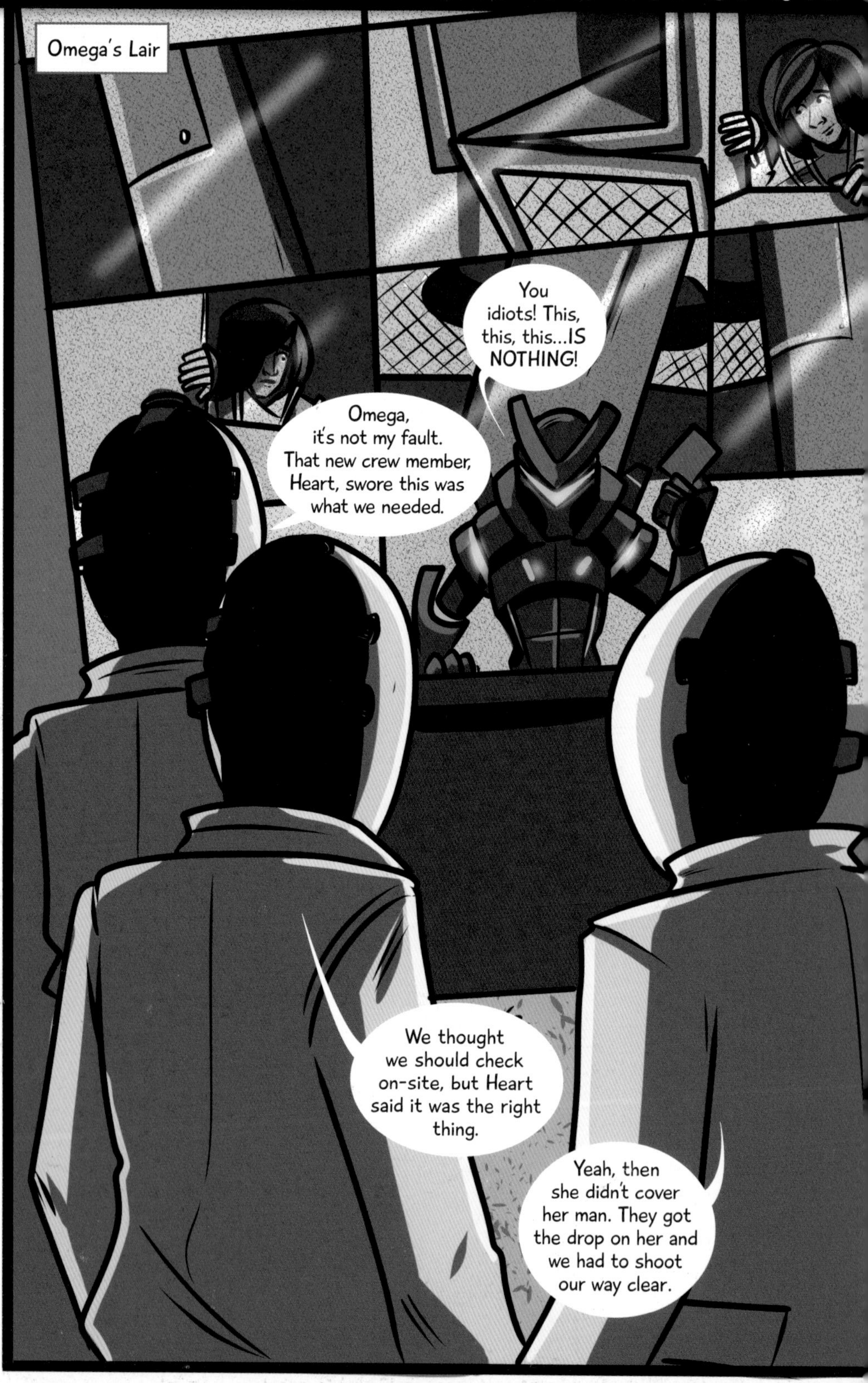

Omega's Lair
You idiots! This, this, this...IS NOTHING!
Omega, it's not my fault. That new crew member, Heart, swore this was what we needed.
We thought we should check on-site, but Heart said it was the right thing.
Yeah, then she didn't cover her man. They got the drop on her and we had to shoot our way clear.

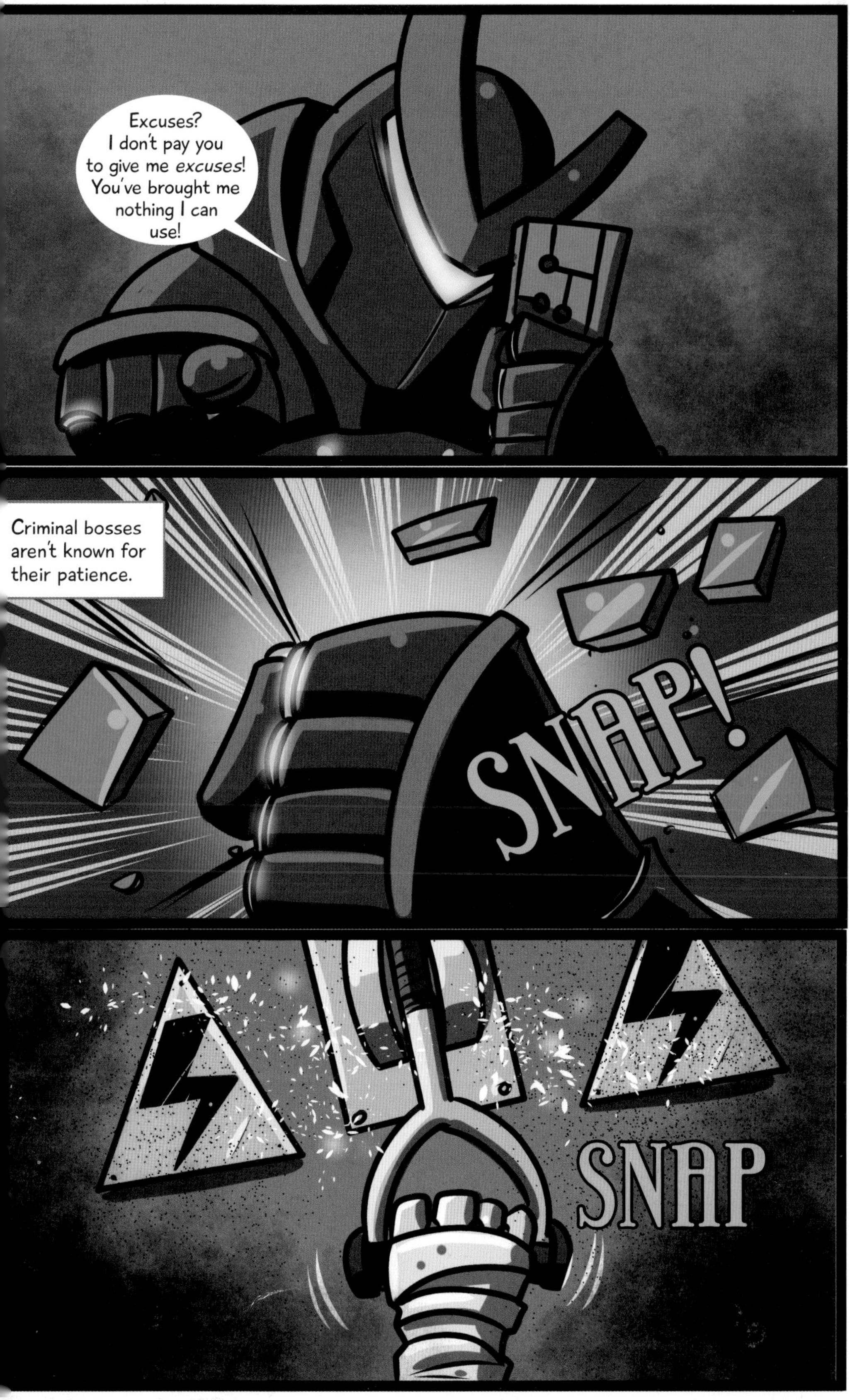
Excuses? I don't pay you to give me *excuses*! You've brought me nothing I can use!
Criminal bosses aren't known for their patience.
SNAP!
SNAP

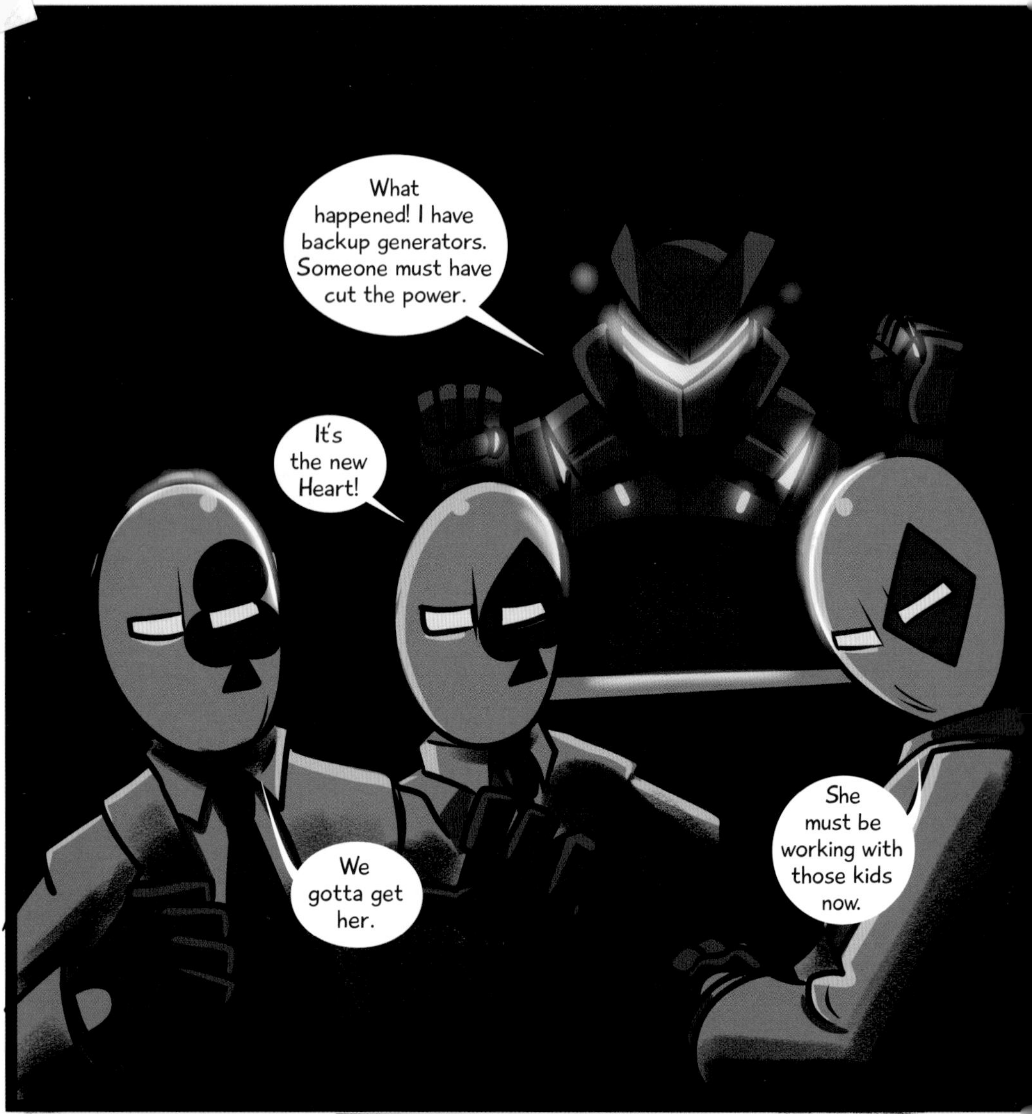
What happened! I have backup generators. Someone must have cut the power.
It's the new Heart!
We gotta get her.
She must be working with those kids now.

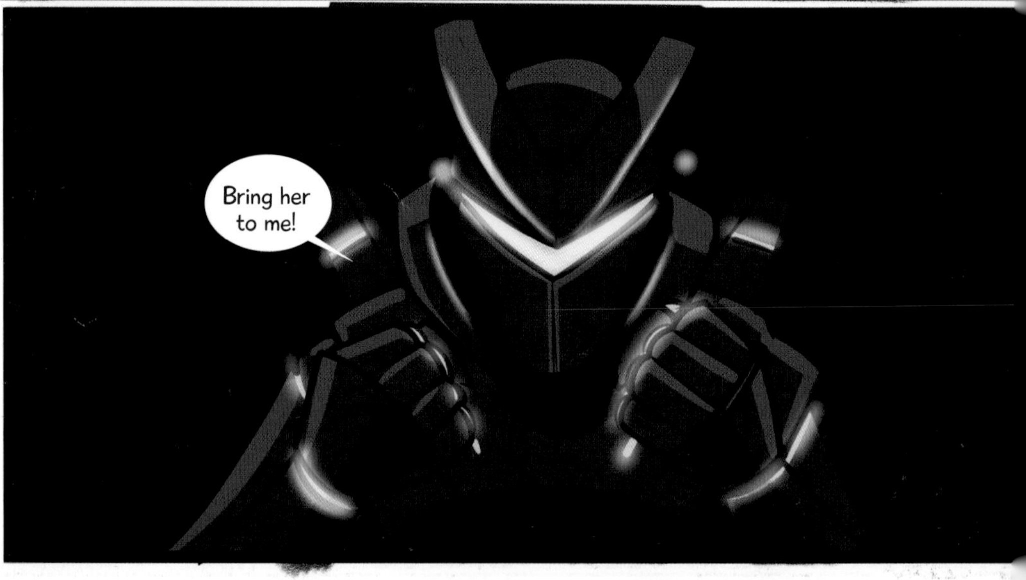
Bring her to me!

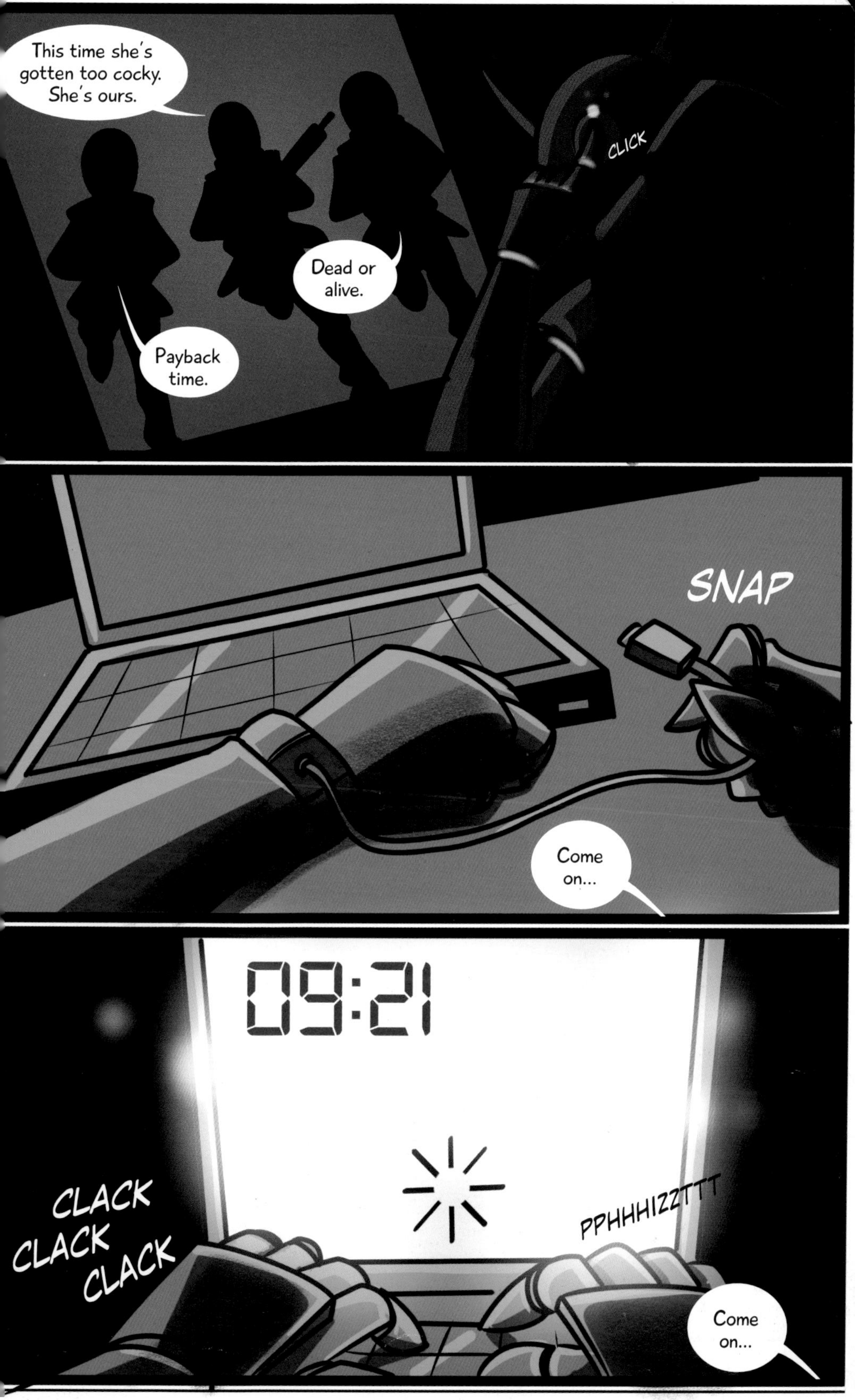
This time she's gotten too cocky. She's ours.
CLICK
Dead or alive.
Payback time.
SNAP
Come on...
09:21
CLACK
CLACK
CLACK
PPHHHIZZTTT
Come on...

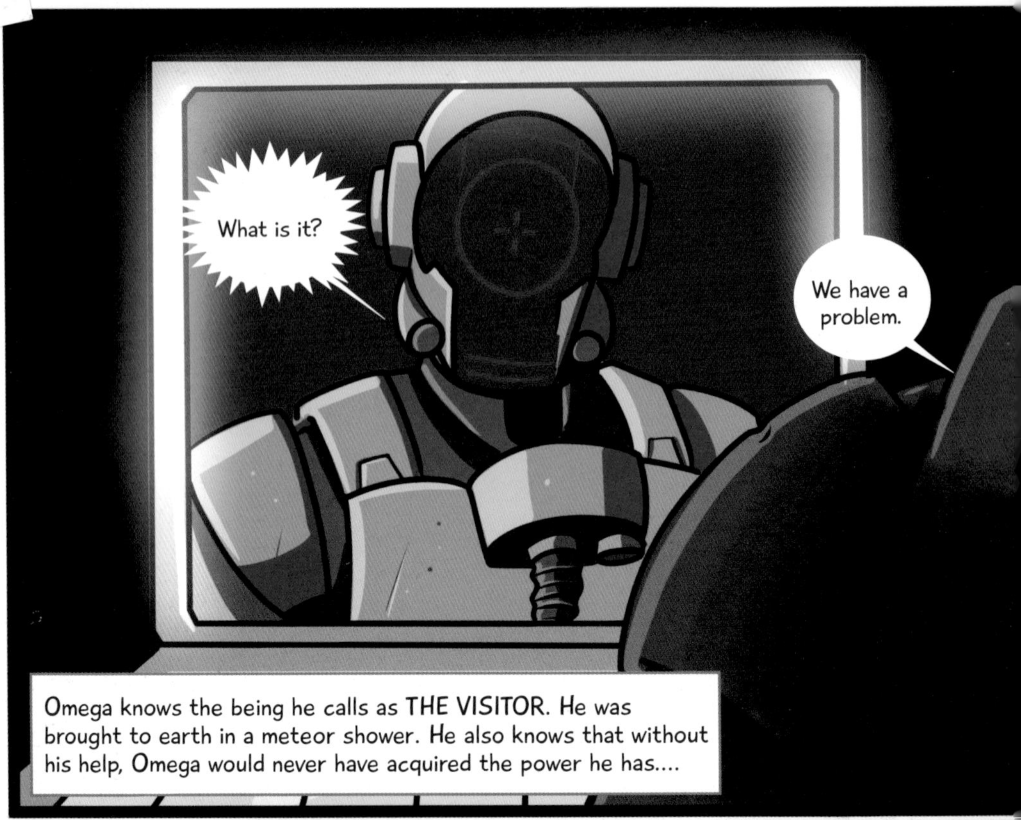
What is it?
We have a problem.
Omega knows the being he calls as THE VISITOR. He was brought to earth in a meteor shower. He also knows that without his help, Omega would never have acquired the power he has....

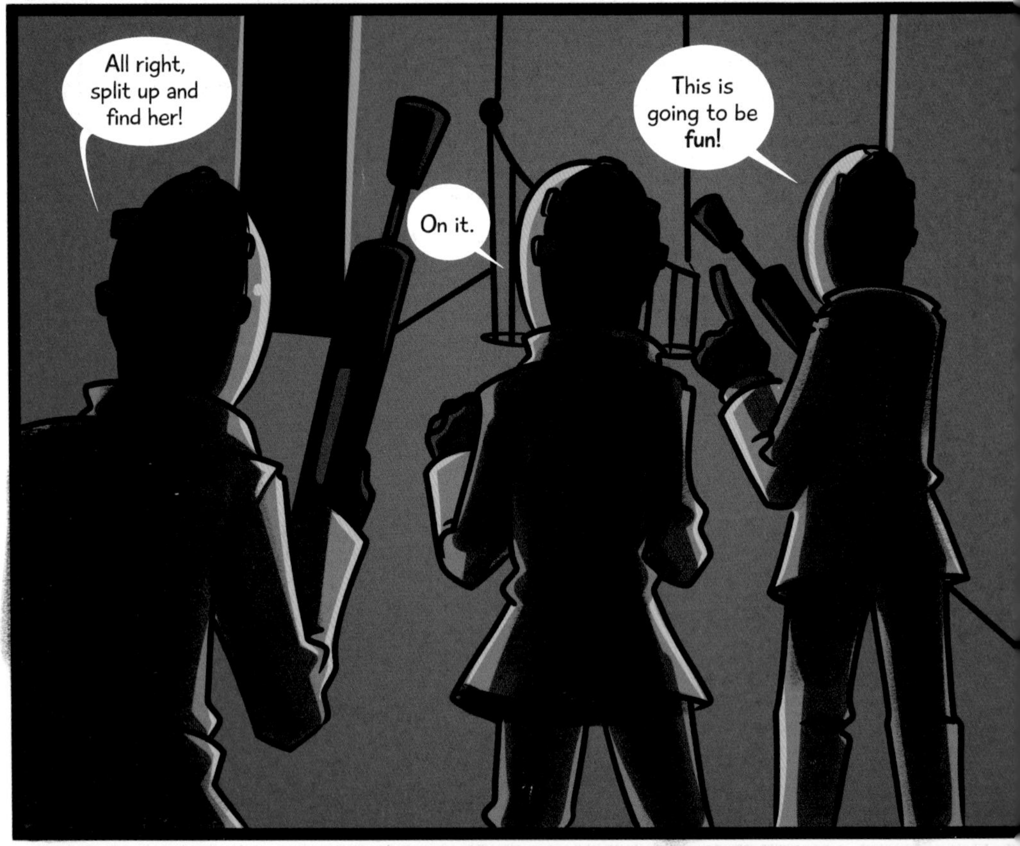
All right, split up and find her!
On it.
This is going to be fun!

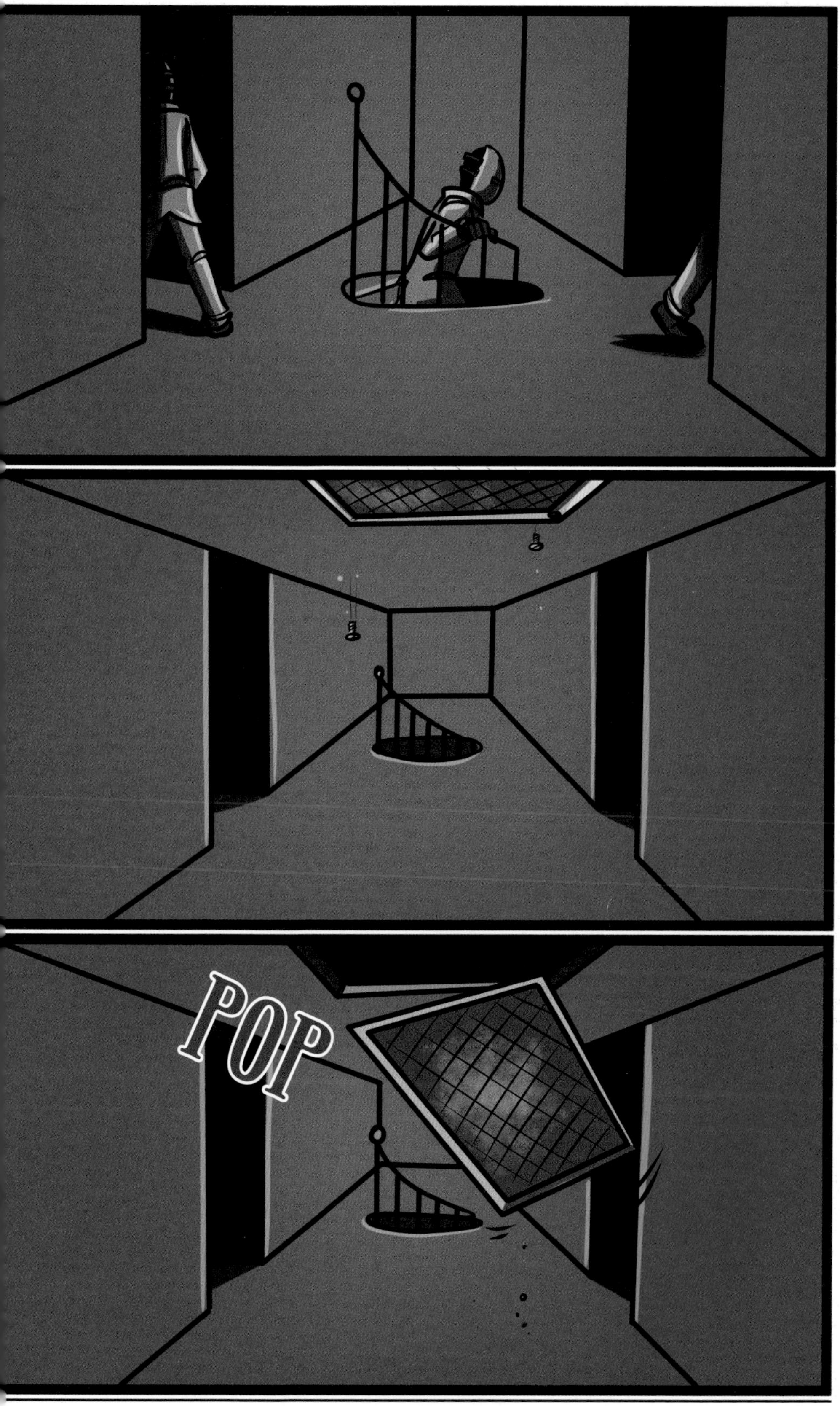
POP

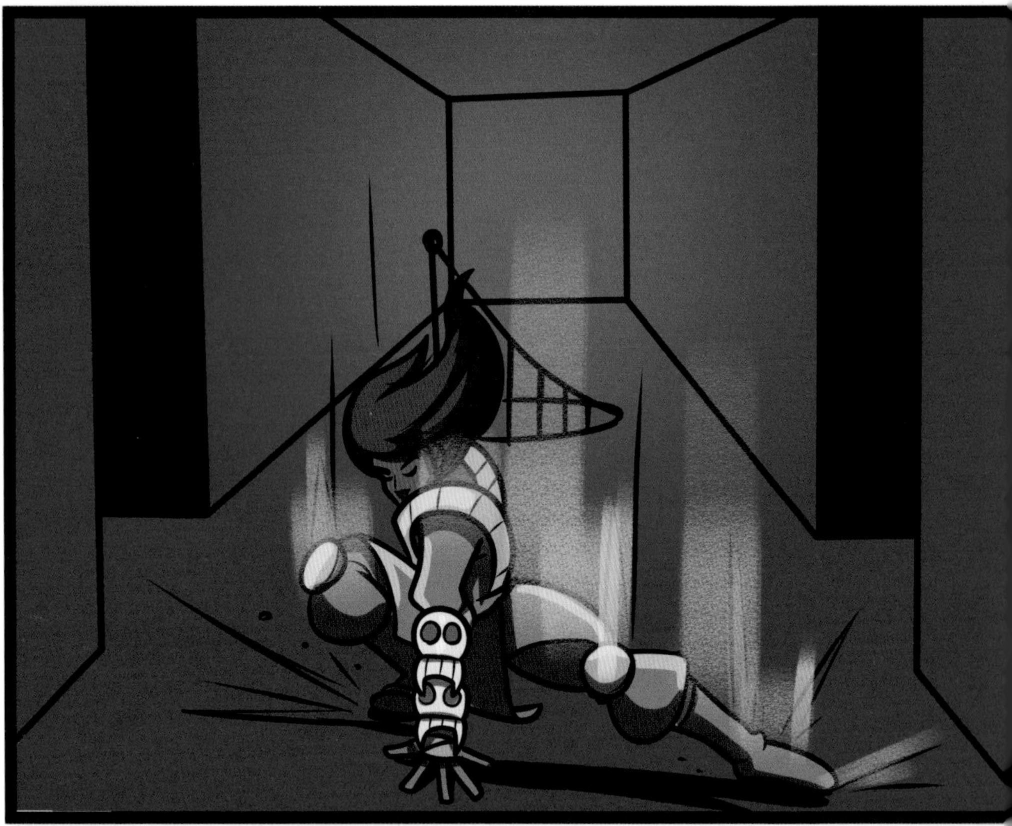

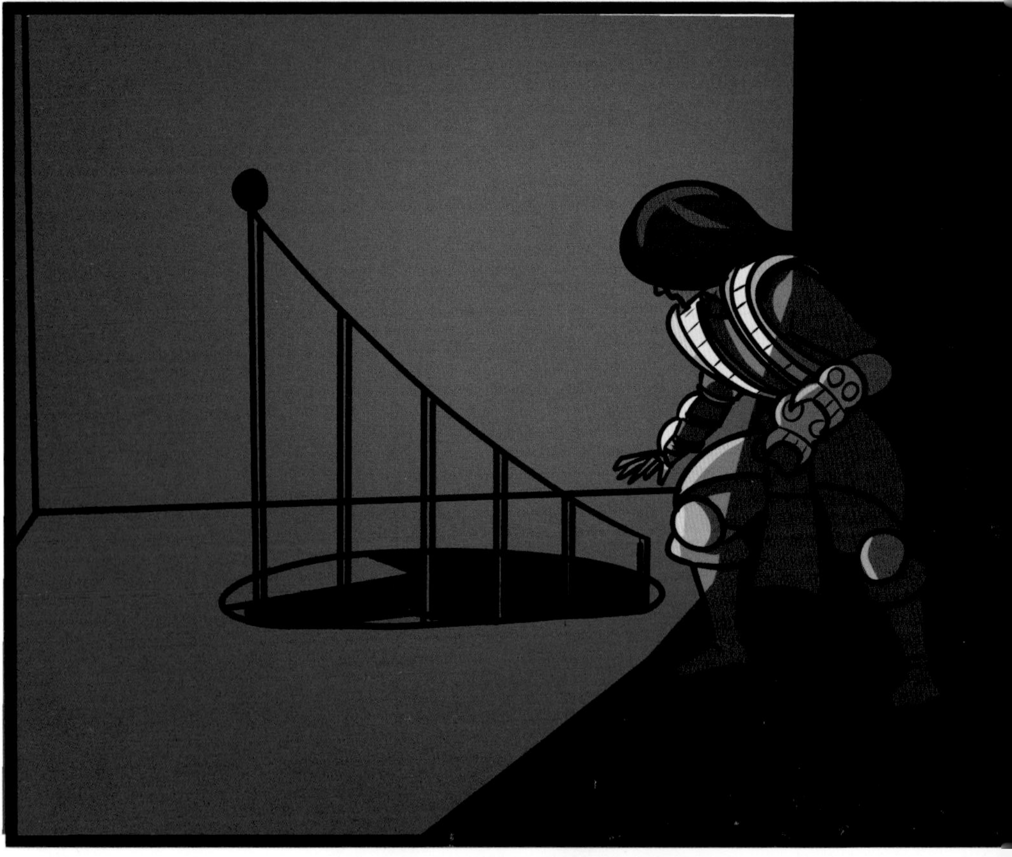

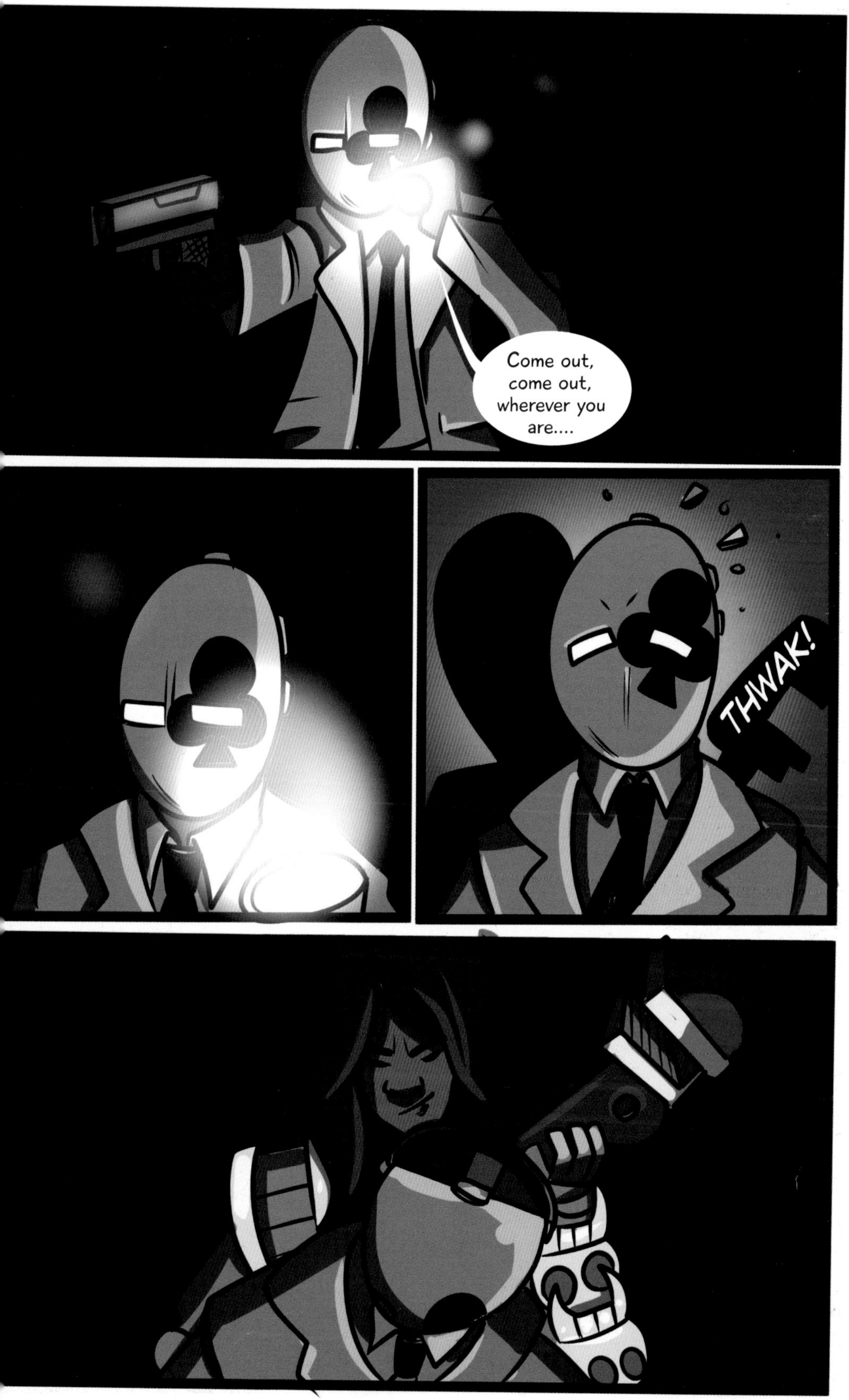
Come out, come out, wherever you are....
THWAK!

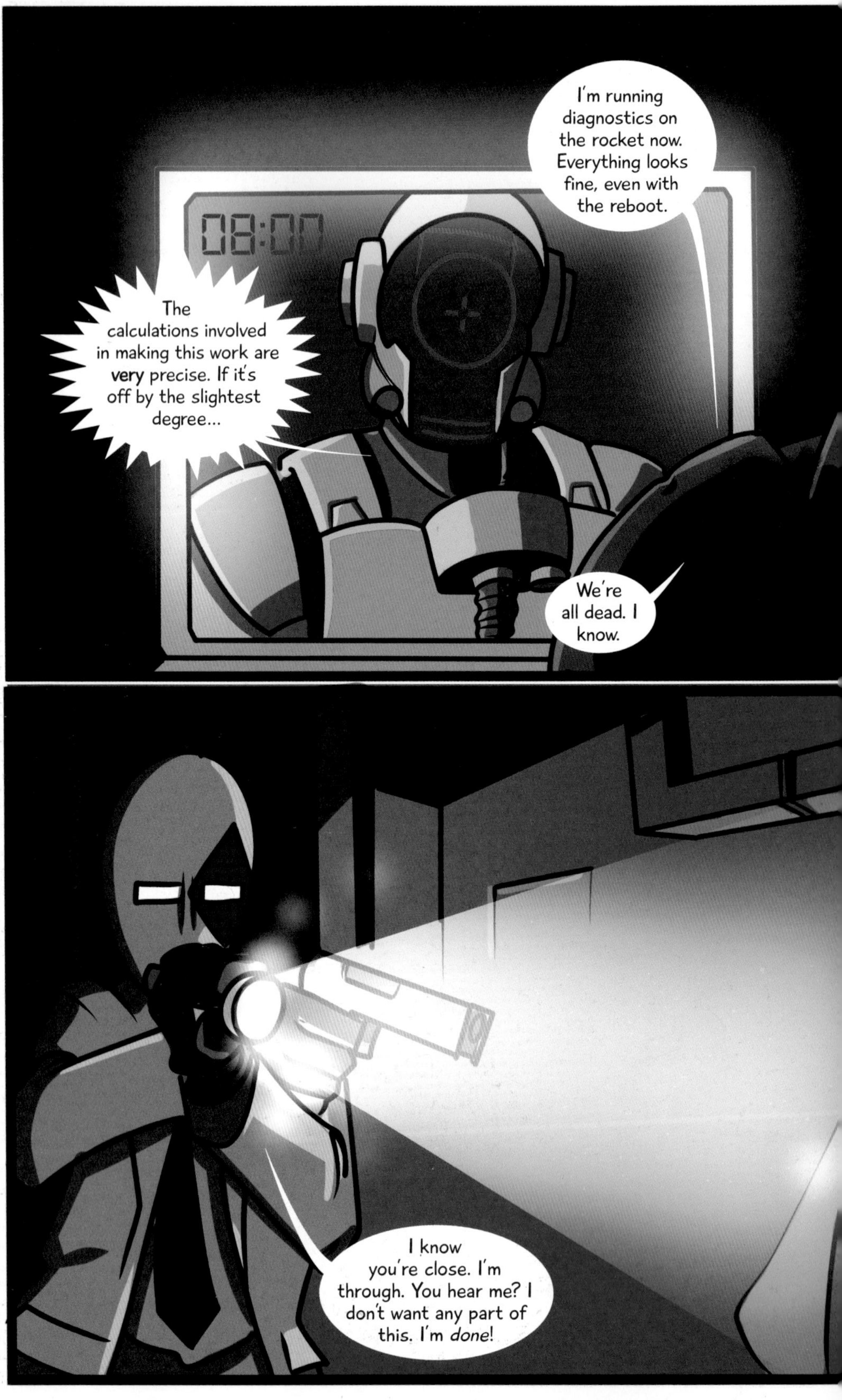
I'm running diagnostics on the rocket now. Everything looks fine, even with the reboot.
08:00
The calculations involved in making this work are **very** precise. If it's off by the slightest degree...
We're all dead. I know.
I know you're close. I'm through. You hear me? I don't want any part of this. I'm *done*!

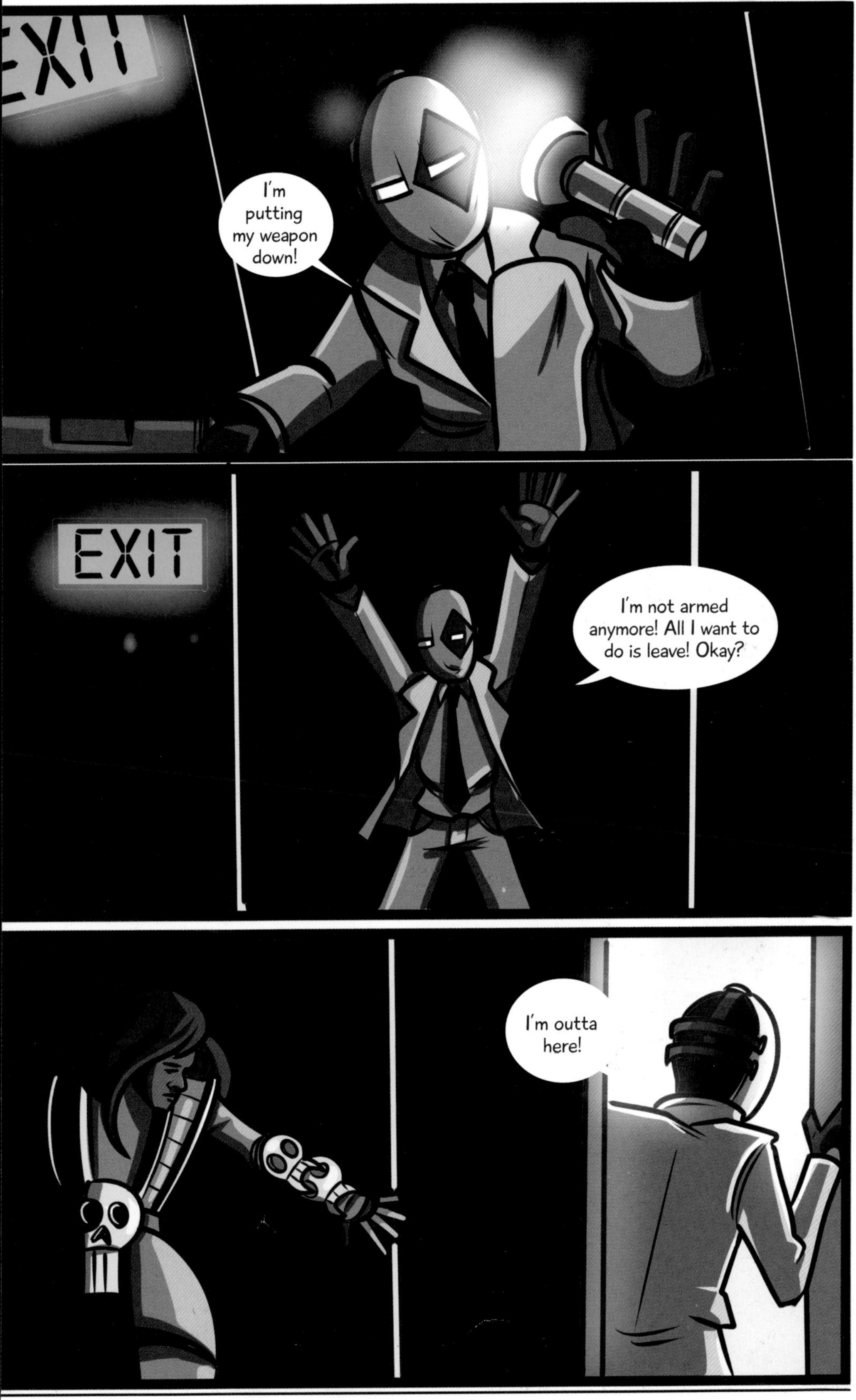
EXIT
I'm putting my weapon down!
EXIT
I'm not armed anymore! All I want to do is leave! Okay?
I'm outta here!

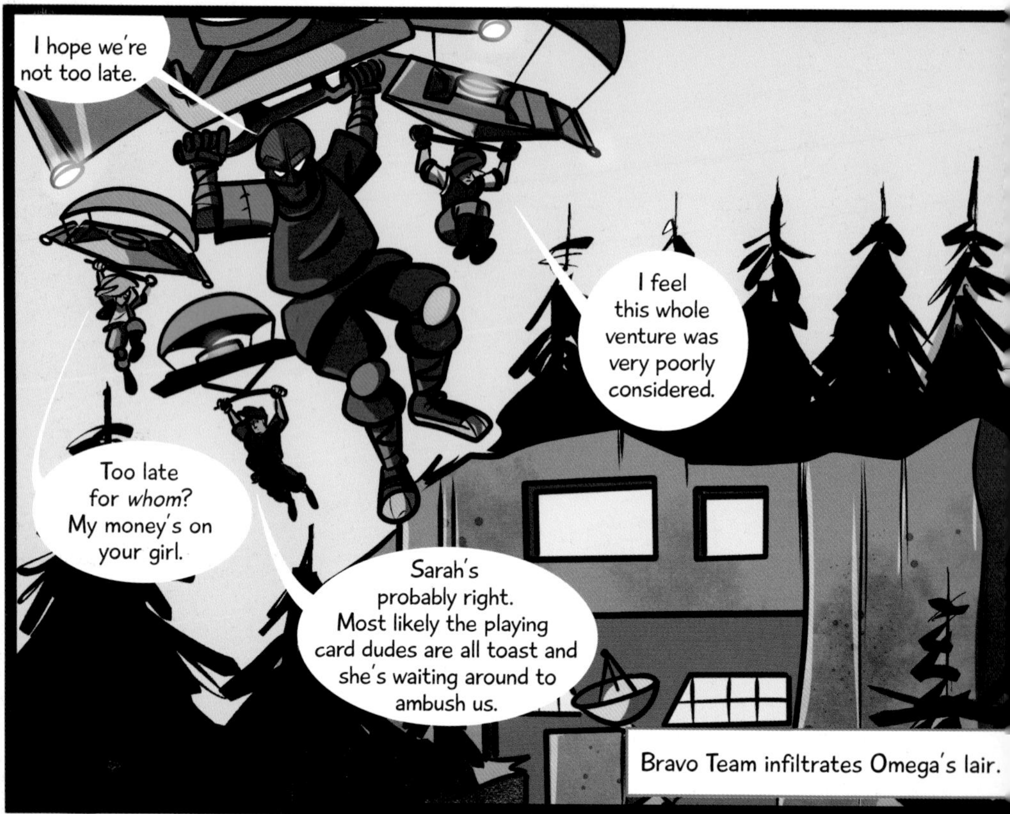
I hope we're not too late.
I feel this whole venture was very poorly considered.
Too late for *whom*? My money's on your girl.
Sarah's probably right. Most likely the playing card dudes are all toast and she's waiting around to ambush us.
Bravo Team infiltrates Omega's lair.

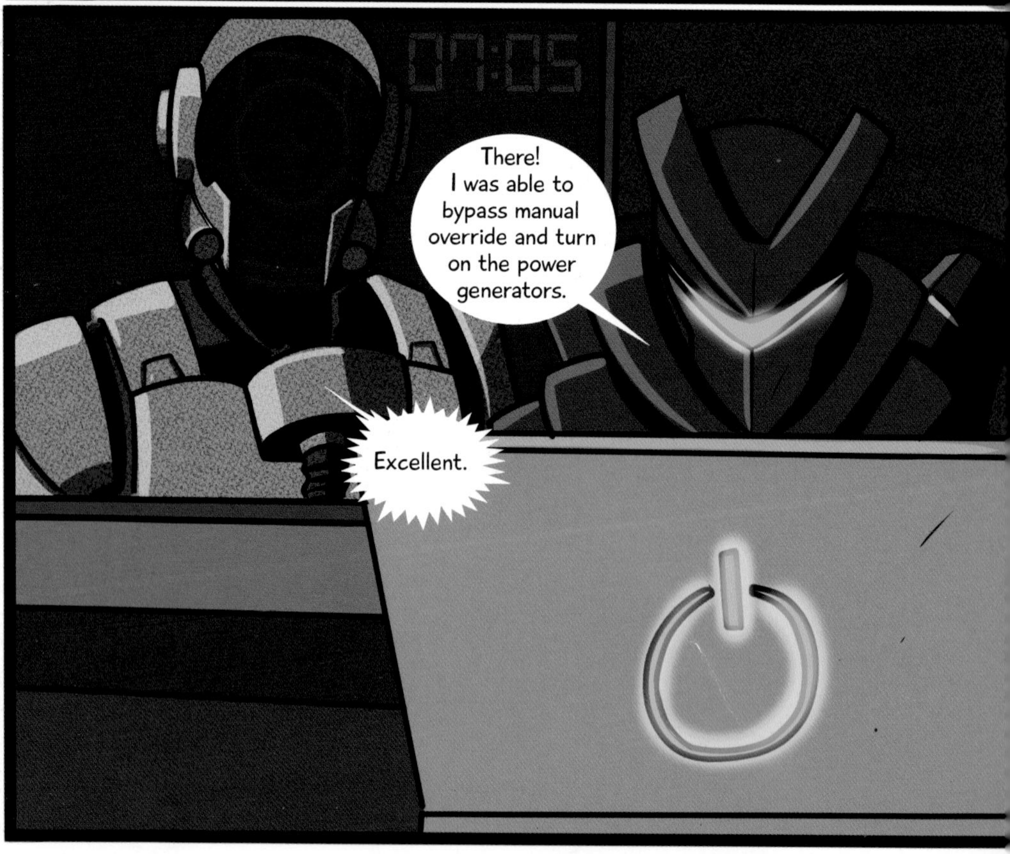
07:05
There! I was able to bypass manual override and turn on the power generators.
Excellent.

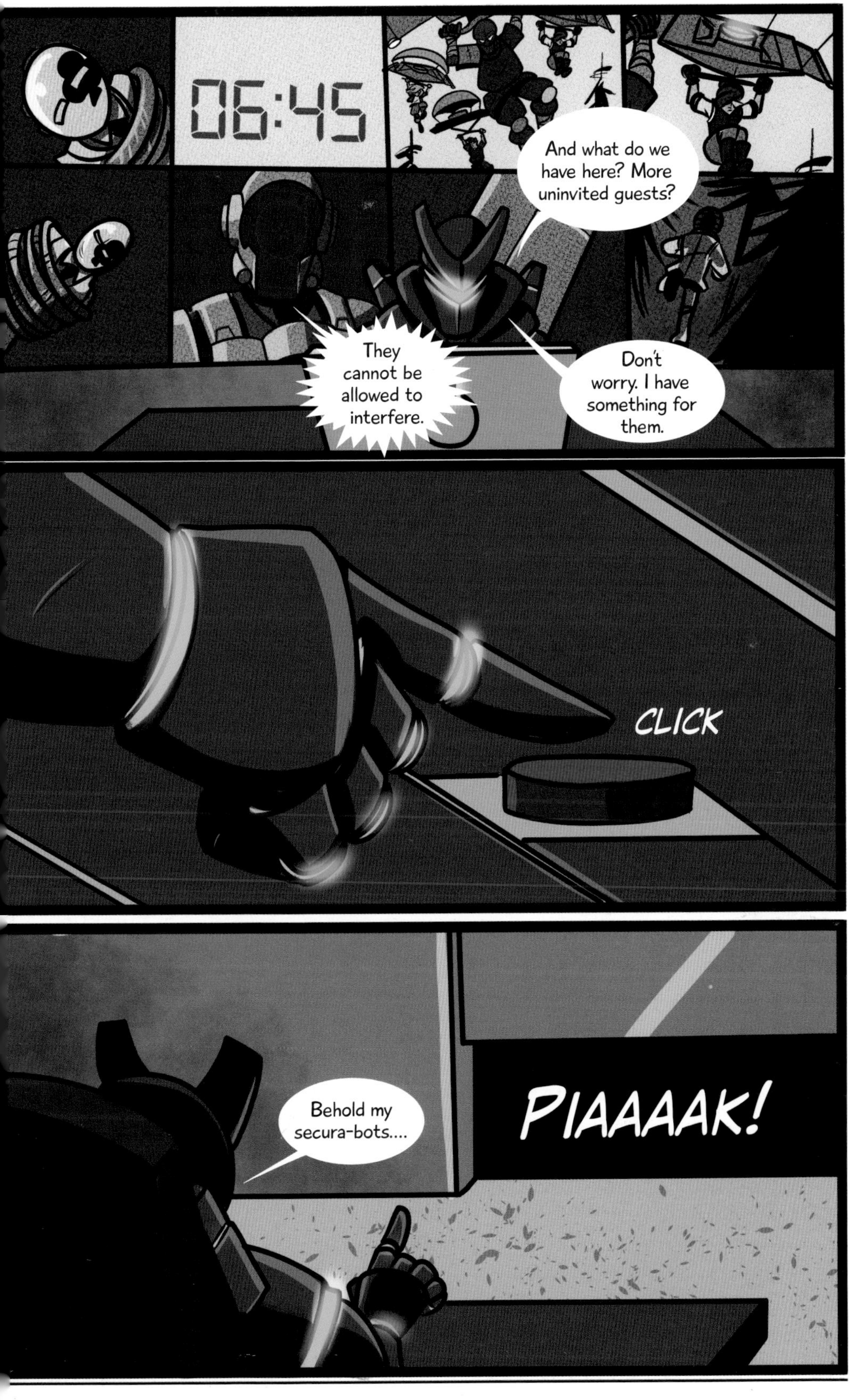
06:45
And what do we have here? More uninvited guests?
They cannot be allowed to interfere.
Don't worry. I have something for them.
CLICK
Behold my secura-bots....
PIAAAAK!

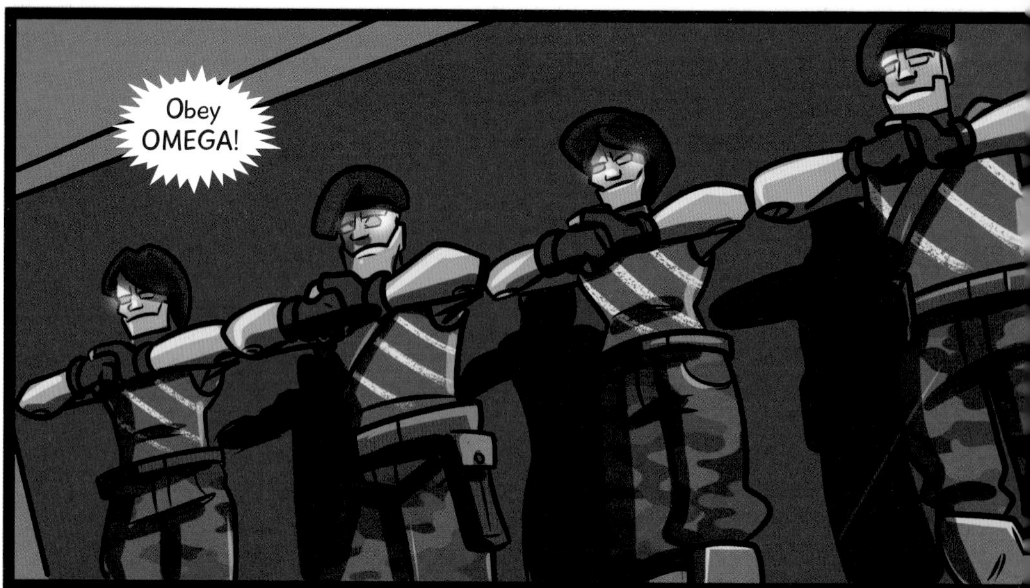
Obey
OMEGA!

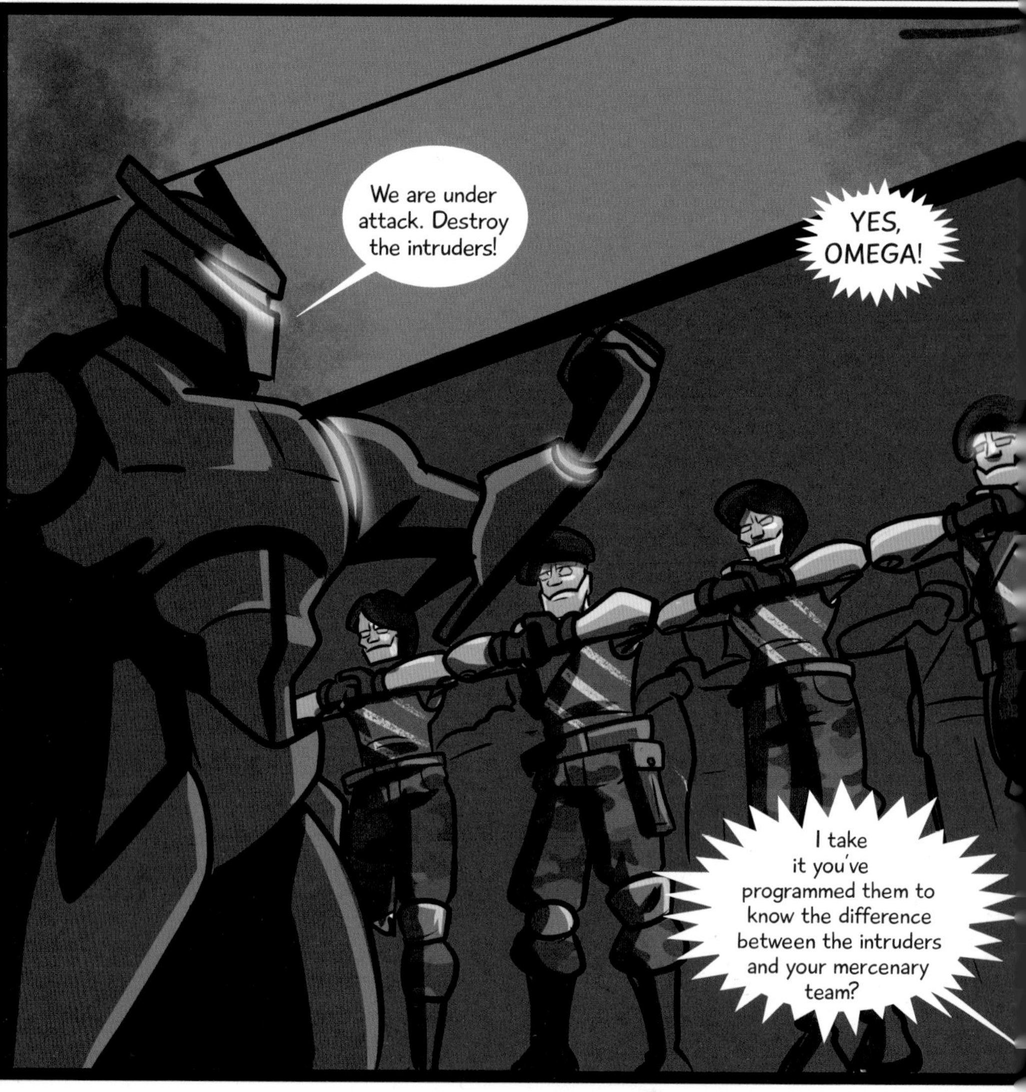
We are under attack. Destroy the intruders!
YES, OMEGA!
I take it you've programmed them to know the difference between the intruders and your mercenary team?

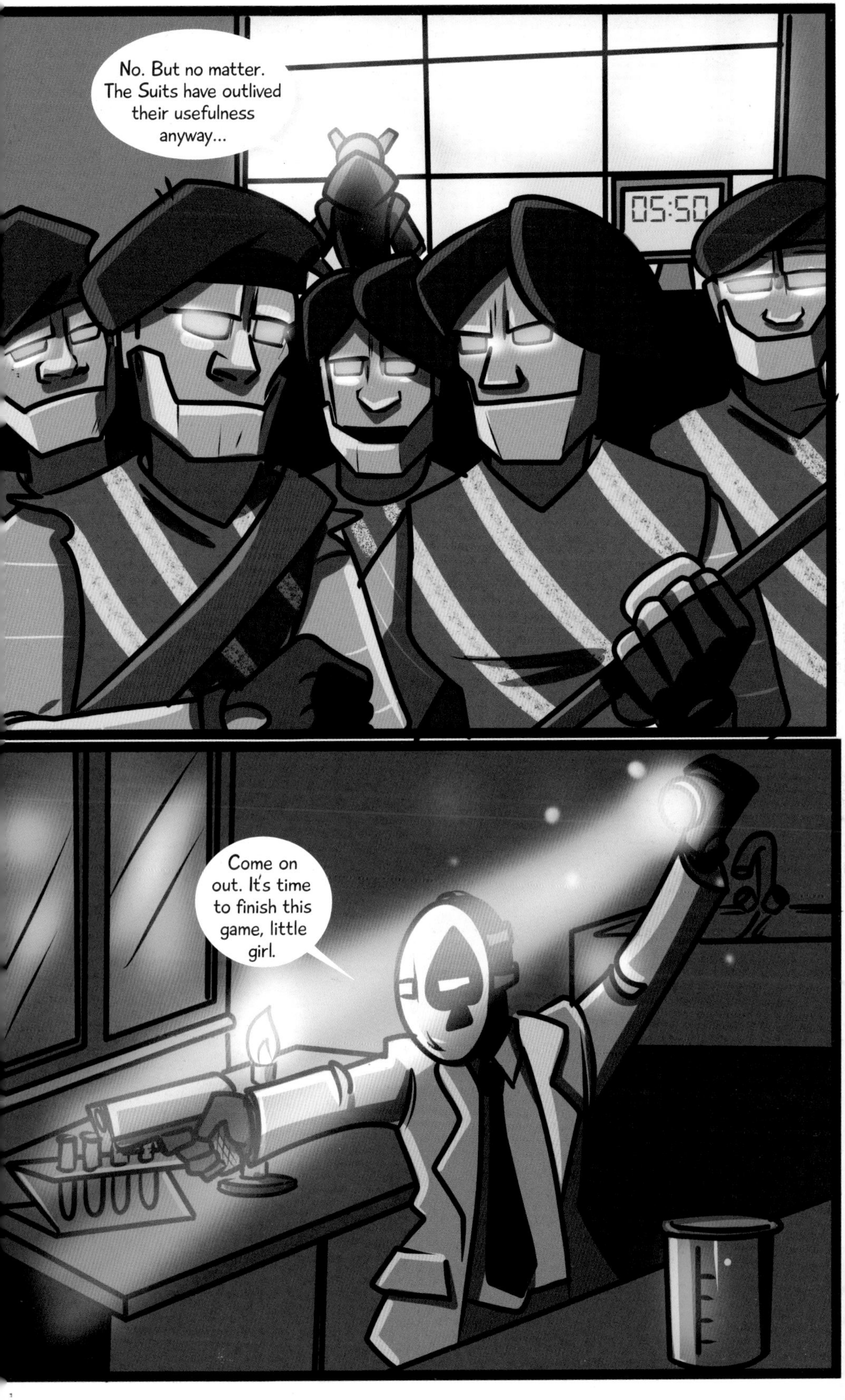
No. But no matter. The Suits have outlived their usefulness anyway...
05:50
Come on out. It's time to finish this game, little girl.

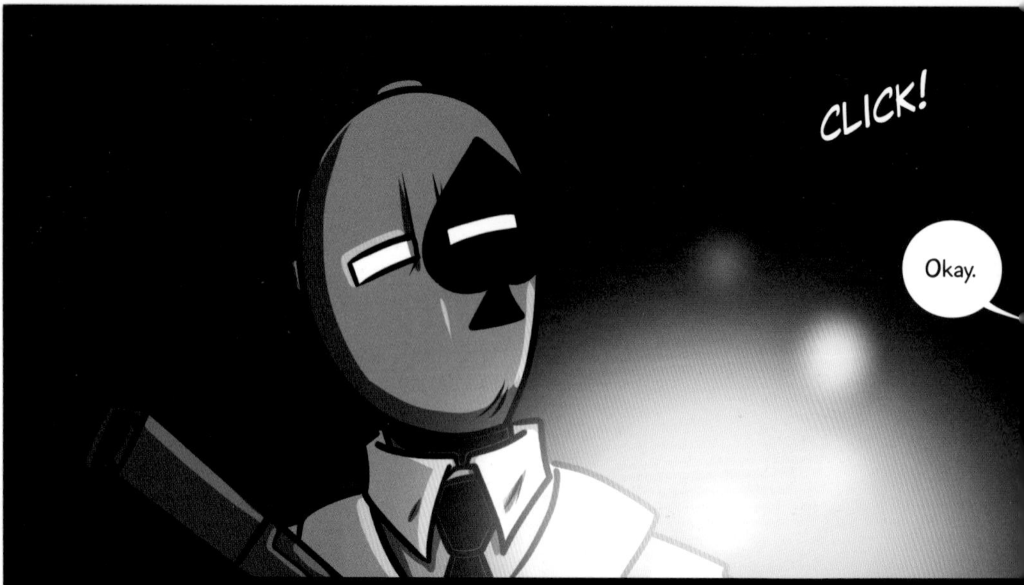
CLICK!
Okay.

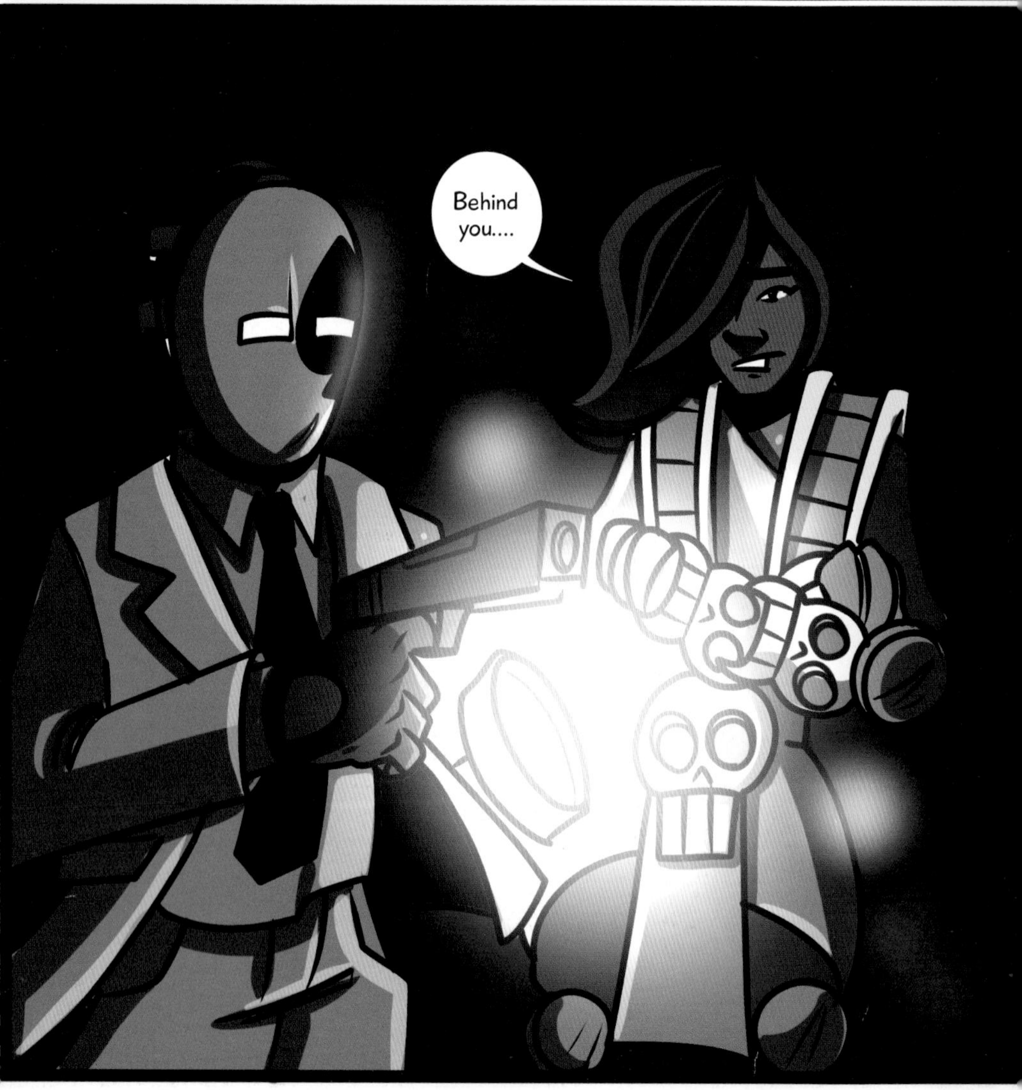
Behind you....

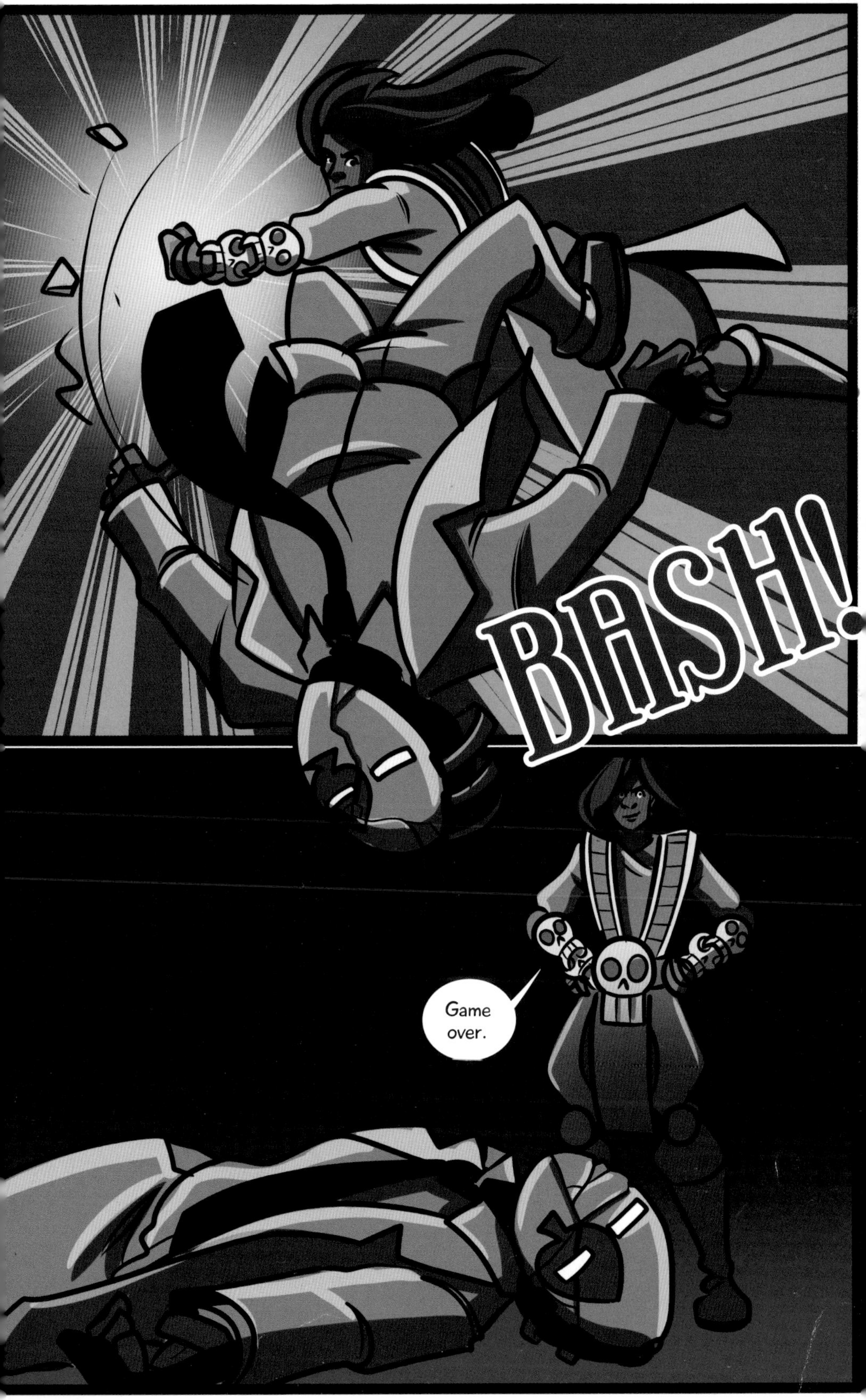
BASH!
Game over.

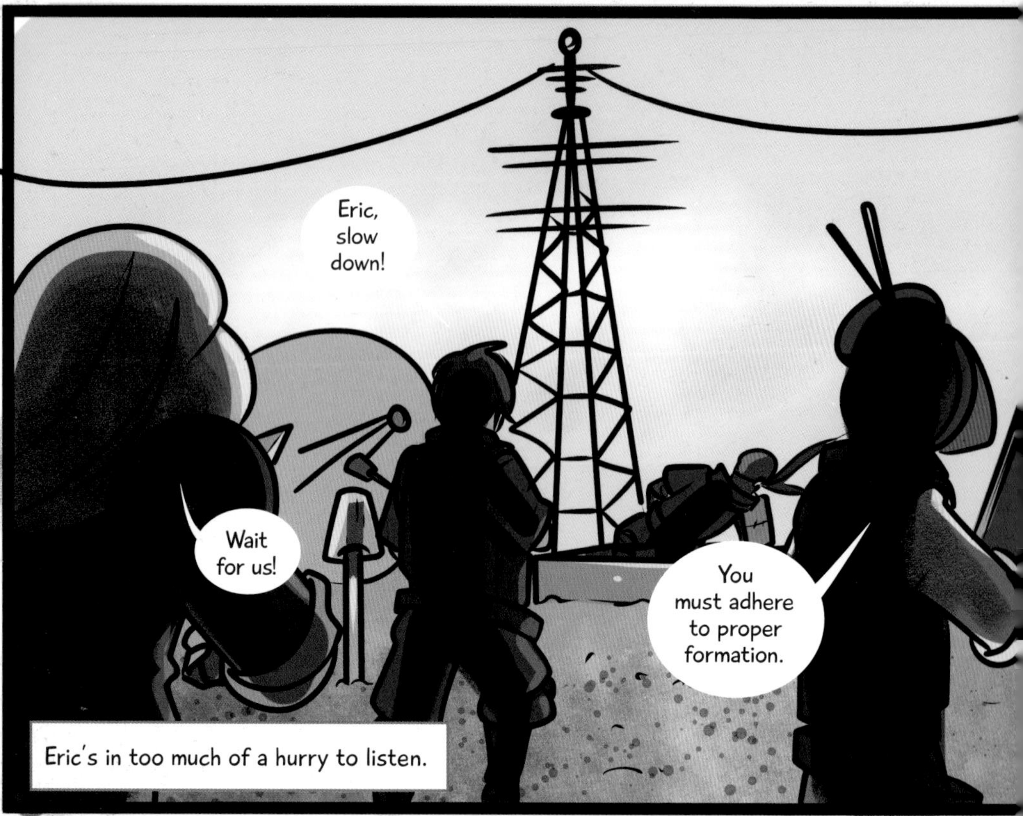
Eric, slow down!
Wait for us!
You must adhere to proper formation.
Eric's in too much of a hurry to listen.

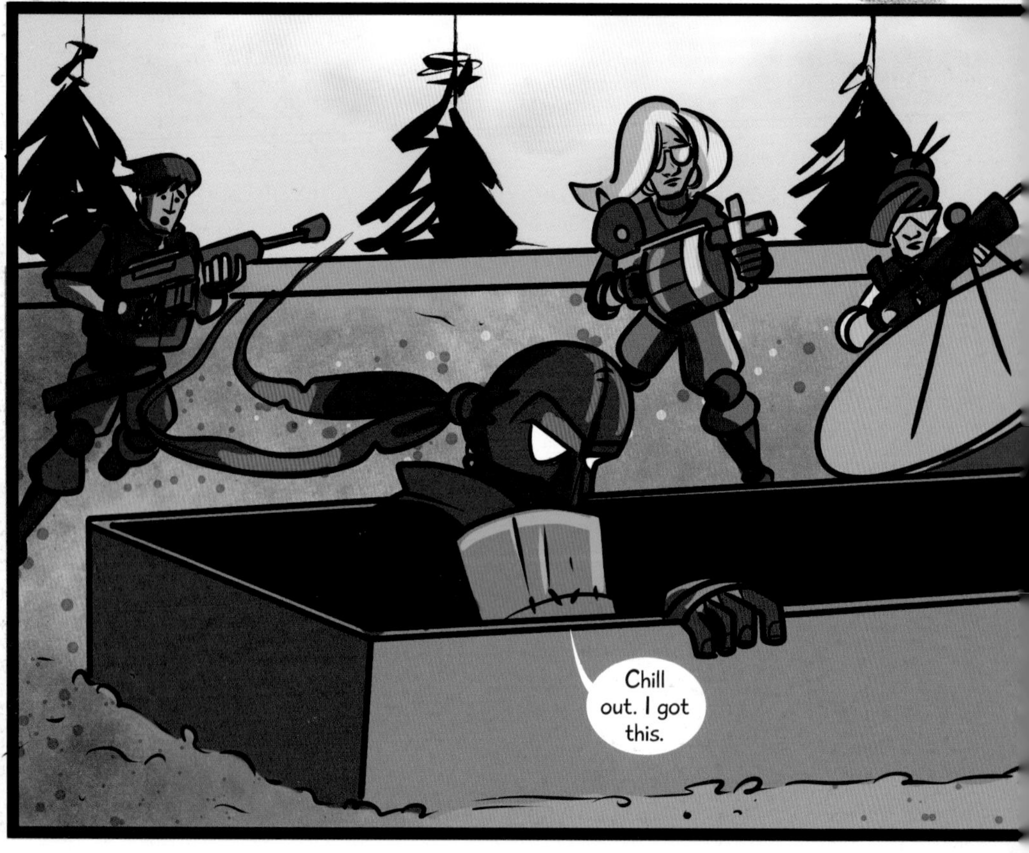
Chill out. I got this.

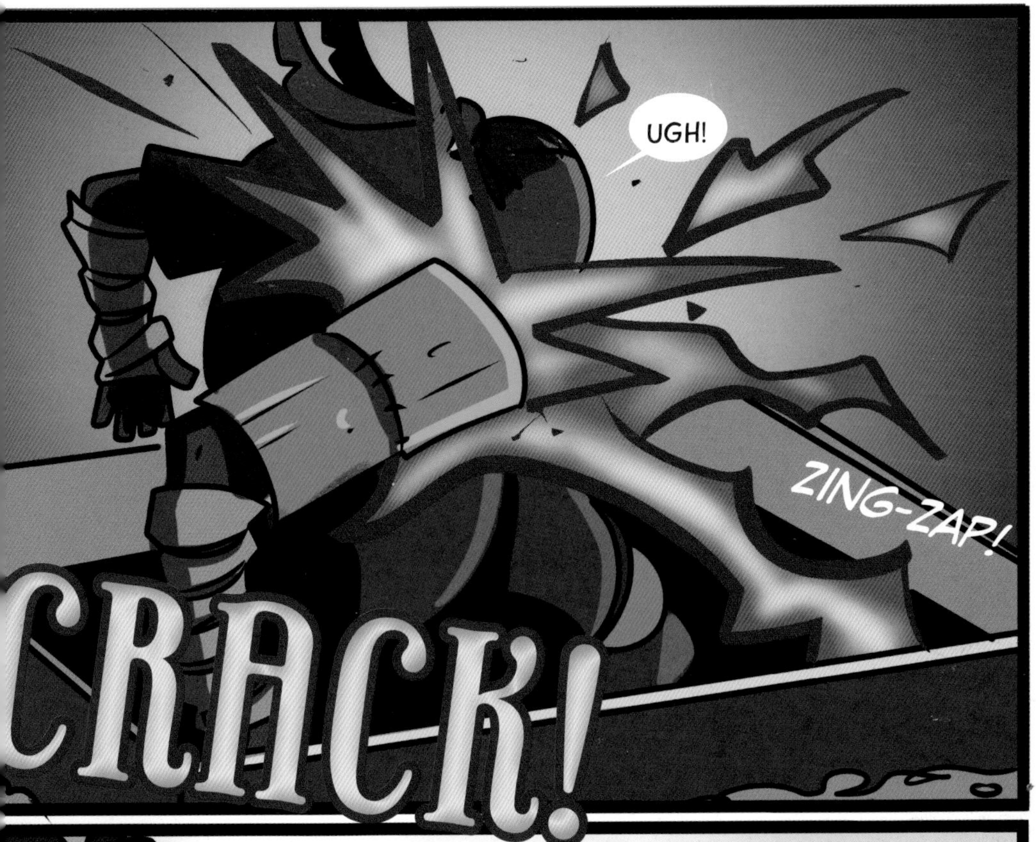
UGH!
ZING-ZAP!
CRACK!
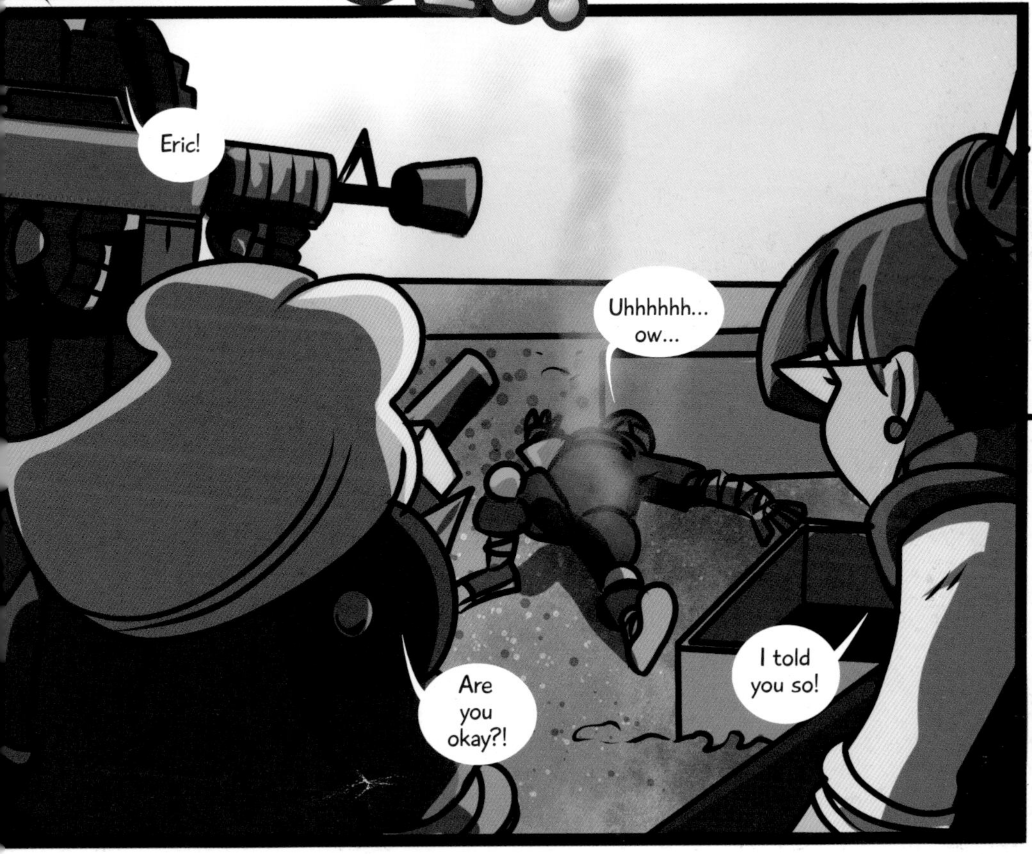
Eric!
Uhhhhhh... ow...
Are you okay?!
I told you so!

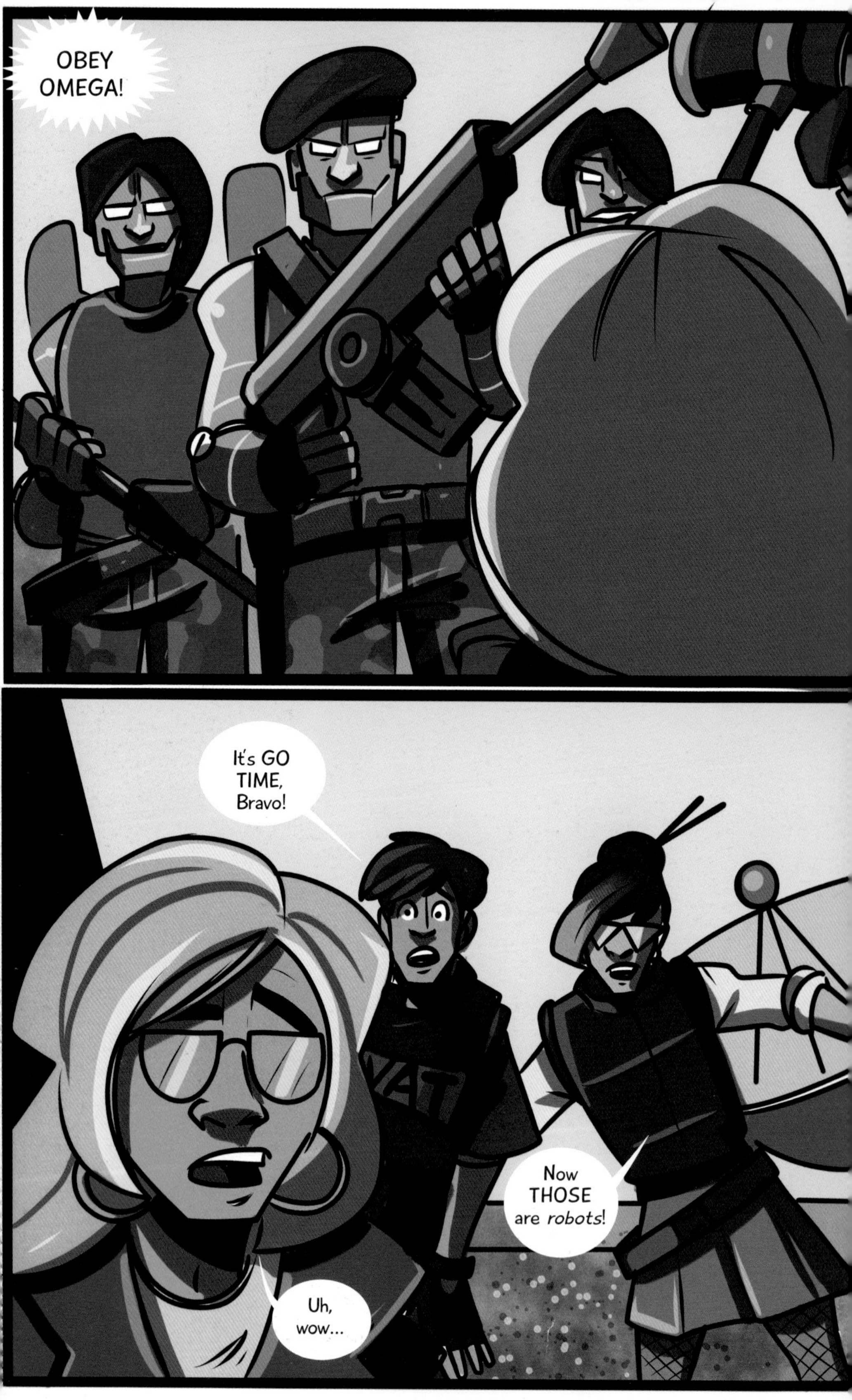
OBEY OMEGA!
It's GO TIME, Bravo!
Now THOSE are *robots*!
Uh, wow...

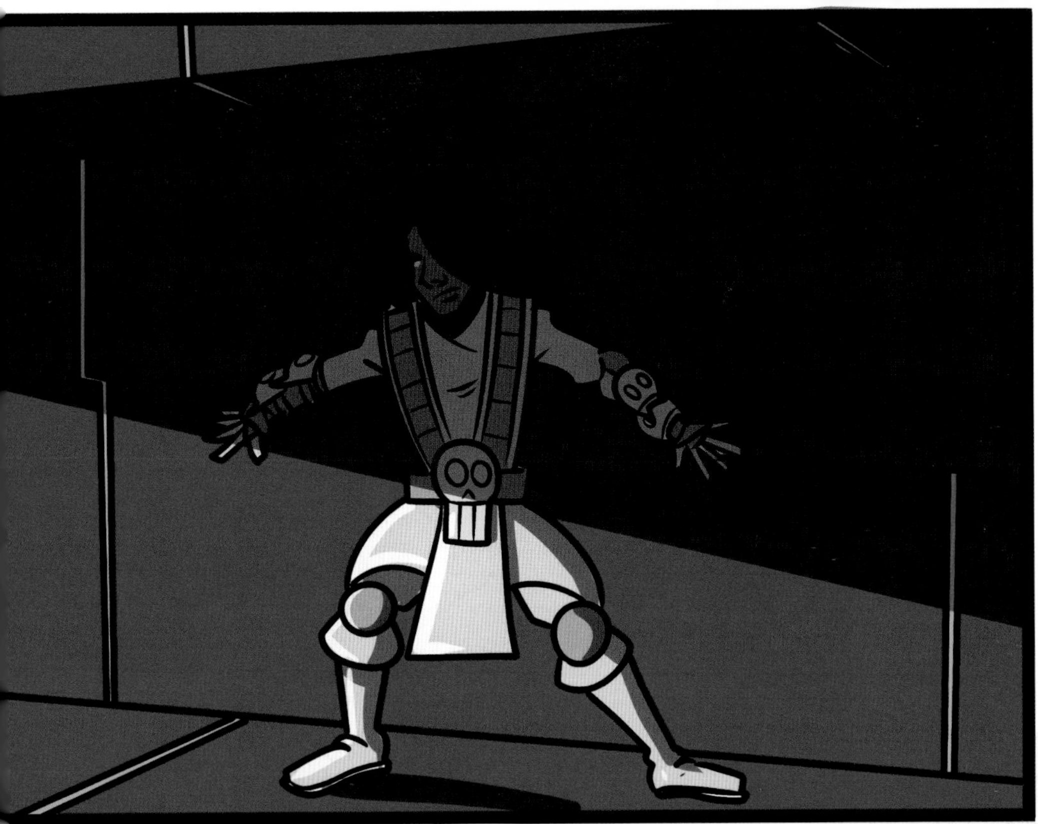

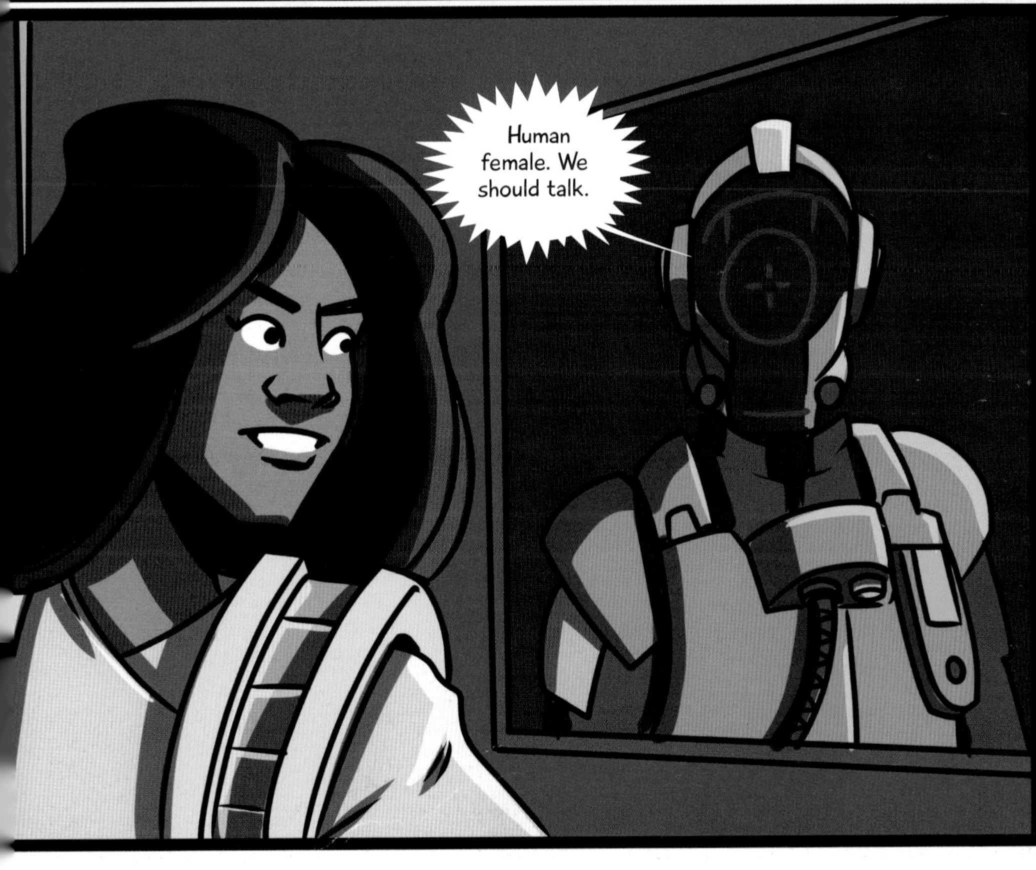
Human female. We should talk.

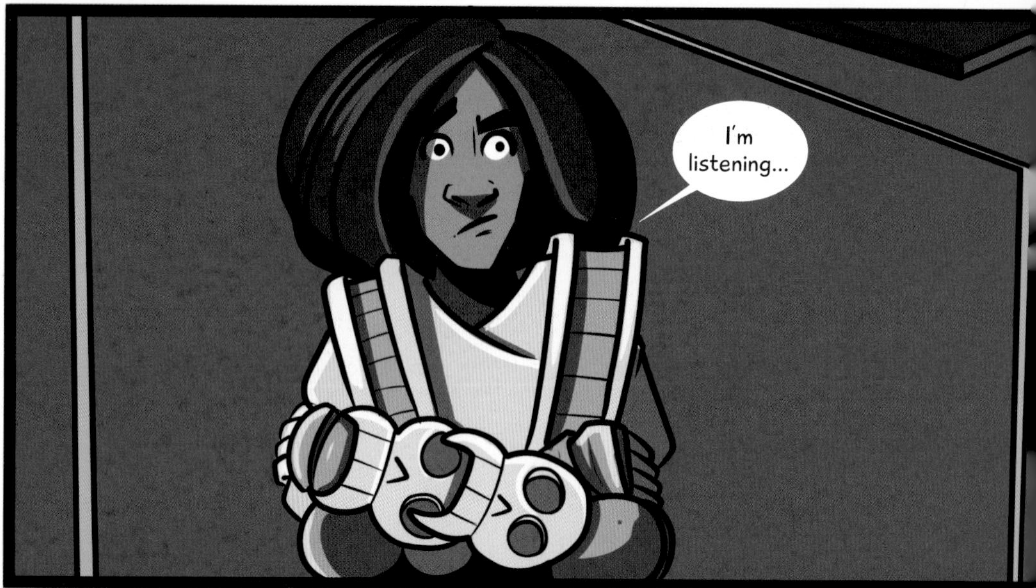
I'm listening...

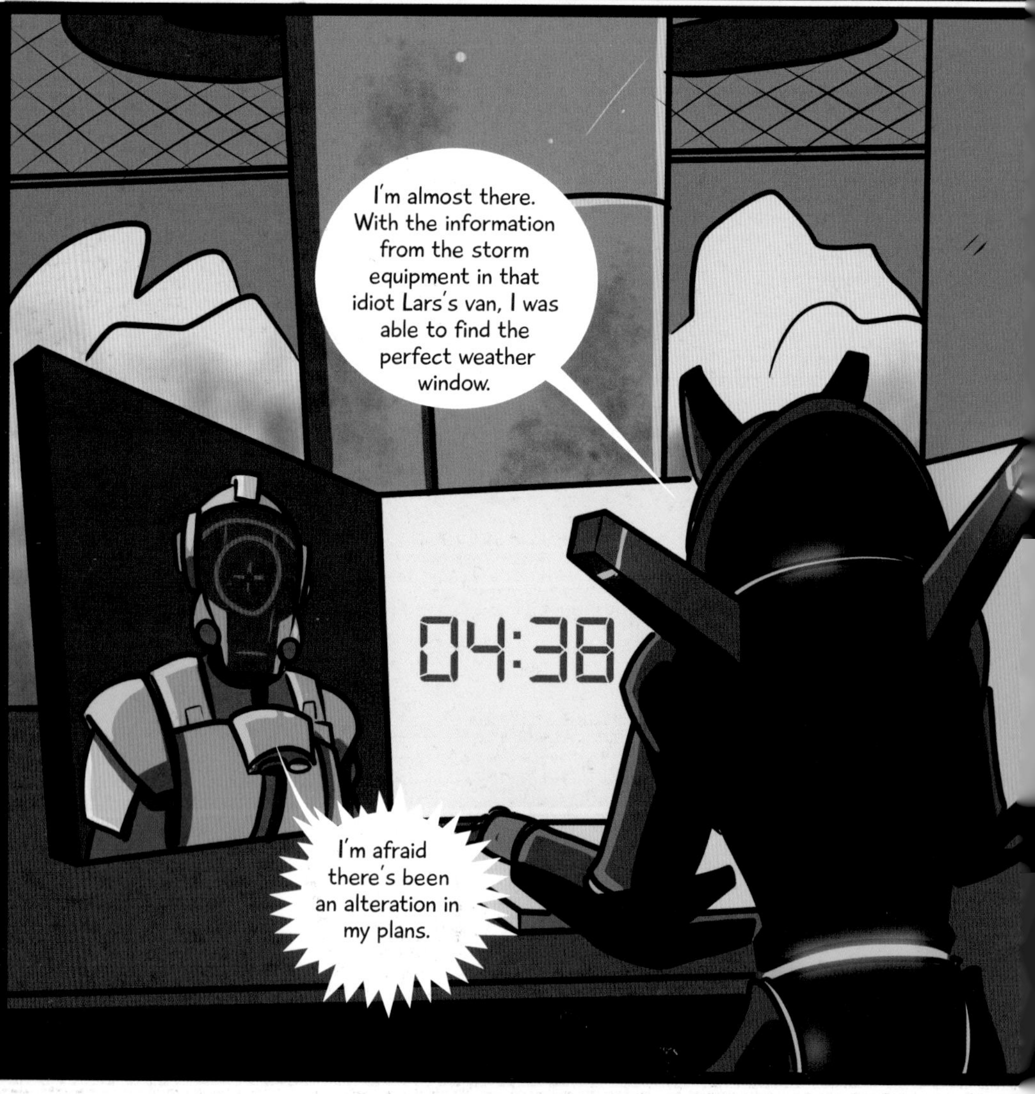
I'm almost there. With the information from the storm equipment in that idiot Lars's van, I was able to find the perfect weather window.
04:38
I'm afraid there's been an alteration in my plans.

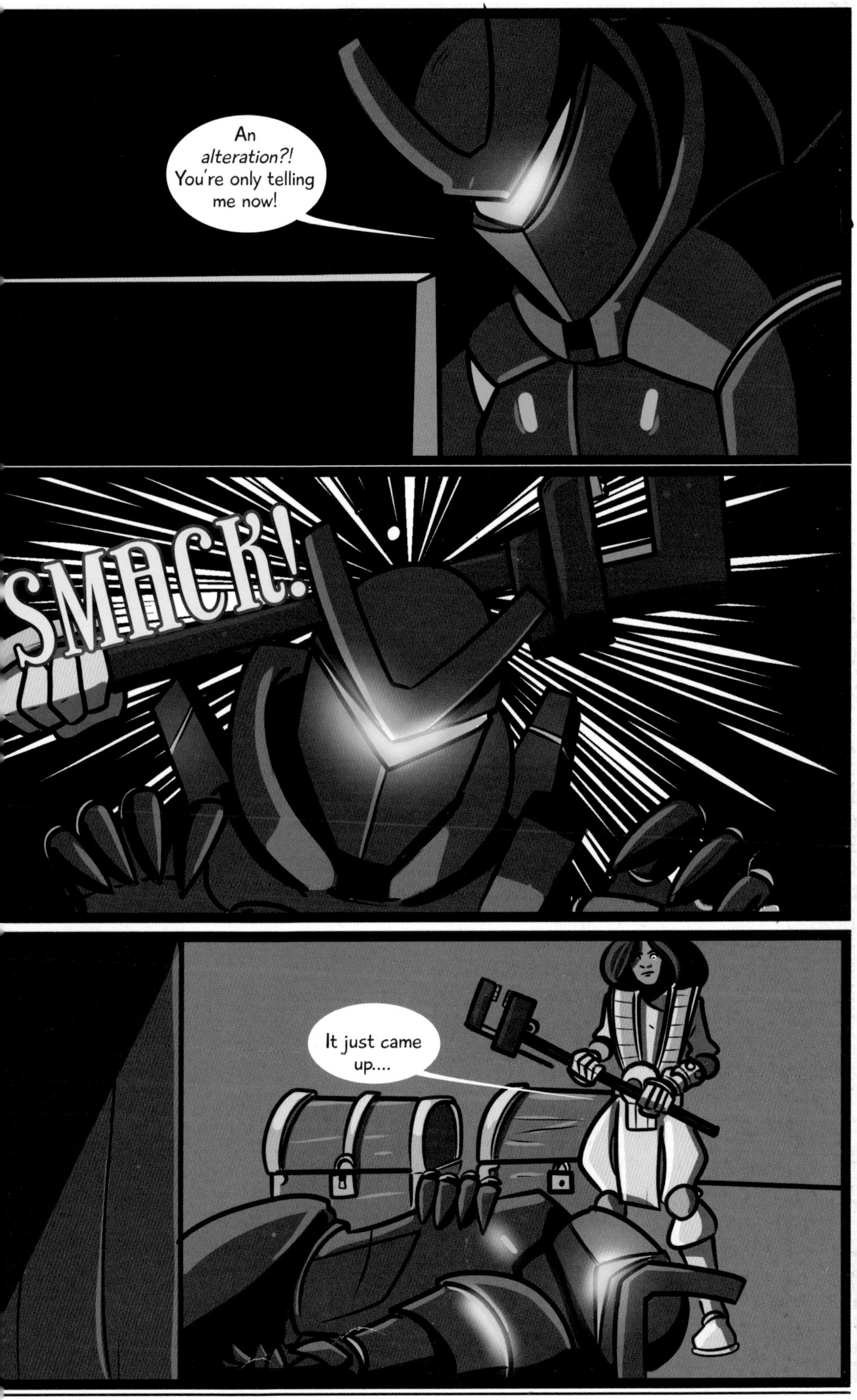
An *alteration?!* You're only telling me now!
SMACK!
It just came up....

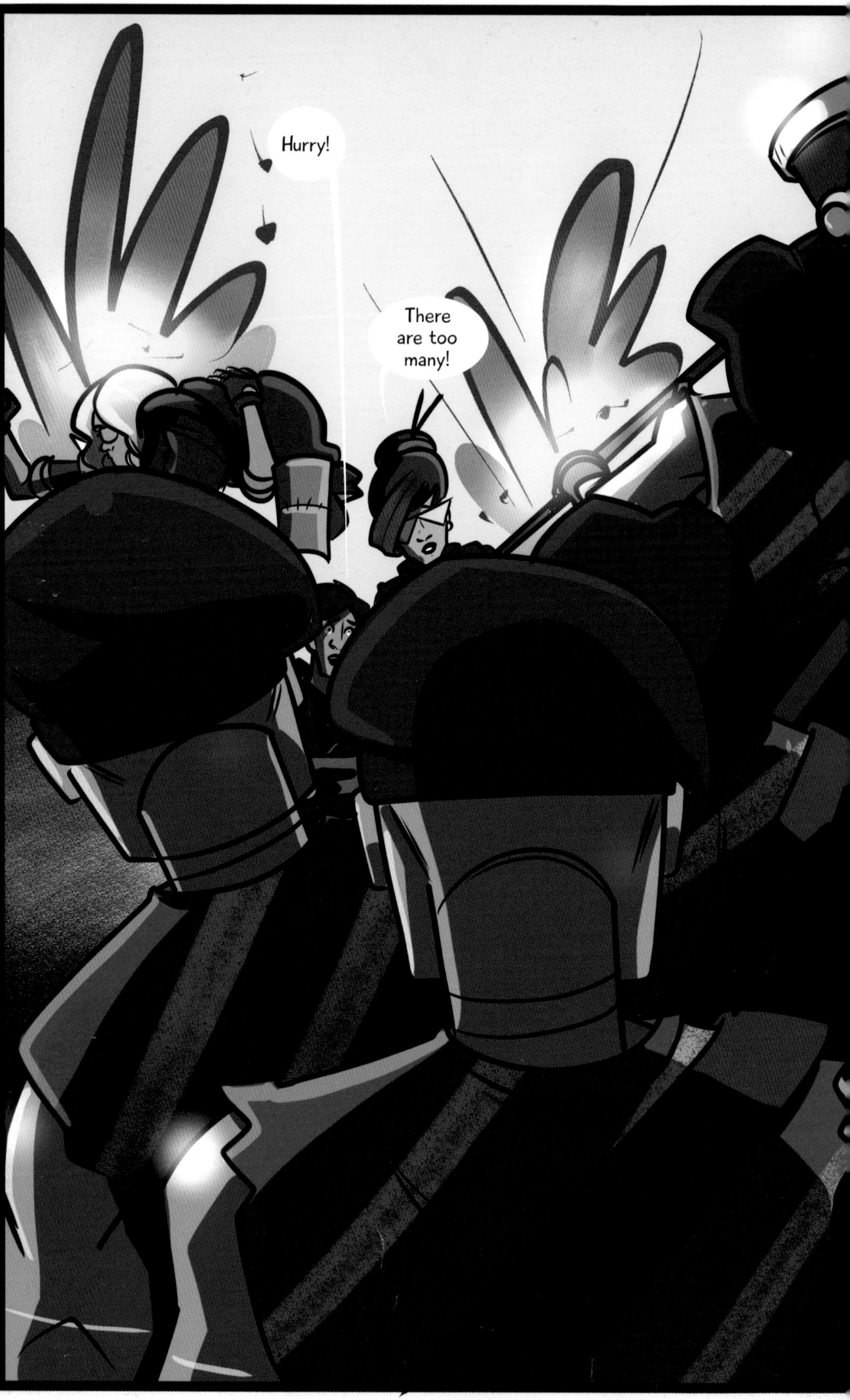
Hurry!
There are too many!

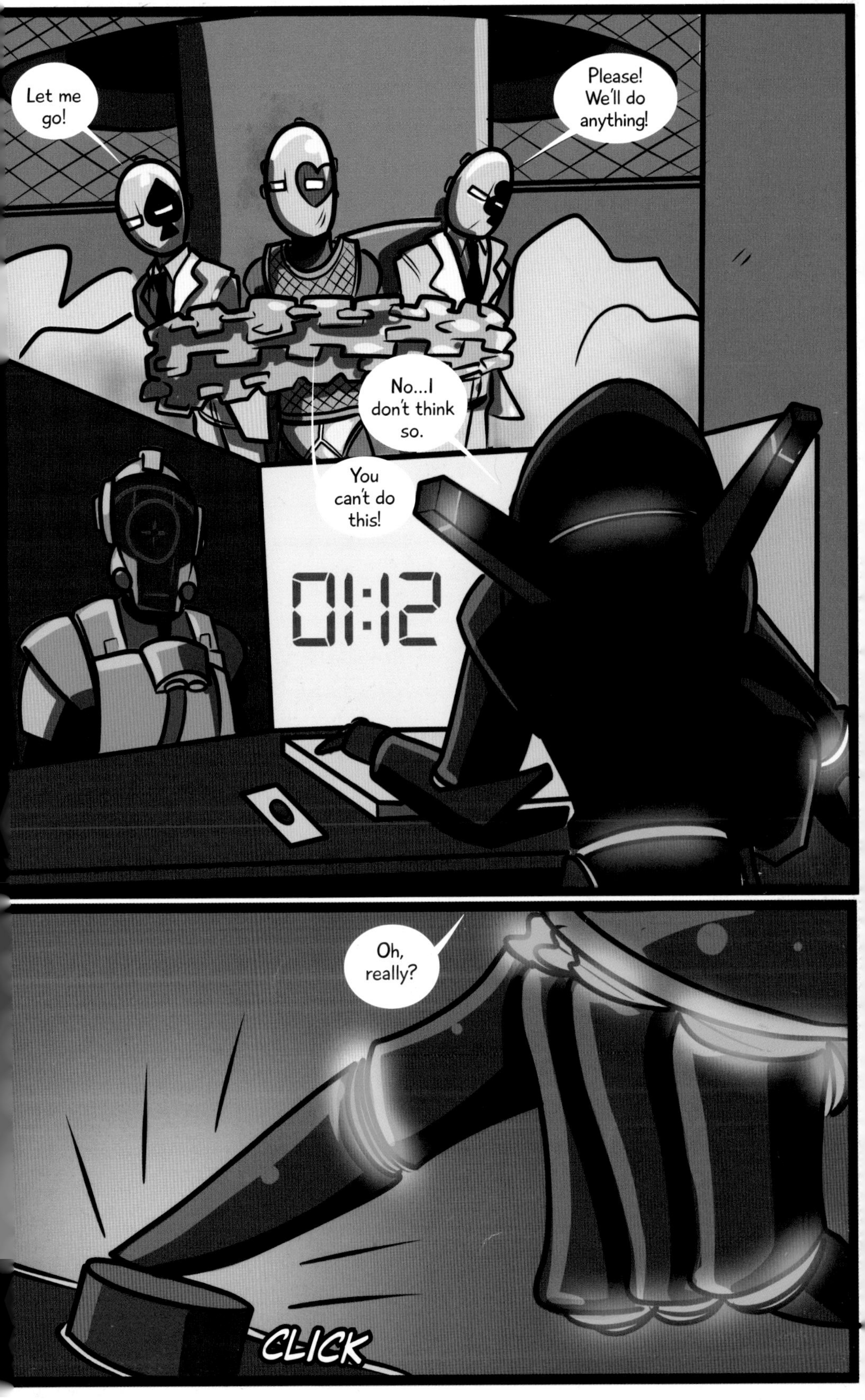
Let me go!
Please! We'll do anything!
No...I don't think so.
You can't do this!
01:12
Oh, really?
CLICK

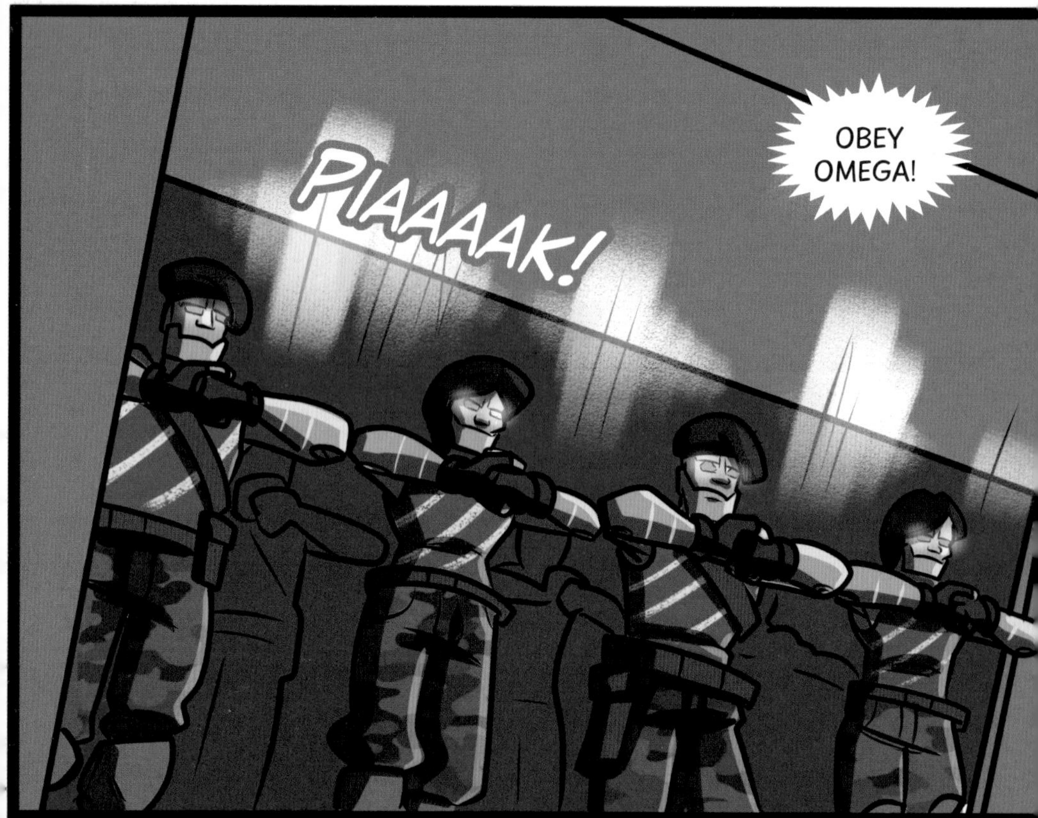
PIAAAAK!
OBEY OMEGA!

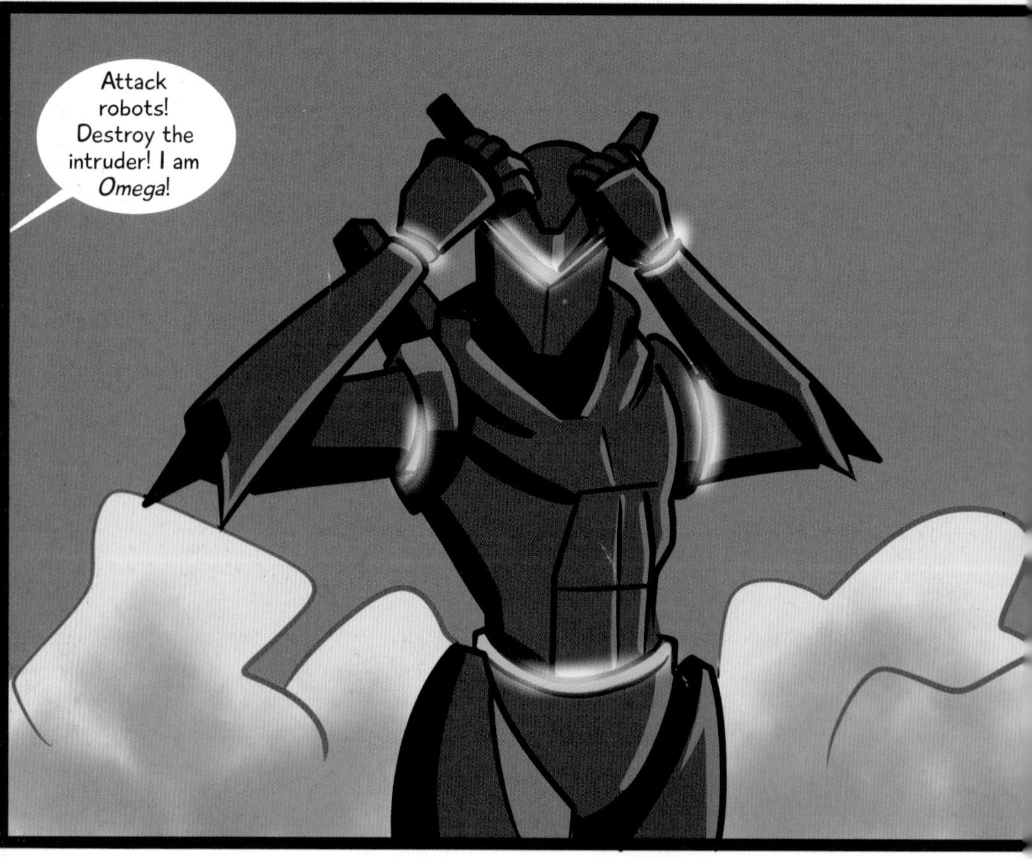
Attack robots! Destroy the intruder! I am *Omega*!

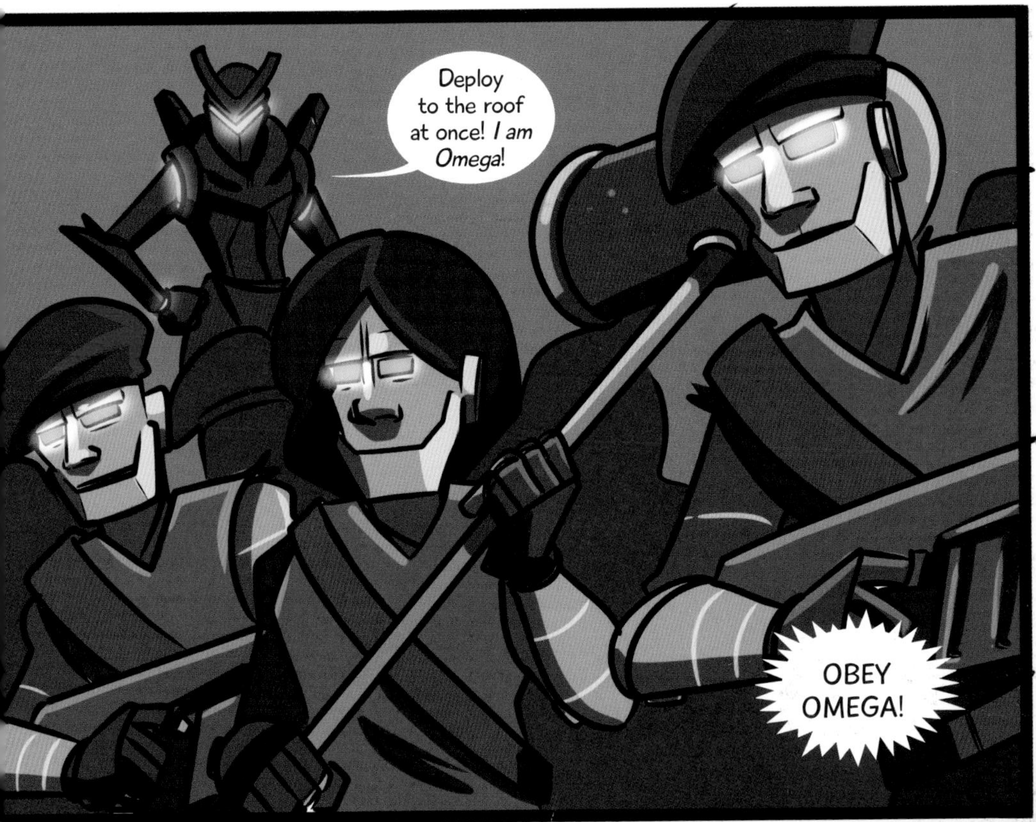
Deploy to the roof at once! *I am Omega*!
OBEY OMEGA!

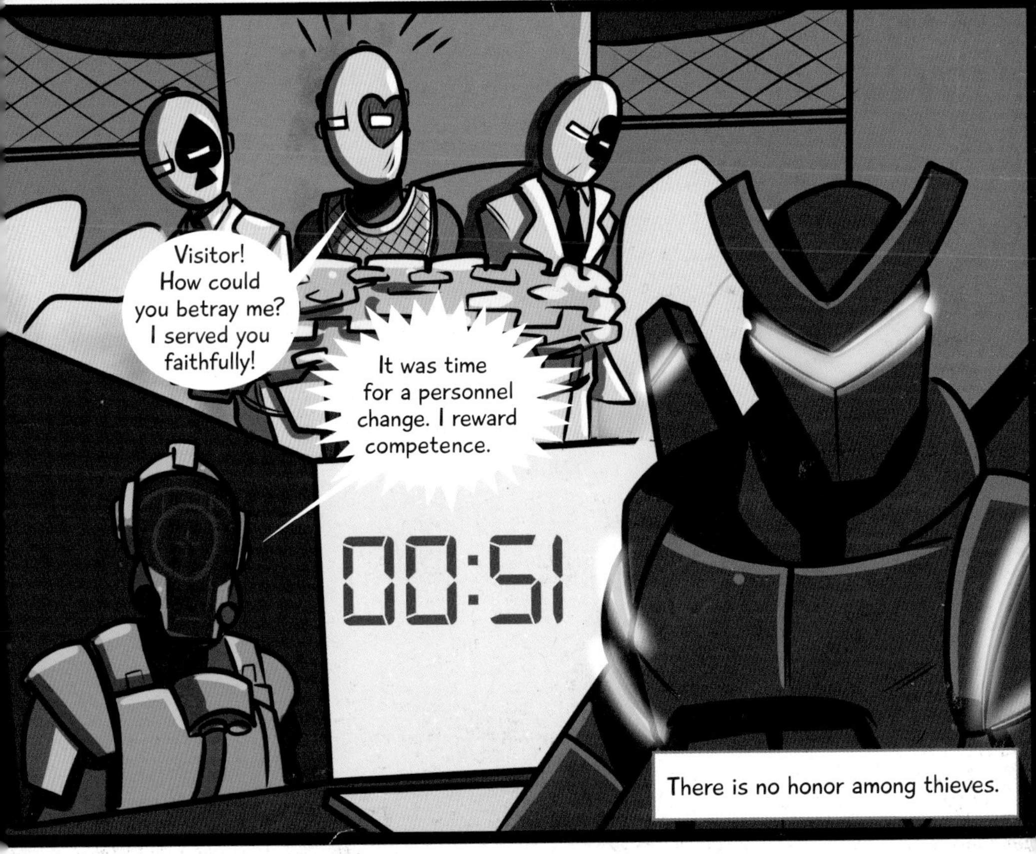
Visitor! How could you betray me? I served you faithfully!
It was time for a personnel change. I reward competence.
00:51
There is no honor among thieves.

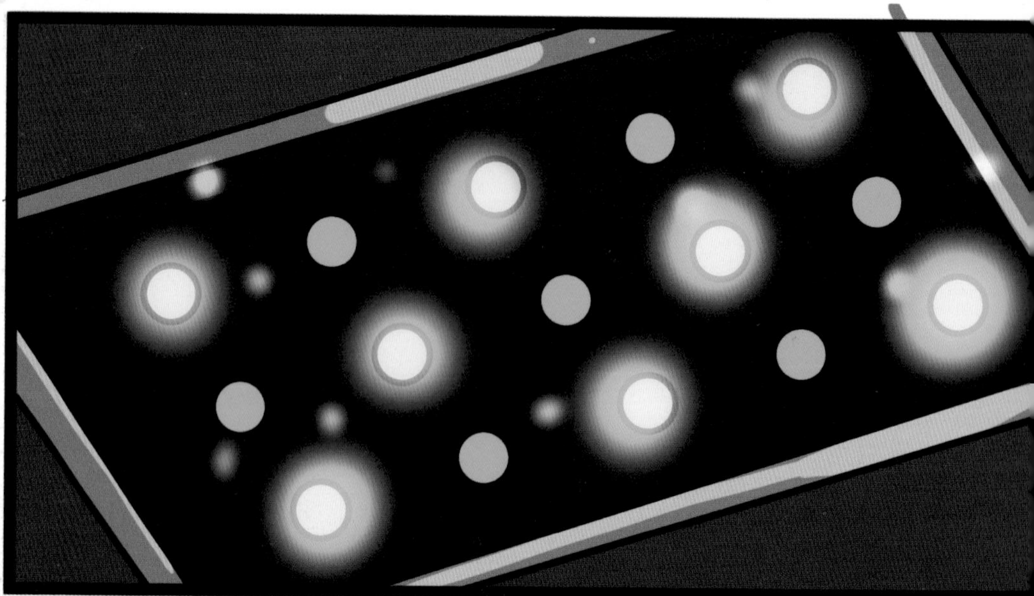

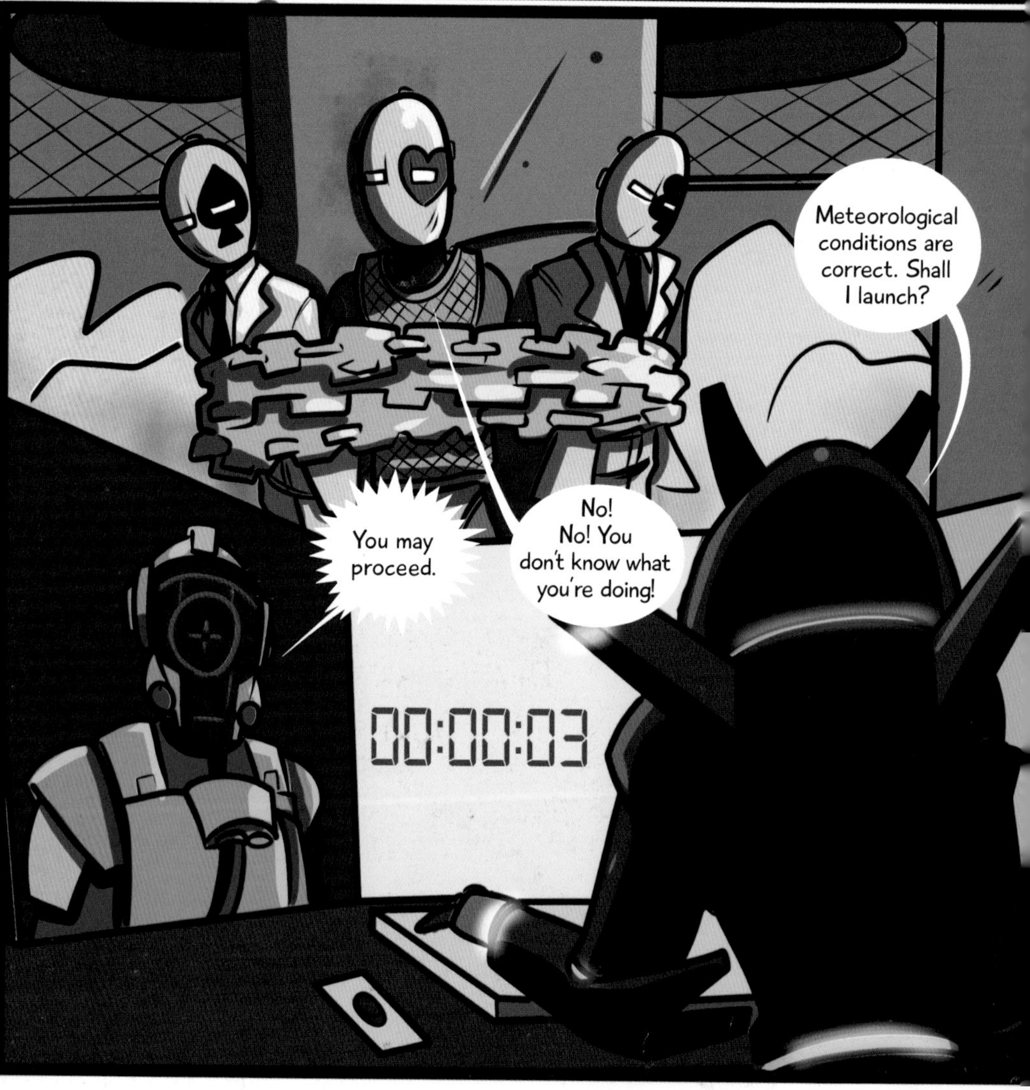
Meteorological conditions are correct. Shall I launch?
You may proceed.
No! No! You don't know what you're doing!
00:00:03

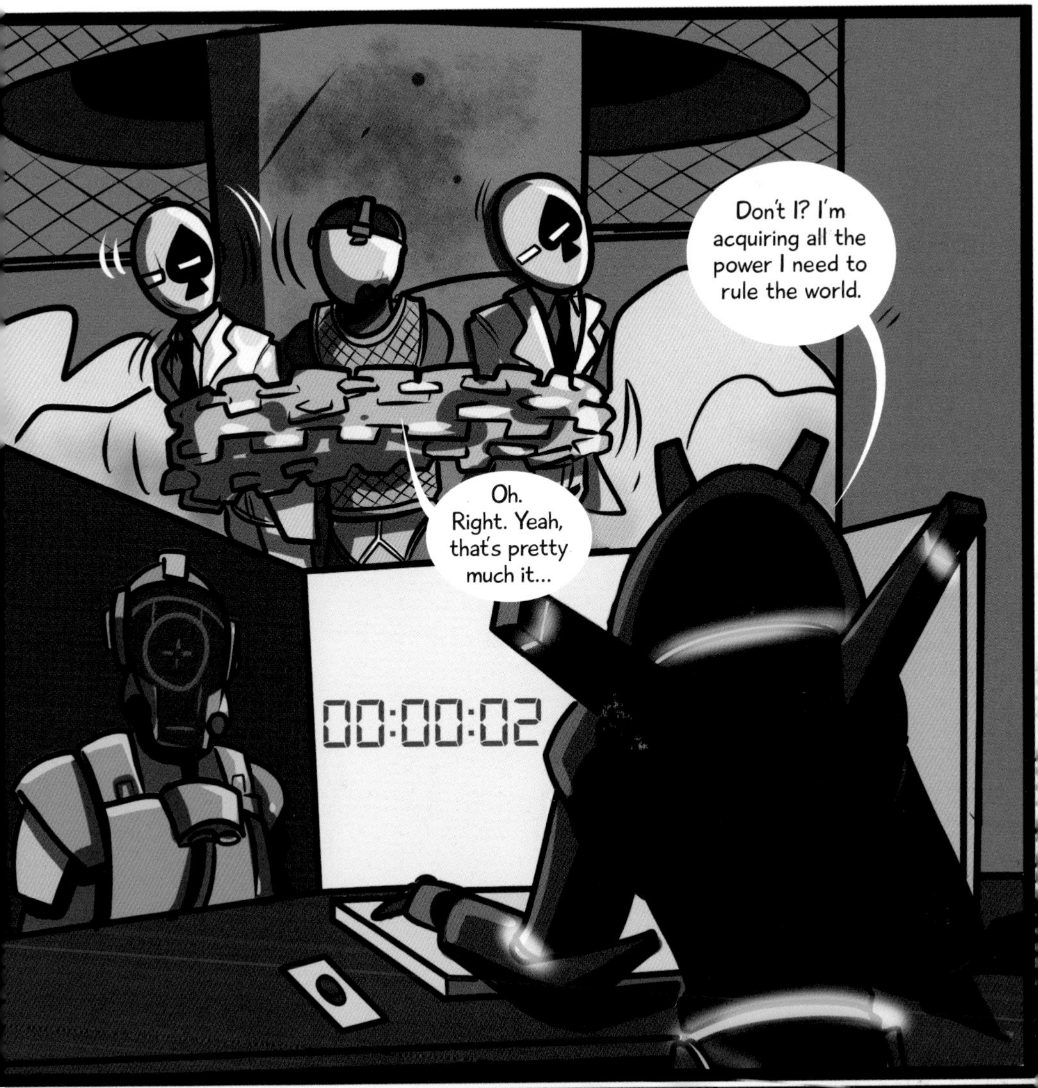
Don't I? I'm acquiring all the power I need to rule the world.
Oh. Right. Yeah, that's pretty much it...
00:00:02

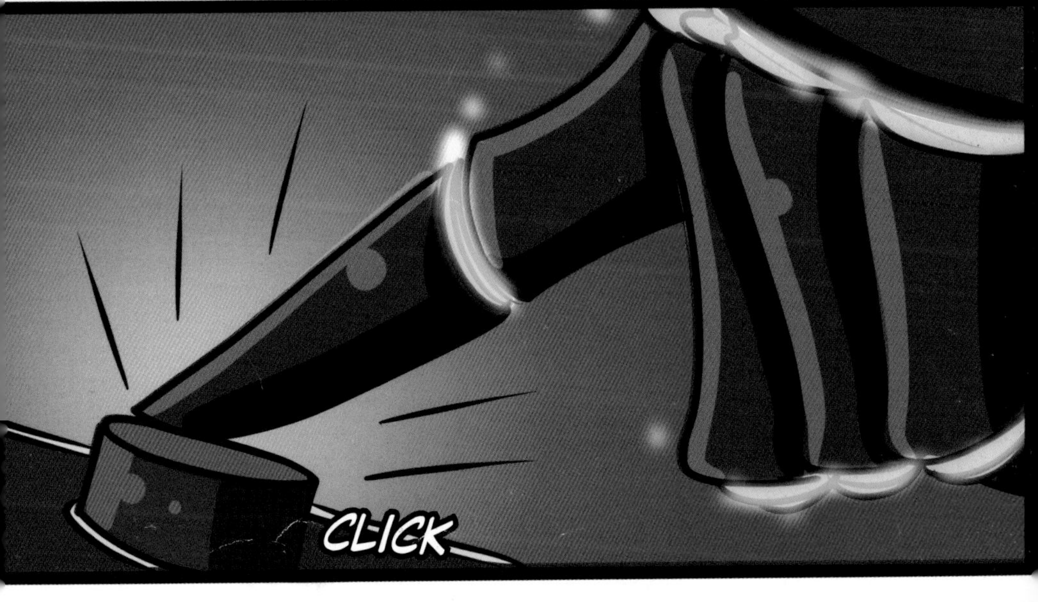
CLICK

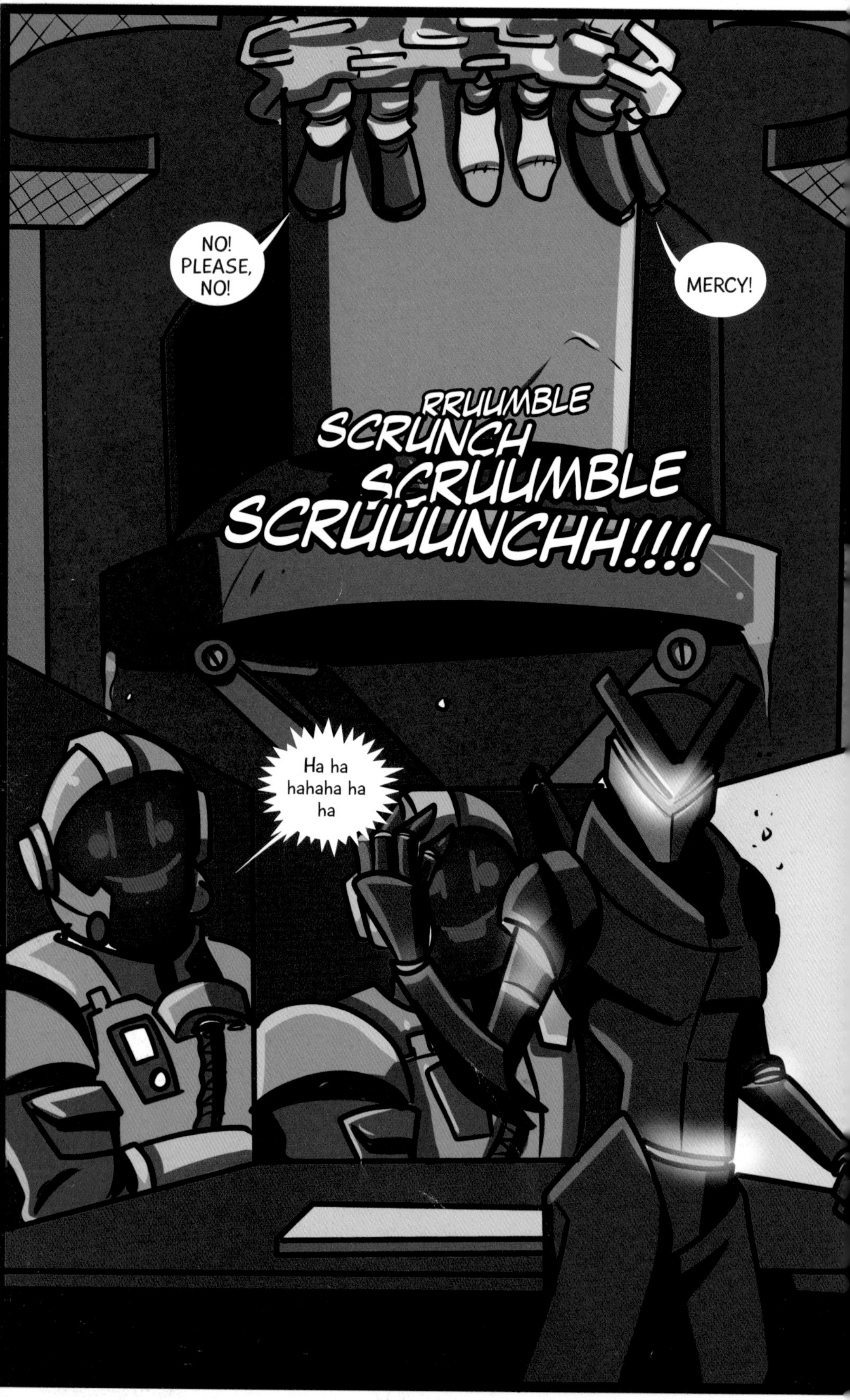
NO! PLEASE, NO!
MERCY!
RRUUMBLE
SCRUNCH
SCRUUMBLE
SCRUUUNCHH!!!!
Ha ha hahaha ha ha

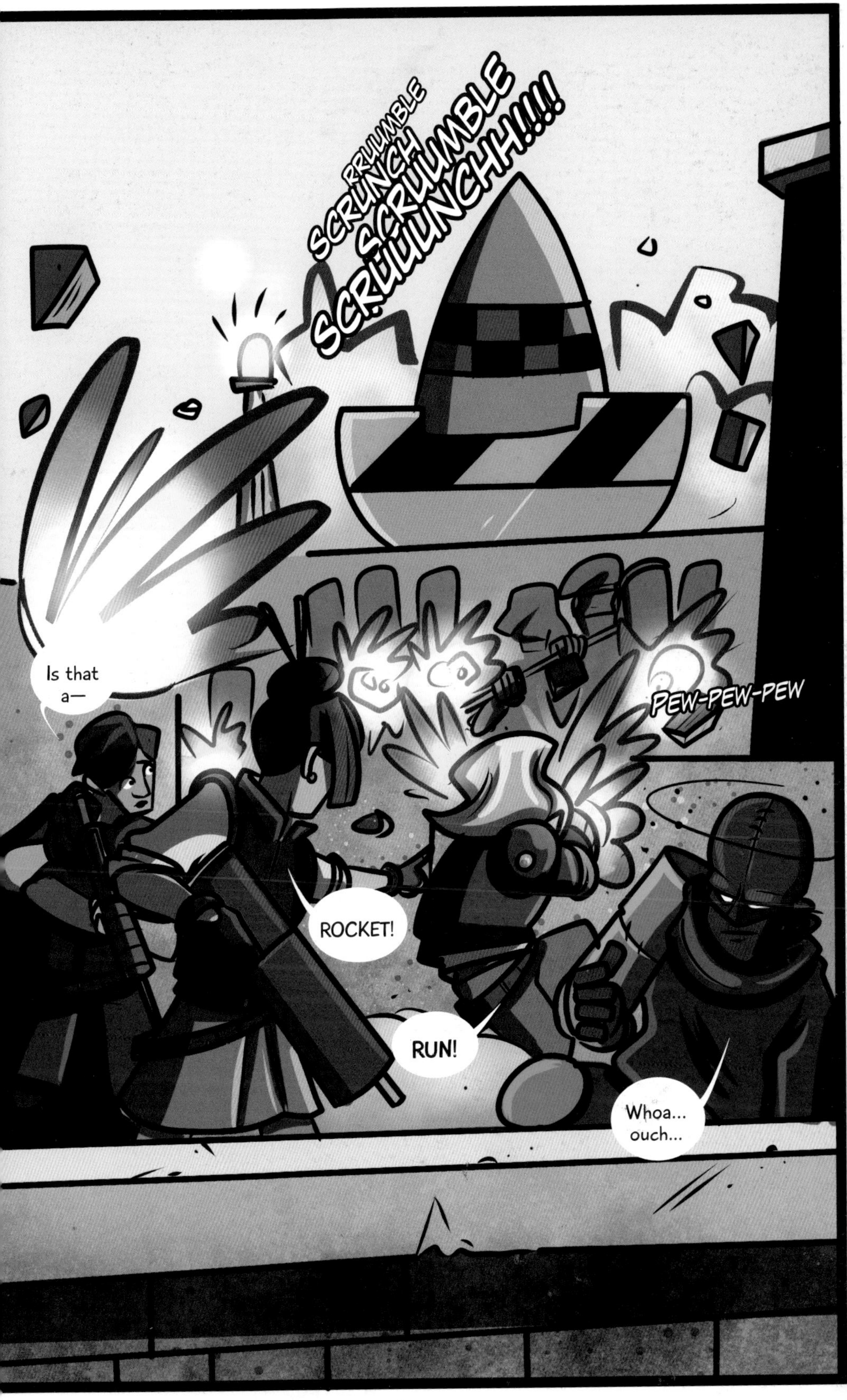
RRUUMBLE
SCRUNCH
SCRUUMBLE
SCRUUUNCHH!!!!
Is that a—
PEW-PEW-PEW
ROCKET!
RUN!
Whoa... ouch...

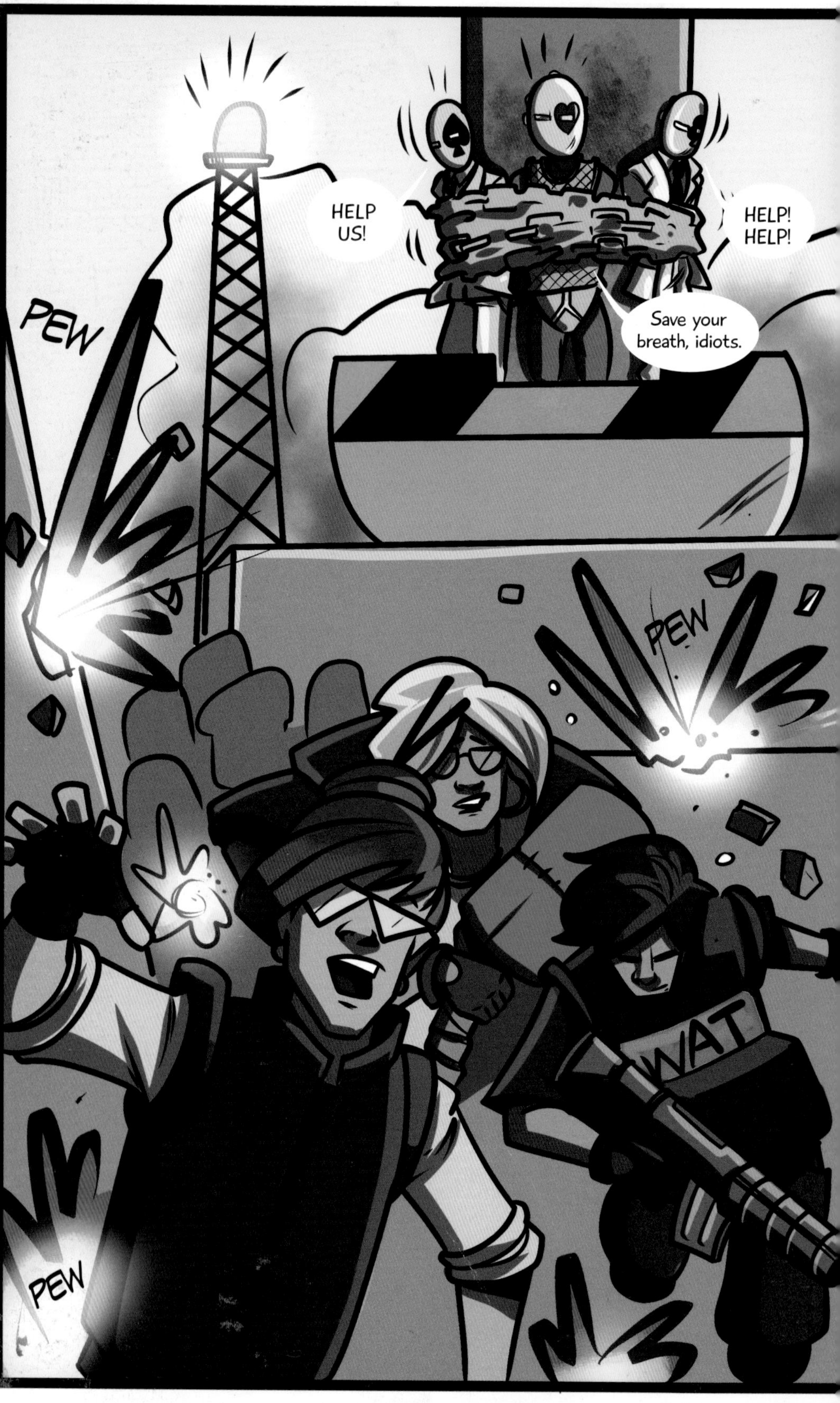
HELP US!
HELP! HELP!
Save your breath, idiots.
PEW
PEW
PEW
SWAT

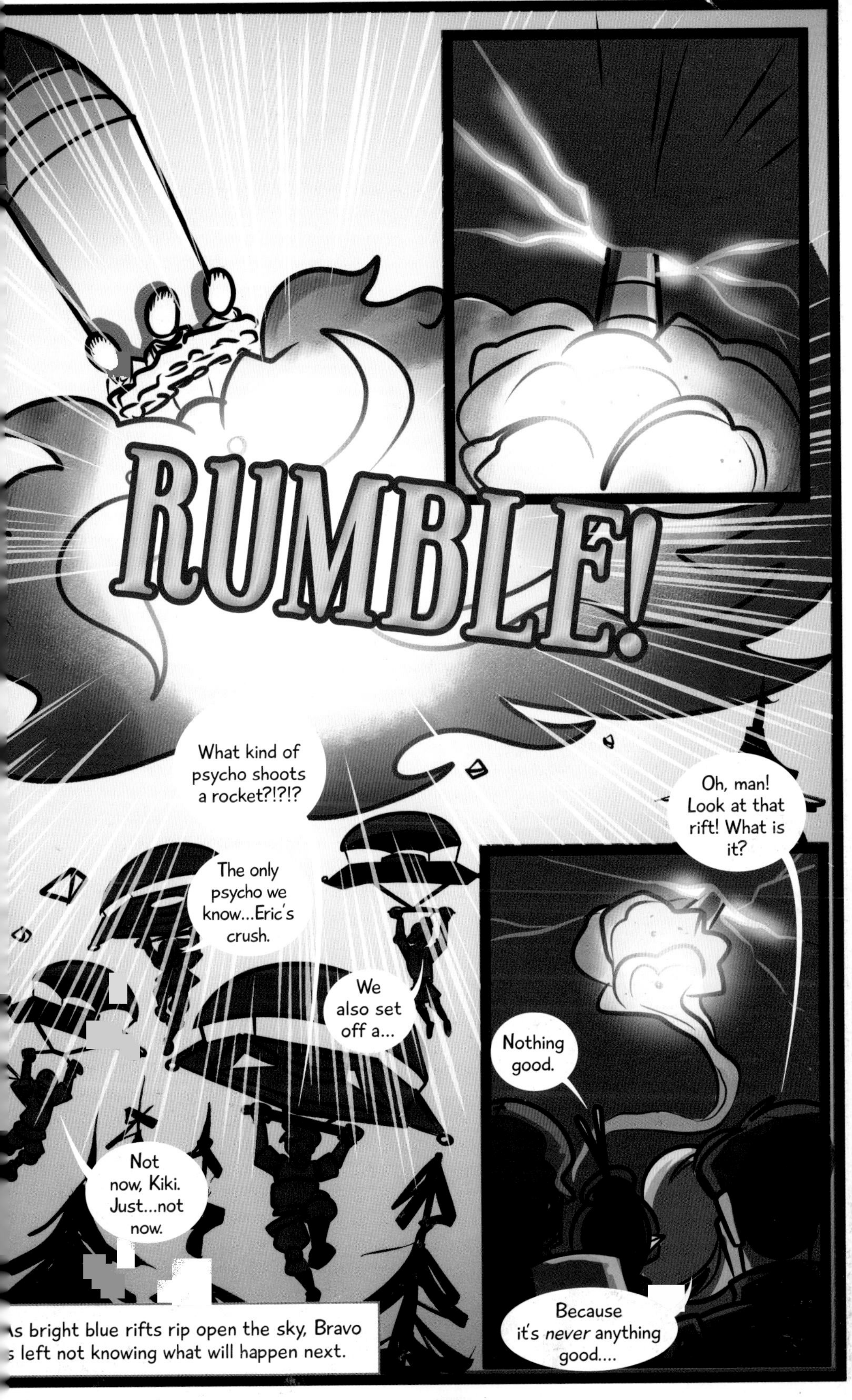
RUMBLE!
What kind of psycho shoots a rocket?!?!?
The only psycho we know...Eric's crush.
We also set off a...
Not now, Kiki. Just...not now.
Oh, man! Look at that rift! What is it?
Nothing good.
s bright blue rifts rip open the sky, Bravo
s left not knowing what will happen next.
Because it's *never* anything good....